The Tent

Shrouded King Book 1
by Sandell Wall

The Tenth Reaver © 2018 by Sandell Wall
Published by Sandell Wall

Cover art by Ricky Gunawan
Map by Ricky Gunawan

Proofed and edited by Matt Feisthammel

First Edition

ISBN: 978-0-9990384-7-5 (print)
978-0-9990384-6-8 (e-book)

Please visit Sandell's website at
http://www.sandellwall.com
And sign up for his newsletter at
Sandell's Newsletter Signup Form

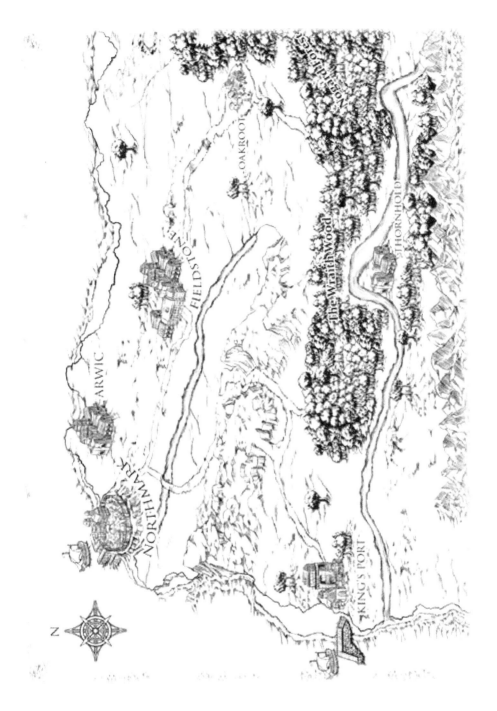

For myself, because without writing, life just isn't frustrating enough.

Prologue

GUSTAVUS STARED WITH UNSEEING eyes at the open tome before him. The great book took up most of the desk. The smell of its ancient pages conjured images of forgotten glory and hidden truths. Gustavus's thick fingers drummed the dark wood of the desk as he contemplated his findings. Beneath the tanned skin of his massive forearms, muscles contracted and released in time with his tapping.

Under Gustavus's feet, the floor rocked with the gentle motion of the sea. The *Golden Dawn* would soon arrive in King's Port, the westernmost port of the Kingdom of Haverfell. He refocused his eyes on the pages in front of him. What had started as a simple trading voyage might soon become something far greater.

Gustavus closed the tome, careful not to tear the brittle parchment of its pages. A rigorous study of its contents were beyond him, and the answers to the questions in his heart remained hidden, but he understood enough that they could not be ignored.

The door to his cabin creaked open and the head of his first mate poked into the room. Even the dimly lit cabin did not diminish the luster of Niad's brilliant red hair. Gustavus beckoned, indicating that she should enter.

Niad slipped through the door and approached Gustavus's desk. "King's Port is on the horizon, cap'n."

Gustavus rubbed a hand across his face. "I've no love for this cursed kingdom, but the pay was too good to turn down. Have the crew unload the goods as planned. I've got business in the city."

Niad's gaze flicked to the giant book on the desk and then back to his face. She raised her eyebrows. "Can't shake the dreams?"

"They only get stronger," Gustavus said. "I think I know what they mean. All signs point to Thornhold, but a scryer would be able confirm my suspicions."

"Be careful, cap'n. Mystics are outlawed in Haverfell."

"You're my first mate, not my blessed mother," Gustavus growled.

"And for that, I say thanks every day," Niad said with a grin. "I couldn't bear the shame of having a degenerate smuggler for a son."

Gustavus grunted to cover a laugh.

A shout rang out. They were moving in to dock. After a quick salute, Niad left Gustavus alone in the cabin to go supervise their arrival in King's Port.

Gustavus lifted himself out of his chair, plucking the huge tome off the table with one hand. He placed the book into a chest at the back of the cabin and closed the iron-banded lid, locking it away.

Outside, he heard the commotion of his crew stowing sails and preparing for landfall. Gustavus buckled his sword belt around his waist. The familiar weight of his scimitar slapped against his thigh. He slipped a flintlock pistol into the holster on his opposite side, pausing to double-check that it was loaded. Something would have gone terribly wrong if he had to discharge the weapon in King's Port, but he had long ago learned to not carry a weapon unless you were prepared to use it.

Once the ship had been secured, the crew started to unload the cargo without delay. The gangplank hit the dock with a solid thud. Gustavus exited his cabin and stepped down the wooden plank, leaving the *Golden Dawn* behind. Niad would see that they received payment and make sure that the next shipment was loaded without issue.

Chasius the harbormaster stood on the dock, waiting his turn like a carrion crow perched over a hunter's kill. Gustavus had an understanding with the man. He made Chasius rich, and the harbormaster failed to notice the smuggled goods that flowed in and out of the *Golden Dawn's* hold.

"You're earlier than I expected," Chasius said. "This is going to create complications."

"You'll get your fair cut," Gustavus growled.

Chasius sniffed.

"If you want to earn extra, you can take me to a scryer," Gustavus said.

"I might know a man," Chasius said after a long moment. "But he's not cheap and taking you to him is a risk. Five hundred marks."

"Two hundred, and I'll not bash your skull in for insulting me with such a high price," Gustavus said.

"Three hundred. I'll not go lower. Even talking about a mystic is enough to get a person arrested these days."

"Damnation," Gustavus said, turning to look out over the harbor as he contemplated the price. Finally he said, "Three hundred it is, you bloodsucking eel. I'll pay you when I get the funds from this delivery. Now tell me how to find this man."

Chasius cast a furtive glance around the docks. "I can do better than that," he said. "I can take you to him."

Gustavus fell into step with Chasius, and the two of them left the harbor behind. Chasius led him to a nearby slum. The church might try to outlaw mystics, but it could not separate people from their superstitions. If there was a scryer to be found in King's Port, it was here.

At the dead end of a dark alley, Chasius paused in front of a dilapidated door. A small, lidless eye had been drawn in charcoal at the bottom of a door jamb. After a quick glance around to confirm no one had followed them, Chasius pushed through the rotting door. Gustavus followed close behind.

The small room on the other side held nothing but a table and two chairs. A single candle burned on the little table. Next to the candle, a tiny brass bell waited to be rung. At the rear of the room, another door led deeper into the interior of the building.

Chasius indicated the chair, and Gustavus sat. The rickety piece of furniture creaked under his bulk. Chasius picked up the bell and gave it a shake. After three rings, he returned it to the table.

"Just a minute, I'm coming," a voice called out from behind the second door.

Footsteps thudded against the wooden floor as someone approached the room where Gustavus waited. "I can manage from here, Chasius," he said. "Scurry off and wait for your payment."

"You'll need me to make introductions. Mystics are a skittish lot in Haverfell."

Gustavus grunted his displeasure but held his tongue. When the door swung open, a plain-looking man stepped through. He stopped in his tracks midway into the room. They were obviously not who he had been expecting.

"We're closed," the man snapped, turning on his heels as he prepared to bolt to safety.

"Hold a moment," Chasius said, raising a hand toward the scryer. "This man is a friend of mine. I told him you're worth whatever price you ask, and he's agreed to pay it."

The scryer paused with his back to them. "You were instructed to never bring anyone here without warning me first," he said.

"You can trust me," Gustavus said. "Here, sit down and I'll prove it."

Gustavus imagined he heard the wheels spinning in the man's mind. Finally, the scryer turned and sat opposite Gustavus. He folded his hands neatly on the table and looked at Gustavus with a blank face.

"There's nothing you can say or do that will change my mind," the man said.

"I thought you might say that," Gustavus said. The scryer flinched as Gustavus reached underneath his coat and withdrew something from an inside pocket. Gustavus tossed the object onto the table, where it landed with a heavy thunk. Gold glittered in the candlelight.

"Do you know what that is?" Gustavus asked.

The man did not answer. Instead, he stared in open-mouthed shock. Attached to a long strip of leather, it was an amulet the size of his palm. Formed from solid gold, a dragon stood frozen in a silent roar, its great wings stretched wide.

Finally, the scryer looked up at Gustavus, his eyes narrowed. "It's pretty enough, if that's what you're asking," he said. He seemed to have trouble speaking, his words were stilted and sharp. The man's face twitched, the corners of his eyes spasming out of control.

"Are you okay?" Gustavus asked slowly. Underneath the table, his hand crept toward the hilt of his scimitar.

"I-I-I can't scry for you t-today," the man stammered. "Y-you need to leave. R-right now."

"My apologies," Gustavus said. "I didn't mean to startle you. We'll go." Gustavus reached across the table to pick up his amulet. Instead, he flicked it into the scryer's lap.

The man screamed and leapt away from the table. He fell backward over his chair, flinging the dragon amulet as far away from himself as possible.

Gustavus lunged to his feet, sword in hand. He hurled the table aside and stood over the convulsing seer.

"What the hell are you doing?" Chasius demanded in alarm.

Gustavus ignored Chasius. He leaned down and took a fistful of the scryer's shirt, pulling the man up toward his face. "Tell me who your master is, or I'll shove that amulet down your throat," he growled.

"Praise be to Abimelech, King of Darkness, Lord of Dragons," the scryer babbled.

"That's what I thought," Gustavus said. He let the man fall back with a thud. In the next instant, Gustavus slammed his scimitar into the scryer's chest, puncturing his heart and ending his life. The man's body jerked once and then went still. Black blood spilled from the wound and covered the wooden floor.

"God's balls!" Chasius swore, a look of horror on his face. "What have you done?"

"This man wasn't a seer," Gustavus said as he cleaned his sword on the dead man's shirt. "He was bait in a trap."

"The only trap I see is the one you've set for us! There are consequences for murdering a man."

"Not a man," Gustavus said as he stood. "See for yourself."

Chasius moved around the table and looked down at the body. In death, the man's face was no longer human. Instead, the features of a dragon stared up at them. Brown scales covered a thick snout lined with teeth. The open eyes were unmistakably reptilian, pupils a slash of darkness in a red iris.

"This can't be real," Chasius said, stumbling backward with a hand over his mouth.

"It'll probably go better for you if you believe that," Gustavus said. "You'll need to clean this up. I'll double your fee. If you value your life, don't speak of this to anyone."

Chasius had gone pale. All he could do was nod.

Gustavus moved across the room to recover his discarded amulet.

"Now we're all properly introduced," Gustavus said, holding up the golden dragon pendant so that Chasius could see it. "This isn't the emblem of a smuggler. It's the mark of a Dragonslayer."

Chapter 1

KAISER LISTENED TO THE muted roar of the crowd above his head. Twenty feet of wood and stone could not quiet the cry of a hundred thousand voices. Dust floated down from the exposed rafters as the mob stamped their feet, working themselves into a state of frenzied anticipation.

With his arms outstretched, Kaiser stood motionless as servants hurried to strap on the last pieces of his armor. He bunched the muscles of his shoulders under spaulders of dark steel, making sure that the armor sat properly on his back. Gauntlets were pulled onto his hands, and Kaiser flexed his fingers before clenching them into fists.

Satisfied, Kaiser lowered his arms and stepped forward. A servant approached with the final piece: his helmet. Six twisted horns adorned the dread helm, and as it clicked into place, Kaiser's world reduced to two eye slits. His breathing echoed in the confines of the cold metal.

Kaiser took hold of the proffered shield and sword. A ruby winked on the pommel of his serrated blade. The shield covered most of his body, and he hefted it with an effortless strength earned in long years of training and combat.

Without a word, the servants fell away, leaving Kaiser alone. His heart fluttered in his breast as he started forward. No matter how many times he did battle in the arena, it never lost its thrill. At the end of a long corridor, Kaiser stopped in the middle of a wooden platform. When he was in place, the platform lurched into motion, hoisted upward by a system of ropes and pulleys.

Sunlight penetrated the gloom as Kaiser rose, and he tilted his head back to look up. Overhead, a perfect square of brilliant blue sky beckoned to him, the rays of the sun falling upon his dark armor like the blessing of heaven. As the platform creaked ever higher, the roar of the crowd surged in strength. Kaiser's soul soared on the crescendo of voices.

Kaiser closed his eyes for a heartbeat when his head cleared the floor of the arena. The white sand reflected the sun with blinding intensity. Rather than show weakness by shielding his eyes, Kaiser suffered the tears that leaked down his face.

When the platform lurched to a stop, Kaiser stood in the center of the arena, his sword grounded in front of him, shield in his hand. All around him, the stands towered over his head, pillars and arches of stone supporting the bloodthirsty citizens of Northmark. To Kaiser's right, Regent Trangeth watched from a throne in the royal box.

The regent stood and raised his hands for silence. In response, the roar of the crowd lowered to a dull murmur.

"The Ninth Reaver has challenged his only superior for the position of High Reaver," Regent Trangeth bellowed out across the arena. "Let the trial commence!"

The crowd thundered its approval.

Thirty paces in front of Kaiser, another armored figure already stalked the arena floor. Clad in dark armor similar to Kaiser's, with a helm that bore wings instead of horns, the Ninth Reaver wielded a savage trident in both hands. When Kaiser appeared, the man turned from the crowd and advanced on him.

Kaiser did not move as his opponent surged toward him. The crowd loved it, taunting his attacker on. When his opponent closed within striking distance, the Ninth Reaver planted a foot and aimed a hard thrust at Kaiser's chest.

At the last instant, Kaiser exploded into motion. He batted the trident aside with his shield and spun toward his assailant, his serrated sword a blur of motion. The enemy leapt back and out of range.

When the Ninth Reaver's back foot touched down, he lunged forward, the three prongs of his trident seeking Kaiser's face. Kaiser parried the blow with a swing of his sword, diverting the attack down and away. He whirled again, trying to close the distance between them, but the Ninth Reaver danced away. His enemy had the advantage of reach and had no intention of giving it up.

The Ninth Reaver circled Kaiser, his trident held low. Kaiser no longer heard the crowd. He did not even see the arena. His opponent filled his vision. This man had challenged him. This man wanted to take away everything Kaiser held dear. This man had to die.

With a roar, Kaiser raised his shield and charged forward. He felt the Ninth Reaver's trident glance off his shield, but he did not slow. Kaiser changed course, first angling left, and then right, hoping to confuse his opponent. Once inside the trident's reach, Kaiser lowered his shield and lashed out in the direction of his enemy.

Disoriented by Kaiser's reckless charge, the Ninth Reaver could not jump back in time. He twisted his body away from Kaiser's sword, but the teeth of the blade still carved a jagged gash on the armor of his left bicep. The man cried out in pain as he spun away. Blood seeped through the punctured armor.

The crowd cried in delight at the sight of first blood.

Wounded now, the Ninth Reaver backpedaled away from Kaiser. Kaiser swore. The man was going to draw this out as long as he could, hoping to wear Kaiser down before striking the killing blow. Rather than dance around the arena for an hour, Kaiser decided to change his tactics.

Kaiser grounded his sword in the arena floor and unstrapped his shield. When the shield fell onto the sand, he took his weapon back into his hands, this time in a strong two-handed grip. He flourished the blade for the crowd, and they rewarded him with a hearty cheer.

Not to be outdone, the Ninth Reaver twisted the hilt of his trident with both hands, and it came apart in the middle. The bottom half of the shaft separated to form a vicious short spear with a gleaming tip of sharpened steel. He struggled to keep the head of the trident aloft with his wounded arm.

Kaiser advanced on his opponent, sword held out in front of him. The Ninth Reaver backed away. Without the encumbrance of his shield, Kaiser surged forward, forcing the wounded man closer and closer to the perimeter wall of the arena.

The Ninth Reaver risked a quick glance over his shoulder—he had ten more paces before he reached the wall. They both knew that if Kaiser trapped him against the wall, the fight was over. A hail of half-eaten fruit and rocks pelted the back of the Ninth Reaver. The crowd had grown tired of his refusal to fight Kaiser head-on.

With a cry, the Ninth Reaver sprinted right, trying to get around Kaiser and into the open arena. Kaiser anticipated this—he lept toward his opponent, sword extended in a powerful two-handed thrust. The blade struck only a glancing blow, but it was enough to knock the Ninth Reaver off balance. The man stumbled and fell.

As he charged forward to finish the Ninth Reaver off, a warning cry shouted in Kaiser's mind. Kaiser's attack should not have felled him. The man had fallen on his back, facing Kaiser, and made no attempt to roll away from the killing blow sure to follow. Instead, he raised his weapons in a futile attempt to ward Kaiser off.

Kaiser's eyes found the tip of the spear drawn from the shaft of the trident. It gleamed in the sun with a sickly sheen. The weapon was poisoned! At the last instant, Kaiser abandoned his attack and twisted away. The poisoned tip scratched across his armor, but did not penetrate to pierce his skin.

The crowd gasped at Kaiser's evasion. They were not strangers to poisoned weapons in the arena. By the time Kaiser recovered, the Ninth Reaver had regained his feet. With his ruse failed, he rushed toward Kaiser, intent on closing the distance and plunging the tainted weapon into Kaiser's flesh.

Now Kaiser gave ground, his sword flashing in the sun as he parried the Ninth Reaver's lightning-fast stabs. He swore again, cursing himself for abandoning his shield. The Ninth Reaver had baited him to try and end the fight quickly, and he had fallen for it.

Kaiser's arms burned with the effort of keeping his blade moving. The clash of their weapons rang out across the hot sand. Pressing the attack, the Ninth Reaver's speed flagged as he favored his wounded arm. Kaiser worried it was another trick, but he had to take the chance.

When the Ninth Reaver struck next with the top of the trident, Kaiser did not parry the blow. He let the triple prongs strike his chest armor. The weapon impacted with no strength behind it and slid away without doing damage. Kaiser stepped into the blow and chopped at his opponent's neck with a savage two-handed swing.

Armor crunched under his sword. Kaiser leapt away, twisting his body to avoid the point of the poisoned spear as it thrust toward his crotch. The Ninth Reaver dropped the head of the trident into the sand, his body sagging as he favored his injured side. His left arm hung limp and useless.

The roar of the crowd surged in anticipation, sensing an end to the fight.

"Come on then," the Ninth Reaver rasped behind his helmet. "Finish this."

Kaiser took a step forward and spun on his toes. His sword arced around him in a great swing, the blade tearing at the air with a ripping sound. The Ninth Reaver tried to get inside the attack, to skewer Kaiser on his poisoned spear, but he was too slow. Kaiser's weapon smashed into the Ninth Reaver's right elbow—metal crumpled with the force of the blow. With a cry, the Ninth Reaver lost the spear.

Unarmed now, and bleeding from multiple wounds, the Ninth Reaver swayed on his feet as he stared at Kaiser. Now the noise of the crowd came back to Kaiser's ears. They cried for blood to be spilled on the sand.

"Kill me and be done with it," the Ninth Reaver said, his voice almost pleading.

Kaiser grounded his sword in the arena floor and raised a beckoning hand toward the royal box. The crowd groaned, understanding that Kaiser would not deliver the killing blow.

"You brought this onto yourself," Kaiser said, his voice ringing in his own ears within the confines of his helmet. "No one forced you to challenge me. Now you'll suffer the ministrations of the priesthood."

"You self-righteous bastard," the Ninth Reaver snarled. "One day you're going to lose, and everything you love will fall with you."

"Save your words," Kaiser said. "Make peace with your god, for you will stand before him soon."

Chapter 2

KAISER LOOKED AWAY FROM the doomed man, his attention drawn by the cheering crowd. On the perimeter of the arena, doors opened in the stone walls. Eight dark knights strode onto the sand, each more fearsome than the last. Armor adorned with metal skulls and spikes gleamed in the sunlight. The other eight reavers marched out to where Kaiser and the Ninth Reaver stood and formed a square around them. Once the eight reavers were in position, a procession of women stepped out onto the arena floor.

These women wore long, heavy robes that disguised their forms. The dark fabric of these garments seemed to absorb the sunlight. An embroidered image of a twisted, seven-branched tree shimmered on the chest of each robe, every limb bowed under the weight of single giant, misshapen fruit. The acolytes were women of astonishing beauty, their hooded cowls doing little to hide the perfection of their faces.

In contrast to the beauty of the women that followed behind her, the woman at the head of the procession was a brute. High Priestess

Parenthia had the face of a disgruntled mastiff and the temperament to match. The heavy vestments she wore could not hide the bulk of the body beneath.

Parenthia led her acolytes into the square formed by the eight reavers. She marched right up to Kaiser, inspecting him with an impish grin on her wide face.

"Congratulations, Lord Reaver, you've bested yet another opponent," Parenthia said.

"Swallow your praise," Kaiser said. "It grows tiresome."

Parenthia smirked. "False humility doesn't become you. You're the champion of the arena, and the people love you."

"And yet I must come when called and kill when challenged," Kaiser said.

"There are worse fates," Parenthia said, dark humor dancing in her eyes.

"I'm not here to trade words with you, High Priestess," Kaiser said, nodding toward the doomed Ninth Reaver. "Do what you must."

Kaiser saw malice in Parenthia's eyes, but she let the matter drop. She turned toward the Ninth Reaver and barked a command to her acolytes.

"Strip him," Parenthia commanded.

Without a word, the robed acolytes descend upon the Ninth Reaver. Each woman bore a sharp dagger in her hand, and they took turns cutting away pieces of the doomed reaver's armor. The crowd roared with every piece of armor that dropped into the sand.

The Ninth Reaver made no move to resist, and as the armor fell away, what remained was a terrified shell of a man. His wounds throbbed an angry red against his pale flesh. He shivered under the heat of the sun. Only his eyes betrayed the hatred that burned within—they never left Kaiser's helmeted face.

When the Ninth Reaver had been stripped of all but a loincloth, the acolytes stepped back, hiding their daggers in the folds of their dark robes. Parenthia stepped forward and raised her hands to quiet the crowd. She stared at the Ninth Reaver while she waited for the voices of the mob to lower to a murmur.

"The fate of men and kings is decided in the arena," Parenthia said, her orator's voice booming out across the open space. Her words were echoed by criers positioned in the stands to spread her message through the crowd. "One lives, and one dies. This pleases Abimelech. As victor, the Tenth Reaver has delivered his opponent unto us for sacrifice. He does us great honor by allowing us to share in his glory."

As Parenthia's words died away, great doors on the north side of the arena swung open, and the city of Northmark was visible on the other side. At this signal, the eight reavers started to march toward the doors. Still positioned in the center of the square formed by the reavers, Kaiser and Parenthia, along with the acolytes and the Ninth Reaver, moved in step toward the city outside the arena. The stands above them emptied at a rapid pace as the citizens of Northmark raced to reach their destination first.

Kaiser left his sword and shield on the arena floor for his servants to collect. He marched alongside Parenthia, his stomach twisting at the thought of what came next. When they cleared the arena and stepped into the street, Kaiser tilted his helmeted head back to look upward. The spires of the Tarragon Cathedral cast long shadows over the arena.

The doors to the cathedral's courtyard were already open, and citizens lined the street, eager for a glance at their procession. Parenthia led them through the gates of the cathedral with a flourish. The citizens of Northmark spilled in behind them, filling the grand space.

In the center of the courtyard, a great, twisted tree reached toward the sky. It looked like no tree Kaiser had ever seen, and every time his gaze touched upon it, he felt sick. Its bark was smooth like skin, the color a sickly white instead of brown. Kaiser had never touched the tree, but he imagined it would throb with the warmth of flesh. Seven grotesque, swollen fruits hung from the leafless branches, the same as the image embroidered on the robes of the priestesses.

Beneath the tree, ensnared in its roots, lay an ancient tomb. The stone tomb might have been grand once, but whatever likeness of king or hero it bore had been buried under decades of filth. Bones and skulls littered the roots around the tomb. Parenthia made straight for this sepulcher.

Kaiser came to a halt when Parenthia stopped before the tree. She turned with her hands raised, and he turned with her. At their back, thousands of citizens had crammed into the cathedral courtyard. Ten thousand more would be filling the streets outside.

"You, who venture into this holy place, venerate the name of our god with me," Parenthia called out.

"Praise be to Abimelech," the crowd said in unison, repeating the words on Parenthia's lips. "He provides and protects, and his blessings endure forever."

With a huge smile on her face, Parenthia turned to Kaiser. She produced a wicked-looking dagger from within her robe and offered it to him hilt first. Kaiser took the blade without hesitation.

Two of the acolytes grabbed the Ninth Reaver by the arms and carried him toward the stone tomb with a strength that belied their slight forms. Now he struggled. His legs flailed as he tried to drag his heels into the stone of the courtyard floor. Without a word, Kaiser followed after, dagger held low by his side.

"Blood begets blood!" Parenthia thundered behind him. "No reward comes without a price. Behold, the blessing of Abimelech!"

With those words, Parenthia fell silent. The crowd waited with bated breath, hanging on Kaiser's every move. Ahead of him, the acolytes stretched the Ninth Reaver across the lid of the stone tomb. His chest heaved as panic gripped him.

Kaiser stepped up to stand over the frantic man. He stared down at his defeated opponent, disgusted by this display, but knowing he had no other choice.

"Yesterday, I was like you," the Ninth Reaver said, finding the last of his courage. "I had power, wealth, and a future for the taking. Now the whole world is against me. They'll turn on you just as easily. Not even you can escape the tree."

Kaiser ignored the man's words. He raised the dagger above his head and plunged it into the Ninth Reaver's chest. The jagged blade parted flesh and scraped bone as it sank deep into its victim's body. With a savage sawing motion, Kaiser pulled the blade downward, making a ragged incision from sternum to crotch. The Ninth Reaver gasped, his spine arching skyward, and then sank back as he moved beyond the pain.

Kaiser stepped back, away from the tomb, to avoid the blood spilling down the sides. Parenthia darted past him, accompanied by her acolytes. Kaiser turned his head away, not wanting to see them pull the man's organs out and arrange them atop the grave.

Instead, he watched the tree. As the Ninth Reaver's blood trickled between the pale roots, they drank deep of the crimson liquid. Instead of pooling in the dirt, the blood disappeared, absorbed into the sickly wood. Veins of dark red appeared in the flesh of the tree, climbing upward from the roots. Behind Kaiser, the crowd gasped as the tree slurped up the Ninth Reaver's lifeblood.

Robed acolytes streamed toward the white trunk. Each carried a sharp dagger in their right hand, and a golden chalice in their left. With ceremonial reverence, they pierced the flesh of the tree with the tips of their blades, and caught the sap that poured forth in their gilded cups. The tree's sap flowed like wine, and then the wounds left by the daggers closed before Kaiser's eyes.

When ten cups had been filled, the acolytes distributed them amongst the reavers, giving the last to Parenthia. Kaiser refused to take the chalice offered to him, which prompted a severe frown from the High Priestess. The other reavers had removed their helmets, revealing leather masks that hid their faces, but left their mouths uncovered.

Parenthia stepped toward the crowd with her own chalice raised high toward the sky.

"Behold, the blood of Abimelech!" she cried. "Drink deep, sustain your soul, and preserve your life."

As one, Parenthia and the other eight reavers lifted the goblets to their lips, tilted their heads back, and drained the contents. The crowd cheered at the display. Kaiser remained silent, watching it all from within his helmet.

Once the first part of the ritual was complete, an army of acolytes began to distribute goblets amongst the gathered crowd. Citizens gulped the liquid down greedily. Kaiser watched as priestesses of stunning beauty draped themselves over the other reavers, enticing the men deeper into the cathedral where they could satiate the physical need brought on by the bloodletting.

Parenthia alone approached Kaiser. He could see the lust in her eyes—even the High Priestess felt the effects of Abimelech's blood.

"You claim to believe, yet you spurn His sacrament," Parenthia said. "The people see your refusal to partake. Your stubbornness is exceedingly vexing."

"I'll not drink the blood of a man I just killed," Kaiser said.

"It's no longer his blood. The tree takes the essence of the slain and translates it into a blessing from Abimelech. Taking the cup is nothing like drinking the blood of a dead animal."

"I've no desire to taste it, nor experience its effects."

"Ah, foolish man," Parenthia purred. "You don't know what you're missing." She placed a finger on his armored chest and slowly traced a line down toward his crotch. "Come, let me show you the pleasures that the other reavers enjoy."

Kaiser grabbed her wrist before her hand went lower than his waist. He expected to feel her bones grind beneath his gauntleted grip, but instead he felt surprising strength.

"You know I'll take no bed but that of my wife," Kaiser said.

Anger flared in Parenthia's gaze. "You buy leniency with victory, but don't think Abimelech will overlook your disdain for his blessings forever," she snarled.

Parenthia turned away and moved toward the crowd where Kaiser knew she would find a more receptive audience. He set his mouth in a grim line behind his helmet. The power and influence of the High Priestess was growing, and he did not know how long he could afford to defy her wishes.

Chapter 3

MARIEL GAZED OUT OVER the rooftops of Northmark. She stood on the highest battlement of her fortified home. It was supposed to be a mansion, but in truth it was a small castle. As the wife of Kaiser, the Tenth Reaver, she lived her life behind the thick stone walls, almost never venturing out into the city beyond. Mariel traded her freedom for safety from Kaiser's enemies.

Their home was one of ten fortified mansions in the royal district. Each palace housed a reaver and his family. As the High Reaver, Kaiser's home stood at the far end of the district, at the end of a long street that terminated in an iron gate to the west. To the immediate east, high walls separated the reavers enclave from the rest of the city.

To the north, the stone arches of the arena and the spires of the Tarragon Cathedral dominated the skyline. The roar of the crowd had quieted half an hour ago, and the familiar dread was starting to worm its way through Mariel's bowels.

A noise behind her caused Mariel to turn. She found Garius, captain of Kaiser's guard, climbing the long wooden staircase to reach her perch. Mariel moved to the side to give him room to climb up onto the small platform. When he stood next to her, he cocked his head and listened.

"How long has the crowd been quiet?" Garius asked.

"It's not been more than an hour," Mariel said.

"We'll know the outcome soon, then."

"I wish he would allow at least one runner at the arena, to warn us if he lost."

"To do so would admit the possibility that he could be defeated. Your husband refuses to give his opponents even that."

"Are the children okay?" Mariel asked.

"Tarathine and Saredon are barricaded in the cellar," Garius said. "I've got my best men in front of the door. If they come for us, they'll have to pay in blood to reach the children."

Mariel turned her gaze back to the distant cathedral. Whether he won or lost, Kaiser would be there now. She forced her mind away from visions of what Kaiser would suffer should he lose.

"You know your husband doesn't like you coming up here, m'lady," Garius said gently.

"I'll not cower in darkness while I wait to learn our fate," Mariel said. "I want to watch it come. If I must die, I'll die with my honor intact."

Garius shook his head in wonder as a grim smile spread across his face. "There are not many women that could survive a single year as consort to a reaver, yet you've survived ten as his wife, and borne him two children."

"He gave me my life back," Mariel said. "Standing by him is the least I could do. Ever since that day, I've resolved to not let fear control me. To do so is to live as if I'm already dead."

"I remember—I was there," Garius said, leaning his arms against the top of the battlement. "Reavers had more power back then. He'd never get away with that today, snatching you from the clutches of the inquisition. Parenthia would have his head."

"I thought he was going to kill me," Mariel said, remembering Kaiser standing before her, terrible, bloody, and silent. Her uncle Shadwin had gone mad, manifesting strange and horrible powers. Shadwin had decided he was chosen by a god and set himself up as ruler in the city that Mariel's family had governed for generations. In his insanity, Shadwin murdered any who questioned his authority.

At the head of an inquisition from Northmark, a young reaver had come to make Shadwin pay for his crimes. After a long and bloody battle, Kaiser had beheaded Shadwin in the public square. Law required that the rest of the heretic's family be purged as well. Mariel had been marched out into the square with her mother and father, and the rest of her extended family, to be exterminated under the inquisitor's axe.

Kaiser had stopped the proceedings when he saw Mariel. With the blood of her uncle still splattered on his dark armor, he had stood before her, staring at her from within his dreadful, six-horned helm. Rather than cower, Mariel had met his gaze with defiance.

Kaiser had spared her life, and her family, on the condition that she become his ward. He convinced the inquisition that he would watch over her, and if she ever showed signs of heresy, he would kill her himself. Only years later did Mariel understand that her uncle had been a magus, driven mad by power he did not ask for and could not hope to control.

"I've never asked why he saved me," Mariel said, her thoughts returning to the present. "It's enough that he did."

Garius did not respond. Mariel glanced in his direction. He was looking to the west—the blood had drained from his face. She whirled to follow his gaze. At the gate to the royal district, dark-armored soldiers were returning from the city. They strode down the center of the street, and as they came, troops streamed from the mansions they passed to join their ranks.

"The reavers have returned," Mariel whispered.

"I don't see Kaiser," Garius said, his voice hard.

"That doesn't mean anything," Mariel said. "If he was victorious, he would be detained by the ceremony."

Mariel took no comfort from her own words, and she sensed that Garius did not either. Soon, the reavers and their household troops filled the street. They passed the Fifth Reaver's palace, and still they came.

"They're going to the ninth mansion," Garius said without confidence. "They have to be."

The small army passed the Seventh Reaver's home. Mariel struggled to breathe as fear threatened to overwhelm her. They were close enough that she could make out the horrifying features of each reaver's helmet.

At last, they reached the front of the Ninth Reaver's mansion and stopped. Mariel sagged against the battlement, tears spilling down her cheeks.

Garius let out a huge breath. "He won. Kaiser won."

The relief and joy that surged in Mariel's heart ashamed her. Kaiser had bested the Ninth Reaver and ensured the safety of his own family at the cost of the loved ones of the man he defeated.

Even as she watched, the armed mob below prepared to assault the house guards of the Ninth Reaver's mansion. From her vantage point, Mariel saw a woman and her children rush into the palace while guards ran toward the gate.

"Poor souls," Garius said, shaking his head. "They don't stand a chance. The death of a ninth is the only time eight other reavers will ever work together."

Garius placed a comforting hand on Mariel's shoulder before turning toward the stair. "I'll go inform the men of Kaiser's victory. Don't watch for too long. It won't be pretty."

Mariel nodded, but did not turn to watch Garius leave the battlement. She knew she should look away, but she could not tear her gaze from the scene below. Reavers were the kingdom's greatest warriors, and the highest station a man could attain short of regent or king. But only the best held the title, and they were allowed to challenge one another to combat in the arena. The loser died in dishonor, and the winner moved up a position in the hierarchy.

However, the family and troops the slain reaver left behind must first be ousted from their fortified home. The eight reavers below were working together because the loss of the Ninth Reaver meant that each would ascend one rank. All they had to do was murder the Ninth Reaver's family and anyone who might raise a sword to defend his name.

Such a fate awaited Mariel and her children if Kaiser ever fell in the arena. She looked away when the first screams of the dying floated on the air up to where she stood on the battlement. Mariel's cheeks were still wet with tears, but now she cried for the innocent lives who would suffer and die only a stone's throw from her home. She hated this city and this kingdom, yet without Kaiser's help, she could never leave. And in her heart, Mariel knew that she would never leave without him.

After a time, movement at the district gate caught Mariel's eye. She lifted her face and wiped away her tears. Only one man could march through the district like he owned it: Kaiser had returned. Mariel lingered on the ramparts for only a moment, then she made her way down the stairs and toward the gate of the compound. She wanted to be the first to greet her husband.

The grounds were quiet as Mariel made her way through the compound. News of Kaiser's victory had yet to spread through the household troops. They still wondered if they would be forced to fight and die tonight. Mariel reached the front gate and ordered it unbarred.

"I'm sorry, m'lady," the gatekeeper said. "I'm under strict orders not to open the gate unless the Lord High Reaver himself returns."

"Kaiser is out in the street," Mariel said. "Now open the gate, or step aside so I can do it myself."

The soldier went white. He hurriedly unlocked the gate and resumed his post.

"Make yourself scarce," Mariel said. "I wish to speak to my husband in private when he arrives."

The soldier looked uncertain, but he decided not to argue. He moved along the wall until he stood thirty paces away, still in sight of the gate, but out of earshot. Mariel stepped forward and cracked the gate so that Kaiser would see that it was open. She did not have to wait long before his shadow blocked the light streaming through the open door.

Kaiser pushed the gate aside and stepped through. He stopped short when he found Mariel waiting for him. His ornate armor was crusted with dried blood. He carried no weapon or shield, but that did nothing to diminish the menace of his presence. Mariel knew him and loved him, and yet she still had to resist the overwhelming urge to shrink away from Kaiser's dread visage.

They stared at one another without speaking, and the memory of their first meeting returned to Mariel's mind. She had intended to congratulate Kaiser and to welcome him home, but her anger and sorrow got the better of her.

"You stink of blood and death," Mariel said. "Don't think to come to me or the children without cleaning yourself up first."

Kaiser inclined his helmeted head in acknowledgment. Mariel turned on her heel and strode away, not trusting herself to speak further. A rage gripped her, and she did not want to say anything she might regret.

Mariel encountered Garius in the hallway, walking fast toward the gate.

"He has returned?" Garius asked when he saw the look on Mariel's face.

Mariel nodded. "Tell him I'll be in the cellar with the children when he's ready to see us."

"As you wish, m'lady," Garius said.

Garius continued on toward the gate as Mariel turned toward the stone steps that led into the bowels of the mansion. Guards no longer manned the stout double doors, and for the moment, the threat had passed. Mariel pushed one of the doors open and slipped into the cool cellar beyond.

Mariel paused to let her eyes adjust to the dim lighting. Barrels and sacks lined the walls, and the exposed foundations of the house above formed a crude ceiling. Torches lit the cavernous space, with a single brazier providing extra light and warmth where the children played. A few servants attended them.

Together, Mariel and Kaiser had two children. Tarathine, a girl of twelve summers, and Saredon, a boy two years younger. Unaware of their mother's presence, they sat in the center of the cellar on a blanket that had been spread across the cold stone floor. Mariel smiled as she watched them play together. They were blissfully unaware of the dangers on the other side of the compound walls.

Drawing strength from her love for the children, Mariel stepped forward into the light. They both noticed her at the same time and scrambled to their feet. Saredon tackled her midsection while Tarathine held back for a more reserved, mature embrace. Mariel squeezed her daughter tight.

"Has father returned?" Saredon asked, looking up at Mariel's face.

"He has," Mariel said. "I expect he'll join us soon."

"Are you okay?" Tarathine asked, frowning with concern. "You look like you've been crying."

"I'm fine," Mariel said. "It's nothing to worry yourself over."

Mariel ushered the children back to the blanket, and they sat while Mariel answered all the questions they had about why they were hiding in the cellar.

"You're down here to keep you safe," Mariel said. "There's no threat that Garius and his guards can't handle, but it makes his job easier if he knows you're in here."

So far, the children had not seen through the lies Kaiser and Mariel told them. But Mariel knew Tarathine was beginning to suspect that they were prisoners in their own home. The girl would start asking questions that had no good answer soon.

Kaiser joined them within the hour. Freshly washed and scented, he wore a simple cloth shirt and pants. He padded barefoot across the stone floor. While still a hard man, he appeared nothing like the frightful persona he donned when wearing the armor of the Tenth Reaver. Underneath his harsh exterior, he possessed a tenderness that Mariel had grown to love dearly.

Once Kaiser appeared, he became the center of the children's attention. Mariel reclined on the blanket and contented herself with listening to their conversation. The children adored their father.

"Did you fight in the arena, father?" Saredon ask, his eyes shining brightly.

"I did indeed," Kaiser said.

"Did you win? Did the crowd cheer?"

Kaiser laughed. "Yes, and yes."

"When can I watch? I want to see you fight!"

"Someday, son. When you're old enough."

"There's more to life than fighting," Tarathine said, with all the gravity a girl of twelve summers could muster. "You need to train your mind too."

"You only say that because you can't beat me with a sword anymore," Saredon said.

"No, your sister's right," Kaiser said with a smile. "The strongest sword arm is useless without an experienced mind to wield it."

This prompted Tarathine to stick her tongue out at Saredon, who escalated the argument by pinching his sister. Kaiser joined in the tickling and soon all three were rolling on the floor.

"Your father has had a long day and needs his rest," Mariel said, raising her voice to be heard over their squeals. "Say goodnight and follow Pelly upstairs. She'll see you into bed."

The serving girl named Pelly stepped forward with her head bowed. Tarathine and Saredon groaned in unison, both appealing to Kaiser for just a little more time. He grinned at them.

"I might be the champion of the arena, but your mother is boss," Kaiser said. "Get upstairs, you two. I'll see you in the morning."

Mariel and Kaiser watched as Pelly ushered the reluctant children up the cellar stairs. The rest of the servants followed, and soon the two of them were alone. The silence stretched as neither spoke.

"It was a good victory?" Mariel finally asked.

"Not as clean as I'd like," Kaiser said. "He tried to stick me with a poisoned weapon."

Mariel glanced at Kaiser in alarm.

He raised a palm to reassure her. "He didn't get past my armor."

"You bled him beneath the tree?" Mariel said.

Kaiser sighed. "You know I don't have a choice. The public ritual appeases the priesthood and keeps them out of our hair about your... past."

Mariel set her mouth in a grim line and did not respond. She wanted to plead with Kaiser to find a way to cast off the office of reaver and deliver them this dreadful existence, but she knew this was not the right time.

Kaiser gazed at her with undisguised longing, and Mariel sensed his need. It was the same after every trial in the arena. A need for closeness. A need for catharsis. The other reavers quenched their fire within the priesthood's prostitutes. Kaiser came home to her.

"You should block the cellar doors," Mariel murmured.

After a heartbeat of confusion, Kaiser took her meaning. With a grin, he hopped to his feet and moved toward the double wooden doors. By the time he had them secured, Mariel had stood and slipped out of her dress.

When Kaiser turned, he stopped in his tracks, gazing at her naked body. She stepped forward, walking slowly, stoking the flames of his arousal. He did not move as she approached. When Mariel stood in front of him, she reached out and drew the cloth shirt over Kaiser's head. He lifted his arms to help.

Mariel let the garment fall to the floor as she traced her fingers down Kaiser's bare torso. Her fingertips brushed across the scars of a hundred battles. When he could wait no longer, they came together with a desperation borne of living life on a knife's edge. For a time, nothing else existed.

Afterward, they lay intertwined on a blanket in the center of the cellar. "I know you're unhappy," Kaiser said. His fingers traced random symbols on Mariel's bare thigh as he spoke. "It pains me every day that I cannot give you a better life than this."

"I know," Mariel murmured.

"In the ten years that I've been High Reaver there's not been one mention of putting a king on the throne," Kaiser said. "The regent has ruled for as long as anyone can remember, and yet he has no claim to the crown. I travel the entire kingdom, enforcing his will with an iron fist, but nothing ever changes. In truth, things only get worse. When I pass through the countryside, I cannot shake the sense of a growing desperation. It's like there's an invisible hand on our throat that's slowly squeezing the life out of us."

Mariel rolled over and looked at Kaiser. "What will you do?"

"Whatever ails the kingdom is beyond my power to change," Kaiser said. "All that matters now is keeping you and the children safe. Perhaps if I survive another five years, the regent will let me retire, and we can find somewhere to live that's free of this madness."

Mariel lowered her head to Kaiser's chest to hide her tears. In her heart, she knew they would never survive another five years. Even if they did, a reaver had never been allowed to retire. To pin their hopes on that dream seemed beyond foolish.

Beneath her head, Kaiser's breathing slowed and the rise and fall of his chest took on the rhythm of deep sleep. Mariel listened to the beat of his heart as she thought about the future. How could she make him see? How could she make him understand? As long as they stayed in Northmark, they had no hope.

Mariel closed her eyes. In the midst of her despair, she knew where to find hope. The priesthood would burn her alive if they ever learned of her faith, but that did not deter her. Not even Kaiser suspected.

"Watch for his coming," Mariel whispered under her breath. "For the Shrouded King returns."

Chapter 4

MAZAREEM CONTEMPLATED THE EASEL in front of him. He held no brush, and the paint was long dry. Suspended on the canvas in subtle hues, a woman of peerless beauty stared back at him. Clothed in a simple white dress, with her hair pulled back from her face, she looked like an almost perfect replica of his last memory of her. A thousand years separated him from that moment. He recalled her face, her scent, and her touch, but not her name. Mazareem knew she was long dead, but he could not bring himself to destroy the unfinished painting.

For hundreds of years, Mazareem had labored on this one work, painting, starting over, and painting again. Now, when he visited her, his brush remained still. He had changed. The passage of time had stripped Mazareem of his humanity while leaving the flawless beauty of her memory untouched. In his heart, Mazareem knew that the woman in the painting would recoil from him as a monster if she saw him now.

An odd sound interrupted Mazareem's thoughts and shattered his contemplation. He cocked his head to one side, trying to remember what the noise signified. When he found the memory, the edges of his mouth turned up in a satisfied smile. Footsteps. It was the sound of footsteps.

In the main room of his prison suite, a deep, throaty bark meant that Worm heard the sound too. Mazareem stepped away from the painting and went to join the hound.

Whatever breed Worm had once been was lost under a hundred years of experimentation and mutation. A steady diet of the concoction that Mazareem survived on had turned the beast into a monster. Mazareem stood taller than most men, and the top of Worm's head reached his shoulders. Powerful muscles wrapped the dog's neck and trunk. On their last foray into the outside world, Mazareem had seen Worm snap a horse's neck between his massive jaws.

"Steady, boy," Mazareem said to the dog. "Visitors are rare down here. Let's not frighten them away." He scratched under the animal's massive jaw.

Worm sat back on his haunches, content to wait to see what came through the door before tearing it apart. The footsteps slowed as they approached, and soon Mazareem heard the sound of a key grinding in the lock. When at last the thick iron door scraped open, a fat woman wearing a black robe stepped through.

The woman stopped short, her mouth hanging open but no words coming out. Mazareem smiled to himself. Worm had that effect on people.

"To what do we owe the pleasure, Parenthia?" Mazareem asked in his most polite voice.

Parenthia's jaw clacked shut. She turned to close the door behind her before speaking. When she faced him again, she had recovered from her shock.

"You will address me as High Priestess," Parenthia said.

"Certainly, Parenthia," Mazareem said with a grin. The fear in her eyes pleased him.

Parenthia glowered, but decided not to argue. "The signs and portents are strengthening," she said. "My prophets believe that the appearance of a magus is imminent."

"Has it been twelve years already?" Mazareem asked.

"Don't mock me," Parenthia snapped. "You knew why I was here as soon as you heard my footsteps."

"Why don't you tell me?" Mazareem asked, his smile widening.

Parenthia glared daggers at him. "I've been instructed to release you. The prophets believe the magus will rise in the east. You're to travel to Oakroot in the Nogard Forest and hunt him down. You have two months. If you fail, my priesthood will be called upon to deal with the threat. If you're not back sixty days from now, you'll not be allowed entry into this sanctum. Without a steady supply of the blood of Abimelech, you'll whither and die."

As she spoke the last words, her lips twisted in a cruel smile.

"Why do you despise me so, sweet Parenthia?" Mazareem asked. "We serve the same master."

"You're not one of his children!" Parenthia said, her words almost a shout. "You're a foul, twisted thing. You're an abomination."

Worm growled and Parenthia cringed, much to Mazareem's delight. "Such harsh words cut us deep, don't they, Worm?"

Mazareem said, laying his head against the beast's ragged coat in mock sadness.

Parenthia's mouth twisted in a grimace. She raised her right hand, revealing a ring forged from black metal. Around the band, draconic script glowed with red fire. "You have two months."

She exited the room, leaving the heavy iron door open behind her. Mazareem shuddered as the binding power that compelled him to obey tightened on his soul. The yawning portal called to him. He held himself still for a long time, relishing the denial of the overwhelming impulse to dash through the door with a shout.

Worm's thick tail slapped the floor. The dog looked up at Mazareem, big black eyes pleading with his master to move.

"Yes, yes," Mazareem finally said. "We're going."

Mazareem donned a long, black travel cloak, plucked his walking staff from the corner, and secured a belt of vials around his waist. Dark liquid sloshed in the glass tubes. Neither he nor Worm needed food, but Parenthia was right: without the vials, they would both perish. When he was certain that all was in order, Mazareem strode through the door with Worm at his side.

Mazareem smiled to himself as he climbed to the surface. Parenthia and her kind hated him, for he was older than most of them and had served Abimelech far longer. He had been hunting magi for hundreds of years. Parenthia's priesthood was a new invention, an ostentation to appeal to the masses. Let her revel in her frivolous role. She might be Abimelech's own priestess, but Mazareem was his assassin.

Chapter 5

LACRAEL SLIPPED THROUGH THE trees with long-practiced ease. Branch and bush parted at her passing with a gentle caress of her leather armor. Gripped in her left hand, the smooth, polished wood of a hunting bow instilled a familiar confidence. She held an arrow nocked, ready to draw in the blink of an eye.

Thirty paces to the south, a large stag grazed in a clearing between the trees. Lacrael had been stalking the animal for the better part of the morning. She needed to make the kill here or the day would be a waste. The deer jerked its head up and looked straight at her. Eight points of bone reached for the sky above its head, a magnificent crown for a forest prince.

Not daring to breathe, Lacrael stopped in her tracks. It was not the shot she wanted, but she had to try. Careful not to spook the animal, she raised the bow in front of her. The stag's tail twitched in agitation, and Lacrael imagined it bounding away at the last instant.

Lacrael drew the string back to her ear, the pull of the bow overpowered by the strength in her arms. She sighed and let fly. The bowstring whispered past her ear, sending the arrow speeding toward her target. Her eye tracked the bright red fletching as the broadhead slammed home. A perfect shot. The arrow buried itself in the stag's side.

The animal leapt into the air in surprise, its body convulsing with the shock of the impact. When its feet touched the ground, it bolted for the woods. Lacrael made no hurry to follow. The deer would not get far with a punctured lung.

Lacrael took the time to unstring her bow and wrap the cord before stowing it in her pack. She secured the bow on her back and drew her sword. It seemed distasteful to slaughter an animal with so elegant a weapon, but she had discovered it to be an effective way to strike the killing blow.

When she stepped into the clearing, Lacrael found a trail of blood leading away to the east. Sword in hand, she followed the path of the dying stag. She did not have to walk far. The deer had collapsed about a hundred paces from the clearing. It lay on its side, chest heaving with great, wheezing breaths. White spittle flecked its mouth.

Lacrael stepped to the animal's side. It saw her coming, and eyes already wide with terror rolled back in its head. She placed the tip of her sword on the deer's heaving chest above the heart. With a sharp twist and plunge, she drove the blade deep into the stag's body, piercing its heart and ending its life. Four hooves twitched once and went still.

Pleased with the clean kill, Lacrael pulled her sword from the animal and set it aside. She drew a hunting knife and set to butchering her prize. The process took a good two hours and was far harder than the hunt had been. When she finished, Lacrael leaned back on her heels, swiping a bloody hand across her forehead to wipe away the sweat.

She could not carry all the meat with her, but she knew the carcass would not go to waste. Scavengers would pick it dry before the sun rose next morning. Ready to be on her way, Lacrael unfolded the large satchel she carried for just this purpose and packed the raw meat inside. This done, she collected her sword, hoisted the satchel over her shoulder, and strode away from the bloody scene.

The forest town of Oakroot was less than an hour's walk to the north. Lacrael did her hunting near the town so that she could carry the meat in to sell before it spoiled. She had enough venison here to fetch a tidy sum from the innkeeper.

Lacrael paused at a small stream to clean the blood from her hands and wash the gore from her sword. She did not want to walk into town looking like death. Satisfied with her reflection in the water, Lacrael hefted her burden and continued toward Oakroot.

Cut out of the Nogard Forest, Oakroot sat on the eastern border of the Kingdom of Haverfell. The small town was home to only a few hundred souls. In the summer months, the population swelled as laborers traveled from all over the kingdom to harvest lumber and transport it west.

The last of the winter's snow had thawed the previous week, and Lacrael knew the town would soon be bustling with activity. The thought filled her with anxiety. Several hundred lonely and curious men brought problems for her. Her appearance did little to help. Lacrael's dark skin, raven black hair, and impressive stature marked her as a foreigner from some distant and exotic land. She stood a head taller than most of the men of Haverfell, and they were drawn to her like ants to honey.

Lacrael lived in the deep forest and only ventured into Oakroot several times a month to purchase the few supplies she needed. For the past four years Lacrael had managed to keep the location of her home a secret. She wanted to keep it that way.

The outskirts of Oakroot appeared between the trees in front of her. Soon, Lacrael found herself striding down the dirt street that marked the center of the town. She nodded at those she passed, returning their gestures but not lingering to speak with any of them. The regulars knew her and did not bother her, for which Lacrael was grateful.

Built from the ready supply of wood taken from the nearby forest, Oakroot boasted an impressive assortment of buildings and storehouses. Most went unused until the lumber harvesting season. In the center of town, the Acorn Inn stood the tallest, a three-story structure with enough rooms to house an army.

Lacrael had an arrangement with the owner, Monty. He would purchase whatever wild game she hunted for a fair price, which allowed her to buy what goods she needed from the general store.

The inn was quiet when Lacrael entered. Strewn with stout tables and chairs, the huge main room could have fit Lacrael's entire home inside of it and then some. A fire smoldered in a giant fireplace on the far wall.

A serving girl noticed Lacrael and smiled. "Monty's in the kitchen."

Lacrael nodded her thanks and dropped everything but her meat-laden satchel by the door. She found Monty standing at a high counter, gnawing on a piece of bread while he looked over a ledger. He looked up when he heard Lacrael approach.

"Lacrael!" Monty said with a smile. "I was wondering if we'd see you today. How's your grandfather?"

"He's well," Lacrael said after a brief pause. Monty's jovial demeanor and polite, but persistent questions always made her uncomfortable. She dropped her satchel on the floor with a thump. "I've brought meat."

Monty chuckled. "You butcher conversation as viciously as you do dead animals."

"It's a long hike back," Lacrael said, not accustomed to witty banter.

Monty peered into the satchel as he muttered to himself.

"This is a good haul," Monty said when he finished. "I'll give you ten marks for this."

"That sounds fair," Lacrael said, masking her surprise. Ten marks was more than he had ever paid.

Monty counted ten coins out of a pouch on the counter and then dropped them into Lacrael's waiting palm. He made a mark in his ledger while she stored the money in her belt pouch.

"It'll be lumber season soon."

"That it will," Lacrael said patiently.

"Can't come fast enough," Monty said. "My ledger tells a sad tale through the cold months. The warmth of summer brings with it the promise of gold, and I don't mean flowers."

Lacrael said nothing. Summer would only make her life harder, but she did not want to say it.

"Say, I was thinking that you might earn some extra coin this season," Monty said, glancing at her out of the corner of his eye.

"I've no use for it," Lacrael said. "I earn more than enough to buy what little I need."

"Come now, everyone can find a use for more wealth," Monty said. "Store it away in that forest home of yours, or buy your grandfather something nice."

"I don't... we get on just fine, Monty, really—"

"With how much time you've spent in these woods, you must know where the best lumber can be found. What do you think of hiring yourself out as a guide to the crews this season?"

His features softened as he smiled at her. "I don't doubt that your grandfather needs you, but you shouldn't hide yourself in the deep forest forever. I think you could do quite well as a guide."

"I'll think on it," Lacrael said.

"It would give you the chance to spend more time in town," Monty said with a wink. "Maybe you could even help out at the store."

"I should go," Lacrael said, suddenly embarrassed. "I've got to pick up a few things before I head back into the forest."

"Of course," Monty said with a smile. "Think about what I said. Safe travels and give my regards to my son."

Lacrael left Monty to his ledger, hoping he did not see her blush at the mention of his son. Once back at the front of the building, Lacrael gathered her gear and stepped out into the street. The sun had started its descent toward the western horizon. If she wanted to be home before nightfall, she needed to leave Oakroot within the hour.

She set out down the road, heading toward the general store. The ten marks jangled in her pouch as she walked. Her steps grew

lighter as she neared her destination, and the wings of a hundred butterflies started to flutter in her stomach.

The owner and operator of the Oakroot store was Monty's son Brant, the most handsome man Lacrael had ever seen. Getting to see his face and hear his voice was the highlight of every trip into Oakroot. Lacrael knew it was foolish, but she would often invent a reason to hike into town just for the chance to exchange a few words with Brant.

With its wooden porch facing the road, the general store caught her eye long before she reached it. Brant kept the place spotless. Wedged between two dingy buildings, the store almost seemed to glow in contrast. There was a series of woven mats leading up the open doors. The first lay in the dirt of the street, the next on the steps of the deck, and then the last on the porch itself. The implication was clear: Lacrael carefully wiped the dirt off her boots.

The storefront was open and inviting. Once inside, Lacrael could not help but marvel at how everything had its place. Racks lined the wall, holding tools sorted by size and purpose. Bags of flour and grain were stacked in intricate pyramids. Not even a single kernel of corn could be found on the spotless plank floor.

In Lacrael's mind, the only thing more perfect than the store itself was Brant, who watched the place from the counter at the back. He stood a head taller than Lacrael. With his light brown hair, strong jaw, and shoulders as broad as an ox, Brant looked more like a knight than a shopkeeper. Only his soft midsection betrayed his profession.

Brant's face lit up when Lacrael entered. He smiled at her. Lacrael nodded, returned his smile, and turned her attention to shopping. She took her time, pretending she had no idea that Brant was watching her. This was the game they played. She lingered in the store, happy to be in the same room with Brant, and he waited patiently for her to finish and approach the counter.

The forest provided for most of her needs, but there were a few items that she liked to buy to make life a little easier. Lacrael placed a small bag of flour, a handful of iron nails, six eggs, and several packets of seeds into her pack before moving toward the counter. Brant never took his eyes off of her, and now Lacrael returned his gaze.

"How much for all of this?" Lacrael asked in the most serious voice she could muster.

"Six marks," Brant said, too shy to look directly at her now that she was close.

Lacrael withdrew six marks from her pocket and plunked them down on the counter.

Brant scooped the coins up. The marks disappeared into a pouch, and he finally dared to look at Lacrael's face.

"Good day to you," Lacrael said with a nod before their interaction could descend into awkwardness.

"Your business is always appreciated," Brant said, returning her nod.

Lacrael gathered her goods and walked out of the store. She felt Brant's eyes on her back the entire way. With the obvious attraction they had for each other, Lacrael knew he wanted to take it further, but she would not give him the chance. There was no way she could risk any sort of relationship. Lacrael knew that flirting with him was foolish, but she was so lonely.

Once back in the street, Lacrael breathed easier and tried to push thoughts of Brant aside as she set her feet to the long path home.

Pleasant as it was to daydream, no good could come of a ridiculous infatuation with a storekeeper. Before coming to this strange land, Lacrael had been a warrior. She still practiced with the sword she carried. She needed to be ready and able for her destiny, and unattached.

The sun would dip below the western treetops soon. She would have to travel hard to reach the deep forest before nightfall. Lacrael smiled to herself, relishing the strenuous hike ahead of her.

Oakroot dwindled behind her, finally vanishing behind a wall of trees. Lacrael yearned to show the woods her heels and never return. She had no desire to stay here any longer than necessary. Soon, Lacrael's purpose would be accomplished and she could leave this unfamiliar place. As she hiked through the trees, Lacrael lost herself in thoughts of the future, imagining the day when she would be free of the forest's omnipresent shadow.

Lacrael's legs ached with the wonderful soreness of hard exercise. She did not know the exact distance from Oakroot to her home in the forest, but she guessed the trip took at least four hours at a quick pace. She made the last hour of the trek in the dark. Lacrael did not carry a torch, preferring to slip through the shadows like a silent predator. Every so often, she paused to listen, her senses attuned for any sound in the nearby trees. Only when she was certain that she was alone did she move toward her secret home.

The small cabin she lived in was nestled at the bottom of a wooded ravine. Hundreds of years ago, a powerful river had carved a path through the heart of the forest. Now all that remained was a winding canyon with a small stream at its bottom. Constructed next to this bubbling brook, the log house was invisible from the forest floor above. Lacrael knew this part of the forest better than her own face and it still sometimes took her several passes to find the hidden cabin.

Fortune favored her tonight. Lacrael found the path down into the ravine without having to search for it. She stood at the top of the trail and listened to the subdued sounds of the forest. Suspended in that quiet place between day and night, the trees were still as tired animals crawled into burrows to wait for the dawn. The creatures that owned the darkness would soon start to sing their quiet symphony. Lacrael might be sick of the forest, but on nights like this, she could not deny its beauty.

With a small smile, Lacrael descended into the secret valley. She found the small stream, the descendent of a once mighty river, and followed it north. After several hundred paces, Lacrael arrived at her home.

In the darkness, the cabin looked like just another shadow. Its roof stood only a head taller than Lacrael, and trees grew close on every side but the front. Mossy and snug, the cabin beckoned, promising comfort and warmth if she would stoke the hearth.

Pleased to be home, Lacrael pushed open the creaky door and deposited her packs on the floor. Her happiness faded when only silence greeted her. Out here in the deep woods, she was the only living soul for miles. Thoughts of Brant returned as her loneliness surged.

Lacrael lit a lantern and stored the items from her travel pack, but she could not quiet the restlessness in her soul. She stood in the center of the small cabin and tried to envision the four walls as something other than a prison. Frustrated, she left the shack and followed the little stream north. Meditation would clear her head.

After a hundred paces, she pushed aside the thick bushes to reveal a secluded pool at the base of a small waterfall. Lacrael had chosen this ravine for her home because of this spot. When she meditated here, the veil separating her from the spirit plane felt thinner. She liked to imagine that the spirit of her grandfather could find her in this place. Lacrael hoped he was pleased that she had not abandoned the quest he set her on.

— —

Lacrael sat on the bank of the pool and crossed her legs. The chill of the earth penetrated her leather leggings and bit into her flesh. She raised a hand in front of her and focused on the outstretched palm. Five tiny flames sprang to life on the tips of her fingers. Lacrael smiled and wondered for the hundredth time what Brant would think if he knew the truth about her. With a flick of her wrist, Lacrael sent the fire plunging deep into the core of a nearby log. The wood crackled and burned. She closed her eyes and sighed as the warmth washed over her.

The steady gurgle of the stream plummeting into the dark pool slowed the chaos of Lacrael's thoughts. When she felt ready, she fished the amulet she wore around her neck out from beneath her shirt. Gold glimmered in the flickering firelight. She held the amulet in her palm, staring at it in wonder.

Hammered from the richest gold, carved with intricate detail, a miniature dragon roared up at Lacrael. Its outstretched wings spread across her hand. It had claws of emerald and eyes of ruby. The little stones caught the light and winked up at Lacrael, tiny pinpricks of color.

Unshed tears filled Lacrael's eyes. The amulet had been her grandfather's. Seven years ago, Lacrael had manifested the powers of a magus. In her homeland of Vaul, these powers were used for destruction and tyranny. Her family had been overjoyed to possess so terrible a weapon in her and made grand plans to make war on their rival clans.

Lacrael's grandfather, Garlang, had abducted her. Together, they escaped deep into the blasted wastelands of Vaul. For three years, her grandfather had instructed her on the proper use of her power. Lacrael's family had hunted them, but thanks to Garlang's ability as a warrior, they always stayed one step ahead.

Until one fateful day, when her clan's warriors stumbled onto them by accident. Garlang had thrust this amulet into her hand, told her that she was ready, and instructed her to flee to the standing stones in the field near their hiding place.

The power of the memory gripped Lacrael as it played out in her mind. She had sprinted to the field as her grandfather commanded. She knew the place well. They had trained in the shadow of the great standing stones for years. It was a sacred place, a place of power. On that terrible day, the stones had reacted to her presence. A swirling vortex of green energy appeared in the center of the menhir. Confused and afraid, Lacrael had hesitated.

She wanted to close her eyes and shut out the memory of what came next, but all she could do was watch.

Garlang had held off ten men to cover her escape. He made his last stand on the field of the standing stones. When he saw Lacrael hesitate, he had bellowed at her to enter the portal. In the next instant, an enemy's blade found a gap in his defenses and he suffered the wound that would be the end of him. With a roar, her grandfather had charged the warriors to buy Lacrael a few more heartbeats.

With tears streaming down her face, Lacrael had stepped into the maelstrom of light in the center of the stones. She could still feel the sensation of being pulled apart as if it had just happened. Her vision went black, and her soul was ripped from her body. She had hurtled through the endless void, lost and terrified. When she had crashed back to reality, she found herself on the bank of this pool. That had been four years ago. In that time, no one had followed her through the portal.

Lacrael did not have her grandfather to ask, but she knew she was in a different world. She had never imagined that trees could grow so high, or water run so clear. Thanks to her grandfather's training, Lacrael had survived, and then thrived. She had discovered Oakroot, and after overcoming her fear, she had been astonished to find that one of the languages her grandfather taught her allowed her to communicate with the people here.

Garlang had been preparing Lacrael to come to this strange land. Perhaps he had intended to come with her. During the three years they spent in hiding, he taught Lacrael that her powers were neither curse nor gift, no mere weapon to be used against rivals, but a tool given to man to fight against a great evil. Garlang had claimed to be a member of an ancient and sacred order, sworn to fight this threat wherever it might arise. He had recruited Lacrael to his cause and impressed upon her the urgency of their duty.

Cross-legged on the bank, Lacrael stared into the dark pool in front of her and saw a vision of the homeland she had forsaken. Nomadic clans wandered a sundered wasteland. Black clouds blotted out the sun. A sentient miasma covered the earth, twisting all life that it touched into poisoned abominations. Before obtaining her powers, Lacrael had spent most of her life fleeing before this darkness and fighting the monsters it spawned.

Her grandfather had insisted that Vaul had once been a lush, beautiful realm, describing a world that Lacrael had never understood before the forest. He had said that their homeland was dying and only Lacrael could save it. According to Garlang, others with powers like hers would rise. She had to wait and watch for their coming. For four years Lacrael had lived in a state of constant vigilance, ready to act when the time came.

"I'm still here, grandfather," Lacrael said to the dark water. "I'm still waiting for the next sign."

Lacrael hoped that her grandfather could see her, hoped that he could see that she had not abandoned the duty he had trained her for. Her faith did not waver, but on days like today, she felt weary. She had been living in the forest for four years. How much longer did she have to wait?

With a heavy sigh, Lacrael pulled herself to her feet. She tossed the burned-out log into the water, where it hissed and smoked as its embers were quenched, then tromped back to her little cabin.

Inside, Lacrael prepared a meal in her small kitchen. In honor of her grandfather, she fried a few eggs. She smiled to herself. Fried eggs had always been his favorite.

Chapter 6

MAZAREEM APPROACHED OAKROOT FROM the west. Needing neither rest nor food, he and Worm had traveled day and night along the highways of the kingdom. As his tireless feet devoured the miles between him and his destination, Mazareem could not wipe the smile off his face. It was such a small thing, this brief gift of freedom, but oh how he relished it.

The other travelers on the road gave the dark stranger and his monstrous hound a wide berth, which suited Mazareem just fine. His passing would be marked, and rumors would spread through the countryside, but this was no concern of his. By the time the locals worked up the courage to confront him, Mazareem would be once again locked within his sanctuary beneath Northmark.

Thoughts of his gilded prison almost soured Mazareem's mood, but when the trees of the Nogard Forest rose on the eastern horizon, he set his mind to the task at hand. He had survived a thousand years as a servant of Abimelech, and he could endure another thousand if need be. A slave could escape and win back his freedom; a dead man had no such hope.

"It's been a hundred years since we've come this way," Mazareem said to Worm as they passed under the branches of the first leafless trees. "Do you think anyone remembers us?"

Worm gave no sign that he heard. The dog was more interested in the scents of the forest and the rustling in the undergrowth.

"You should heed the words of your master, you disrespectful mutt," Mazareem said in amusement.

The morning sun rose overhead as they traversed the forest road. Mazareem quickened his pace, eager to reach Oakroot by noon. His black cloak fluttered around his long legs as he stretched his stride to cover the last few miles.

When the first wooden building came into view between the trees, Mazareem pulled the cowl back from his head. He knew that with his pallid skin and hairless head, he looked like a vision stepped from a nightmare. Mazareem preferred it this way. People tended to be more accommodating when they were terrified.

Together, Mazareem and Worm entered the isolated forest town. The few citizens in the road stopped and stared. Mazareem strode down the center of the main thoroughfare toward the largest building on the street. His eyes found the sign hanging at the front: *The Acorn Inn*.

"They've added a third story and changed the name," Mazareem said. "I suppose that means it's under new management."

Mazareem did not hesitate, climbing the steps of the porch and pushing his way through the swinging doors. Worm padded along at his side, his long claws clicking on the wooden floor.

Inside, Mazareem found a great room strewn with round tables and chairs. All were unoccupied. Along one wall, a small fire crackled in a hearth large enough to turn a boar on a spit. On the other side of the room, opposite the fireplace, stout wooden stairs led up to the second story.

Behind the counter at the back of the room, a serving girl looked up. She visibly started, and Mazareem suppressed a smile.

"C-can I help you?" the girl managed to squeak.

"Indeed you can," Mazareem said. "I wish to speak to the owner of this fine establishment."

Eyes huge, the girl's gaze flicked back and forth between Mazareem and Worm. "I'll see if he's available."

"If you would be so kind."

The girl dashed out of the room like a frightened fawn. While he waited, Mazareem turned his attention to the decorations that adorned the inn's great room. Several paintings on the wall caught his eye, and he moved closer to inspect them. One in particular, the portrait of a woman, arrested his gaze, and Mazareem could not look away.

Mazareem rested both hands on the top of his walking stick as he stared at the painting. Frozen in time by paint and canvas, she stared at the object of her affection with a small smile on her lips. The sort of smile reserved for a lover in a moment of intimacy. The artist had captured the essence of unconditional love in the woman's gaze.

Sudden rage gripped Mazareem. His hands twisted on the head of his staff as his entire body trembled.

This simple painting hanging on the wall of an inn paled in comparison to Mazareem's own work. The brush strokes were crude, inconsistent. The tone was haphazard and flat, lighting the woman's face as if from multiple angles, and none to her benefit. The pigments themselves were cheap, pink overtones of flesh

SANDELL WALL

already fading into the green underneath. The painting was boorish, forgettable. Impermanent.

Locked in a dungeon for a millennium, Mazareem had honed his craft to the point of surpassing all who came before him. The mortal who sketched this work would live and die in less time than Mazareem had spent capturing a single brooch from his memories of her. Yet he could not portray the raw humanity of this woman's gaze. He could make her eyes *look* but he could never make them *see.* It was lost to him. He had bargained it away, perhaps forever.

"Can I help you?" a stern voice said from behind Mazareem.

Mazareem stilled the turmoil in his heart. One lesson that a millennium of servitude taught was that anger accomplished nothing. With a smile on his face, Mazareem turned toward the voice. The instant he made eye contact with the owner of the inn, he knew the man would be difficult. Short and burly, the man showed no sign of fear, and before Mazareem spoke one word, he sensed a mutual disrespect between them.

"Where did you get this painting?" Mazareem asked. "It's quite remarkable."

"I painted them all myself," the man said as he wiped his hands on the apron that every innkeeper seemed to wear.

Mazareem made a show of being both surprised and impressed. "I didn't think to find such talent in the far reaches of the kingdom."

"Business is slow during the winter months," the man said, unphased by Mazareem's flattery. "I paint to keep my mind occupied."

"Do you know the woman in the portrait?"

"She's my wife. Before you ask, she's been dead for years. Now, did you need something, or did you travel to Oakroot just to inspect my art?"

"Ah, my apologies," Mazareem said, extending his hand. "Let me introduce myself. My name is Mazareem, and I've come from the central kingdom on the behalf of a group of investors. We're of a mind to buy a stake of the operations here in Oakroot."

"My name's Monty," Monty said, shaking Mazareem's hand with a fierce grip. "I'm the owner and operator of this inn, and what passes for a mayor in this town. I can answer whatever questions you may have, but I'm going to have to ask that your... dog waits outside."

"My good man, I mean no offense, but I cannot be parted from my hound," Mazareem said. "Think of him as my manservant, if it helps. He'll not disturb your establishment, I assure you."

Monty blinked several times as he contemplated how to react to Mazareem's blunt refusal to comply. Worm sat back on his haunches and stared at the innkeeper. Even sitting, the animal's snout sat level with the shorter man's face. A trickle of blood seeped from around Worm's crusted eye. A defect to be sure, but Mazareem thought it suited him.

"Ask your questions and be on your way," Monty said. "I've work to return to."

"Certainly," Mazareem said with an understanding smile. "This is just a formality, a matter of due diligence. I'm here to investigate security in Oakroot. My group of investors are primarily concerned with banditry. Do you have recourse to deal with them, this far from the center of the kingdom?"

SANDELL WALL

"You'd be surprised how hard it is to rob a logging camp full of men armed with axes," Monty said. "That doesn't stop a few idiots from trying every year, but they never manage to steal much."

"Splendid. One last question, which I'm required to ask. Being one of the remotest towns in the kingdom, I imagine a certain type of undesirable might seek safe harbor here. Are you aware of anyone in Oakroot that might attract the attention of Northmark's reavers or the priesthood's inquisition? My investors wish to avoid altercations with both groups, as I'm sure you can appreciate."

Monty gave Mazareem a long look before replying. When the innkeeper did speak, Mazareem heard tension in the man's voice.

"We're all upstanding citizens out here," Monty said. "I'll not have you prying into our personal business just to satisfy some shady investors from the west."

"Of course you are," Mazareem said, baring his teeth in a humorless smile. "And I'm sure your word is as solid as this inn."

"If that's all?" Monty asked, turning his body away from Mazareem to indicate the conversation was over.

"For now," Mazareem said. "I'll be in touch if we decide to pursue this venture."

Already several paces away, Monty did not reply. Mazareem frowned at the innkeeper's back. Five hundred years ago, he would have strode into Oakroot with fire in one hand and death in the other. Several thousand innocents slaughtered was a good bargain to kill one magus. Now, however, such a heavy-handed approach seemed like a needless waste to Mazareem. Perhaps he was getting old.

"Come, boy," Mazareem said to Worm. "We've worn out our welcome for the time being."

Worm got to his feet as Mazareem stepped toward the exit. Near the double doors, the serving girl swept the dust on the floor out onto the porch. She paused her work and stared at Mazareem with wide eyes as he approached.

Mazareem reached into a pocket beneath his cloak and plucked out a solid gold mark. He stopped in front of the girl and passed the coin across the knuckles of his hand, making sure she noticed. The soft yellow metal gleamed in the sunlight streaming through the door. Mazareem and Worm forgotten, the girl stared at the gold in awe.

"Tell me, miss, what's the biggest item of gossip in Oakroot?" Mazareem asked.

The girl glanced at the door Monty had disappeared behind.

"He'll have no idea you spoke to me," Mazareem said. "And there's a coin in it for you, if you can tell me something particularly juicy."

A solid gold mark was worth more than the girl would make in two years of hard labor at the inn. He could see her doing the calculation in her head.

The serving girl glanced toward the back of the inn one last time and then leaned toward Mazareem. "There's this woman that lives in the deep forest with her grandfather. She came out of nowhere four years ago. She's got dark skin and hair, like the desert people you see in books. The whole town talks about her but no one knows who she is or where she came from."

"Is that so?" Mazareem said, suddenly very interested. "Is there anything else you can tell me about this mystery woman?"

"Yeah," the serving girl said with a smirk. "Brant, Monty's son, is in love with her. She visits his shop every time she comes to town, but he hasn't got the guts to make a move."

"Very good," Mazareem said, slipping the golden mark to the girl. "Very good indeed. Where might I find this shop?"

"Oh, it's just down the road to the right," the serving girl said, snatching the coin and hiding it away in her dress. "Big porch, clean as a cat's paw, you can't miss it."

"You'd best keep that gold secret if you want to hold on to it," Mazareem said.

With Worm at his side, Mazareem left the serving girl staring after them in wonder. True to her word, they found Oakroot's general store without trouble. The immaculate painted porch, spotless mats, and perfectly arranged storefront indicated that Monty's son was a stickler for appearances.

Mazareem grinned to himself.

"I don't think the innkeeper's son is going to like us, boy," Mazareem said to Worm as they climbed the steps of the store.

Inside, the place was immaculate. Every item had its place, neatly labeled with a title and price. Mazareem had seen throne rooms given less care than this store. Brilliant sunlight streamed in through large glass windows—an expensive luxury for a small-town merchant.

From the counter at the back of the store, a broad-shouldered man looked up. Brant bore an unmistakable resemblance to his father, but stood at least two heads taller than Monty. The man had size and strength, yet Mazareem sensed a timid softness that made Brant seem smaller than his impressive stature. The fragility of his perfect dollhouse of a shop was almost enough to make Mazareem giddy.

Brant's eyes grew wide as Mazareem wound his way through the store toward the counter. He could not tear his gaze from Worm. Brant winced as Worm's claws scratched the polished hardwood floor.

"Sir, would you mind leaving your animal outside?" Brant said in a tiny voice.

"I'm afraid that's not possible."

Like his father, Brant stared at Mazareem for a few heartbeats as he processed the bold defiance.

"My name's Brant," Brant said with a frown, "I'm the owner of this store. Can I help you find something?"

"Actually, I'm here to speak with you," Mazareem said. "I've just come from the inn where I met your father. He directed me to your store and said that you might be of help to me."

Mazareem turned and raised an arm at the well-stocked store behind him. "I must say, your father's words didn't do this place justice. I'd wager there's not a better furnished shop in the entire kingdom."

Brant glanced at Worm and then quickly away. Now close enough to inspect Mazareem's features, Brant could not hide a grimace. "I do my best. What did you want to speak with me about?"

"It's a long and complicated story," Mazareem said, resting both of his hands on top of his walking stick. "A shop as fine as this must have wine for the weary traveler. Do you think you could fetch me a cup to chase away the dust of the road?"

Brant's hands kneaded the apron at his waist. After a moment of thought he said, "Sure, I can spare some wine."

"Good man," Mazareem said with a smile.

Mazareem waited as Brant ducked through a door into the back of the store. He gave Worm and absentminded pat on the head. Soon, Brant returned with a bottle and a wooden cup. He filled the cup and handed it to Mazareem. Mazareem drained the wine in a single gulp and wiped his mouth with the back of his hand.

"Many thanks," Mazareem said. "You've done an old man a world of good. Now, about why I'm here. I come from a desert country far to the south. I won't bore you with the name as you won't be able to pronounce it. Five years ago, a bloody revolution swept through my homeland, and the royal family had two choices: flee or die. The crown princess, and heiress to the throne, escaped into the wilderness with only her most trusted bodyguard. After months of hard fighting, the rebels were put down, but the princess had disappeared.

"I've been traveling far and wide for the past few years, seeking news of her fate. Today, from the mouth of your father, I've heard the first words of hope that she might still be alive. He told me that a young woman lives in the deep forest with her grandfather, and that she frequents your shop when she comes to town. Based on his description, my old heart dares to believe that this woman might be the lost princess I seek."

Mazareem stopped talking to allow Brant time to think. The poor man looked like he might faint.

"I-I-I knew she was special, but I had no idea!" Brant finally stammered.

"So your father spoke the truth," Mazareem said.

"Yes, of course he did," Brant said. He raised both hands to his head to rub his fingers through his hair in exasperation. The sudden motion prompted a growl from Worm, which caused Brant to freeze. His eyes narrowed—he dropped his hands to his side.

"What's her name?" Brant asked.

Mazareem cursed under his breath. So the man had some spine.

"Her given name would mean little to you," Mazareem said. "I've no doubt she's assumed a different identity in this land."

"Tell me anyway," Brant said. "When I see her next, I'll tell her that you're looking for her."

"Your foreign tongue would twist and mangle the beauty of her name," Mazareem said. "Do you have a scrap of parchment? I'll inscribe it for you."

Brant reached beneath the counter and produced a torn shred of parchment. Mazareem scratched out a few arcane symbols with a piece of charcoal, confident that they would mean nothing to Brant. When he picked up the piece of parchment, Brant frowned at Mazareem's writing.

"Show that to her," Mazareem said. "She'll be able to read it."

With his free hand, Mazareem dipped his fingers into his pocket and grabbed another golden mark. He placed the coin on the counter between them.

"For your trouble, and your discretion," Mazareem said. "I'd appreciate it if this conversation stayed between us. I didn't even reveal everything I've told you to your father."

"I don't know what sort of place you think Oakroot is, but you can't buy friends here," Brant said, making no move to pick up the coin.

Mazareem gave Brant a pained smile, resisting the urge to command Worm to sink his teeth into the man's tenders.

"For your wine and hospitality, then," Mazareem said. "Think on it, that's all I ask." He left the coin on the counter as he turned to exit the store.

Brant said nothing as Mazareem and Worm made their way into the street. Once outside, Mazareem turned his feet toward the forest. Best to lie low for a while. Brant and Monty would soon confer, and they would no doubt conclude that he had lied to both of them. No matter. Mazareem sensed his quarry was close.

Now all he had to do was wait.

Chapter 7

KAISER DID NOT LEAVE his compound for a week. He watched from the walls with his guards as a new reaver took possession of the ninth's palace. Mariel did her best to hide it, but Kaiser knew she was distraught. She always grieved when another reaver's family suffered. It was far too easy to imagine the same fate befalling their family.

Seven days after his trial in the arena, Kaiser sat eating breakfast with his wife and children. Mariel picked at her food, and Kaiser stared off into the distance, mulling over the day's tasks. Tarathine and Saredon were subdued, mimicking the moods of their parents.

"I want to be free of this place," Mariel said suddenly, looking up from her uneaten meal.

Kaiser jerked his thoughts back to the present. "What do you mean?" he said.

"I'm tired of this palace, this city, and this entire forsaken kingdom," Mariel said. "Why can't we just leave? I don't want to see our family dragged out into the street and slaughtered."

"Mariel, be silent!" Kaiser commanded. He glanced at the children, who were staring at the two of them open-mouthed.

Mariel glared at him, her face set in defiance.

"Children, go find Garius—ask him to start your lessons early," Kaiser said to Tarathine and Saredon.

"Yes, father," they said in unison before shoving themselves away from the table and bolting from the room.

"You can't talk that way in front of them," Kaiser said when the children were gone.

"Why not?" Mariel said. "Don't they have a right to know? Shouldn't they be aware of what's at stake every time you enter the arena?"

Kaiser set his mouth in a hard line. "Do we have to go through this after every trial?"

Mariel wilted under his harsh countenance. "I'm so afraid, Kaiser. I never imagined I'd live my life in a prison, fearing for the lives of my husband and children."

Kaiser's face softened. "This isn't the life I imagined either, but you know we cannot leave. Remember Zimon?"

Mariel nodded through her tears. He knew she would never forget Zimon. Seven years ago, Zimon had been the Fifth Reaver. He had decided that he no longer wanted to be a reaver and managed to smuggle his family out of Northmark. He fled south, seeking asylum in one of the small tropical kingdoms. Word of his treason preceded him, and no kingdom or country would take him in, until one warlord, desiring to curry favor with Haverfell, tossed Zimon and his entire family in a dungeon.

"The fate of Zimon and his family is known only to the priesthood," Kaiser said. "But the tale from the south was that the warlord sealed the dungeon and never used it again because of the atrocities committed once their inquisitors arrived."

"So there's no hope for us?" Mariel asked. Kaiser's heart broke at the despair in her voice.

"You know I don't believe that," Kaiser said, leaning forward to place a hand on her arm. "Everything I do, everything I am, is to give you and the children hope. Stay strong for a little longer. With as much upheaval that the death of the Ninth Reaver caused, I shouldn't have to defend against another challenge for at least a year. I may not be able to retire at that point, but perhaps I can convince the regent that I've earned security for my family."

Mariel nodded as she wiped unshed tears away from her eyes. Before either of them could speak again, Garius stepped into the room.

"Apologies, m'lord, m'lady," he said, inclining his head. "A summons was delivered at the gate." He handed Kaiser a black leather envelope and backed out of the room.

Kaiser opened the flap and drew out the heavy parchment. He scanned the written message and then placed it on the table.

"A summons so soon after a trial?" Mariel said. "What does it say?"

"It's a formal proclamation of an inquisition," Kaiser said, making no effort to hide the frustration in his voice.

Mariel looked pale. "An inquisition means people will die."

"People die every day," Kaiser said, rising from the table. "I have to appear at the cathedral within the hour. I'll make sure to return to say goodbye before I depart."

After holding Mariel in a long embrace and kissing her goodbye, Kaiser went to the armory. Official business in the Tarragon

Cathedral required a full reaver's dress. With the help of his servants, Kaiser donned his sinister armor in preparation for the ceremony. He opted to carry his helm under one arm, wearing a leather mask to disguise his face. The mask covered everything but his eyes and lower jaw, with a small slit cut out for the nose.

Kaiser found Garius waiting for him by the gate.

"The children were terrified when they came to me this morning, m'lord," Garius said. "Did they overhear something they shouldn't have?"

"I don't know anymore. Maybe we should tell them the truth. Watch over them, Garius. They need a steady hand."

"With my life, m'lord," Garius said, saluting Kaiser.

Kaiser returned the salute and stepped into the cobblestone street. He hesitated for a heartbeat as the gate was secured behind him. The orderly row of fortified compounds showed no evidence of the brutal assault carried out two nights ago. Kaiser sighed, hefted his shield, and set out down the street.

The Tarragon Cathedral lay on the opposite side of the city from Castle Vaulkern. A more recent construction than the castle, funded by the priesthood after their rise to prominence, the cathedral dominated the eastern skyline of Northmark. Thousands of citizens had been displaced to make room for the structure's massive footprint. Kaiser had never explored the place, but he heard rumors that a vast system of catacombs lay below the cathedral.

Outlined against the rising sun, the cathedral towered over the city like a man-made mountain. Kaiser walked in its shadow long before he reached it. Its spires and towers scratched at the sky far overhead, shining like exposed implements of torture. Kaiser hated the building, with its profusion of hard edges and sharp angles. The architecture hurt his eyes to look at, and every time he drew near, something in the core of his being heard a whispered promise of pain.

Kaiser made it to the cathedral without distraction. The few citizens he saw in the street gave him a wide berth. He found the great doors of the center of the priesthood's power thrown open and a large crowd gathered outside the gates. Kaiser strode through the middle of this throng. People scrambled over each other to get out of his way.

High Priestess Parenthia stood on a podium in front of the cathedral, looking out over the crowd. Her powerful voice echoed off of the high walls behind her as she preached. Kaiser listened as he approached.

"The priesthood of Abimelech stands ready to defend Haverfell against the heretic, the practitioner of dark arts, and the lovers of abomination that would bring us low," Parenthia thundered. "Hand in hand with the regent's reavers, we have rooted out and crushed every cult and rebellion that has dared raise its head in the past twenty years. We do this to keep you safe, and to honor the one true god who watches over us. Abimelech be praised!"

"Abimelech be praised," the crowd answered.

"But there is a far more insidious threat than the simple nonbeliever and the harmless dabbler in mischief," Parenthia said. "Do you know of what I speak?"

"Magus!" the crowd roared in response.

Parenthia smiled and clasped her hands together in approval. "Indeed, the deplorable *magus!* Those who take unto themselves the forbidden power seek to sunder the very foundations of our great kingdom. They attempt to wield power that they cannot control and with it destroy everything that we hold dear. Would you allow them to do this?"

"No!" the crowd cried.

By this point, Kaiser had reached the front of the throng. Parenthia spotted him and delivered her next words as if she were speaking directly to him.

"Then be vigilant, brothers and sisters, for the lust for power can take root in any soul, and even the meekest of men can seek to throw off the yoke of his betters," Parenthia said. "Guard yourselves against thoughts that would weaken your resolve. Drink long of the cup of Abimelech, for there you will find succor and strength. Suffer not the man who denies the cup."

On Parenthia's cue, an army of hooded acolytes emerged from the cathedral and moved into the crowd, each one bearing a goblet of Abimelech's blood. Kaiser never took his gaze from Parenthia's as the surrounding crowd gulped at the dark liquid with greedy mouths.

Parenthia waited long enough to see that he would not drink and then she stepped down from the podium and entered the cathedral. She turned her back on Kaiser without ever beckoning for him to follow.

Annoyed, Kaiser moved after her. On the other side of the huge black gates, he found the cathedral courtyard just as crowded as the street outside. The huge, pale tree dominated the open square. Red tendrils climbed the white trunk as blood from a fresh sacrifice pooled amongst the roots.

Kaiser guessed that every minor noble and governor from the surrounding countryside had made the trip. Along the inner wall, the regent stood looking out over the gathered dignitaries. On his left stood a row of nine armored figures, each one a vision of terror wrought in metal. Kaiser's annoyance grew when he saw that the other reavers had arrived before him. He would have to take his spot before the entire crowd.

The acting regent of the Kingdom of Haverfell had already noticed Kaiser, and the man nodded pointedly at the empty spot nearest him. Regent Trangeth was a tall, dour man with black hair that formed a severe widow's peak on his high forehead. He watched the world like a raptor. He was the predator and everyone else his prey. In the absence of a true king, Trangeth spoke for the throne.

A hush fell over the courtyard as Kaiser strode forward. Parenthia and Trangeth might find him insufferable, but everyone else gave Kaiser the respect a Tenth Reaver was owed. When Kaiser took his place at the regent's side, he glanced down the line of reavers, his mind finally registering that there were nine others instead of eight. How could the first position be filled so soon and without his approval? Tradition and regulation had been violated. He made a mental note to speak with the regent about it.

Parenthia stood on Trangeth's immediate right, along with the highest ranking priests and priestesses of her order.

"So good of you to join us, High Reaver," Parenthia said.

Kaiser said nothing, refusing to be baited into looking petty.

"Our assembly is complete," Trangeth said. "You may begin, High Priestess."

Parenthia cleared her throat. Her jowls quivered as she began to speak.

"As you know from your summons, we're launching a formal inquisition," she said, projecting her voice so that it filled the courtyard. "It has been over ten years since the last true inquisition. The signs of prophecy point to a magus arising every twelve years, and those portents are strengthening once again. We believe the threat will arise in the far east. With the regent's blessing, we'll begin the inquisition in the forest town of Oakroot and work west.

"You've been gathered here to be reminded of your commitment to our cause. Don't forget that the last time a magus rose to power unchecked he destroyed the southern half of the kingdom. It's in your best interest to see that we reach our destination with all haste. The travel path of the inquisition will be provided you, and if you find yourself on our route, we expect to be accommodated."

A low murmur filled the courtyard as the nobles complained amongst themselves.

"Make no mistake, the throne fully supports the inquisition," Trangeth said, his powerful voice overriding the grumbles of discontent. "Afford her the respect and submission you would give to the king, because she carries the blessing of the crown with her."

The crowd fell silent, but the tension did not ease. Kaiser wondered how many other minds burned to ask the same question: how long until the regent abandoned his flimsy pretenses and claimed the throne for himself?

Parenthia seemed to anticipate the agitation. After Trangeth spoke, she signaled to acolytes who had been waiting on the perimeter of the courtyard. These acolytes had their hoods down, revealing a stunning array of beautiful hair and faces. They mingled through the crowd, offering sips out of the golden goblets they carried.

The effect this had on the gathered nobles was immediate and profound. Laughter filled the courtyard as inhibitions were stripped away faster than Kaiser could believe possible. As the concoction took hold, their concerns over the inquisition were forgotten. Soon, the acolytes paired up with men and led them away to nearby private rooms. Kaiser watched them disappear into the cathedral in disgust. The priesthood ran the place like a brothel.

With the nobles appeased, Trangeth and Parenthia turned their attentions to Kaiser.

"As High Reaver, you will be tasked with leading the inquisition," Trangeth said. "I'm aware that you defeated a challenger three days ago, but the inquisition waits for no man. I expect you to carry out your duty with the excellence expected of your station."

"I will do as you command," Kaiser said, inclining his head.

"Parenthia tells me you hesitate to embrace the priesthood," Trangeth said.

Kaiser frowned. "I was not aware it was expected of me, Lord Regent."

"Let me simplify things for you then," Trangeth said. "You have until you return from the inquisition to align yourself with Abimelech. While you're gone, the throne will decree that all citizens of Haverfell must partake of his blood. Even you, High Reaver."

"And my family?" Kaiser asked.

"Will have have received the blessings of Abimelech by the time you return."

Kaiser ground his teeth and said nothing. Parenthia's wide smile hung over Trangeth's shoulder.

"One other thing," Trangeth said. He raised a hand as he spoke, beckoning someone behind Kaiser to step forward. "The new First

Reaver will travel with you on the inquisition. Use this opportunity to mentor him. I expect to hear a good report of his progress."

Kaiser opened his mouth to protest, but the words would not come. Not only had the First Reaver been selected without his input, now he was supposed to mentor the man? This was unprecedented. Kaiser had never heard of such a thing being done. He resisted the urge to glance at the First Reaver, knowing he would only see a visage of hammered steel.

"We'll leave with the dawn," Parenthia said. "Be outside the cathedral no later than sunrise."

After saluting the regent, Kaiser stalked from the courtyard. His mind reeled. Too much was happening too fast. He had one more night with his family before leaving them alone for weeks. The words of the regent gnawed at him. His family would be required to drink the blood of Abimelech before he returned. Perhaps it would not be as bad as it sounded. Plenty of others partook regularly, and they were not turned into slavering demons.

Kaiser feared the ritual because he could not anticipate how it would affect him. He had survived this long as High Reaver because of his absolute commitment to discipline of mind, body, and soul. To introduce something to his being that might influence how he made decisions could mean the difference between life and death. His family did not have to do battle in the arena. Maybe they could drink of the priesthood's cup and no harm would come to them.

Lost in his thoughts, Kaiser turned a corner and crashed headlong into a man coming from the other direction. The frail creature bounced off Kaiser's armored form like a pebble hitting a barrel. Kaiser glanced down at the fallen man to find a beggar named Ursais grinning up at him. He offered a hand to help Ursais rise.

When the old man regained his feet, he brushed himself off and gave Kaiser a quizzical glance. The senile old man claimed friendship with Kaiser's wife, and for some reason she trusted him. Ursais seemed to be oblivious to the dangers of befriending a reaver.

"Where's the High Reaver off to in such a hurry?" Ursais asked.

Kaiser opened his mouth to tell the old man to mind his own affairs, then snapped it shut as a thought crossed his mind.

"You've taken the blood, haven't you?"

Ursais's face fell. "Against my will I have, yes."

"And it didn't change you? It had no lasting impact on your being?"

Ursais stared at his feet for a long time. When he looked up, Kaiser almost took a step back at the sorrow in the old man's eyes.

"You want me to tell you that it's harmless," Ursais said. "You want me to tell you that your family can drink and be safe. I'm sorry, son, but I can't. That foul liquid magnifies every base instinct that plagues the heart of man. Lust, greed, rage, pride—it all bubbles to the forefront of the mind after but one sip from that cursed cup." The old man's next word were almost a whisper. "And it feels so good."

Ursais wiped a tear out of the corner of his eye. "You become a god in your own mind and all that matters is glorifying yourself. The priesthood preaches that this pleases Abimelech. I've learned to lock myself away until the ritual wears off. I thought I was strong enough to resist the first time. To my shame, I did some terribly hurtful things to people I love. I cannot bear the thought of repeating that mistake."

"Why do they insist on forcing this on us?" Kaiser asked, not really expecting Ursais to answer.

"That's easy," Ursais said, looking at him in surprise. "Reduce a man to the worst parts of his nature, control his source of pleasure, and what do you get?"

"A slave," Kaiser said.

Chapter 8

KAISER WRESTLED WITH URSAIS'S words as he walked the rest of the way to his fortified home. He thought of Zimon and the man's failed attempt to escape the responsibilities of being a reaver. Mariel would have Kaiser follow in Zimon's footsteps and try to smuggle their family out of Northmark, but she had never seen the bloody remains of an inquisitor's victim. Kaiser had, and he would do everything in his power to keep his wife and children out of their clutches.

Garius met Kaiser in the small courtyard of his palace. "Is everything alright, m'lord?"

"No, Garius, it's not," Kaiser said. "Go find my wife and bring her to my study. The three of us need to discuss the future."

After disarming, Kaiser sat behind the writing table in his study and stared unseeing at the parchments scattered on its surface. Each document represented a request for mediation from a citizen of the kingdom. Kaiser understood the importance of his role as High Reaver, but his official duties seemed insignificant in light of recent events.

He did not have to wait long before Mariel and Garius entered the room and took up seats opposite his. Garius must have warned Mariel of Kaiser's mood, because both of them remained silent, waiting for him to speak.

Kaiser raised his gaze from the table and looked at the two of them in turn. "As you know, the priesthood is launching an inquisition. As High Reaver, I'm required to lead the military force that will accompany it. I'll be gone for at least a month. While I'm absent, the regent is going to make a proclamation to the entire kingdom. Every citizen of Haverfell will be required to partake in the ritual consumption of the blood of Abimelech. Including the nobility and the reavers."

Garius cursed and Mariel's face turned ashen.

"He can't do that," Mariel said.

"Who's going to stop him?" Kaiser said. "The priesthood grows in power by the day." Kaiser gestured at the pile of parchments on his desk. "Half of these are from citizens reporting people who openly criticize the priesthood. I've no choice but to round them up and deliver them to the cathedral for imprisonment. There they stay until they've had a change of heart and proclaim faith in Abimelech."

"And those that don't?" Mariel asked.

"They're never seen again."

"What would you have us do?" Garius asked.

"You will comply with the decree," Kaiser said, his voice as hard as steel. "We've defied the wishes of the priesthood for as long as we can. I don't care what you think of Abimelech; the safety of my family is paramount. If we must participate in the ritual to preserve our lives and what limited freedoms we enjoy, so be it."

Garius's face fell as Kaiser spoke.

"Do you anticipate any objection among the men?" Kaiser asked.

"Most of them would die for you," Garius said after considering the question. "But there are a few newer recruits who might not take kindly to having this forced on them."

"See to it that they are prepared to obey," Kaiser said. "If you think they'll cause trouble, get rid of them."

"What about me and the children?" Mariel asked, her voice quavering.

Kaiser met her gaze, dreading what he had to say next.

"You're going to have to drink the blood," Kaiser said. "I've never seen it given to children, so I think they'll be safe for the time being."

Garius grimaced. Mariel dropped her eyes to the floor and went very still.

"I'm told the effects are only temporary," Kaiser said. "You won't become addicted the instant the liquid touches your lips. Will you do this to save our family? Can you?"

Mariel nodded but said nothing.

"I'm your man to the end," Garius said. "I'll see to it that the household troops understand your wishes."

"I know you will," Kaiser said. "Now leave us. I wish to speak with my wife in private."

Garius stood and raised a fist to his breast in a crisp salute. Kaiser acknowledged the gesture with a nod. He waited until the man's footsteps faded in the hallway before speaking again. Mariel stared at him, her eyes filled with sorrow. Kaiser met her gaze without flinching.

"There's no other way," Kaiser said at last. "Perhaps if it were just the two of us, we might escape Northmark and live on the run for a few frantic years, but we'd never make it with our children in tow."

"Is this it?" Mariel asked, fire in her voice. "Is this the life you wanted when we brought Tarathine into the world? When she was born, you told me there was hope for change, that you believed we could give our children an existence free of fear. Just this morning, you told me to be strong, to not give up hope. And now this. You don't even believe in Abimelech anymore!"

Mariel's last words were almost a shout.

Kaiser looked away from his wife. He stared at the muted colors of a stained glass window set in the wall. "What I believe doesn't matter. It hasn't for years. Abimelech used to reward the strong and grant honor in victory. Now, if Parenthia is to believed, he cares only for those who curry favor with her priesthood."

"What we believe is the one thing they cannot take from us," Mariel said, despair starting to creep into her voice.

"Can't they?" Kaiser asked, returning his hard gaze to her face. "Will you risk the pyre to refuse the cup and leave your children motherless? Will you condemn yourself to torture and death to defy the priesthood's will? Tell me: what will that accomplish?"

Rather than hold Kaiser's gaze, Mariel buried her face in her hands. After a moment of silence, Kaiser's heart softened.

"I'm sorry," Kaiser said. "I've no desire to cause you hurt, but I must know what you'll do. Can I trust you not to jeopardize your life and the lives of the children while I'm gone?"

Mariel raised her face from her hands. Tears flowed down her cheeks, but she did not sniffle or sob. "I'll do what I must."

"No, this is not the life I wanted for our children," Kaiser said in a gentle voice. "There's no way I could have anticipated Parenthia's quick and relentless rise to power. I've used every bit of my influence to insulate you and the children from her schemes. As the reaver in charge of the inquisition, at least I can ensure that you and your extended family are safe."

"And what of the innocents you'll slaughter by her command?" Mariel asked. "Who watches for their safety?"

"Tell me, which child would you sacrifice to save the life of an innocent man? Tarathine, or Saredon?"

Mariel said nothing.

"There's only one way forward now," Kaiser said. "We must be as ruthless as those who would do us harm. This is the lot that's been given us. We can stand and face it, perhaps winning freedom for ourselves and our children, or we can cower and die."

Mariel took a great shuddering breath and wiped at her face with the back of her sleeves. She rose from her chair and moved toward the door. Kaiser said nothing, content to let her go in silence.

Before she left the room, Mariel paused in the doorway and looked back. "If you fall to the magus, then all is lost."

"I'll return to Northmark with his head before the summer is over," Kaiser said.

Mariel lingered in the door for a heartbeat as she contemplated Kaiser's words. With a nod and a tight smile, she ducked into the hallway and disappeared.

With a sigh, Kaiser tried to focus on the pile of work that needed to be done. It was impossible. The discussion with Mariel and Garius played over and over again in his head. Frustrated, Kaiser rose from his seat and went to find his children. This time of day they should be sparring with Garius in the training yard.

Servants bobbed their heads at Kaiser as he walked through the halls of his home. He smiled at them as he passed and hoped that they would not grow to hate him when the priesthood came to impose the ritual on his household.

He heard the clack of wooden swords before he reached the doorway into the yard. Set in the center of the fortified palace, the large dirt square was open to the sky. Racks of weapons and armor lined the high stone walls. Kaiser trained with them all. In the center of the yard, Saredon squared off with Garius, each gripping a practice weapon.

Rather than interrupt their training session, Kaiser hung back and watched. He rested his shoulder on the solid door frame and admired Saredon's technique. The boy had skill and strength for a ten-year-old. Sweat dripped from Saredon's face as he lunged at Garius, trying to find an opening in the man's defenses.

Garius parried Saredon's attacks with ease and thumped the boy on his leather breastplate every time Saredon left himself exposed. Saredon did not get angry or frustrated—he got determined. His face a mask of intense focus, Saredon launched a flurry of attacks at Garius. The veteran guardsman jerked his blade up to defend himself. Kaiser smiled at the look of surprise on Garius's face. The sudden attack forced Garius to take a step back and that was victory enough for Saredon.

Saredon grinned as he lowered his wooden sword and shouted, "I'm High King Rowen, savior of Haverfell!"

Kaiser's smile froze on his face. His jaw clenched so hard that his teeth creaked. Garius looked up, scanning the courtyard to see if anyone overheard. His gaze stopped on Kaiser. The guard captain gulped.

"Saredon, leave us," Kaiser commanded as he strode into the yard.

Saredon jumped at the voice of his father. One glance at Kaiser's face was enough to convince him that he should vacate the training yard as quickly as possible. Garius stood rooted in place as Saredon scampered out of sight.

Kaiser stood before Garius, struggling to rein in his fury before he opened his mouth to speak. "What was that?" he finally asked.

"It was nothing, m'lord. Just a boy playing at being a hero."

"Did he hear that name from you?"

Garius looked everywhere but in Kaiser's eyes. "I don't know, m'lord. Maybe he overheard it somewhere."

"I'll give you one more chance," Kaiser said. "Did he hear that name from you?"

Garius fidgeted like a man cornered by a viper. As Kaiser waited for the man to speak, he heard someone approaching from behind. Garius glanced at the newcomer and exhaled a great sigh of relief.

"Kaiser, he heard that name from me," Mariel said as she stepped to his side.

"Are you trying to give Parenthia a reason to throw your entire family into prison?" Kaiser asked. "What insanity would cause you to fill Saredon's head with such dangerous lies?"

Mariel's eyes blazed. "You don't know that they're lies. The children need hope. They need to believe in a world where good things can happen."

"So you fill their heads with tales of a mythical king that will rise from the grave and right all the wrongs in the world?" Kaiser said.

"You might as well tell them that they can grow wings and fly. All it takes is one of the guards to hear Saredon speaking like that and they'll report it to the priesthood for a reward."

"The children know it's a secret. They don't speak of it when they shouldn't."

Kaiser hesitated as he processed the implications of her words. He glanced at Garius. "You damnable fool."

Garius squared his shoulders and said, "My father's father remembers tales of when the High King's glory still graced our kingdom. A time before the priesthood covered Castle Vaulkern with the twisted emblems of Abimelech. It wasn't even called Castle Vaulkern back then, it was called—"

"Stop," Kaiser said, raising a hand to cut Garius off. "I don't care what it was called. What you're talking about is ancient history. The only bearing it has on the present is that it could get my family *killed*. Is it worth that risk?"

"No, m'lord," Garius said, looking at his feet.

"If a single *whisper* of your High King were to reach Parenthia's ears, she'd have you up before the inquisitors, and I'd be forced to preside over your trial," Kaiser said. "I don't care how much faith you have in some foolish legend. It's not worth having the skin stripped off your back."

Kaiser turned his ire on Mariel. "How can you be so careless? Is this why you've grown so restless? You know the oath I swore when I took you in. Heresy means execution, *by my hand*."

Mariel stared at the dirt of the training yard, refusing to meet Kaiser's gaze.

Kaiser struggled to control his anger. As a man of discipline and self-control, he exercised rigid control of his temper, but right then, he wanted nothing more than to scream at the two of them.

"I'll deal with this when I return," Kaiser said, his voice strained with the effort of holding himself in check. "Until then, you will speak of this to no one, and you'll not say that name again in this compound. Swear this to me now, or I'll lock the both of you in chains while I'm gone."

"I swear it, m'lord," Garius said.

Mariel finally looked up. Her look of defiance stabbed like a knife in Kaiser's guts. If she refused to obey, he would have no choice but to follow through on his threat.

"I swear it, husband," Mariel said after a tense pause.

Not trusting himself to speak further without losing control of his temper, Kaiser left the subdued Mariel and Garius standing in the training yard. He used his anger as motivation, tackling the work that waited for him in his study.

Kaiser labored long into the night, assigning work to the lower reavers to be completed in his absence. When he finally went to bed, he laid himself down next to Mariel as quietly as he could, hoping not to wake her. After a few long heartbeats, she rolled over and pressed herself up against his body. She clung to him, and Kaiser felt her fear and desperation. He fell asleep with Mariel cradled in his arms.

Kaiser woke before the dawn. Mariel had risen before him. A small platter of food waited for him beside the bed. Kaiser wolfed down cold cheese and meat before leaving the room. As he wiped sleep from his eyes, Kaiser trudged to the armory. The servants were waiting for him.

With his shield strapped to his back and his helmet under one arm, Kaiser walked toward the door that opened onto the street. He found Mariel, Garius, and the children waiting for him in the small courtyard before the fortified gate.

Kaiser leaned in close and kissed his wife on the forehead. He pulled back and gazed into her eyes. She gave him a small smile which he returned. There was still tension between them, but also an understanding that each would do what must be done to keep their family safe.

Next, he patted Saredon and Tarathine on the shoulder and ruffled their hair. They grinned up at him. Garius offered his hand, and Kaiser clasped the man's forearm in a firm grip. They nodded at each other but did not speak.

Their parting ritual complete, Kaiser donned his helm and hid himself from the world. Without looking back, he opened the door and stepped into the street. He paused, waiting to hear the gate secured behind him. Only when the bar slid into place and Kaiser heard the click of the locking mechanism engage did he start down the road. With his family secure, he could set his mind to the task at hand.

The streets were deserted in the predawn stillness. Only a few torches still burned, most having guttered out hours ago. Kaiser navigated the city by starlight. Even in the darkness, Kaiser's mind registered the physical presence of the Tarragon Cathedral. It blocked out the stars in front of him, a single jagged mountain rising out of a sea of rooftops.

As Kaiser neared the cathedral, he saw torchlight spilling out of the open gates. He heard voices and the sound of commotion coming from the courtyard. Sucking in a deep breath, Kaiser stepped through the high archway and joined the inquisition.

Soldiers from the garrison were already formed up in the shadow of the great tree. Their dull mail and steel breastplates gleamed in the torchlight. Kaiser counted ten rows of twenty men. The count of two hundred soldiers surprised him until he remembered that a second reaver would join them. Kaiser would command a hundred soldiers, and the new First Reaver would command the second hundred.

Kaiser found the First Reaver already mounted on his warhorse. The man struck an imposing figure, his dark, spiked armor matched by the barding on his horse. His helmet, a grinning metal skull, stared down at Kaiser. The First Reaver said nothing as Kaiser approached.

An attendant moved close with Kaiser's own warhorse and he mounted the massive black destrier. From his new vantage point, he gazed out across the courtyard.

He spotted Parenthia near the western wall. Her attention was focused on an ornate, windowless carriage. Adorned with gold and silver, and bearing the tree of Abimelech's priesthood on every surface flat enough for it to be carved, the wagon would carry the inquisitors on the road.

As Kaiser watched, the inquisitors shambled out of the cathedral and into the dark box of a coach. The three dark-robed figures were stooped like old men. Black masks covered their faces with only a slit cut at the nose to allow them to breathe. They often stopped in their tracks and turned their faces to the courtyard as if catching scent of something foul. Parenthia walked alongside them and shooed them forward anytime they lagged.

SANDELL WALL

When the last bent inquisitor had been ushered into the carriage and the door sealed behind them, Parenthia turned to assess the rest of the preparations. She gave Kaiser a knowing smile when she saw him on the back of his horse.

Parenthia moved to stand in front of the gates, raised her open hands above her head and shouted out, "Abimelech is pleased by your faith. Let us go forth and rid the kingdom of the heretic. You are tasked with this holy mission. Do not waver. Do not err. The inquisition has begun!"

To Kaiser's surprise, the soldiers behind him responded with a cheer. He looked over his shoulder to see acolytes wandering through the ranks, offering drinks from golden cups. Kaiser raised a hand, pointed out the gates, and kicked his horse into motion. At the head of two hundred soldiers and thirty priests, blessed by the crown, Kaiser left Northmark in command of an inquisition for a god he did not believe in.

Chapter 9

KAISER'S MOOD DARKENED THE farther he traveled from Northmark. The Kingdom of Haverfell had long ago paved the highways with cobblestones, so they made good time, but even that made him angrier. The extent of his duties in the inquisition was to babysit the hundred soldiers under his command.

Regent Trangeth had ordered the newly appointed First Reaver to join him under the pretext that Kaiser would mentor the man, yet the First Reaver never spoke to Kaiser. Kaiser found this acceptable. He had no desire to ever hear the man's voice, let alone train him. Parenthia seemed obsessed with the First Reaver, and that suited Kaiser too. The less she bothered him, the better.

In fact, as Kaiser reflected on it, he had not spoken to a single soul since leaving Northmark a week and a half ago. He brooded atop his horse all day and retired to his tent every evening. He knew all the soldiers under his command by name, but he was the High Reaver to them. They would have been terrified if he ever addressed them personally.

Thunder rolled overhead, causing Kaiser to glance at the sky. The clouds promised rain. He rode in the vanguard of the column. At his back, the inquisitors carriage creaked and groaned as it rolled across the cobblestones. From his horse Kaiser had a good view of the surrounding countryside. Their little procession wound through the rolling hills, a black worm wriggling between mounds of green.

Kaiser twisted in his saddle to make sure his packs were secured against the threat of rain. He cinched the leather bindings tighter, just to be sure. The first fat drop hit his helmet when he faced forward again. In the next instant, a wall of water hit him. Kaiser hunched in his saddle as the water found the cracks in his armor and trickled down his back.

After a few miles of this misery, a mounted figure appeared at Kaiser's side through the driving rain. He glanced to his left and found the First Reaver's metal skull of a helmet staring at him. The man raised a closed fist, clearly indicating that he wanted the procession to stop.

Kaiser snorted inside his closed helm. This man would never make it as a reaver if he could not suffer a little rain. Before Kaiser responded, another mounted figure appeared on his right. It was Parenthia. Her drenched hood dripping water, she yelled over the rain at Kaiser.

"The First Reaver requests that we halt," Parenthia shouted. "He has a matter of discipline amongst his men that he needs to deal with.

Annoyed, but outnumbered and uncaring, Kaiser stopped, wheeled his horse, and raised a closed fist over his head. The column stopped at his command and stood staring at him, blinking in the rain.

"What's this about?" Kaiser shouted back at Parenthia.

The High Priestess only nodded at the First Reaver's back, who had trotted his horse back down the column toward where his soldiers marched. Curious now, Kaiser spurred his mount to follow. Parenthia urged her own horse forward and stayed at his side.

They reached the First Reaver's horse to find him dismounted. Two soldiers stood before him, holding a third captive between them. The restrained man stared at the First Reaver in terror. As Kaiser edged his horse closer, the rain eased to a light drizzle.

A fourth soldier stepped forward to present the First Reaver with something in his hand. "This was found in his pack, M'lord Reaver," the man said.

The First Reaver reached out a gauntleted hand and plucked the item from the man's outstretched fingers. He held it up in front of the grinning skull of his helmet to inspect it. Kaiser squinted through the slits of his helm, trying to identify the source of this conflict. They had halted the procession for a crudely carved wooden figurine?

Parenthia took the offered figurine when the First Reaver held it up to her. The First Reaver's gaze paused on Kaiser before returning to the man in front of him.

"Do you know what this is?" Parenthia asked, still inspecting the trinket in her hand.

"It's just a silly thing I carved for my kids, High Priestess," the terrified soldier stammered. "I don't mean nothing by it."

"Last night around the fire, he regaled us with tales about how the kingdom used to be ruled by a proper king, High Priestess," one of the soldiers holding the unfortunate man said.

"Did he now?" Parenthia said slowly, raising her gaze from the wooden figure to stare at its owner. "What's your name, soldier?"

"My name's Trenner, High Priestess, second corporal in the King's Army," Trenner said.

"Which king?" Parenthia asked, one eyebrow raised.

"There's no... I mean, of course —," Trenner spluttered. He stopped and composed himself, choosing his next words with care. "I'm loyal to the regent, High Priestess."

"We shall see," Parenthia said. She turned her head toward the carriage and raised a hand. "Bring an inquisitor!"

"What is this?" Kaiser said in disbelief. "You cannot subject one of our own soldiers to an inquisitor!"

Every head turned toward him. Hope for deliverance lit Trenner's face.

"Why can't we?" Parenthia asked in a bemused voice.

"There are laws to observe," Kaiser said. "The formal process must be followed."

"What do you think an inquisition is? The inquisitor's ruling *is* law."

Kaiser clamped his mouth shut. His was the only voice of opposition. When he said no more, Trenner struggled against the men that held him.

"M'lord High Reaver, take me into your custody!" Trenner shouted. "I submit to your authority and judgment."

Parenthia smiled wide at Trenner's words, although her gaze never wavered from Kaiser. "This man appeals to you for judgment. Perhaps he thinks to find mercy at the hand of the High Reaver?"

Kaiser ground his teeth. He could not refuse the plea for arbitration in front of the entire inquisition. The First Reaver stepped back as the hunched form of an inquisitor drew near.

The men holding Trenner forced him to stoop, and the inquisitor shuffled forward until their faces almost touched. Behind his leather mask, the inquisitor sucked in each breath with a terrible, gasping wheeze. With a gnarled hand raised to the sky, the inquisitor snatched at the air, his twisted fingers plucking at the strings that bound the doomed man to the mortal plane. Trenner stopped struggling. Instead, he bowed his head and closed his eyes. He jerked in time with the inquisitor's dancing fingers. His face tightened in pain, and he screwed his eyes shut, as if he could fight off the inquisitor with the power of his mind.

No one moved. It seemed to Kaiser that no one even breathed as they waited for the inquisitor to finish. The inquisitor's black, eyeless mask stared at Trenner so long that the man started to whimper. Finally, the inquisitor stepped back, gave a single nod to Parenthia, and shuffled back toward the carriage.

"Trenner, second corporal of the King's Army, the inquisition has found you guilty of treason," Parenthia said, her voice booming out before Trenner could even raise his head. "Regent Trangeth rules our kingdom with Abimelech's blessing. Faith in a false god or king is punishable by death."

"No!" Trenner cried. "I've got a family. I've got children!"

Kaiser gripped the horn of his saddle so hard that the leather creaked. The men holding Trenner pushed him forward before stepping back into formation. Trenner whirled, looking for an ally or a way out. Soldiers blocked him on every side but one. When he found no sympathy in the faces of his comrades, Trenner turned to face the First Reaver.

The First Reaver drew a wicked, two-handed sword from over his back.

"No," Kaiser said, raising a hand to stop the First Reaver. "He appealed to me for judgment, and I'll see it delivered by my hand."

The First Reaver gave Kaiser a nod and stepped back. Kaiser lifted one leg over his horse and dropped to the ground with a thud. He pulled his sword from its sheath next to the saddle. No one spoke—the soldiers watched Kaiser's every move.

"This is the mercy I offer," Kaiser said as he moved to stand ten paces before Trenner. "Trial by combat. Someone give the man a blade."

Someone in the crowd tossed a sword into the mud at Trenner's feet. The blade flashed in the sun before it hit the ground and sank into the wet earth.

Trenner knelt and plucked the weapon up with fingers made clumsy by panic. He never took his eyes from Kaiser. With an anguished cry, Trenner rushed at Kaiser. Kaiser stepped aside, his movements as casual as a stream flowing around a bend. Trenner's wild swing found only empty air.

Kaiser's serrated sword flashed down, the jagged edge biting deep into the back of Trenner's knee as the soldier stumbled past. Blood ran down Trenner's left leg. Hobbled now, he turned to face Kaiser again. Tears streamed down his face.

"Tell my girls I love them!" Trenner shouted at the crowd of soldiers behind Kaiser. He raised a fist to the sky and looked to the heavens. "Glory to the High King!"

Trenner charged again. Kaiser pivoted on one foot and swung his killing blade in a huge arc. The sword whistled through the air, slamming into Trenner's throat with tremendous force. A gasp went up from the watching soldiers as Trenner's head left his neck. The dead man's body fell forward, and his head landed with a splat in the mud several paces away.

Rather than crying out in triumph, Parenthia stared at the dead man from atop her horse, lost in apparent sorrow. No one spoke as rain washed the blood from Kaiser's sword. Finally, Parenthia raised her head and addressed the soldiers who had just witnessed the execution of one of their own.

"Abimelech finds no satisfaction in this," Parenthia said. "He would much rather you join him than die a needless death. Those of you who reported this man will be rewarded. Come to my tent when we stop for the night."

Kaiser marveled at Parenthia. The High Priestess had a deft touch. Her false sorrow and appeal for reason would do more to sway these men to her cause than any fiery rhetoric.

Something in the mud caught Kaiser's gaze. He looked down to see the figurine that Trenner had died for. It was a crude carving of a knight with his hands resting on the hilt of a down-turned greatsword. Kaiser could see the tines of a crown on the knight's head. Blood stained the wooden knight's face like tears.

With a start, Kaiser jerked his gaze away from the carved figure. He looked around, making sure no one else had noticed. When he glanced toward the carriage, he found the sightless gaze of one of the masked inquisitors watching him.

— —

After the delay, the inquisition had to travel hard to reach the town of Fieldstone by nightfall. The halfway point of their journey, the small city stood in the center of the kingdom. By the time the rooftops came into view, Kaiser wanted nothing more than to strip out of his soaking armor and sit next to a fire. The rain had finally stopped an hour ago, but his gear would be damp for days.

A campsite had been set up for them on the outskirts of town. Fires were already burning, tended by volunteers from the city. As Tenth Reaver, Kaiser commanded the biggest tent, and he went straight to it. He hoisted himself out of the saddle with great effort and handed his horse off to a local stable hand.

Kaiser staggered into the tent and took the offered assistance from servants to help him remove his armor. He donned his leather mask as soon as his helmet came off. The town had sent their prettiest young women to attend him, no doubt hoping to find favor in his eyes. Kaiser shooed them away when they lingered too long.

He held his hands over the brazier in the center of the tent, grateful for the warmth of the fire. Try as he might, Kaiser could not put the events of the day out of his head. What had Trenner's crimes been? Who cared if he made crude carvings of kingly knights? To spill a man's blood because he believed in myths was madness. His thoughts returned to Saredon in the training yard and a chill ran down his spine in spite of the fire.

Outside the tent, a voice began to chant a hymn. The voice sang alone at first, but was soon joined by a choir. Kaiser knew the melody. He usually ignored it. Tonight, he was restless. He moved to the door of his tent to observe.

Between the inquisition campsite and Fieldstone, a group of robed acolytes sang their haunting hymn. In front of them, a long line of people stretched out of sight into the streets of the city. They took their turns stepping forward and drinking deep of the cup of Abimelech.

Kaiser saw his own soldiers waiting their turn. The men would descend into a few hours of drunken debauchery and rise in the morning with no memory of it. When they woke, each would march with the strength and stamina of three men before the effects of the ritual wore off in the afternoon.

As Kaiser stood and watched what must have been the entire population of Fieldstone drinking from the cup, a figure approached his tent in the darkness. He knew Parenthia by her bulky shape, but did not acknowledge her presence. She stepped into the faint firelight cast by the brazier.

"Thinking of partaking tonight?" Parenthia asked with her eyebrows raised.

"I'll only drink from the hand of the High Priestess herself," Kaiser said.

"How chivalrous. I had to delegate the ritual tonight. I was forced to arrange some... rewards."

A moan of pleasure slipped from a nearby tent. Parenthia smirked.

"Why give a man gold when you can offer him the one thing he wants more?" Kaiser said in disgust.

"It does keep us from having to dip into our coffers," Parenthia said. "Most men aren't as fastidious as you are. Your dear wife must be so thrilled."

Kaiser crossed his arms and did not respond.

"You're not pleased about what happened today," Parenthia said.

"Whether I'm pleased or not is unimportant," Kaiser said, refusing to give in to her attempts to bait him.

"You're the most stubborn man I've ever met," Parenthia said, shaking her head and smiling. "I like that about you. But you're also a fool. I know you care about your family, yet you risk their lives every day that you resist my friendship. Do you think that as Tenth Reaver you're immune to the inquisition?"

"Are you threatening my family?" Kaiser said, his voice tight.

"We're a long way from Northmark. Who knows what might happen to them while you're away?"

Kaiser whirled toward Parenthia, his hands clenched into fists. He stopped short when he looked into her face. Grim humor danced in her eyes. She was taunting him. Kaiser forced himself to relax.

"Blood running hot tonight?" Parenthia purred. "Come, set aside thoughts of your wife and let me show you the pleasures all the other reavers enjoy."

"Go find someone else to torment," Kaiser said. "Did the First Reaver spurn your advances too?"

Parenthia's face hardened as her humor faded. "You should be thankful he's here. If all goes according to plan, we'll arrive in Oakroot before the magus appears. If we're too late, we'll be forced to fight. Depending on what sort of magus we find, two reavers and two hundred soldiers might not be enough."

Kaiser laughed. "How long are you going to keep up this charade? Do you truly believe that we're going to find someone in a small logging town capable of defeating our entire force?"

Parenthia gave him a strange look. "You're more of a fool than I expected. You know less than you think you do, Kaiser Pellathor."

Kaiser paused, and not just because she used his full name. He saw something in Parenthia's eyes he had never seen before. He saw fear.

"I've killed a magus before, or did you forget?" Kaiser said. "The man was a lunatic, barely able to speak in coherent sentences, let alone fight off an entire inquisition."

"Be silent and listen," Parenthia snapped. "Perhaps you will learn something. Reality is not limited to the physical plane. The spiritual plane covers everything that we can see and touch like a blanket, inhabiting the same space but invisible to us. There are demons that roam the spiritual plane, seeking a way to break into our world. Every twelve years the barriers between these planes weakens, and the demons try to take control of a weak-minded host. These people that they inhabit are granted great and terrible powers. We call them 'magus.'

"Your wife's uncle was a failed possession. A magus stillborn on this plane. I promise you, you've never faced anything so terrible as a fully transformed magus. Our only hope of surviving is to find them before they grow too great in power. This 'high king' that Trenner spoke of before he died was a magus, one of the first. Anyone who holds magi in high regard is susceptible to possession. When the barriers between planes are weak, we've no choice but to kill such people. You may despise our priesthood, but we're all that stands between this kingdom and complete destruction."

"And if we find no magus in Oakroot?" Kaiser asked.

"Then we pray that Abimelech protects us," Parenthia said. "The last time a magus got loose, he consumed the southern half of the kingdom in fire."

In front of them, the last townsperson accepted the cup and then the ritual was over. The acolytes returned to the campsite. With their feet hidden beneath long robes, they appeared to glide across the ground. They required Parenthia's attention.

"I can see it in your eyes that you doubt me," Parenthia said as she walked away. "You're too well-trained as a reaver. Ignore my words if you wish, but when you find yourself facing a magus, you'll wish you listened."

Kaiser entered his tent and closed the flap behind him. He stretched himself out on the provided cot, grateful that he did not have to sleep on the hard earth. He tried to focus on all that Parenthia had said, but instead his thoughts were drawn of their own accord to Trenner.

No matter how hard he tried, Kaiser could think of nothing else. Thousands of men had died at his hand and been forgotten where they fell, yet Trenner's face stuck in his mind and would not give him peace. He closed his eyes and drifted off to sleep with a vivid image at the forefront of his thoughts: smashed into the mud, the bloody, carved figurine of the High King looked up at the sky, and when the sun touched the tines of the crown, they shone like gold.

Chapter 10

LACRAEL HAD INTENDED TO return to Oakroot within the week, but time had a way of passing without notice in the deep woods. As the ground thawed and the forest awoke from long months of winter, Lacrael found herself fully occupied with repairing her cabin and preparing for summer. Three weeks passed before she thought to hike back into town.

One morning she woke, and the first thing that popped into her mind was Brant's face. She decided to make the trek into Oakroot that day, for no other reason than to see his smile. Lacrael hummed to herself as she pulled on her supple leather boots, strapped her sword to her hip, and hefted her pack.

The brilliant morning sun filtered down through the naked trees as Lacrael climbed up out of the ravine that hid her home. As she walked through the forest, Lacrael looked for the last glimpses of white snow hiding in the cold shadows, but she saw none. Winter had well and truly gone. Lacrael smiled to herself. Spring always brought change with it. She felt good, and she sensed in her bones that her long wait in the forest was nearing an end.

About an hour out from Oakroot, Lacrael heard voices on the trail ahead of her. To stumble on other people in the woods was not uncommon, but Lacrael preferred to be cautious. She left the trail and crept forward through the undergrowth. Her green tunic and brown leggings would hide her from all but the most determined scrutiny.

When she drew near to the voices, Lacrael peered through the bushes. Five men were loitering on the trail, four of them leaning against trees, and the fifth kicking a pinecone around in the center of the path. They did not look like loggers, and they were definitely not locals. Crude weapons of wood and iron hung at their hips. Lacrael noticed one man carrying a shiny new axe and frowned.

"We've been at this for weeks," one of the men said. "There's no one out here but filthy loggers."

"That creepy bastard is paying us good money to watch these trails," the man in the center of the path said. "This is the easiest work we've ever had, so stop your whining."

Lacrael moved back, careful to make no noise. She gave the men a wide berth and continued on her way to Oakroot. Rough men were a nuisance that came with the sudden increase in population in the forest. She made a mental note to warn Monty about their presence.

The final leg into town passed without issue, and Lacrael stepped out of the forest in good spirits. She had made good time. The sun had not yet reached its zenith in the sky. Tents and makeshift dwellings were popping up on the outskirts of Oakroot. Men traveled from hundreds of miles away to rent out the strength of their arms for the logging season. While not yet crowded, the quiet town showed definite signs of life.

Usually the new faces would dampen Lacrael's spirits, but not today. She strode into town with confidence, heading to the inn first to speak with Monty. Before she reached the big wooden building, Brant intercepted her in the street. He hurried down the steps of his store when he saw her coming and raised a hand requesting her to stop.

Surprised, Lacrael paused and waited for Brant to reach her. At first her heart did a little flip at this break from their routine, but when she saw his face, Lacrael knew something was wrong.

"You need to get out of the street," Brant said in a hushed voice. "Come with me, we can talk in the back of my store."

Brant grabbed her elbow and guided her toward the steps of his store. Alarmed now, Lacrael followed. She glanced up and down the street. What was Brant was so concerned about? As far as she could tell, no one seemed interested in her.

They did not speak again until they were standing in the privacy of the small storeroom at the back of the store. After checking that no one had followed them inside, Brant turned to Lacrael.

"The town's no longer safe for you. There's a strange man poking around, and I'm certain that he's looking for you."

Lacrael smiled to try and put Brant at ease. "I appreciate the concern, but I don't see how anyone could be looking for me. No one but you, your father, and a few others even know I'm here."

Brant shook his head. "You don't understand. This man is dangerous. Maybe he thinks you're someone else, but he strikes me as the sort to take what he wants and ask questions later. You've got to lie low for a while until he gives up and moves on."

"Your father agrees?"

"The man lied to both of us, asking after you," Brant said with a nod. "My father thinks it would be best for everyone if he doesn't find you."

Lacrael could not hide her skepticism, but if both Monty and Brant were in agreement, she would be a fool to ignore their concern. "Alright, I'll avoid Oakroot for a month or two. How will I know when it's safe?"

Brant fumbled for an answer. As he tried to get the words out, he actually blushed, and Lacrael realized that they were alone in the back of his store. Her stomach did a little backflip.

"I was hoping that we could agree on a meeting place somewhere in the forest," Brant finally got out. "I could leave you a sign when the coast is clear, and maybe... maybe we could meet and talk from time to time, at least until this blows over."

Warning bells went off in Lacrael's mind. She had never allowed anyone to follow her into the forest, and if the danger in Oakroot was real, she did not want Brant mixed up in it. And yet... all the reasons she had to say *no* seemed insignificant when she gazed up at his hopeful face. What harm could it do? He was right: she would need to know when the danger in Oakroot had passed.

"I'd like that," Lacrael said with a smile.

"We should get you out of here," Brant said. "I can sneak you out the back of the store. Do you need any supplies before we go? Take whatever you want, no charge."

"I could use a few things, if you don't mind."

"Not at all. I'll go close the blinds and lock the door while you gather what you need."

Together, they returned to the store, and Lacrael quickly gathered the few items she needed. When she returned to the counter, Brant took note of what Lacrael had taken and marked it down in a ledger.

"It's just to track the inventory," he said.

After securing the items in her pack, Lacrael moved toward the rear of the store, but Brant stayed behind the counter. She stopped and looked back at him. He had an odd look on his face, like he wanted to say something but lacked the courage.

"What is it?" Lacrael asked.

"This man that's looking for you, he told me a story," Brant said. He reached down behind the counter and produced a scrap of folded paper. "I know it's nonsense, but he wrote a foreign word on this paper. He said it was your true name and that you would be able to read it. I'm just curious: does it mean anything to you?"

Lacrael stepped forward and took the piece of parchment. She unfolded it and looked down. The strange symbols on the paper blazed like fire, searing themselves into her eyes like the afterimage of the sun. With a gasp, Lacrael dropped the scrap—the flames from the symbols spread, consuming the paper before it hit the floor.

"What was that?" Brant asked, alarm in his voice.

"I don't know," Lacrael said, shaking her head to clear her vision. "I think the symbols reacted to me."

"I'm sorry—I shouldn't have given it to you," Brant said. "Come on! Let's get out of here. I'll show you the way."

Lacrael stumbled as she followed after Brant. They moved through the storerooms at the back of the store toward the exit at the back of the building. Brant paused at the door and poked his head out. After scouting the area, he gave Lacrael a nod, and they stepped into the sunlight. Once in the open, they ran for the nearby treeline, only stopping when they were hidden from the town by a wall of towering trunks.

"Can you leave the store for an hour or two?" Lacrael asked. "If you walk with me a ways into the forest, I can show you a place where we can meet."

Brant looked over her head, back toward his store. She watched him think it over and then make a decision.

"It's still early in the day," he said. "And I closed and locked it before we left. I can leave the store unattended for a bit. Come on, let's go!"

They set out again and were soon hiking south on the trail out of town. Neither of them spoke. Lacrael sensed that like her, Brant was too caught up in the wonder of the moment to cheapen it with words. Her heart sang as the loneliness she had carried for the past four years faded to a distant ache.

A mile or two out of town, Brant started to talk. He rambled, and Lacrael was content to listen. He told her about his childhood, about growing up in Oakroot. Once, he had thought to make his fortune in the inner kingdom. But the little forest town always called him back.

With the topic of his childhood exhausted, Brant launched into telling her the history of his store, and the challenges of being the only merchant on the edge of the kingdom. Lulled into a state of contentedness by Brant's voice, Lacrael forgot where they were and how long they had been walking.

They stopped short when a man stepped out from behind a tree and blocked the trail. Brant looked at the stranger in confusion. Lacrael swore under her breath. She had totally forgotten about the bandits.

"Nice day for a stroll," the man said, eying Lacrael up and down.

"It is that," Brant said. "Now if you'd please step aside."

Brant was twice the bandit's size. He stepped forward in an attempt to intimidate the man.

Lacrael placed a restraining hand on Brant's arm. He glanced back at her in surprise. She gave him a small shake of her head. Brant was no warrior. Despite his size and strength, he possessed a softness that Lacrael did not want to see tested against the wiry brigand.

The bandit spat onto the trail. "Smart girl," he said, ignoring Brant. "I've got no quarrel with your man, but if you don't come quietly with me, he's going to get hurt."

"Like hell I will!" Brant shouted.

Brant jumped forward, hands reaching as if he intended to throttle the life out of the man. A second bandit stepped from behind a tree. This man was a brute, almost a match for Brant in size. He swung an axe as he came, and the blunt side smacked into Brant's skull. Brant hit the ground hard.

Lacrael drew her sword. The bandit with the axe stood over a groaning Brant. Three more brigands revealed themselves. Lacrael said a silent prayer of thanks that none of them carried a bow or spear.

"Don't be foolish," the leader said when he saw Lacrael's blade. "There's five of us and one of you. If you fight, it's only going to go worse for you and your friend here."

"I'm only going to warn you once," Lacrael said, her voice tight. "You may outnumber me, but if you attack, I'm going to kill at least one of you. Which one of you wants to die today?"

The men hesitated. None of them wanted to trade their lives.

The leader sneered at her. "You think you know how to use that blade? Come on, show me what you got."

Surrounded and outnumbered, Lacrael gripped her sword. She could charge the man nearest her, but that would expose her back to the bandit with the axe. One tap of that steel axehead to her skull and she would join Brant in the dirt.

Lacrael sized up the leader. The man crept toward her, rusted sword held out in front of him. His arms were rigid, knuckles white on the hilt of his weapon. This man had no idea how to fight. She glanced at the others and saw the same ineptitude. These men were as much a danger to themselves as they were to Lacrael.

With a tight smile, Lacrael advanced toward the leader. He stopped in his tracks, surprised, then snarled and pulled his sword back for a mighty swing. Lacrael darted through the opening, free hand thrust into the man's pommel as she slashed through the bicep of his sword arm. He shouted and dropped his weapon, leaping back to clutch his bleeding arm.

Before Lacrael could speak to tell him to stop this foolishness, a pair of arms grabbed her from behind. The man wrapped crushing arms around her and lifted her off her feet. Lacrael screamed in frustration, her legs flailing as she tried to kick her attacker. She could not twist to strike at the man who held her.

The bandit leader's eyes lit up and he stepped forward, blood seeping between his fingers.

"We were supposed to take you alive, but you've proven more trouble than you're worth," he said. "Toss me that chopper!" he shouted at the man with the axe.

The bandit leader caught the axe with his good arm. He gave Lacrael a knowing glance.

"Hold her," the leader said to the man behind her.

Lacrael saw what would happen next. She gritted her teeth as the bandit leader cocked the axe back for a huge swing. He pivoted on one foot, both hands locked around the base of the weapon's handle. The metal head arced toward Lacrael's face, nothing but a silver blur.

At the last instant, Lacrael threw herself forward and ducked her head. The axe whistled past her ear and struck the man's skull behind her. She heard the horrible crunch of bone and then a gurgle as the man died. Warm liquid spilled down her back.

The bandit leader's mouth went slack as his eyes filled with horror. He stepped back, his axe falling from numb fingers. Lacrael shook off the dead weight of the dying man and stepped toward the bandit leader with her sword raised.

"I told you—," Lacrael tried to say.

Her words were cut off by a tremendous roar. Something huge hit her, and the trees overhead spun as she crashed to the ground. Her vision went black for an instant. When her sight returned, she looked up to see the brute of a bandit pummeling her.

His massive fists pounded her face, chest, and stomach. She could not breathe under his weight—she felt herself losing consciousness under the onslaught. Her head bounced off the ground from the force of the blows. Lacrael's hand scrabbled for her sword, but it was out of reach.

With a silent prayer, Lacrael placed her open palm on the bandit's chest and tapped into the power sleeping inside her. Fire rushed through her veins and exploded from her hand. The man grunted like he had been kicked by a mule. His crushing weight disappeared as his body launched backward. He started to burn as he hit the ground.

Lacrael scrambled to her feet and found her sword. She turned to face the remaining bandits, but the fight had gone out of them. They stared open-mouthed as their comrade screamed. The big man flailed in the dirt, rolling back and forth as he tried to quench the fire. Nothing he tried worked. Soon, he went still as flames consumed him from within. His dead eyes stared at the sky as they melted in their sockets.

The smell of charred flesh filled the forest. The three surviving bandits looked at Lacrael in horror.

"She's a magus!" the leader cried.

His words snapped the others out of their stupor. They left the dead man behind and ran for the trees. Lacrael did not give chase. They would not be back. She groaned as she tested her limbs. Her chest and arms had taken a brutal beating.

Lacrael could not bring herself to look at Brant, so she stared down at the smoldering corpse. The flames had died down, but the body still burned from within. Blackened bones were starting to poke out of liquified flesh. She averted her gaze. This was bad. Word of this would spread, and soon the whole kingdom would know of a magus hiding in the Nogard Forest.

Finally, she worked up the courage to shift her gaze to where Brant lay. He stared up at her from the dirt. Lacrael saw the bandits' horror at her power mirrored in his eyes. Blood dripped down his face from the nasty wound on his forehead. It had started to swell.

"Can you stand?" Lacrael asked, kneeling at his side and raising a hand to his injury.

"Don't... don't touch me," Brant said, flinching away from her fingers.

Lacrael recoiled. Tears filled her eyes.

"I'm sorry. There's no way I could have told you. I shouldn't have let you come out here with me."

"No... you shouldn't have," Brant said, speaking slowly as he struggled to his feet. He swayed where he stood. He reached out a hand to steady himself on a tree.

"What will you do?" Lacrael asked.

"I'm going back to Oakroot," Brant said. He hesitated, finally meeting Lacrael's gaze. "I'll keep your secret, but you should leave this forest and never return. You stay away from me and my father."

Lacrael nodded, unable to speak. Without another word, Brant turned and staggered away. He could barely walk at first, but after a few steps he managed a ragged gait.

When Brant disappeared around a bend in the trail, Lacrael took a great, shuddering breath. She did not blame him for turning away. Tales of the inquisition had reached her even in Oakroot. Befriending a magus meant certain torture and death.

With tears blurring her vision, Lacrael left the trail and ran through the forest. She hurdled creeks and jumped over logs, pushing herself to the limits of her strength. Branches scratched at her face and caught in her hair. Lacrael ran for miles, not caring where she ended up. When she could run no further and her chest felt like it would burst, she collapsed in the hole left by the roots of an upturned tree.

While the sun slid toward the western horizon, Lacrael sobbed as the loneliness came crashing back. After a time, even the strength to cry had gone, and she slept.

Chapter 11

MAZAREEM OPENED HIS EYES. He blinked as the world came into focus. With a feeble arm, he reached toward the crevice of light a foot in front of his face. Groaning, he pulled his stiff body into the evening sunlight. Mazareem smirked to himself. Had anyone been present to witness his waking, they would have seen an old, dead tree giving birth to a skeletal phantom.

Once free of the hollow trunk, Mazareem stretched to his full height. Spiderwebs and dust covered his long black cloak. Judging by the lethargy in his limbs, Mazareem estimated he had slumbered for at least two weeks. Numb fingers fumbled at one of the vials on his belt. He pulled the stopper and lifted the glass tube to his pale lips. The liquid disappeared down his throat in one gulp.

Fire spilled down his gullet and detonated in his stomach. Mazareem gasped as his thirsty flesh absorbed the life-giving concoction. He sat cross-legged before the tree. It would take most of the night to nurse his body back to full strength.

Hibernation was the only method Mazareem had at his disposal to extend his journey into the world outside his prison. At the cost of a great deal of pain and discomfort, he could buy himself several extra weeks to complete his task. To wake early meant that someone tripped one of his triggers.

A slow grin spread across Mazareem's face: a magus had read the draconic script he left in the fat merchant's care. Mazareem had not entered Oakroot for weeks, and no doubt they thought him gone. Come morning, he would pay the general store a visit.

Darkness crept through the trees as the sun slipped below the horizon. Night sounds began to fill the surrounding forest, and yet Mazareem sat in a sphere of silence. No animal or insect disturbed him. Once, the twin glowing orbs of a forest cat's eyes inspected him from the nearby shadows.

"Here, kitty, kitty," Mazareem called to the animal. The eyes winked out and did not appear again.

Throughout the night, Mazareem occupied himself with drinking careful sips from the vials he carried and massaging life back into his limbs. A hibernation of two weeks or more was long enough for rigor mortis to set in.

"Can you see what I've become, Rowen?" Mazareem said into the darkness. "Some might call me a monster, but I've found this body has its uses. Although I fear not even the mistress of death himself would take me into her bed now."

Mazareem cackled at his own joke. The wind rattling the tops of the trees was the only response. As the night wore on, strength returned to Mazareem's limbs. Soon, he stopped kneading his cold, pale flesh and sat back to watch the moon pass overhead.

She had loved the moon. He remembered the wonder of her naked flesh framed by its celestial light. Once, the intimate mystery of her curves had held him in greater rapture than any ancient text.

The memory teased him with a promise of lost humanity, but sparked no lust within his husk of a body.

While he waited for the coming of the sun, Mazareem brooded. Abimelech owned him body and soul, and the power of the dark god's authority extended to a few chosen children. Mazareem was a tool, hidden in shadow until the time came to loose him like an arrow at the target of Abimelech's choosing.

At the beginning, this arrangement suited Mazareem, and he had revelled in his newfound longevity. With it had come the time to study and learn, infinite lifetimes without sleep or hunger to delve into mystical riddles that were inconsequential to mortal men. And with learning came knowledge. Perhaps even knowledge that Mazareem's captors preferred he not possess, for Mazareem had learned that his current state of undeath need not be permanent. The recovery of his lost humanity might be possible. Since that revelation, the memory of the woman in the painting had haunted his every step.

What had her name been? It seemed cruel, petty, that Mazareem could never recall it. He had understood the price so little when he had agreed to pay it, all those centuries ago.

The lightening of the eastern sky roused Mazareem from his grim musings. He had idiots to use and desert princesses to kill. Humanity would have to wait.

With a grunt, Mazareem got to his feet and stretched his now-supple limbs. Twenty paces from his hollow tree, Mazareem knelt over a pile of dead tree limbs. After a bit of digging, he spotted Worm's snout poking through the fallen branches. Mazareem cleared the twigs and debris from the rest of the hound. Worm's body was still—no breath issued from his mouth.

"Sorry, boy," Mazareem muttered. "I know this isn't pleasant."

With one hand, he pried open Worm's jaws. With the other, he popped the stopper off a vial and poured the contents down the dog's throat. Mazareem sat back on his heels and waited for the liquid to work its magic.

After a moment, one of Worm's paws twitched. Soon, the animal's entire body spasmed as empty lungs filled with air. Worm sucked in ragged gasps of breath through his mouth. Finally, the hound's eyes opened, and he raised his head to look at Mazareem.

"Welcome back to the land of the living," Mazareem said, rubbing the dog's head.

Worm struggled to his feet on unsteady legs. When he found his balance, he took a step. He sneezed and shook his head, dripping bloody snot.

"There's a good dog," Mazareem said. "It took me all night to get my muscles working again."

Mazareem collected his walking stick from the same pile of branches that had hidden Worm, got to his feet, and started out toward Oakroot. Worm followed after, slow at first, but soon catching up and trotting alongside his master.

The streets of Oakroot were deserted this early in the morning. Mazareem and Worm made straight for the general store. Finding the front door still locked, Mazareem made short work of it with the lockpicks he kept in his cloak. He held the door open for Worm to enter and then closed it softly behind them. Despite his attempt at stealth, the little bell above the door tinkled to announce their presence.

Drawn to the sound of money crossing his threshold, the thick-witted shopkeeper appeared from the back room. He stared at

Mazareem and Worm with an incredulous look on his face. A bloody bandage wrapped his head.

"That looks like a nasty wound," Mazareem said.

Without a word, Brant whirled and made to dash out the back of the store.

"Worm, get him!" Mazareem barked.

Worm's claws scrabbled at the wood floor as the hound surged forward. The animal disappeared through the door, and Mazareem heard Brant cry out from the backroom. Mazareem strode forward without hurry.

Mazareem found the shopkeeper backed against a wall in the storeroom. Worm bared his teeth, growling low in his throat anytime Brant tried to escape.

"L-let me go!" Brant shouted when he spotted Mazareem. "You've no right to do this!"

"Why, whatever do you mean?" Mazareem asked in mock surprise. "I don't see any chains that prevent you from leaving. Feel free to walk out yonder door."

Brant's horror-filled eyes never left Worm.

"What do you want from me?"

"I want to know who read that little note I left in your care," Mazareem said. "Was it your mystery love from the deep woods?"

"I don't know what you're talking about," the fool said after a heartbeat of hesitation.

Mazareem sighed. "Contrary to what you might think, I'm a reasonable man. I've no quarrel with you or anyone else in this cute little town. But if you don't cooperate, I'm going to hurt you."

"You can go to hell," Brant said.

"I've been there. They didn't want me." With a snarl, Mazareem lunged forward and slammed a bony fist into Brant's gut. The big man doubled over as the air left his lungs. Mazareem gripped the back of his neck in iron fingers, dragging him to the center of the storeroom.

"You stink of magus fire," Mazareem said. He threw Brant to the floor between two metal storage racks that stretched from floor to ceiling. Brant's injured head hit the floor hard.

Brant tried to struggle—Mazareem smacked him hard across the face. While the shopkeep was dazed, Mazareem secured his wrists and ankles to the base of the racks with lengths of rope from a nearby shelf.

"One last chance. Who read the note?"

Brant stared up at Mazareem with mortal, frightened eyes and said nothing.

"This place is just as tidy and organized as the front of the store," Mazareem said, gazing around the storeroom. "I appreciate order. There's something comforting about it." He glanced back down at Brant. "You brought this upon yourself. I hope whatever you're hiding is worth what you're about to endure."

Brant could only groan in reply.

Mazareem leaned over him, gleaming dagger in hand. With several quick cuts, he sliced the shirt away from Brant's chest, then rummaged around in a pouch hanging from his belt. He withdrew a small clay pot, removed the stopper, and dipped a fingertip inside.

When Mazareem pulled his finger from the pot, a foul-smelling ichor coated the tip. Using this substance as ink, he started to draw a symbol on Brant's chest. Brant struggled to raise his head so that he could see what Mazareem was doing, and Worm sniffed at

Brant's chest with his huge snout. Mazareem shooed the animals away. With swift, sharp strokes, he painted a jagged heptagram on Brant's exposed skin.

"If you don't survive, let me apologize in advance," Mazareem said as he leaned back to inspect the completed symbol. "It's not my intent to kill you. You're no good to me dead. Probably."

Brant tried to mumble a response. Mazareem chuckled.

"Don't worry. This'll fix that pain in your head." Mazareem stowed the clay pot back in his pouch and slipped a small glass vial from his belt. The stopper came out of the vial with a small pop. Mazareem poured the black liquid out onto Brant's chest.

Brant screamed. Green fire blazed on his skin where the contents of the vial touched the symbol drawn on his torso. He thrashed against his bindings, but the knotted rope held strong. Brant's flesh sizzled, the flames tracing the shape Mazareem had drawn.

"Don't fight it," Mazareem said. "If you struggle, it excites them."

Mazareem stepped back. Above Brant's body, a dark shadow appeared out of thin air. The shadow grew until it stretched between the storage shelves. It hung over Brant, a swirling oval of solid black. Even in the midst of his pain, Brant stared up in horror at the colorless void.

A face appeared in the portal, and then another. Soon, a crowd of heads ringed the dark oval. They stared down at Brant, their features nothing but shapes in the swirling shadow. One of the heads leaned forward, and a body the size of a man oozed out of the murk. It floated down toward the wooden planks like smoke. It rotated in the air, landing without a sound; the floor turned black where its feet touched. Mazareem could see through the thing's body.

The shadow being leaned over Brant, the empty sockets of its eyes searching for something only it could see. It reached out a single hand, the phantom limb passing through Brant's skull. Brant's screams stopped abruptly—his eyes rolled back in his head. Mazareem knew what those icy talons felt like. They did not touch flesh and bone but instead carved the soul, sundering even the most tightly held memory from their victim's grasp. Mazareem's lips began to curl in spite of himself.

At last, the shadow creature pulled back its hand. Its examination of Brant complete, the thing leapt back up into the dark portal and disappeared. The rest of the faces vanished along with it, and the swirling vortex started to collapse in on itself. After a few heartbeats, it blinked out of existence, gone as suddenly as it had appeared. The green flames on Brant's chest dwindled and died.

"So you're not the magus," Mazareem said. "I didn't think you were, but I had to be sure."

He squatted on his heels next to Brant's head.

"Now, you're going to tell me what I want to know, or I'm going to let Worm chew on your face."

— —

Lacrael ransacked her little cabin as she prepared to leave it behind forever. With relentless efficiency, she cataloged every item that had come into her possession over the last four years, packing only what she could carry on her back. Lacrael's sadness grew with the pile of items to be discarded. Now faced with hiking out of her secret ravine never to return, she realized how much this place felt like home.

After running away from the incinerated bandit, Lacrael had spent a miserable night in the forest. Overwhelmed by exhaustion and despair, she had slept until dawn. Her body still ached where roots had jabbed into her side.

As she had hiked through the trees, one truth had dominated her thoughts: her life in the forest was over. She would never be welcome in Oakroot again. Even if Brant kept her secret, the surviving brigands would soon spread their tale near and far. They might even return with hunters, eager to assist in the capture of a rogue magus. They might return with an inquisition.

Lacrael stuffed the last morsel of food into her pack and wiped at her wet eyes with the back of a hand. This was not how she wanted to leave, but now she had no choice. She did not know where to go. The portal from her homeland had deposited her in this forest, and Lacrael had felt compelled to stay near to the place where she had arrived in this realm. Her grandfather would have known what to do.

With an angry yank, Lacrael cinched the straps of her pack closed, hefted the burden onto her back, and strode from the cabin. She shut the door behind her but did not lock it. Maybe some other unfortunate soul would find shelter here once she was gone. Lacrael paused next to the little stream that trickled through the bottom of the ravine. She looked up at the trees, breathing in the smell of the deep forest one last time. There was peace here, a quiet strength that had sustained her during the long, lonely years.

Lacrael heard her grandfather's voice in her mind, chiding her for her sentimental nature. She smiled at the imaginary reprimand, lowered her gaze, and set her feet to the path up and out of the ravine. Soon, the cabin was lost in the overgrowth behind her.

At the top of the trail, Lacrael stopped. Where should she go? She had no friends outside of Oakroot. Lacrael had heard many tales about the kingdom beyond the forest, but she had never set eyes on it. Could she survive out there? She knew her exotic appearance would draw curiosity wherever she went. People knew she was an outsider, that she did not belong.

Without making a conscious decision, Lacrael started walking. In her heart, she knew her destination, but her mind had not yet accepted it. She could not leave Oakroot behind forever without talking to Brant one last time.

Perhaps he feared her now, and perhaps that fear was justified, but Lacrael wanted to hear it from his own mouth. She wanted to look in his eyes and see for herself if fear had consumed his affection for her. They had been drawn to each other from the start, and their shared, unspoken attraction had forged a unique kinship between them that Lacrael was not willing to let die alongside the bandit slain on the trail.

Chapter 12

KAISER SUFFERED THROUGH THE last leg of the journey to Oakroot in complete silence. He avoided Parenthia and steered clear of the First Reaver. After the execution of Trenner, the mood of the soldiers darkened. Parenthia sensed the growing disgruntlement amongst the men and spent the evenings preaching about the dangers of the magus they were hunting. These men had no reason to doubt the truth of the High Priestess's words. Kaiser watched as the soldiers were whipped into a righteous fervor as they neared their destination.

With every mile of road that passed beneath his horse's hooves, discontent grew in Kaiser's heart. A seed of doubt had taken root in his being, and although he could not yet determine the source, it dug its way into his soul and turned his world black. Confidence gave way to despair, and hopelessness beset Kaiser on all sides. He could not banish Mariel's plea to escape from Northmark from his mind.

The anger smoldering in Kaiser's soul troubled him. He had survived ten years as Tenth Reaver because he refused to let emotion influence his decisions. Every man he struck down in the arena was as much a victim of his own rage and arrogance as he was of Kaiser's blade.

As they neared Oakroot, Kaiser rose early every morning to meditate, trying to soothe the slow boil of his fury, but when his gaze invariably found Parenthia or the First Reaver, his efforts proved useless.

When they finally reached the Nogard Forest, Kaiser's patience had worn thin. Trenner's killing loomed large in his mind. For the first time in his life, Kaiser felt guilty, and as the weight of this new emotion pressed down on his shoulders, the thousands of souls reaped by his blade cried to him from the past. Was he a monster?

They marched for several hours under the trees. Beneath their feet, the cobblestones gave way to hard-packed dirt. A steady stream of travelers clogged the road, many of them carrying axes and saws over their shoulders. When the inquisition appeared, these travelers stood to the side and gaped at their procession as it passed. Kaiser swore under his breath. The logging season would soon be under way. Oakroot would be packed.

Sure enough, when the forest town appeared between the trees, the streets were crawling with people. The sound of axes striking hardwood rang out from every side, and the shouts of work crews echoed through the woods. Crude tents and sleeping pallets covered every square foot of open ground. As the procession of the inquisition snaked from the treeline, the forest fell silent. Word of their arrival passed through the work camps faster than wildfire.

As the first target of the inquisition, Oakroot had not been warned of their coming. No furnished campsite waited for them. Parenthia intended to rectify this, and she marched their column into the center of the little forest town. Citizens and laborers were forced to quit the road or be trampled. All activity stopped as the two reavers, high atop their armored destriers, rode at the head of the inquisition down the main street.

Runners dashed from the city and disappeared into the trees, no doubt going to tell the outlying work camps of their arrival. Parenthia trotted her palfrey up to the head of the column, moving in front of Kaiser and the First Reaver. She let the silence settle before she spoke. Kaiser knew she enjoyed the suspense.

Parenthia's jowls quivered when she spoke. Her orator's voice boomed off of the walls of the buildings. "Where is your mayor? Do you intend to leave us standing in the street like vagabonds?"

No one spoke, but a woman ducked into the nearby inn. Several heartbeats later, a stout man hurried from the door of the three-story building. He stepped into the street, wiping his hands on the apron that hung from his waist. He took in the soldiers loitering in the street with a glance and then squinted up at Parenthia. Kaiser smiled behind his helmet. The man was not intimidated.

"My name's Monty," the man said. "I'm the owner of the Acorn Inn, and I'm the closest thing to a mayor that Oakroot's got."

"I am Parenthia, High Priestess of Abimelech," Parenthia said. "By the order of Regent Trangeth, the inquisition has come to Oakroot. Every man, woman, and child will be examined by an inquisitor. Any who are caught trying to flee will be tested by fire."

Monty blanched. His gaze flicked to the two reavers behind Parenthia, falling last on the gilded carriage.

"We're all law-abiding citizens here, priestess," Monty said.

"*High* Priestess," Parenthia corrected him. "If you're all loyal subjects to the crown, then you've nothing to fear."

Monty gulped and nodded his agreement.

"We passed by a clearing on the outside of town," Parenthia said. "We'll be claiming it for the inquisition. I expect every single one of my soldiers to be treated as a royal guest for as long as we stay in Oakroot. As agents of our holy mission, they represent both Abimelech and the throne. Treat them as such, or suffer the consequences."

"That field is already full of tents," Monty stammered. "As you can see, the logging season has started. There's no more room. I'll do my best to furnish your men, but we've already too many mouths to feed and not enough food to go around."

Parenthia leaned forward in her saddle, piercing Monty with a withering gaze. "The empty stomachs of a few filthy laborers are none of my concern, little man. Rest assured that if I'm disappointed with your efforts to accommodate us, the regent will hear of it. He has little patience for any who disrespect Abimelech's chosen. Don't worry yourself about the trash covering my field. I can deal with that."

Before the innkeeper could respond, a noise from the nearby store drew the attention of everyone in the street. A tall man in black leathers stepped onto the building's porch. The biggest hound Kaiser had ever seen padded along at the man's side. Kaiser did not recognize the man, but Parenthia jerked so hard that she almost lost her seat on her horse. The dark stranger examined their column of armed soldiers with undisguised contempt before turning on one heel and striding away down the street. The monstrous dog followed close at his heels.

"Send a pair of soldiers to check out that shop," Parenthia snapped. "He was in there for a reason."

Parenthia's orders were relayed back to the column, and two men stepped out of ranks to investigate the store. They vanished inside. Monty stared after the two soldiers, his face pale with fear.

— —

Lacrael told herself that she would be discreet. She could sneak into Brant's store through the back and wait for a moment to speak with him in private. No one else would see her, and once she had spoken with Brant, she would follow the road west out of Oakroot.

She had approached the town from the south where the undergrowth grew the thickest. Before Lacrael had grown brave enough to enter the town, she had spent months observing its people from afar. Her favorite spot to spy from had been a tree with low-hanging branches in the middle of a briar patch. She stood at the base of it now, confident it would give her a view of whatever was happening in town.

After taking a deep breath, she dropped her pack between its roots, grasped the lowest limb, and hauled herself skyward. Her hands remembered the shape of the tree, and she scampered up the branches with practiced ease. She stopped well short of the top. Stripped of its leaves by the winter, only the tree's thick trunk hid her from anyone in the town who might look her way. Lacrael anchored herself to a branch and peered around the tree, looking into the heart of Oakroot.

Lacrael's brow knit in confusion. She stared for a long time, trying to make sense of what she saw. In the center of town, standing at the head of a column of soldiers, stood a pair of massive horses. On the backs of these beasts, two dark knights stared down in silence at the assembled townspeople. For all the time that Lacrael watched, she never saw the knights move.

Between the mounted knights sat a plump, robed woman on a smaller steed. Something about the woman's face bothered Lacrael. Behind her, a group of women adorned in similar black robes stood around an ornate, windowless carriage.

A crowd had gathered to watch these sinister figures confront a single man in the street. Lacrael recognized Monty standing in the road, and her heart skipped a beat at his bravery to face the strangers so calmly. She was too far away to overhear the conversation, but she could tell from Monty's posture that he was upset. They were all turned to look toward Brant's store.

Lacrael held her breath as she clung to the tree, fascinated. After a few moments, two soldiers emerged from Brant's shop. They were carrying a man between them, supporting his limp body on their shoulders. Even with his head lowered and his feet dragging the ground, Lacrael recognized Brant.

Like a thunderbolt from the sky, the identity of these soldiers hit her. This had to be the priesthood of Abimelech. This had to be an inquisition. Lacrael gasped and almost cried out. How had they come so fast? How had they known to find her here? She shook her head in angry frustration. Somehow they had found out that Brant knew her.

Lacrael gritted her teeth. She could not let Brant suffer for being her friend. Would these soldiers torture everyone in Oakroot who had showed her kindness? These people deserved better. Lacrael weighed her options and made a decision. If the priesthood had come seeking a magus, she would give them one. For every person they hurt, one of their own would burn.

Chapter 13

KAISER STARED AT THE man hanging between the two soldiers with disinterest. The crowd had gasped when he appeared. Whoever he was, he looked to be in a bad way. The innkeeper stepped forward, his mouth open to object, but Parenthia pounced before he could speak.

"You know this man?" Parenthia asked.

"He's my son," Monty said.

Kaiser frowned behind his helmet at the anguish in Monty's voice.

"How fortuitous," Parenthia said with a smile. "I'm placing him under the custody of the inquisition. Cooperate with us, and perhaps he'll be returned to you in one piece."

Parenthia glanced at Kaiser. "Take the First Reaver and clear the rabble from the campsite. I want the prisoner secure and my tent set up within the hour."

Kaiser nodded his acknowledgement of Parenthia's orders. Monty glared up at them as Kaiser turned his horse away from the column and started to trot back the way they had come. Kaiser's anger surged—he was fed up with Parenthia ordering him around as if he was her dog.

Kaiser dismounted on the edge of town. The First Reaver stayed on his horse, his grinning metal skull of a helm staring down at Kaiser. Kaiser ignored the man's show of disrespect and turned his attention to the field. Tents, cooking pots, and travel packs covered every single blade of grass. Women tended the camp, waiting for their men to return from the days work. A few terrified children peered around the skirts of their mothers.

"I don't know who you are or how you came to be First Reaver without my consent," Kaiser growled, "but in the field, you answer to me, not the High Priestess. Get off your horse or I'll drag you down."

Not a small part of Kaiser wanted the First Reaver to defy him. It would give him an excuse to challenge the man, and he would take great pleasure in spilling the First Reaver's blood in front of Parenthia. The First Reaver stared at him for a long time, the gaze of the metal skull never wavering from Kaiser's face. Finally, the First Reaver hoisted a leg over the saddle and slid to the ground. The man never spoke—he just stood there, waiting to see what Kaiser would do next.

Annoyed, but determined to not let the First Reaver know, Kaiser said, "I only see women and children here, so I don't expect resistance. Don't draw steel unless I do."

Without waiting for a response, Kaiser strode toward the group of women that had gathered to watch their approach.

"I am the Tenth Reaver of Northmark," Kaiser said to the women. "Do you know what that means?"

A few of them nodded. The rest just looked at him with wide eyes.

"I've come to Oakroot at the head of an inquisition," Kaiser continued. "The High Priestess of Abimelech has claimed this field for our troops. You need to have your belongings removed from it within the hour. She won't be as understanding as I am. Leave. Now."

One or two women tried to raise their voices in protest, but they were quickly shushed by their more astute companions.

"Our thanks, Lord Reaver," one of the older women at the front of the crowd said. "We'll be cleared out in no time."

A commotion from one of the nearby tents caused both Kaiser and the First Reaver to whirl toward the noise. Children in tow, a woman was making a desperate dash for the forest.

"Stop her!" Kaiser commanded.

The First Reaver sprinted forward. He caught the woman easily, felling her with a savage blow from behind. The three small children crowded around their fallen mother, looking up at the First Reaver in terror.

Kaiser moved to stand over the woman. When he looked down at her, his breath caught in his throat. She could have been Mariel's sister. Kaiser forced himself not to look at the tear-streaked faces of the children.

"Are you trying to flee the examination of the inquisition?" Kaiser asked, his voice ringing deep in his helmet.

"Please, M'Lord Reaver, just let me go," the woman begged, now on her knees. "We've done nothing wrong. We'll disappear into the trees and you'll never see us again."

"If you're free of the taint of heresy, then you've nothing to fear," Kaiser said. "You've earned yourself the right to be the first to face the inquisitor."

Kaiser turned his back on the woman as she started to wail.

"See that she does not leave," Kaiser commanded the First Reaver.

Kaiser walked back to his horse. There had been no confrontation, yet adrenaline surged through his body. Why had he saved Mariel, so many years ago, only to condemn this woman now? He harbored a heretic in his own home while he condemned others to torture and death.

Parenthia arrived at the field an hour later. The inquisitor's carriage creaked to a stop in the center of the clearing. Her troops seemed unmarred, and Kaiser assumed she had reached an agreement with the mayor without bloodshed.

"What's this?" Parenthia said when she spied Kaiser. "You dispersed the mob without bloodying your blade? I thought for sure you'd cut down a few women, maybe skewer a youngling or two."

"Women and children might die by your hand, but not mine," Kaiser said.

Parenthia laughed. "Your wife and brats have made you weak. What's the harm in putting a little terror into them? Fear primes the mind for the inquisitor."

Kaiser did not respond.

"We still have a good six hours of daylight," Parenthia said, focusing on the task at hand. "We'll begin the process now. I informed that pitiful excuse for a mayor to start gathering people. You'll preside over the testing along with the First Reaver. This isn't a request."

"As you wish," Kaiser said.

Parenthia moved to the carriage and opened a gilded door. A gnarled hand reached from the darkness inside. Parenthia took the hand in her grip and helped one of the bent inquisitors descend from the wagon. She knelt so that they could speak without being overheard. They conferred quietly for some time before Parenthia stood straight and nodded to Kaiser.

With a sigh, Kaiser returned to his horse. He placed a foot in the stirrup and pulled himself back into the saddle. Next to the mounted First Reaver, Kaiser waited in the road for Parenthia's little procession to form up.

Four robed acolytes joined the High Priestess and the inquisitor. Each one of the hooded women carried a golden chalice filled to the brim with the blood of Abimelech. Woven belts of gold hung from their waists, lined with clay pots containing a black, foul-smelling ichor. The seven-limbed tree of Abimelech glittered in silver embroidery on the front of their robes.

At Parenthia's signal, Kaiser and the First Reaver started their horses forward at a slow walk. Between them, the four acolytes flanked Parenthia and the inquisitor, two on each side. With the golden chalices raised before them, the acolytes chanted an eerie hymn in a language that Kaiser did not recognize. The unknown words tickled at something primal in the center of Kaiser's brain and shot shivers of fear down his spine.

They returned to the center of Oakroot to find a line of people already waiting. Parenthia led their strange group to the head of the line. When they were in position, the acolytes stopped singing and the inquisitor stepped forward. Parenthia stood at the bent man's side, with Kaiser and the First Reaver towering over their heads several paces behind.

Soldiers dragged the woman from the camp to stand in front of the inquisitor. She sobbed as the masked inquisitor peered into her face. After a moment, he made a cutting motion with his right hand and turned away from the woman.

The soldiers lifted the screaming woman by her arms and carried her back toward the camp. Watching from a nearby porch, Monty grimaced.

Parenthia turned her face toward the Oakroot mayor. "For your sake, you'd best pray that's the last heretic we find."

Kaiser rested his gauntleted hands on the horn of his saddle and settled in for a long wait. The next citizen of Oakroot stepped forward to submit himself to the inquisition. The inquisitor stared into the man's face for a few heartbeats before turning his head away with a sharp jerk. Found innocent, the citizen breathed a sigh of relief and moved forward into the care of the acolytes. One of the robed women dipped a finger into a clay pot hanging on her sash and used the ichor to mark the innocent man's forehead. The putrid gunk stuck fast, a black smear on the man's skin. To complete the ritual, the man drank from an offered chalice.

This process repeated itself fifty times in the span of an hour. Soon, people bearing the black sign of the inquisition were mingling with those yet untested. Over the course of the next few days, every man, woman, and child would suffer through the ceremony, and every soul in Oakroot would bear the mark.

As the day wore on, Kaiser's frustration grew. He could not shake the sense that this was wrong, that this was not where he was supposed to be. What he had once overlooked as inconsequential now seemed intolerable. How had he ignored the priesthood's insanity for so long? Why had he spent years hunting down infidels at their behest?

Parenthia had told him that an inquisition never failed. She claimed that the signs of prophecy were always right, and the priesthood always found the magus they sought. As Kaiser watched the inquisitor examine the steady stream of people, he understood why an inquisition never returned to Northmark empty-handed. All the inquisitor had to do was signal that he had found a heretic, and the prison cells would fill. No one but the guilty parties cared if it was not the truth.

Kaiser counseled himself to hold fast. He had endured much, and he would survive this too. If others must die to keep his family safe, so be it. Trenner's terrified face tried to surface in his mind, but Kaiser vehemently suppressed the memory.

When the sun finally sunk below the treetops in the west, Parenthia called an end to the day's examinations. She dismissed those citizens still waiting in line, informing them that the inquisitor would return with the dawn. Kaiser turned his horse, and along with the First Reaver, he escorted Parenthia, her acolytes, and the inquisitor back to the camp.

Taking the innkeeper's son prisoner had put the fear of god into him. Several great tables had been set up and draped with white linens. A huge feast had been laid out for the soldiers of the inquisition. Monty himself presided over the banquet, personally directing an army of young serving men and women. A hundred torches lit the scene.

The ravishing acolytes of Abimelech glided between the tables, offering drinks from the goblets they carried. As the potent liquid took effect, the feast started the slow descent into drunken revelry.

"With the right sort of persuasion, even this barbaric little town knows how to treat its guests," Parenthia said as they approached.

Kaiser wanted nothing to do with it. He dismounted and tried to go straight to his tent, but Parenthia had other ideas.

"Hold a spell," Parenthia said to him before he could leave her behind. They waited until the others had spread out into the camp and they could speak in private.

"I don't have to be an inquisitor to sense that you're troubled," Parenthia said when they were alone. "As the Tenth Reaver , you're above reproach. But while we're on an inquisition, my word is law. If your attitude doesn't improve, I'll place you under arrest and let the regent sort it out when we return to Northmark. I don't care what you believe or what you think about what we're doing here, you will do your duty and you will show outward support for my leadership. Do I make myself clear?"

"I will do my duty," Kaiser said, his voice hollow.

Parenthia's lips twisted in a cruel smile. "See that you do. You've amused me thus far, so I've been lenient. Cross me and I'll make your life miserable."

As Parenthia's words penetrated his mind, Kaiser's head started to buzz. Pain lanced through his temples. He rested a hand against the neck of his horse to prevent himself from falling. Kaiser waited for Parenthia to move away before trying to take a step. The last thing he wanted to do was show her weakness. She gave him a self-satisfied smirk when he stayed silent and went to join the banquet.

Kaiser handed the reins of his horse to a servant and staggered to his tent. He stood motionless, arms outstretched, as two men stripped off his armor piece by piece. When they were finished, he waved them away without a word. Food sat on a nearby table, but the growing ache in his head spoiled the thought of eating.

The cot beckoned, and Kaiser collapsed onto it. He tossed and turned for an hour before giving up. Nothing eased the abominable pain in his head.

Kaiser rose from the cot and sat cross-legged on the floor. Meditation brought a modicum of relief. As he turned his gaze inward, Kaiser came face-to-face with the turmoil in his soul. Beneath the surface of his consciousness, ideology and emotion waged a war for his identity. He was changing. He no longer knew himself.

Crouched on the dirt floor of a tent in the far reaches of the kingdom, Kaiser felt very alone. One question dominated his mind, repeating over and over, but he had no answer.

What is happening to me?

— —

Mazareem stood silent in the shadows of Parenthia's tent. Outside, her voice had droned on for hours, preaching an impromptu sermon on the virtues of the priesthood and the righteousness of the inquisition, but now she had fallen silent. He sensed her approach.

An unlit candle waited on a table in the center of the tent. Parenthia carried a burning stick in her hand, which she used to light the candle before tossing it to the ground. As the light from the small flame filled the tent, Mazareem detached himself from the shadows and stepped forward

"I was wondering when you'd make an appearance," Parenthia said, the widening of her eyes the only indication of surprise.

"You said I had two months," Mazareem snarled. "It's not even been six weeks."

"Oh dear," Parenthia said in mock contrition. "I do apologize if our arrival has inconvenienced you."

"You fool. The magus is already here, and I was on the verge of uncovering their identity."

"The man we found in the store knows something, doesn't he?"

Mazareem did not answer.

"You can run along back to your hole," Parenthia said. "I'll take it from here. Did you truly think I'd let you steal the glory of capturing a magus for yourself?"

"I've served Abimelech longer than you've been alive," Mazareem said. "I've accomplished more in his name than a hundred of your kind."

"And yet I am one of his children, and so you must obey." Parenthia raised her left hand, revealing a ring of black iron on her finger. Draconic script glowed red along its circumference as she spoke. "You will return to Northmark and lock yourself away in your prison. I'm sure the regent will reward you like the dog you are. Perhaps he'll toss a piece of choice meat into your cage. You can fight over it with your disgusting hound."

Mazareem stared at her in silence for a long time. Were he not compelled to obey, he would have snuffed her life out like the flickering fire of the candle.

"Abimelech does not suffer failure," Mazareem finally said. "See to it that you don't return empty-handed."

He brushed past her as he moved toward the door of the tent.

"You're not his child," Parenthia said to Mazareem's back. "You can never understand the love He has for me. Abimelech will never let me fall."

Mazareem smirked to himself as he strode through the camp toward the dark trees beyond. Parenthia was a zealot, blind in her naivety. To Abimelech, lesser beings were only tools. Useful ones were rewarded, the rest discarded. Mazareem knew how to make himself useful.

Chapter 14

KAISER DREAMED. FOR WHAT felt like an eternity, he fled across plains of dark grass. A dying sun lit the ghostly landscape. The pale sunlight kissed his skin with the touch of death. Instead of warmth, it blanketed his dreamscape with a frigid cold that ate at his bones. Something hunted him through the night. It called out his name, its terrible voice rending the sky with every shout.

Fear like Kaiser had never known filled his being. He wanted to hide. He screamed at the forests and cursed the mountains. They retreated from him. No matter how hard he ran, he could not reach the safety of a hiding place.

When he could run no farther, Kaiser whirled to face his pursuer. Lightning streaked across the horizon, followed by thunderclaps that shook the foundations of the earth. Kaiser dropped to his knees. Unbidden tears streamed down his face.

An armored rider appeared in the east under the blackened sky. The figure galloped toward Kaiser, racing across the dreamscape. Kaiser stared in awe.

Wreathed with an aura of blue fire, the spectral knight's armor shone like the dawn, and the stars of the night sky twinkled in the black coat of his steed. The hilts of twin swords rose over his shoulders. Kaiser trembled as the charging knight crashed to a stop before him. The celestial warrior stared down, the empty eyes of his helmet piercing Kaiser's soul.

Kaiser woke with a jerk. He was covered in sweat. His dream faded as the pain returned. He sat up on his cot and held his throbbing head. The tent spun in his vision, rotating so fast that Kaiser groaned. Outside, he heard the camp preparing for today's examinations. Parenthia would be expecting him.

The door of the tent twitched as a servant peeked inside to see if Kaiser was awake. Kaiser covered his face with his leather mask and then waved the man forward. A second servant followed close behind the first with a tray of food. Kaiser struggled to his feet and turned down the food. The thought of eating made his stomach turn. He stood in the center of the tent as the servants dressed him.

As the familiar weight of his armor pressed around him, Kaiser tried to get a hold of himself. His best guess was that he had a fever. Sickness on the road was a common enough occurrence. Perhaps he had eaten some spoiled meat. Fortunate, then, that all he had to do today was not fall out of his saddle. Kaiser would suffer through another day of futile examinations and then come back to his tent and sweat out the toxins in his body.

When the last piece of armor had been buckled into place, Kaiser donned his great, horned helmet. He might not feel up to the task, but at least he could look the part. His pounding head protested as he stepped from the tent. Kaiser would have given anything to crawl back to the cot, curl up, and shut out the world. Instead, he forced himself toward his waiting horse.

Parenthia appeared in front of him, blocking his path. She scowled. "Are you unwell?"

Kaiser grunted, not in the mood to banter with the High Priestess.

"If you're unfit for duty, I'll have no choice but to promote the First Reaver to head the inquisition's troops," Parenthia said.

"You'll do nothing of the sort," Kaiser growled.

"The blood of Abimelech can chase your ailments away," Parenthia said, nodding toward where the acolytes were distributing the morning ritual to the soldiers.

Kaiser dismissed Parenthia's words with the wave of a gauntleted hand. He brushed past her and beckoned to a servant to help him into the saddle. Kaiser's vision swam when he placed a foot into the stirrup, but he managed to find his seat without toppling over the other side of the animal.

The First Reaver watched from atop his own mount nearby. Kaiser held onto the horn of his saddle with a death-grip. He clamped his mouth shut and swallowed hard. If he retched, it would splatter all over the inside of his helmet.

Soon Parenthia, her acolytes, and the inquisitor were formed up to march the short distance into Oakroot. A squad of soldiers would accompany them as an honor guard today. Kaiser took up his position on the right, and the First Reaver moved his horse to shadow Kaiser on the left. Together, they escorted Parenthia and the inquisitor down the town's main street.

A crowd had already gathered in front of the local inn. Parenthia wasted no time. She ushered the first person forward, and the inquisitor went to work. The acolytes waited for those who passed the examination, marking their foreheads and offering the cup before ushering them away.

Kaiser closed his eyes as the rays of the morning sun stabbed into his skull, daggers of brilliant pain. He snapped them open an instant later. The vision of his dream lurked on the backs of his eyelids. Night terrors faded with time, he told himself. By sundown today, the celestial knight who haunted his thoughts would have diminished into insignificance, devoured by the forgetfulness that eats away all nightmares in the end.

But now that he recalled the dream, Kaiser could not free himself from its memory. The pain in his head intensified as the spectral warrior galloped through his mind. In his feverish state, Kaiser imagined he heard the echo of hooves on the horizon.

Parenthia's voice droned on as she congratulated yet another citizen for surviving the inquisitor's gaze. The sound of her words rocked Kaiser like a blow to the stomach. Even the tiniest of noises detonated in his ears and made his head ring. In spite of himself, he whimpered, leaning forward in his saddle. His mount sidled and whickered uneasily.

As the sudden bout of sickness overwhelmed him, Kaiser thought for sure that he was about to crash to the earth. But before he could fall from his saddle, sudden relief washed over him. The edges of his vision burned with blue light, and the pain in his head and the ringing in his ears vanished. Spring had erupted unbidden in the dark, wintery depths of his being.

Kaiser wanted to shout for joy. He sat up straighter in the saddle as strength filled his limbs. He glanced at Parenthia to make sure she had not noticed his suffering. It was a small thing to shift his gaze by several feet, but when Kaiser looked at the High Priestess, his heart seized in his chest.

Parenthia's fleshy jowls were gone, as were the rest of the features that would identify her as human. In their place, green scales covered her face. She had the snout of a dragon, with a mouth full of jagged teeth to match. Dark slits split her yellow, snakish eyes. Instead of hair, small spikes protruded from her skull and disappeared into the shadow of her hood.

Kaiser's mouth hung open. He decided that he was seeing a waking hallucination. Doing his best to stay calm, he closed his eyes, counted to ten, and opened them again. Parenthia was still a monster. He glanced at the acolytes. They bore dragon faces too.

The inquisitor in front of Kaiser's horse paused mid-examination and raised his nose to the air. Kaiser watched in disbelief as the bent man turned slowly toward him. When the inquisitor's blind gaze found Kaiser, it stopped.

Kaiser held his breath.

Parenthia had noticed the inquisitor's odd behavior, and she stared at Kaiser with a strange look on her reptilian face. The inquisitor jerked a hand up and screamed, his mad cry shattering the stillness of the morning.

Parenthia's snake eyes went wide. "You," she said, mouthing the word, although no sound came out.

Kaiser struggled to understand.

The First Reaver jerked his horse to face Kaiser, pulling his greatsword from its sheath on his saddle. Parenthia snapped her reins, urging her palfrey into motion as she fled back toward the camp. The inquisitor's scream grew to an impossible crescendo. Kaiser thought his head might burst from the onslaught of sound.

Kaiser did not remember drawing his sword. The blade lashed out with a mind of its own, slashing the inquisitor's face and silencing his demonic scream. The four acolytes howled in unison, drawing long, ceremonial daggers from beneath their robes, but the First Reaver fell upon Kaiser before they could strike.

An inhuman strength filled Kaiser's limbs. He roared with joy at the raw power flowing through his muscles. As the greatsword arced down to sweep Kaiser from the saddle, he spurred into the blow, horses shrieking and biting, and caught the First Reaver's sword in the serrated teeth of his own weapon. The greatsword shattered. Kaiser's blade slammed into the First Reaver's gorget and stuck fast, jagged teeth biting deep into the man's throat. The force of the blow knocked the First Reaver from the saddle. Kaiser released his weapon as it went to the ground with his opponent. The First Reaver did not rise.

As the First Reaver's horse stumbled away, the acolytes rushed at Kaiser. He shouted the kill command to his horse, and the beast exploded into action. Hooves and teeth became deadly weapons. The animal kicked—Kaiser heard the crunch of bone. One of the acolytes dropped to the dirt, her life snuffed out in an instant.

The point of a dagger scraped against Kaiser's armored thigh. As his horse spun, he pummeled the remaining acolytes with his gauntleted fist, teeth and scales and blood showering into the mud. The dragon women screamed as they were beaten down and trampled.

Kaiser wheeled his horse to face the inquisitor's honor guard. They were huddled together, pikes and swords raised to defend themselves. Kaiser saw the terror and disbelief in their eyes. Behind them, Parenthia had almost reached the camp. He could hear her shrieking at the troops. Soldiers were rallying, and soon they would understand that Kaiser was their target.

Kaiser was certain that he had gone insane. He half-suspected that he was still dreaming. But one idea sliced through the turmoil of his thoughts with undeniable clarity: if a single soldier escaped Oakroot to carry news of his betrayal back to Northmark, Kaiser's family would die.

Determined to kill Parenthia first, Kaiser snapped the reins and dug his spurs into his horse's side. The animal lunged toward the camp. Kaiser ignored the honor guard—he would deal with them later.

As Kaiser raced around the clump of soldiers, one man, braver than the rest, jumped into his path. The soldier leveled a pike at the chest of Kaiser's horse and braced for impact. Kaiser wrenched the reins, but it was too late. Two feet of cold steel pierced the animal's ribs. Wood splintered, the haft of the pike shattering under the horse's weight. The animal screamed in pain as it collapsed.

Kaiser pulled his feet out of the stirrups and let his momentum carry him out of the saddle. He landed hard on his chest, rolling as soon as he hit the ground. The newfound strength in Kaiser's limbs made the weight of his armor seem trifling. He leapt to his feet and stared at the soldiers over his dying horse. He had no weapon, and his shield was still in his tent.

In response to his need, the air crackled around Kaiser. The soldiers in front of him murmured in astonishment. Kaiser looked down and found twin scimitars glowing in his hands. The weapons weighed nothing, and yet Kaiser could feel their grips in his palms. Tendrils of blue smoke rose from the transparent blades as if the weapons burned from within.

"Kill the magus!" the brave pikeman cried.

Kaiser dropped into a combat stance, spectral blades up and ready. The soldiers of the King's Army were good—he had trained them himself—but they were no match for the Tenth Reaver. They fanned out as they came, trying to surround Kaiser.

Kaiser attacked. He spun around a pike thrust, glowing scimitars tearing at the air around him. One of the ethereal blades bit into the helmet of his attacker—it passed through metal like water. The soldier dropped dead at Kaiser's feet.

A sword slammed into the armor of his exposed back. Kaiser shrugged off the blow. He whirled, catching the enemy's next swing on one of his blades. The burning scimitar sheared the corporeal weapon in half. With a cry of surprise, Kaiser's attacker stumbled backward. Kaiser lunged forward, stabbing at the man's chest. His sword pierced the man's breastplate without a sound—the soldier died on his feet.

Four soldiers remained. Their attack faltered, and Kaiser saw in their eyes that they would run. The first cast aside his weapon and turned to flee. With one last look at Kaiser, the other three followed suit. Kaiser dashed forward, overtaking the soldiers with ease. He covered ten paces in the blink of an eye.

Kaiser cut down the running soldiers from behind, his blades lopping off heads as easily as separating a flower from its stem. He hamstrung the last man, who fell to his knees in the road. Kaiser stepped into the man's vision and looked down. He recognized one of the men who had been rewarded for reporting Trenner. The doomed man spluttered as he begged for mercy. With a casual backhanded swing, Kaiser took his head and his life.

Heartbeats stretched into an eternity during battle, but Kaiser knew the skirmish had been brief. He raised his horned helm and turned his gaze toward the inquisition camp. Parenthia had reached the tents and was marshalling the soldiers into a shield wall.

Kaiser stood in the road, corpses littered at his feet, twin scimitars burning in his hands. A tiny voice of reason or doubt whispered that Parenthia had come here seeking a magus, so she must have some means of dealing with him, but his newfound power roared only supremacy. Kaiser made no move to advance on the inquisition's troops. Let them come. He would kill them all, and when none were left to protect her, Kaiser would cut out Parenthia's black heart.

Chapter 15

LACRAEL HAD SLEPT AT the foot of the tree and rose with the sun to resume her vigil. All she needed was the tiniest of openings, and she would act. The morning had been uneventful until, without warning, pandemonium erupted in the center of Oakroot.

One instant, a bored crowd of citizens waited their turn to be examined by the inquisitor, then she blinked her eyes and people started screaming and dying. She had no idea what was happening, but Lacrael knew she would not get a better chance to rescue Brant.

In her haste to reach the ground, Lacrael lost her grip on a branch and dropped the final ten feet to the earth. She landed hard on her back. The air went out of her in a great gasp—stars exploded in her vision. Only the soft dirt saved her from a cracked skull. Lacrael's chest heaved as she sucked air into her empty lungs.

When the sky above her stopped spinning, she climbed to her feet, grabbed her pack, and sprinted toward town. She circled around the southern perimeter, aiming for the west side of Oakroot. They had taken Brant in that direction, and Lacrael assumed they had camped in the clearing outside town.

When she stumbled from the treeline, Lacrael stopped in her tracks, staring open-mouthed at the scene in front of her. A fortified campsite stood between her and the town. Soldiers swarmed over the clearing, forming a battle line at the command of a hooded priestess mounted on a horse. In the road on the other side of the camp, a single knight tore into six soldiers with swords that flashed like sunlight on water. The twin blades left glowing trails in Lacrael's vision.

As Lacrael watched, the mass of soldiers in the camp started forward. Two hundred combatants advanced on one warrior. Behind the shield wall, the dark-robed figure leapt down from her horse and began scratching in the dirt with a dagger.

While Lacrael hesitated, the power slumbering inside her roared to life. She gasped as an inferno ignited in the core of her being. Her power had flared before, but never like this. Fire raced through her veins. Heat like she had never known burned behind her eyes. The grass at Lacrael's feet turned black, reduced to ash in an instant. She raised her hands, mesmerized by the flames dancing on the tips of her fingers.

A fireball blossomed into existence above Lacrael's outstretched palms. It grew and grew until she could not fit her arms around it. Lacrael stepped back. Somehow, her skin did not burn in the intense heat, but her armor burst into flame.

Lacrael tore her gaze from the tiny sun in front of her and looked at the backs of the advancing soldiers. She raised both palms, and with a mental shove, sent the fireball hurtling away. It shot through the sky like a cannonball. The shock from its sudden departure knocked Lacrael off her feet and snuffed out the flames on her armor.

The air screamed as the orb of fire arced far over the soldiers' heads and into the roof of a sawmill in the center of Oakroot. The building exploded, sending burning planks of wood scattering in every direction. Lacrael stared in horror. Everyone had stopped in their tracks to watch the fireball pass overhead, and when it struck home, they traced it back its point of origin. Lacrael scrambled to her feet under the gaze of the entire stunned town.

"What the hell was that?" Lacrael muttered under her breath.

Shouts of alarm and confusion split the sky over the campsite. With a magus at their back, the soldiers did not know how to react. The dark-robed woman stared at Lacrael in disbelief. In the chaos caused by the fireball, the woman's hood had fallen back. Lacrael's mouth hung open when she saw the thing's face. She stood on two legs like a human but had the scaly features of a dragon.

The dragon woman snarled and dropped to her knees, renewing her frenzied scratching in the dirt. Behind her, the dark knight with the twin swords tore into the panicked soldiers, deciding their course of action for them.

Lacrael took a step toward the camp, but tent flaps flew open and a mob of robed dragon women charged her. They wielded long, gilded daggers and rushed at Lacrael with no regard for their own lives. Lacrael waited until they were ten paces away before raising her hands to attack.

This time, Lacrael kept the fire under control. Streaks of flame exploded from her hands, incinerating anything they touched. The first wave of dragon women screamed as they dropped to the earth, their long robes billowing dark smoke. The second wave leapt over their fallen comrades and straight into the destruction pouring from Lacrael's hands. She almost felt bad for them.

When the last enemy had stopped writhing on the ground, Lacrael lowered her smoldering hands. She waited several heartbeats to see if any more attackers would burst forth from the tents. A wall of black smoke obscured her vision, hiding the rest of the camp. Lacrael moved forward, stepping gingerly around the charred bodies.

On the other side of the smoke, Lacrael found the first priestess still kneeling on the ground. Before Lacrael could raise a hand to strike the her down, the dragon woman slashed her own palm open with a dagger. Dark blood oozed from the wound and dripped onto the complex symbol scratched into the dirt.

The dragon woman spoke a single word that Lacrael did not understand, and the world stopped. She tried to blink, but her eyelids refused to move. The dragon woman stood, a satisfied sneer on her face, and the vision of the smoking campsite faded before Lacrael's eyes.

— —

Kaiser could not be stopped. The inquisition's soldiers threw themselves at his blades, trying in vain to slow him down. Kaiser's spectral swords split shields and sundered helmets, carving into the flesh and bone beneath. He whirled into their midst, forcing them to retreat or die. When it became obvious that the direct approach would never work, the soldiers changed their tactics.

With a quick thrust and a twist, a pikeman slipped his weapon between Kaiser's legs. Kaiser clawed at the sky as he fell. When he released his ethereal weapons, they vanished into thin air. He hit hard and tried to roll, but the enemy soldiers rushed forward and pinned him beneath their weight.

Flat on his back in the mud, Kaiser's vision was blotted out by the press of armored bodies. Gauntleted hands pummeled him. A flurry of hungry blades scraped against his armor, stabbing and slashing as they tried to find a weak spot. The press of the enemy hindered their attempts to kill him as effectively as they prevented Kaiser from fighting back.

"Give me some bleedin' space," a voice shouted, "I'll jam this pike through his neck."

Suddenly, the man blocking Kaiser's vision moved. A patch of sky appeared. Silhouetted against the brilliant blue, a soldier lunged forward, putting every bit of his weight behind a mighty thrust. Kaiser roared, and the heavens roared with him. Above the battlefield, the clouds turned black.

Kaiser tore his right arm from where it was pinned beneath five men. He caught the shaft of the pike before it pierced his gorget. With the weapon still in its owner's grip, Kaiser slammed the steel point into the nearest face he could find. He flailed against his attackers with the head of the pike. The pikeman tried to pull the weapon back, but Kaiser was too strong. Kaiser felt a frenzy building deep inside as he fought, and when he could hold it no longer, he released it with a shout.

Summoned by his cry, lightning poured from the sky. Jagged bolts of white fire detonated in the midst of the enemy. Kaiser stared in awe as the wrath of heaven flashed down, stabbing into the soldiers piled on top of him. The smell of burning flesh filled his nostrils. Men sprang back, screaming in pain. Blue lightning

coruscated up and down Kaiser's armor. The caress of the dread energy tickled Kaiser's skin.

The weight holding him down vanished. Kaiser climbed to his feet. Charred and blackened bodies were scattered around him. The soldiers who still stood cowered before his gaze. With a thought, Kaiser recalled the spectral swords into his hands.

"Throw down your weapons," Kaiser called to the surviving soldiers. "Stop this madness. Don't spend your lives for Parenthia."

In response, the inquisition soldiers hefted shields and closed ranks. They did not intend to surrender.

"So be it."

Kaiser stepped forward. Thunder rumbled in the sky overhead.

— —

Lacrael saw only blackness. After a few heartbeats, shadows and shapes began to resolve out of the gloom. She stood in the ruins of a castle. The skeleton of once mighty fortifications rose around her. Through the empty gate, she saw a vast plain of dark grass. High overhead, a pale sun shone down, its feeble rays devoid of warmth or life.

Panic surged through Lacrael as she spun, trying to look everywhere at once. Had the dragon woman's spell hurled her into another plane? Lacrael looked down at her body—she still wore the same clothes, but she could see through herself. She reached down to touch her leg, and her fingers passed into her thigh. She was a spirit.

Something huge flew in front of the sun. The great shape of a winged shadow flashed across the courtyard. Lacrael jerked her head up in alarm. Movement flickered in the corner of her vision, but it dipped below the castle walls before she could catch a glimpse of the beast.

Whatever it was, it landed in front of the castle. Before Lacrael could think to act, she felt its presence. Black hatred assaulted her soul like a thousand poisoned spears. She staggered, overwhelmed by the inhuman rage that threatened to sweep her away.

The head of a dragon rose above the wall in front of her. Its long neck soared into the sky with a strength and pride that surpassed even the mightiest of oaks. Crimson scales glinted in the anemic sunlight. Teeth the size of swords filled a mouth that could swallow Lacrael in one gulp. Unholy fire burned in its eyes.

A second head joined the first, and then a third, until there were seven sets of hungry eyes staring down at Lacrael. The dragon reared up, and she caught a glimpse of the creature's body over the castle wall. It was the size of a small mountain.

Lacrael could see through the dragon's body to the sky beyond, yet that did nothing to assuage her fear. She had no doubt that the creature had come to kill her. If she died as a spirit, Lacrael suspected her body would soon follow. She tried to move, but her limbs would not respond. The dragon's gaze held her prisoner.

The seven terrible heads weaved back and forth as they watched Lacrael. Their long, scaly necks wound together before unraveling again, as if each head had a mind of its own. The dragon took a step forward, and Lacrael knew she was about to die.

One of the dragon's heads swooped over the wall, coming at Lacrael low and fast. She stared through the open jaws, straight into the monster's gullet. At the last instant, Lacrael flinched and closed her eyes. She waited for death.

Nothing happened. Confused, Lacrael opened one eye.

The dragon struck at her, its seven heads flailing like enraged serpents. Again and again it tried to devour Lacrael, but every time one of the heads neared her, it deflected away in a brilliant flash of light. She looked down to find her grandfather's amulet glowing like the sun.

Consumed with rage, the great dragon tore at the sky. Over the monster's roars, Lacrael heard a new sound. The clatter of hooves echoed across the horizon. In the next heartbeat, a spectral knight thundered through the empty gate into the courtyard.

He rode on a horse made of night; the stars of a hundred skies twinkled in its coat. His armor blazed with the splendor of the dawn. In his right hand, he wielded a sword that crackled with the fury of a storm, and in his left, he carried a brilliant shield that could hold back winter. Lacrael's heart soared. Everything her grandfather had told her was true. Here was the Shrouded King.

The specter reined his horse to a stop before Lacrael and wheeled his mount to face the dragon. He thrust his sword into the sky. Lightning plunged from the clouds and slammed into the blade. A blinding flash of light exploded in the courtyard.

When Lacrael opened her eyes, she was back in Oakroot. Her foot came down hard, finishing the step she had started before being thrown into the spirit plane. No time had passed. In front of her, the dragon woman's eyes widened in surprise.

"You're supposed to be dead," the woman hissed.

The woman lunged forward with her dagger raised. Lacrael sidestepped the attack and drew her sword in the same motion. Dizziness threatened to undo her. When the woman came for her a second time, she was ready. The dragon woman possessed surprising strength and speed, but she was no fighter. Lacrael caught a clumsy attack on her blade and then slashed at the woman with a quick riposte. The blade caught the dragon woman in the hand, hacking off two fingers and a ring of black iron.

Undeterred, the dragon woman lashed out again. Lacrael let the attack glide past her and smashed a fist in the woman's scaly snout. Her opponent reeled and stumbled backward. Lacrael shook her hand in pain—the dragon woman's face was as hard as rock. She kept up the attack as she tried to corner her enemy and land the killing blow.

When it became obvious that she could not best Lacrael, the woman leapt back and out of range. With an angry hiss, the woman threw her dagger at Lacrael and ran for her horse. Lacrael parried the attack and gave chase, but the creature moved too fast.

Before Lacrael could close the distance between them, the priestess had gained her saddle and aimed her horse into the forest. With a shout and a slap to the palfrey's hindquarters, she galloped away.

Lacrael tried to summon fire to strike the fleeing woman down, but the power did not come. Instead, a wave of nausea washed over her, and she dropped to her knees. Her mind reeled, struggling to accept the sudden transition from the spirit plane.

After a few long minutes and deep breaths, Lacrael opened her eyes. The sounds of fighting had died down. She struggled to her feet and looked around. Behind her, the corpses of the robed dragon ladies were melting into the earth. In the distance, Oakroot burned. She could see townsfolk fighting against the insatiable fire in vain.

Fifty paces in front of Lacrael, the single dark knight stood with his back to her. Two hundred bodies lay at his feet. As she watched, he opened his hands, and his twin spectral blades blinked out of existence.

Slowly, he turned to face Lacrael. She thought he would cry out or step toward her. Instead, he dropped to his knees. Lacrael rushed forward. Her grandfather had been right. This was the man she had waited four years to find.

Chapter 16

LACRAEL APPROACHED THE DARK knight with caution. She remembered obtaining her own powers. She had almost gone insane. There were stories and legends about magi who went crazy and proclaimed themselves gods, or slaughtered thousands in an orgy of blood and fire. If this man proved unstable, she might have no choice but to kill him.

The dark knight's breath rasped behind his helmet. His armor was a work of terror, covered in spikes and skulls, culminating in a sinister horned helm. He watched Lacrael come and made no move to rise. Lacrael stepped around the corpses of the slaughtered men as she neared.

"Are you hurt?" Lacrael asked.

"My soul… is on fire," the dark knight said, his voice ragged.

"You won't believe me right now, but I know what's happened to you," Lacrael said. "I'm the only person in this entire kingdom who can help you."

The dark knight clawed at the clasps of his helmet. When he had released them, he pulled the heavy helm from his head and flung it away. He stared up at Lacrael from his knees, a riot of emotions on his face.

"What am I?" the man croaked.

"You're a magus."

The man's gaze shifted from Lacrael's face to stare into the sky behind her. She could only imagine the thoughts running through his head. A noise nearby caused Lacrael to look up. Monty, at the head of a mob of townspeople, was fast approaching. At their backs, what remained of Oakroot still burned.

At the sight of Monty, Lacrael remembered Brant. Now that the fighting was over, the enormity of what she had done started to sink in. She took one look at Monty's face and groaned inwardly. He was furious.

"What have you done?" Monty asked when he stopped several paces away.

"I'm sorry," Lacrael said, "I never meant to harm Oakroot."

"What you intended doesn't matter. You've brought doom down on our heads."

"We can rebuild. The fire can't have destroyed everything."

"The fire will be a mercy compared to what's coming next. Look around you. You just assisted in the murder of an entire inquisition. How do you think Northmark will respond?"

Lacrael gulped.

"Exactly," Monty said. "Our only hope is to convince them that we're innocent victims, collateral damage in a conflict between powers beyond our understanding."

"You could run," Lacrael said. "You could make a new life somewhere else."

Monty laughed. Lacrael winced at the harsh sound.

"If the priesthood arrived to find only the rotting corpses of their dead, we'd seal our fates," Monty said. "They'd mark us as guilty in their ledger and hunt every last one of us down to exact their blood price. No, our only chance is to remain here and prepare for their coming."

Lacrael hung her head in shame, unable to meet the horrified stares of the townspeople behind Monty.

"How could you do this to us?" Monty asked. "You've profited from our generosity for years, all the while knowing that if the secret of what you are got out, you'd bring only pain and suffering to our town."

"I... I thought if—"

The man on his knees between them groaned and tried to rise. He got one foot beneath himself before tripping and falling face-first into the dirt, interrupting Lacrael's answer. Monty glanced down in distaste, and Lacrael wracked her mind for something to say that would placate him.

"Brant's in one of the tents," Lacrael said. "We should make sure he's okay."

Monty looked pained that Lacrael had found a common cause between them, but he nodded at her words. He told the mob at his back to wait where they stood, and together he and Lacrael went to search the abandoned inquisition camp.

They found only empty cots in the first tent. Monty gave the charred corpses on the ground a wide berth, his gaze flicking back and forth between Lacrael and the slain. She opened her mouth to tell him that the dead women were not human, but the words did not come. The bodies were burned beyond recognition. Monty would never believe her if she tried to convince him the priesthood was run by dragons.

Two more tents revealed nothing, until in the fourth tent they found Brant chained to a massive, iron-bound chest. He had positioned himself so that he could rest his back on the trunk. He stared down at the ground between his legs, showing no sign of having heard their entrance.

"Brant, can you hear me?" Monty said, kneeling at his son's side.

Brant raised his head, looking first at Monty and then at Lacrael.

"Father... Lacrael...," he said, speaking slowly, as if the act of forming words took great effort.

"What have they done to you?" Monty said as he searched the length of chain for the lock. When he found it, he slammed it fruitlessly against the side of the chest.

"Let me," Lacrael said, stepping forward.

She took the lock in her hand and touched the power deep inside her. A small part of her feared that she had lost it for good, but at her call, intense heat poured from her hand and enveloped the metal contraption. Iron sagged, the padlock warping beyond recognition, until gray liquid ran through Lacrael's fingers and splattered onto the dirt.

Monty's jaw sagged as he stared in awe. When Lacrael stepped back, Monty tried to pull Brant to his feet. The big man did not budge.

"Come on, son," Monty said. "You're free of your chains."

"I can feel it... in my head," Brant said. "Fingers like frozen knives, flaying memory from thought."

"Do you know what he's talking about?" Monty asked Lacrael, spitting out the question like an accusation.

Lacrael shook her head. "Just because I'm a magus doesn't mean I know everything."

"And here I thought you might prove useful," Monty muttered under his breath. "Help me get him up."

It took every bit of strength the two of them possessed to lift Brant from the ground and support him between them. They dragged Brant from the tent. As Lacrael struggled to keep Brant upright, her grandfather's golden amulet fell out of her shirt. When the sunlight struck the amulet, the golden wings of the dragon seemed to glow. Brant found his feet, and Lacrael glanced up to find him staring down at the shining pendant.

Brant's countenance cleared before her eyes. He blinked away the faraway look in his gaze, glancing back and forth between Lacrael and Monty in surprise. He shrugged them off, standing by his own strength.

Monty stepped back as he scrutinized Brant's face. Lacrael stuffed the amulet back under her shirt before either of them could remark on it.

"What did they do to you?" Monty asked.

Brant shook his head. "There are gaps in my memory. I remember that pale man with a face like a skull, his terrible hound, and excruciating pain. I think he asked after Lacrael, which means she's in danger if he finds her."

"She's not the only one," Monty said. "Look around you."

Brant raised his head and scanned their surroundings. When his gaze fell on the smoking ruin of Oakroot, he gasped and took a step toward the remains of the town. "By the sacred powers, what happened?"

"She can tell you," Monty said, nodding at Lacrael.

Brant whirled to face her, eyes wide in disbelief.

Lacrael balked, unable to admit to Brant that Oakroot's fate was her doing.

"You tell him, or I will," Monty said.

"I did it," Lacrael said, grimacing as she spoke. "I destroyed the town."

"But... why?" Brant asked in anguish.

"It was an accident," Lacrael said. "I was trying to blast the inquisition troops, but my power surged and I overshot my target."

"You overshot your target," Brant repeated, as if he was struggling to understand. His next words were almost a shout. "You overshot your target, and you wiped out an entire town!"

"I was trying to save you," Lacrael said in a small voice.

Brant's face contorted in agony as he struggled to process her words. "How do you expect me to respond to that? You destroyed my home."

"I'll go, then," Lacrael said. "I hope your lives are easier when I'm gone."

"Not so fast," Monty said.

Incredulous, Lacrael glanced at the older man.

"Don't get your hopes up," Monty said when he saw the look on Lacrael's face. "You've got to put a thousand miles between yourself and this place, and you can never return. But you can do us a favor in your leaving."

"Anything," Lacrael said. "Just name it."

"You can take Brant with you."

Lacrael blinked at Monty's request, but Brant exploded.

"What?" he shouted. "Are you mad? I'm staying here to rebuild."

"You can't, son," Monty said, shaking his head. "I'm sorry, but you're already a fugitive. You were a prisoner of the inquisition. When they return to Oakroot, you must be long gone from here. As it stands now, it looks like the magus freed you from your chains, so I should be safe from suspicion."

"Be reasonable," Brant said. "I'll hide in the forest until they've gone. This is my home, and I've no desire to leave it."

"Damnation, boy, I *am* being reasonable!" Monty shouted. "I'm sending you away because I love you—I don't want to see you in the hands of a vengeful inquisitor. You stand a better chance of surviving in the company of a magus."

Brant glanced at Lacrael and then quickly away. Lines of pain etched his handsome face.

"Will you take him with you?" Monty pressed Lacrael for an answer.

"If he'll come," Lacrael said quietly.

"Go with her," Monty urged Brant. "We'll rebuild Oakroot, survive the inquisition's investigation, and when this all blows over, you can come home. But in the meantime, you've got to stay alive."

Brant's voice was cold when he answered. "If there's no other way to save you from what she's done, I'll go. I made it worse anyhow. Never might've come to this if I hadn't trusted her."

Lacrael turned away, blinking back tears. Brant was right, except it was all her fault and not his. She never should have risked her mission by growing so close with Oakroot. She never should have been so selfish.

"There's precious little to salvage from the wreckage, but I think my storehouse might have survived the fire," Monty said. "Come with me and let's see if I can give you some provisions for your journey."

Monty's invitation was clearly directed at Brant, and Lacrael made no move to follow as the two men walked away. Brant glanced over his shoulder at her, and she gave him a little wave. He frowned in response. The mob of Oakroot citizens followed Monty and Brant into town. Lacrael returned to where the dark knight lay on the ground. She had been prepared to help him, even if she could not help Oakroot.

The man had rolled over onto his back. He stared up into the sky. His cheeks were wet with tears. When Lacrael stood over him, his gaze shifted to focus on her face.

"What's happening to me?" the man murmured. "I feel like I'm lying on the bottom of the sea with a mountain's worth of water pressing down on me."

"The powers of a magus are like a muscle," Lacrael said. "They must be exercised. The first few times you draw on your power, it will leave you drained and weak. It gets better, over time."

The man mumbled something that Lacrael could not understand.

"I'll watch over you until you recover. We've got to get away from this town. I have a place in the deep forest where we can hide."

The man did not respond. His eyes were closed and his breathing had slowed. Lacrael decided to let him sleep until Brant returned. He would need all of his strength to make the long hike to her hidden home.

— —

Mazareem slipped from shadow to shadow, Worm padding along in his footsteps. When the master and his hound passed by, the forest went still. Birdsong ceased, small and fuzzy creatures cowered in their burrows, even the chirping insects went silent. Mazareem smiled to himself. If everyone else were attuned to their superiors as these woodland creatures were, his life would be far easier.

The scent of smoke filled his nostrils long before Oakroot came into sight. Smoke, and the acrid stench of magus fire. Familiar with the smell, Worm growled low in his throat. Mazareem stroked the hound's head to soothe the animal.

The power of compulsion behind Parenthia's order to return to Northmark had vanished a few hours ago. This could only mean one thing: she had faced the magus and lost. No longer bound by her command, Mazareem and Worm had retraced their steps to Oakroot to find out what happened.

Under the cover of the treeline, Mazareem paused to take in the scene. Oakroot had been reduced to a pit of smoldering ash. What remained of the inquisition's troops lay scattered in the road. The black shapes of hungry crows fluttered and hopped amongst the corpses. Nearer to Mazareem, charred skeletons lay twisted in blackened grass between the tents.

Mazareem shook his head in consternation. Parenthia had bungled this worse than he could have possibly imagined. With Worm at his side, Mazareem crept over the corpses of the fallen, a great vulture come for his share of the carrion.

Low in the sky, the sun cast long shadows across the ruined campsite. Mazareem knelt in one of these pools of darkness as he investigated the scorched remains of Parenthia's acolytes. He wanted to make sure they were burned beyond identification. The spell of illusion that Abimelech's children used to appear human failed in death, and Mazareem's master would be furious if his presence were revealed due to Parenthia's carelessness.

Magus fire consumed flesh and bone. A few skeletal remains survived, but nothing that could be used to identify the corpses as dragon spawn. The pity of it was that he could not pick out Parenthia's body among the dead. How she must have sputtered and spat when the fires took her! The thought was almost worth the inconvenient position she'd left Mazareem in.

Confident that Abimelech's secret was safe, Mazareem moved on. He stopped next at the inquisitor's carriage. The fire had spared the gaudy transport. The doors were open wide, and Mazareem poked his head inside. He saw no evidence of a struggle. If the townspeople were smart, they would hold the surviving inquisitors as a peace offering for when the priesthood returned.

Although he knew the exercise pointless, Mazareem moved away from the carriage and walked through the dead soldiers. He had the information he needed and precious little time to travel back to Northmark, but Mazareem's nature would not allow him to be anything less than thorough. If anyone from the town saw Mazareem poking through the wreckage, they gave no notice. He suspected that the lot of them had passed out from exhaustion. Only the most heroic of efforts could have prevented the fire from spreading to the surrounding forest.

Soon Mazareem had seen enough. These men were dead, and unless he wished to expend considerable effort, they were staying that way. He turned on his heel and whistled to Worm, but the hound did not heed his call.

SANDELL WALL

Curious, Mazareem turned to find the dog sniffing at a corpse several paces away from the rest. As Mazareem watched, Worm jumped back and growled, the fur on the back of his neck raising in agitation.

"Jumping at corpses are you, boy?" Mazareem asked as he covered the distance between them.

Worm glanced at his master with a triumphant look on his ugly muzzle before snapping his head back to the object of his interest. The dog growled again as if reminding the corpse not to go anywhere.

When Mazareem drew near, he smelled the same scent that must have been exploding a hundred times stronger in Worm's nostrils. He smelled the cloying sweetness of dragon's blood. Unbidden, a hungry smile spread across Mazareem's face. This unsought bounty would not be squandered.

"Well done, well done indeed," Mazareem said, scratching under Worm's chin.

Mazareem reached down, grabbed the corpse by the breastplate, and heaved it up onto Worm's back. The man inside groaned. Mazareem could not believe his good fortune.

"Still alive in there?" Mazareem said, leaning his head in close to the grinning skull of a helmet. "Hang on a little longer, help has arrived."

Mazareem walked alongside Worm to hold the burden steady. Together, they carried their find into the forest. Soon they were back under the cover of the trees. Mazareem had noted a crevice in the forest floor some ways back, and he guided Worm to it now.

When they reached their destination, Mazareem peered down into the dark fissure and decided that it would suit his purposes. He turned to Worm, grasped the soldier on the hound's back, and heaved the armored body down. Mazareem laid the soldier's back on a flat rock.

The soldier groaned again and tried to raise a feeble hand.

"Be still," Mazareem said. "Just lie back. I know what you are, so there's no need to worry. How do we get this puzzle of a helmet off of you?"

The soldier lifted both hands to his head. He inserted his fingers into grooves along the side of his helmet, and with a series of twists, unlocked the mechanism so that it could be removed. In his weakened state, it took him several tries to get it right. When the helmet clicked open, he fell back, exhausted.

Mazareem leaned forward to pluck the unlocked helmet from the man's head. The face beneath was as pale and chiseled as marble, and Mazareem gave it his best smile.

"My, aren't you fetching? Your kind certainly doesn't skimp when it comes to choosing a face."

"I'm… I'm a reaver," the creature gasped.

"Shush. I know what you are. Don't waste the little strength you've got left."

With gentle hands, Mazareem unclasped the soldier's metal gauntlets. He slid them off, paying careful attention to the naked fingers beneath.

"A hand without a ring—now there's a rare sight," Mazareem said with a satisfied smile. "You've no use for ostentation. I like that in a man."

While Mazareem talked, he removed small leather discs from beneath his cloak. With a tap on the bottom, the edges of the discs popped out to form little bowls. Mazareem positioned these under the man's splayed wrists and ankles. Using a knife so sharp that the man did not feel the cuts, Mazareem severed veins on each of his limbs. Dark blood spilled from the wounds, splashing into the leather bowls below.

"What—what're you doing?" the reaver asked, now too weak to do more than turn his head.

"Your pain is gone, no?" Mazareem asked.

"Yes," the reaver said, his brow knitted in confusion. "I suppose it is."

Mazareem used his knife to cut away the leather straps that secured the creature's breastplate. He pulled the metal away and sawed at the heavy fabric beneath until he reached sweaty flesh. The soldier's breathing slowed, the rise and fall of his chest almost imperceptible.

"I'm afraid this part might hurt a bit," Mazareem said as he raised the knife over his head. "But no more pain after that, I promise."

The soldier's eyes went wide. He tried to struggle, but his strength had drained out of his body into the four leather bowls. "Betrayer," he hissed.

Mazareem sneered. "You're not the first to call me that."

The knife plunged down.

Mazareem's stroke did not kill the reaver outright. He carved the beating heart out of the dragon spawn's chest, cracking ribs in his eagerness. Only when Mazareem ripped the organ out did the life go out of his victim's horrified eyes. He raised the heart to his mouth and tore into the warm flesh with his teeth.

Worm whined while he watched Mazareem devour the prize. Mazareem stopped short of eating the entire thing, tossing the

hound the final scrap. Worm nipped it out of the air and gulped it down. Mazareem nudged one of the bowls in the dog's direction, and the animal lapped the blood up with his tongue.

While Worm ate, Mazareem filled his empty vials from the remaining three bowls. Blood from a dragon spawn was weak fare, but the heart itself was filled with nutrients that Mazareem needed to stay alive. This unforeseen boon extended his timetable. He now had enough sustenance to survive for an extra week before returning to Northmark. With Parenthia and her inquisition destroyed by the magus, her threat to deny him access to the elixir that kept him alive was meaningless.

Whenever Mazareem decided to arrive, trophy in hand, Regent Trangeth would allow him entry into his sanctuary. He smiled to himself as he rolled the dead body to the edge of the ravine. The corpse no longer bore the face of a man. Black scales and wicked teeth covered the dragon spawn's snout. With a violent shove, Mazareem pushed the husk into the ravine. He tossed the helm in after. It bounced from wall to wall as it plunged into darkness. No one would ever find it down there.

Mazareem stood and stretched, energized by the dragon's blood burning in his belly. He had an extra week. He might not be able to catch the magus in that time, but he could follow. The faint outlines of a plan were starting to form in Mazareem's mind. Let the magus run. There was nowhere to hide that Worm would not find.

Chapter 17

KAISER STUMBLED ALONG THE forest trail, unaware of putting one foot in front of the next. He had lost his helmet, but could not recall what happened to it. Ahead of him, two strangers weaved through the trees, a woman and a man. The woman often glanced back at Kaiser with worry on her face. The man scowled.

His name was Kaiser. He tried to cling to that truth, but it did not keep him afloat in a roiling sea of madness. Had he told the dark-haired woman his name? Kaiser thought so, but could not be sure. Memories flashed before his eyes, things that used to be important—should still be important, yet he could not hold on to them. Images of his family came and went in Kaiser's mind, and his heart cried out. They were his only anchor in the maelstrom consuming his soul.

They walked what seemed like an eternity to Kaiser. The creaking of the trees overhead, the shadows lengthening into night, and the rhythm of his footsteps lulled Kaiser into a trance. Soon, the chaos in his heart quieted, and he felt like an empty vessel. He had to reach his family—nothing else mattered. He would walk home without stopping, even to rest, as soon as he could remember the way…

The dark-haired woman stepped in Kaiser's path and placed a gentle hand on his chest, indicating that he should stop. Kaiser went still. He looked into the woman's eyes, but understanding eluded him. She spoke, and the words flowed over Kaiser, yet the sound of her voice seemed no different to him than the cry of the birds flitting through the trees.

The woman shook her head and took Kaiser by the hand. He allowed her to lead him down a steep trail into a ravine hidden in the forest floor. Their male companion followed close behind, scowl plastered on his face.

On the floor of the wooded canyon, they found a bubbling stream winding its way through the bottom of an ancient riverbed. Kaiser smiled at the noise of trickling water. It was a happy sound and tickled a memory that he could not grasp. The woman tugged at his hand, and they walked on.

After several hundred paces, they reached a small cabin tucked back into a thicket. The woman left Kaiser staring up at the trees high overhead as she exchanged heated words with the other man, but their voices meant nothing to Kaiser. He frowned, annoyed that their argument drowned out the sound of the nearby brook.

Finally, the woman turned back to Kaiser, took his hand, and led him into the dark cabin. Once inside, she released him, and Kaiser stood motionless in the middle of the pitch-black room. Soon, a flint sparked in the corner, giving life to a small fire that beat back the shadows. This done, the woman returned to Kaiser's side and gently started to unbuckle his armor.

Her actions triggered a memory in Kaiser's mind, and he raised his arms to give her access to the clasps. Scowling Man stood on the edge of the room, scowling as he watched. Kaiser disliked him.

When the last piece of armor had been removed, the woman led Kaiser to a bed in the corner of the cabin. She pressed her hands on his shoulders. Kaiser sat, and soon his head rested on the crude pillow. He lay there with his eyes open, watching as the woman and Scowling Man conferred quietly on the other side of the room. Kaiser's breathing slowed. The crackle of the fire and the murmur of their voices pulled him toward slumber. Finally, he closed his eyes. Exhaustion claimed him.

At first, Kaiser dreamed of his family. He smiled as Mariel, Tarathine, and Saredon greeted him with happy faces. He knew their names and remembered their voices. Joy filled him as they reclaimed their scattered memories and cemented themselves once again as pillars of his being.

After a time, the dream changed in the manner that only dreams can. One instant, Kaiser was with his family, and the next, he was somewhere else, and it felt that he had been there the entire time.

Kaiser found himself sitting before a small fire in a forest clearing. In his dream, he knew that the trees stretched for miles in every direction, and that he sat at the heart of a great woodland. He wore the armor of a Tenth Reaver, but his head was bare. His sword and shield rested next to him against the log on which he sat. As he stared into the flames, none of this seemed out of place. His awareness within the dream expanded, and he realized that he was not alone. A figure shrouded by shadow sat across the fire opposite him. Curious, Kaiser squinted across the fire at the stranger, but he could only make out the shape of a hooded man.

"Family is a wonderful thing," the stranger said.

Kaiser shivered. The voice carried a quiet strength that could move mountains, and yet the words were spoken with a profound sadness. That the stranger knew Kaiser had just come from visions of his family did not seem odd in this dream place.

"My wife and children are all that matter to me in this world," Kaiser said, returning his gaze to the fire. "Everything else can burn."

"If good men do nothing, everything *will* burn, and your family along with it."

Kaiser's head snapped up. "I've kept them safe thus far. Once I get them out of Northmark, we'll be free of the madness that infects this kingdom."

"That madness will spread, my friend. The evil that infects Haverfell will not stop at one kingdom, or ten. If left unchecked, it will corrupt the entire race of man."

"Who are you, and by what power do you prophesy?"

"I cannot name myself in this place. The enemy watches over this plane like a great spider, his invisible webs spread far and wide. Were I to reveal my identity to you, one of these strands would be plucked, and the beast would be woken by the vibrations. He would fly on wings of destruction to drown us both in fire. Mired in your dream, I'd not be able to resist his power. I've risked a great deal to speak with you here."

"You're the one who gave me the powers of a magus," Kaiser said, the sudden insight coming to him in a flash.

"That's an ugly word, used by dark minds to try and corrupt the truth," the stranger said. "I chose you as one of my champions and bestowed upon you the blessings that follow."

Kaiser's next words were as cold and unforgiving as folded steel. "I don't care what you call it. I don't want it. Choose another."

The stranger did not speak for a long time. Kaiser stared across the fire, daring the stranger to defy him. He would not be the pawn of any spirit, man, or king. The newfound power coursing through Kaiser's being threatened to undo everything he had worked for — it threatened the lives of his family.

"What's done cannot be undone," the stranger finally said.

"Then I'll use the power to save my family," Kaiser said. "No one will be able to stand against me."

"You can try, and when you fail, I'll raise up someone else. I've been locked in an eternal struggle with the enemy for hundreds of years. His agents have become quite adept at killing my champions. You slaughtered a few human soldiers. You've no idea the horrors locked in the bowels of the earth beneath Northmark. Your only chance of survival is to listen to me and do as I command."

"That strikes me as a devil's bargain: I obey, or I die. Why me? Out of all the countless souls in Haverfell, why me?"

"I'm no devil, and when you encounter one, you'll know that to be true. I chose you because I could. Trenner's murder on the road to Oakroot sparked compassion in your soul, and that gave me the foothold I needed. There are other, weaker individuals who would be overjoyed to receive my blessings, but I need you, because I aim to defeat this evil that threatens Haverfell and the rest of humanity. You're the greatest warrior this kingdom has known in a hundred years. With you fighting at the side of the other champions I'll raise up, we might have a chance."

The mention of Trenner's name caused Kaiser to fall silent. Kaiser recalled the horror on the man's face as he died, heard him call out to his wife and children. The plight of the Ninth Reaver's murdered family came back to Kaiser in a rush. He saw Ursais's pained face in his mind, the old man suffering under the forced administration of Abimelech's blood. His shoulders sagged as the weight of a dying kingdom pressed down on him. As Tenth Reaver, he knew how Haverfell suffered. He was not blind to it, but he could not afford to care.

Kaiser closed his eyes. "What do you want from me?"

"The woman in your company is called Lacrael," the stranger said. "She is one of my champions and has waited years in this forest for your appearance. Trust her with your life. Travel west with her, through the Wraith Wood. In Thornhold you will find allies who will know what to do next. Whatever you do, don't return to Oakroot. A creature of darkness hunts you that you're not prepared to face. Go back that way and you'll never see your family again."

"My path takes me home," Kaiser said. "Lead me to Northmark, and I'll follow along. But don't mistake this for compliance—the only thing that matters is my family. Their lives weigh far heavier on the balance than the fate of the kingdom."

Across the fire, Kaiser saw the stranger smile in the shadow of his hood.

"I didn't expect anything less," the stranger said. "Now sleep. You'll need your strength."

Kaiser opened his mouth to respond, but the scene faded to blackness before his eyes. The hooded stranger remained in Kaiser's vision longer than anything else, until he disappeared too. Darkness was all that remained. Kaiser slept and did not dream.

— —

Lacrael watched Kaiser sleep. He had passed out the instant his head touched the pillow. Kaiser's delirium had grown the deeper they ventured into the forest. She worried he might go insane. Not everyone could survive the manifestation of their powers. Weaker minds broke under the strain of sudden and drastic change.

"I don't like it," Brant said for the tenth time. "Why do we need him? It's going to be hard enough with you as a magus. Traveling with a second one is begging for trouble."

Lacrael sighed. Brant was proving to be a bit of a coward. Not that she could blame him. He had just watched his entire hometown burn to the ground, and now he was on the run as a fugitive with the two most powerful criminals in the kingdom.

"I'm sorry about Oakroot," Lacrael said. "I really am. I'll apologize as many times as I have to until you believe it. But I can't change what happened. This isn't going at all the way I imagined. You're going to have to trust me that Kaiser is the reason I've been hiding out here all these years. I've been waiting for him."

"I don't care one wit for magi or your mad quest," Brant said. "I told my father I'd hide out here in the deep forest till this all blows over, and that's all I mean to do."

"After what you've seen already, do you think this will ever 'blow over?' " Lacrael asked, her patience wearing thin.

Brant's wide shoulders slumped. He found a chair and sat down hard, elbows on his knees and head in his hands. He still wore a bandage on his forehead. Lacrael wanted to feel sympathy for the big man, but the truth was that their suffering mattered little, given what was at stake. Her path was finally laid out before her and Brant was only making it more difficult.

"This is insane," Brant said without looking up. "Everything's happened so fast. I'm a merchant, not a fighter. When I was younger, I tried to make my way in the inner kingdom. I wasn't cutthroat enough. I came back to Oakroot because I wanted a simple life." He snorted into his hands. "What a fool I am."

Lacrael left Brant to his thoughts as she moved about the cabin unpacking her gear. If he wanted to sulk, so be it. They would all need to eat before long. Soon, Lacrael had the stove set up and her small collection of pans hanging on the wall.

"There's something I've been meaning to ask you," Brant said from where he sat.

"What's that?" Lacrael asked as she worked. She tensed at his question—there was no kindness in his voice.

"The priesthood preaches that a magus is demon-possessed. They teach that anyone with powers like yours is a danger both to themselves and the people around them. You set Oakroot on fire, but you want me to believe it was an accident. Before two days ago, I had no reason to doubt the priesthood. So tell me: are you possessed by a demon?"

"Would I tell you the truth, if I was?"

Brant's scowl deepened.

"You're going to have to decide if you can trust me," Lacrael said. "I know very little about the powers I control, but I do know that I'm not demon-possessed. My grandfather told me that I've been chosen to fight *against* a great evil. He said that my powers are a weapon to be used in the defense of mankind."

Lacrael's voice trailed off as she remembered her encounter with the seven-headed dragon in the spirit plane. Until that moment, she had not been able to put a face on the enemy. Her powers had been useless. Only her grandfather's amulet, and the appearance of the Shrouded King, had saved her life. The metal pendant felt warm against the skin of her chest. Lacrael glanced at Brant out of the corner of her eye. What spell had he been under when the dragon amulet had cured him in the inquisition's encampment?

Brant looked around the cabin in surprise at the mention of her grandfather. "Where is this phantom grandfather of yours? Was he a falsehood too?"

"He's been dead for years," Lacrael said, shaking her head to dismiss the memory of the dragon. "I lied about him living in the forest with me so nobody would get any ideas."

"What else have you lied about?" Brant asked, anger smoldering in his eyes.

Lacrael ignored Brant's question. "After I gained my powers, my grandfather was the only family I had." She shoved wood into the little iron stove, talking to herself as much as Brant. "He protected me, trained me, and prepared me for the duty I had been chosen to fulfill."

"And he's a part of that?" Brant asked, nodding at where Kaiser snored on the bed.

"He was chosen like me. He'll have questions when he wakes. I'll do my best to answer them, and then we'll have to figure out what to do next."

"Whatever the two of you decide, leave me out of it," Brant said. "I've gone as far as I intended to go."

"You won't be safe here," Lacrael said.

"I'll take my chances. Besides, without me around, there'll be nothing to stop the two of you from rutting like heathens." Brant's words were bitter, and his jealousy and self-deprecation were not lost on Lacrael. Despite this, his words hurt her. Lacrael's hands shook with anger.

The pan in Lacrael's hands slipped from her fingers and dropped onto the stove with a clatter. To cover her sudden fury, she grabbed a pail from a hook and left the cabin. She walked to the little stream and scooped up a bucketful of water.

Before heading back inside, Lacrael paused, staring at her reflection in the surface of the brook. The current distorted her face, but she could still make out her features. Dark skin, dark hair, and dark eyes: the face of a desert nomad reflected in the crystal clear water of a forest creek.

Lacrael could not remember the last time she studied her own appearance. What she saw staring back at her did not match her memory. The face in the water looked older, etched with lines of weariness and smudged with dirt. She dipped her fingers in the water and washed away the grime. She released the rage in her heart over Brant's words, letting it sluice away like the dirt. The man was distraught. She had hurt him and his family enough in the past two days to suffer his words. Whether or not Brant allowed himself to be saved now would be up to him.

Now that her long years of waiting were over, Lacrael wondered if she was ready. The face in the water no longer looked like a child, but Lacrael could not shake the feeling that she still lived in the shadow of her grandfather. He had been a great man. Lacrael hoped she could honor his legacy and the trust he had placed in her.

All of her training had led to this moment, to this secret cabin deep in the forest where the next champion lay sleeping inside. When Kaiser woke, he would need guidance. The next leg of her journey was about to begin, and it started with Kaiser.

Chapter 18

KAISER WOKE FROM SLEEP like a dead man coming back to life. His eyes were open, but the rest of his body remained still. He struggled against the fatigue pulling at him. Weariness whispered promises of restful bliss if only he would close his eyes and submerge himself under the dark waters of unconsciousness. It took long, agonizing minutes for strength to creep into his limbs.

When he could move, Kaiser raised himself to a sitting position, alone on the unfamiliar bed. He looked around the small room. A fire in the belly of a little iron stove provided light and warmth for the tiny space. Kaiser saw his armor neatly arranged on the floor nearby.

With a groan, Kaiser shifted to place his feet on the floor. He held his head in his hands as he sat on the bed and tried to remember where he was. The constant patter of raindrops against the low roof slowed Kaiser's thoughts and calmed his troubled mind.

The door to the cabin banged open. A tall, dark-haired woman stepped inside, followed by a man with wide shoulders, a soft gut, and a sour face. The woman's name surfaced in Kaiser's mind. She was called Lacrael. Her name triggered Kaiser's memory, and his dream of the hooded stranger came back in a rush.

Kaiser watched Lacrael and the man remove wet outer cloaks and hang them on pegs by the door. They were speaking to each other, but their voices were too low for him to overhear their conversation. Lacrael glanced toward the bed, and her eyes widened in surprise when she saw Kaiser awake and upright.

"You're awake!" Lacrael said, stepping across the small room toward Kaiser. "I expected you to sleep for at least another day. How do you feel?"

"Like a tree that's been chopped down and left to rot," Kaiser said. His tongue felt heavy in his mouth. "Where are we?"

"This is the center of Nogard Forest. I brought you here to hide while you recovered."

"You're a… magus," Kaiser said. He stumbled over the word, remembering the dream stranger's distaste for the term.

"Yes, and so are you," Lacrael said. She pulled a chair close to the bed and sat as she talked. The big man moved near to stand and listen.

"I've been waiting for you to appear for four years," Lacrael continued. "I knew I would find you in this forest, but I didn't know where or when. You're not… you're not what I expected."

"My name is Kaiser, Tenth Reaver of Northmark. Do you know what that means?"

Lacrael did not react to this revelation, but the big man at her side did. The blood drained out of his face.

"I do," the big man said in a quiet voice.

"And you are?" Kaiser asked, shifting his gaze to the man.

"My name is Brant. I was a merchant in Oakroot until the inquisition took me prisoner. Now I'm a fugitive, like you."

Lacrael looked annoyed that they had changed the subject. "His name meant something to you," she said, looking at Brant. "Who is he?"

"Behind the regent, he's the second most powerful man in the kingdom," Brant said. "He's killed more men in the arena than anyone else in history. He's… he's a legend."

Kaiser nodded at Brant's words. Lacrael turned back to him with a look of new appreciation on her face. "I suppose I shouldn't be surprised that tales of my victories have spread this far," Kaiser said.

"This is—this is amazing!" Lacrael said, stuttering to get out the words in her excitement. "I had no idea the next champion would be someone of such power and influence. I've been hiding in the forest for years because I'm a nobody. But you, *you* can take the fight to the enemy's doorstep!"

Kaiser's eyes narrowed. "I don't know who you are or where you came from, but this is decidedly *not* amazing. Perhaps the powers of a magus came as a stroke of good fortune for you. For me, they're a death sentence. *Several* death sentences: I have a family at great risk, a wife and two young children surrounded by those who would torture and murder them at the slightest provocation."

Lacrael sobered quickly. "No, my powers didn't come as a boon. They ripped my life away from me and turned all but one of my family into enemies. Forgive me. I got carried away with the thought that we might actually be able to take action now."

"You keep referring to an enemy as if I know what you're talking about. But I've no idea who it is you think we're supposed to be fighting."

"I'm sorry," Lacrael said, turning red. "I'm not doing a good job of explaining. I've rehearsed this moment a thousand times in my mind, but this is nothing like I imagined it would be."

"Slow down, start from the beginning, and tell me what you have to say," Kaiser said.

Lacrael closed her eyes, took a deep breath, and when she opened them again, she started speaking. "I was sent here from another realm by my grandfather. He told me the next champion would arise in Haverfell, and that the magic used to transport me here would place me near where they would appear. So I built a secret home here, explored the nearby forest, and watched and waited.

"Abimelech is the enemy. In my world, the realm of Vaul, we know him as the Lord of Dragons. We've suffered under his wrath for a thousand years. His foul magic corrupts the very earth, and he has hunted the few humans that survive to the brink of annihilation. His children disguise themselves with spells of illusion and infiltrate human society. They seduce humanity, and with the seed of men and the wombs of women, produce dragon spawn instead of human children. You saw them in Oakroot. They stand upright like us, but they're covered in scales and have the face of a dragon. They cannot hide themselves from those of us who have been chosen.

"My grandfather told me that Abimelech wages a war of vengeance against the race of man. He desires to erase us from existence and put his children in our place. Before his fall a thousand years ago, High King Rowen the Dragonslayer protected mankind from the dragons. He hunted them to the edge of extinction, and he ate the hearts of Abimelech's princes to gain immortality. High King Rowen banished Abimelech to the realm of Vaul and set in place a sacred order to guard against the great dragon's return.

"But a thousand years ago, something happened, and High King Rowen disappeared. My grandfather believed that Abimelech found a way to weaken the High King's physical body and imprison him on the spiritual plane. Whatever happened, the High King's throne in Northmark sat empty, and over time, the sacred order tasked with preventing Abimelech from rising to power again faded into insignificance. Outside of Vaul, dragons and their kind were forgotten."

Lacrael fished her grandfather's golden dragon amulet out from beneath her shirt. "However, the descendents of this order still exist, and my grandfather was one of them. He believed that my powers were a gift from the High King himself, and that I'm to use them to fight back against Abimelech. I believed my grandfather, because I saw the destruction Abimelech had visited on my people and my home, but for four years I acted on faith that the High King still lived. I act on faith no longer. During the battle in Oakroot, I *saw* him! One of the dragon spawn cast a spell to banish me to the spiritual plane where a seven-headed monster tried to devour me. High King Rowen himself appeared and released me from the spell. He lives, and he's raising up his champions to fight back against Abimelech and his spawn."

Kaiser listened and observed while Lacrael spoke. He noted her flushed face, the fervor in her voice, how she sat up straighter and gestured with the strength of conviction. She demonstrated all the behavior of a fanatic, the sort that Kaiser was trained to root out. When she produced the amulet, Kaiser's breath caught in his throat.

"Can I see that?" Kaiser asked when Lacrael had finished speaking.

Lacrael extended her arm, offering the amulet. Kaiser took it from her hand and inspected it closely. The dragon roared up at him from his palm. Something deep in his soul stirred, and Kaiser remembered Trenner's carved figure staring up at him from the trampled mud of the road.

"Have you seen one before?" Lacrael asked.

"I've hunted and killed three men that carried these."

Lacrael grimaced, her face going pale.

"One of my primary tasks as a reaver is to root out heresy and sedition," Kaiser said. "At the top of the priesthood's list of dangerous offenders is any man or woman who possess draconic iconography. If what you've told me is true, I now understand why."

"Every word was the truth," Lacrael said.

"I don't care for believers or their truths," Kaiser said, handing the amulet back, "but I'm inclined to believe that some of what you told me is true. I cannot deny the powers we both possess, and… I had a dream."

"Did you see him?" Lacrael asked, leaning forward and suddenly breathless.

"A man came to me in my dream," Kaiser said. "I couldn't see his face and he wouldn't tell me who he was. He told me that I had been chosen to fight a great evil that threatened all of humanity, and he told me your name."

Lacrael looked elated and crestfallen at the same time. "You spoke with him? After all this time I've waited, and he speaks to you first? That's not—," her voice cracked, and she looked away from Kaiser to stare at the wall.

"He said to travel west, that we'd find allies in Thornhold."

"The road to Thornhold would take you through the Wraith Wood," Brant said, fear in his voice.

"I'm aware of that," Kaiser said, annoyed at the stating of the obvious.

"So we have a destination," Lacrael said, having recovered from her disappointment. "I'm sworn to this duty and will follow the High King's guidance until the battle is won or my life is over. What will you do?"

"My family is my top priority," Kaiser said. "I've got to get them out of Northmark before the priesthood figures out what happened in Oakroot. But I can reach Northmark from Thornhold, and the road through the Wraith Wood should be safer than traveling in the open kingdom. I'd not make better time on any other route. Between your fire and my lightning, we slaughtered every last man of the inquisition. It will be at least three weeks before word reaches the capital and mounted troops make their way back here. I'll travel with you as far as Thornhold."

Kaiser waited for Lacrael to say something, but she only stared at him. He glanced up, and the look in her eyes sent daggers of fear stabbing into his gut. "What is it?"

"One of them got away," Lacrael said, the words almost a whisper.

Kaiser resisted the urge to leap from the bed and choke the life out of her. "How long were you going to wait to tell me? Who escaped?"

"The fat dragon woman," Lacrael said. "She's the one who sent me to the spirit plane. When I came back, I was too weak to stop her from jumping on a horse and fleeing into the trees."

Now Kaiser did jump up. "Parenthia escaped?" he roared. "On horseback, she'll reach Northmark in *days,* not weeks, and she's got a head start!"

Lacrael and Brant flinched away from his anger. Kaiser staggered over to his armor and picked up the first piece. With clumsy fingers, he struggled with the buckles and clasps.

"What are you doing?" Lacrael asked, sounding like she did not want to know the answer.

"When Parenthia arrives in Northmark, the first thing she'll do is place my family under arrest," Kaiser said as he wrestled with his armor. "There's no way I can catch her now. I've got to get there before it's too late." He left half the armor on the floor, intent on traveling light.

"And what do you intend to do when you get there?" Lacrael asked. "Fight the entire city? Come with us to Thornhold. We can find horses. You're going to need help if you want to save your family."

"To hell with your quest and your king," Kaiser snapped. "There's not a horse alive that'll enter the Wraith Wood. My only chance is to make it to the other side of that dark forest on foot. The two of you will only slow me down."

"Kaiser, *listen to me,*" Lacrael said. As she spoke, she raised a palm and conjured flame from thin air. The brilliant magus fire blasted away every shadow in the small room. Kaiser paused and looked at her. "You need me. I can help you save your family. Travel with us to Thornhold, and if our new allies won't aid you, I promise I'll go with you to Northmark."

Kaiser cinched the last piece of armor tight on his body as he considered Lacrael's words. She was right: he did need help. If they still lived, his family would be prisoners when he reached Northmark. With his new powers, he might be able to assault the city and kill hundreds before he perished in a blaze of glory, but Kaiser wanted to live, and he wanted to rescue his wife and children. He might be able to fight his way to them, but he would never get them out of the city on his own.

"Alright, I'll travel with you to Thornhold," Kaiser said. "But we're going hard. Your merchant lover looks like he might be unaccustomed to this sort of trial."

His words were answered by an awkward silence.

"We're not lovers," Lacrael and Brant said at the same time.

"No?" Kaiser said with a grunt. "That's too bad. I suspect our lives are about to get very ugly. When things go bad, you might wish you had a memory of pleasure to look back on."

Somehow they managed to look everywhere but at each other.

"I'm staying here," Brant said. "This is where my role in this madness ends. I want no part of your quest to slay a dragon lord."

"You misunderstood me," Kaiser said, eyes narrowed. "I wasn't asking for your preference. As I see it, you've got two options. You can come with us, or I can leave your dead body to rot in this cabin."

Brant took a step backward.

Lacrael's face darkened. "What the blazes are you talking about?"

"I don't leave loose ends. I don't care how well you think you're hidden out here—Parenthia and her creatures will find you. In fact, I'd wager you crawl back to Oakroot within a day. I'm not leaving you behind to tell them where we've gone."

Fire danced on Lacrael's finger tips. "I won't let you do this."

Kaiser summoned the spectral blades into his hands. "Don't test me, girl."

"Stop!" Brant almost shouted. "I'll go, I'll go, just don't start fighting each other in here. All three of us would die."

"So be it," Kaiser said. He stepped past them and strode out the open door into the rain.

"We need to pack supplies!" Lacrael called after him.

Kaiser did not reply. With a few more long strides, he moved out of earshot. He did not look back. They could catch him on the road if they wanted to take the time to stuff food into a pack. He would find subsistence in the forest, or he would go hungry. Water could be had from puddles and streams. The only thing that mattered to Kaiser was reaching Northmark and saving his family.

— —

Mazareem paused at the top of a secluded ravine in the deep forest. Rain tumbled from the treetops above to splatter on his hood. He leaned on his black walking staff and waited patiently as Worm sniffed around the edge of the ancient wooded canyon, fresh blood mingling with the rain to drip off his oozing snout. The hound had picked up the trail outside of Oakroot that morning, and they had followed it all day. Worm could track the lingering scent of magus fire through a hurricane.

Worm raised his head and gave a muffled bark. Before Mazareem could say anything, the dog disappeared over the lip of the gully. Mazareem stepped forward and looked down. Worm had found a trail hidden in the foliage.

"If people could look past the fact that you're a zombified killing machine, they'd see what a good dog you are," Mazareem said as he set a foot on the path.

The two of them half-hiked, half-slid down the muddy trail. When they reached the bottom of the ravine, Worm bounded out of sight into the bushes. Mazareem followed, more cautious than his animal companion.

When he pushed aside the last wet branch, Mazareem found Worm sniffing at the outside of a small cabin. Set back in the undergrowth, the little structure would have been invisible from the forest floor above. If someone had been inside, Worm would be howling and throwing himself at the door, so Mazareem ventured close and went inside.

It did not take a dog's sense of smell to detect the magus fire within the cabin. Mazareem stood in the center of the small room and closed his eyes. He breathed deep, soaking his senses in the subtle hints of those who had stood here only hours before.

"*Two* magi," Mazareem said to himself. "And a third..."

A smile spread across Mazareem's face, and his eyes popped open.

"Fire, lightning, and shadow," he said to Worm, who had followed him inside and was sniffing at the bed. "Our friend from the Oakroot store is a long way from home, isn't he boy?"

Worm responded to Mazareem's question with a reverberating woof and went back to snuffling his way around the cabin.

Mazareem sat at the tiny table as he pondered this new evidence. He suspected his prey would travel west, seeking the coast. They would try to be discreet, which meant avoiding the well-traveled highways of the inner kingdom. That left only one road: through the Wraith Wood.

Mazareem grinned to himself. This was going better than if he had planned the entire thing. In the Wraith Wood, the barriers separating the physical from the spiritual were tenuous. Hungry spirits haunted the dark paths under the trees. The merchant from Oakroot had been marked by shadow, and the demons of the forest would be drawn to him. All Mazareem had to do was give them a little nudge.

Chapter 19

LACRAEL AND BRANT CAUGHT up to Kaiser several miles away from the cabin. She had thrown what few items she could think to grab into her pack and dashed out the door with Brant close behind. Fortunately, the wet ground made Kaiser easy to track. The hard soles of his boots left deep imprints in the damp soil. Lacrael could not believe how fast the man covered ground, and when his armored back appeared between the trees ahead of them, she breathed a sigh of relief.

They tried to fall into step next to Kaiser, but neither Lacrael nor Brant could match his stride. Kaiser threw himself across the forest floor, loping along with a long-practiced gait that devoured mile after mile. Lacrael had to jog to keep up. Brant tried to walk alongside Kaiser, fell behind, and had to run to catch up.

The incessant rain discouraged talking, so Lacrael put her head down and concentrated on regulating her breathing. Brant had said that Thornhold was a seven-day journey from the heart of Nogard Forest, but at this pace they might cover the distance in four. She started to wonder if Kaiser intended to stop for sleep.

Kaiser hurtled through the wet forest for the better part of the day until he was forced to stop by an obstacle in his path. They battled their way through a soaked thicket to find an engorged stream blocking their progress. Kaiser paused and looked up and down the muddy bank. The water of the flooded creek rushed past, carrying a carpet of woodland debris on its surface.

Lacrael's legs quivered. She had been running for hours. On the other side of Kaiser, Brant stood bent over at the waist, hands on his knees. He looked like he wanted to puke.

"Did you bring food?" Kaiser asked, glancing at the pack on Lacrael's back. It was the first thing he had said since leaving the cabin.

"What I could grab," Lacrael said.

"I need a mouthful," Kaiser said, holding out an expectant hand. "You and the merchant should take some too. Eat only what will fit in the palm of your hand. You've both got plenty of fat to burn." He cast a disapproving glance at Brant's thick midsection.

Lacrael stared at Kaiser's extended hand in disbelief. He had rushed out of the cabin without waiting for her to pack, and now he was demanding food. Not only that, but he was instructing her on how to ration it.

"I have a name, you know," Brant said when he finally had the wind to speak.

"Where I come from, names are earned, not given," Kaiser said.

Lacrael decided not to argue. She slipped the pack off her back and rummaged around inside. When she found a hunk of cheese that would break into three equal parts, she handed the pieces to Kaiser and Brant, keeping one for herself.

Kaiser devoured the morsel in two bites without a word of thanks and returned his attention to the stream. Lacrael made eye contact with Brant, who grimaced at her behind Kaiser's back. She stuffed the cheese into her mouth to hide her own frown.

"If this is deeper than I am tall, you're going to have to fish me out," Kaiser said.

With no other warning, Kaiser launched himself into the flooded stream. Dumbfounded, Lacrael watched him wade toward the center of the creek. The water rose to his chest, and then to his neck. He looked silly, a disembodied head floating inches above the current. Kaiser still wore some of his armor. One wrong step and he would disappear beneath the roiling surface. Despite his command to save him, Lacrael knew that if he slipped, he was dead.

Lacrael held her breath as Kaiser passed through the middle of the stream and started up the far side. When he finally climbed out of the water onto the far bank, Kaiser glanced behind to see if they had followed.

"I'm not waiting," Kaiser called. He turned and plunged into the foliage, gone from sight in an instant.

"Spirits take this man," Brant said with a groan. "I hope he stumbles into an angry bear."

"I'd feel sorry for the bear," Lacrael said. "Come on, he'll be a mile ahead of us before we get across."

Kaiser had made fording the stream look easy. When Lacrael stepped into the dirty water, she realized that the weight of his armor had helped anchor him against the strength of the current. As the water rose to her chest, she struggled to keep her feet on the bottom. On the next step, she lost her footing. With a yelp, Lacrael flailed in the water as the current snatched her body up like a twig.

Before she was swept away, one of Brant's strong arms looped around her midsection and held her fast.

Together, Lacrael and Brant fought their way out of the creek and up onto the far bank. They crawled out of the water soaked and exhausted. Brant collapsed on his back in the mud, and somehow Lacrael found herself lying on top of him. Their wet clothes stuck together, and Lacrael felt the heaving of his chest beneath hers.

"Thanks," Lacrael gasped.

"Get off of me."

Lacrael rolled off of Brant and stared up at the gray sky for a heartbeat. She wondered how long he would stay mad at her. Perhaps he did not have it in him to forgive what she had done.

"We've got to catch Kaiser," Lacrael said, heaving herself to her feet and charging into the thicket that had swallowed Kaiser. Behind her, she heard Brant groan, but she knew he would follow.

Kaiser pushed hard for the rest of the day and well into the evening. When it finally grew too dark to see, he called a halt. "We sleep until dawn. I'll be up and away as soon as it's light enough to see where I'm going."

Lacrael wanted to argue. Kaiser had made no effort to find a campsite or light a fire. He had simply stopped and said it was time to sleep. But she could not muster the strength to complain. Instead, she dropped to the ground, shifted until she found a comfortable spot, and closed her eyes. She tried to ignore her growling stomach.

"We've four more days of this ahead of us, so don't waste the food," Kaiser said into the darkness. "I know you're hungry, but you'll survive."

In the cold, wet darkness, Lacrael shivered. If she had not been exhausted, rest would have been impossible. Before sleep claimed her, she glanced over at Brant. He had curled himself into a ball with his back facing them. Lacrael thought she should say something to him, but before she could find the words, she passed out.

It seemed that she opened her eyes a heartbeat later to find Kaiser on his feet and ready to move. The faint light filtering through the trees and the ache in her muscles told her that time had passed, but Lacrael's mind struggled to accept it. She could have slept for another ten hours.

"If you need to break your fast, take a few bites of food," Kaiser said as they set out.

With one eye on the ground in front of her, Lacrael fished a piece of hard bread out of her pack and broke off three pieces. Brant took one and wolfed it down, but Kaiser declined her offer.

"I'll eat when we reach the Wraith Wood."

Lacrael's muscles burned as the three of them sped across the forest floor. Brant's stride had turned into a stagger. From the way he limped, Lacrael knew Brant's feet were blistering. He grimaced with every step, but he did not slow down. If Kaiser noticed their struggles, he said nothing.

They reached the border of the Wraith Wood at noon. The line of demarcation between the two forests was obvious. On the eastern side, the trees of Nogard Forest towered high overhead, naked limbs reaching for the sun. The hint of a thousand green buds were visible on the skeletal branches. Everywhere Lacrael looked, she saw a swelling of life that heralded the coming of spring.

To the west, the stunted trees of the Wraith Wood seemed to cower beneath the sunlight. Black thickets covered in wicked thorns choked the forest floor between the trunks of the trees. A thick canopy of dark leaves blocked out the sun. Winter's chill held no power over the corruption that flowed through the woodland's infected veins.

Kaiser paused on the edge of the shadowy forest. He reached out an expectant hand toward Lacrael, and she handed him the hunk of bread.

"Even in my haste, I'll not risk the uncharted paths of the Wraith Wood," Kaiser said between bites of bread. "We need to find the road."

Without another word, he started south. Lacrael and Brant glanced at each other and then followed after. They walked along the edge of the Wraith Wood for about an hour before finding the overgrown road that connected Nogard Forest to Thornhold. Kaiser stopped in the middle of the manmade path and waited for them to catch up.

Lacrael stumbled out of the trees with Brant at her side. The hard-packed dirt of the road felt wondrous beneath her throbbing legs and feet. She did not think she could lift a foot high enough to climb over another fallen log. To her left, the sunlit trail wandered out of sight around a bend to the west. To her right, the gnarled trees of the Wraith Wood converged over the path, forming a dark tunnel.

"They call it the Wraith Wood because the locals claim that hungry spirits wander between the trees," Kaiser said. "It's superstition, of course, but these woods are dangerous. The trees choke out any view of the sky, so visibility is limited even in the middle of the day. Don't wander away from the trail. It's easy to get lost in there, and I'm not wasting the time to come looking for you."

Kaiser started forward, then paused and added, "In case it's not obvious, stay away from the thorns. The plants respond to vibrations. If they sense prey, they'll move in to smother us. If you get snagged, cut yourself free with a dagger—don't disturb the thicket."

Lacrael took a step to follow after Kaiser, but she stopped when Brant did not move. She turned to see him staring down the road into the Wraith Wood with a look of unease on his face. "What is it?" she asked.

"I can *feel* this forest," Brant said. "I can feel it watching me. There's... something in my head, some trace of shadow, compelling me to enter those trees."

"Don't lose your nerve now, merchant," Kaiser called over his shoulder. "It's a long walk home."

Brant shuddered and started walking. Lacrael fell into step alongside him. They had a much easier time keeping up with Kaiser on the dirt road.

"Are you sure you're okay?" Lacrael asked.

"I'm-I'm fine. Kaiser's right; it's just nerves."

Lacrael did not press the question, but she watched Brant out of the corner of her eye with concern. He was not himself. As they entered the shadows of the Wraith Wood, Brant hunched his shoulders and started shivering. He stopped talking, and no matter what Lacrael tried, she could only get one-word answers out of him. Finally, she gave up and hiked along in silence.

The hours slipped past with each mile they covered. Twice, Kaiser ordered them to eat a small portion of food, but he never stopped to rest. They emptied the last of Lacrael's waterskin, which left only the water Brant carried to hold them until Thornhold.

While they traveled, Kaiser practiced controlling his newfound power. He would summon and dismiss the spectral swords from his hands, sometimes carrying them for a full hour. Lacrael had never seen anyone with more determination and stamina. He peppered her with questions, and she told him everything she knew about the strange powers they shared. The strain of learning to use his power alone should have been enough to exhaust him, yet Kaiser explored his abilities while covering many miles on foot every day.

Thanks to the road they walked, Kaiser traveled until it was pitch black under the trees. He called a halt then, unwilling to risk the thorns that lined the sides of the trail. Without a word, Lacrael collapsed onto the hard dirt and closed her eyes. Brant's paranoia had infected her—Lacrael imagined she felt the trees watching them.

Lacrael would be glad to be free of this place.

— —

Mazareem stood on the edge of the Wraith Wood. At his side, Worm twitched his snout at the dark treeline, every muscle in his massive body tense. The animal did not like the look of the sinister forest. Mazareem did not blame him.

"Don't worry, boy," Mazareem told the hound. "There's nothing under those trees that I cannot subdue."

Worm grumbled low in his throat, voicing his objections to this plan. Mazareem patted him on the head and started forward. As he neared the thorny undergrowth that carpeted the ground between the twisted trunks, Mazareem reached beneath his cloak and withdrew one of the glass vials he had filled with the dragon spawn's blood. He withdrew the stopper and poured the dark liquid over the head of his walking staff, soaking the gnarled wood with the blood of his victim.

Mazareem held the walking stick low to the ground so that the head of the staff preceded him. When he neared the thorns, the black plants reacted violently to the bloodstained wood. With an audible rustling, the thicket parted before Mazareem, allowing him and Worm to walk between the trees. Mazareem smiled to himself. Even after a thousand years, the old ways still worked.

Tracking their quarry had not proven difficult. Worm never wavered from their trail, even when they had crossed that sevenfold-accursed stream. Catching up to them, however, proved a different story. Mazareem traveled fast, but these magi somehow outdistanced him. They tore through the woodlands with a speed that Mazareem could not match unless he wanted to expend all of his strength in the chase. He started to wonder if they suspected his presence.

It had been hundreds of years since Mazareem had reason to tread the paths of the Wraith Wood, but he knew the forest well. There was power here, and grave danger waited for the unwary. Mazareem had seen to that himself. If he did not fear the Wraith Wood as men did, it was not out of ignorance, or because the perils were imagined, but because Mazareem had conquered this ground already.

Master and hound made good time through the forest. As they neared the heart of the blighted woodland, the trees themselves shrank back from their passing. Dark, twisted, and grotesque, the once mighty sentinels shrieked and sighed as Mazareem passed under their branches. Worm cared little for this, snarling and growling at every trunk they walked by.

Suddenly, the trees fell away and Mazareem stood on the edge of a small clearing. He paused. The history of this place throbbed like an old wound. An ancient skeleton of a dragon prince glowed in the pale moonlight at the center of the glade. A thousand years ago, Mazareem had felled the beast in a titanic struggle that had lasted for three days. When Mazareem had finally stood victorious, Rowen had denied him his prize. The self-proclaimed High King had taken the heart of the last dragon prince for himself, ensuring that Mazareem would never attain true immortality.

Mazareem sneered at the memory. Funny that he still walked the earth while Rowen had not been seen for a millennium. He hoped the traitor king did not rest easy in the grave. The king of worms had his fill of blood now—Parenthia and her ritualists had been seeing to that. Ah, but now she too was gone before her time. Mazareem's enemies had made that into a habit. He wrapped his cloak around himself and stalked forward. Worm refused to enter the clearing, and he decided to let the hound be.

The white skull of the dragon stood as high as Mazareem was tall. At the sight of the terrible teeth, an involuntary shudder stopped Mazareem in his tracks. A slow smile spead across his face. He had thought himself beyond such ancient fears. To feel anything at all in his dessicated soul was a delight to be savored.

"The sight of your dread visage still quickens the heart, after all this time," Mazareem said as he stopped before the moonlit skull. He favored the dead beast with a look of compassion. "Ah, but the years have not been kind to you."

Mazareem brushed his fingertips across the row of teeth, each as long as his forearm. Reaching up, he caressed the hilt of his old sword, still buried in the monster's forehead and glinting with stars.

Rowen's last gift to Mazareem, before his kingly pride had damned them all. Before he had betrayed Mazareem's oath of fealty.

The present and the past merged, and Mazareem watched a waking vision of the dragon's final moments. He looked into the beast's eyes and saw the unholy fire that burned in the dragon prince's soul, till he had snuffed it out. He smelled the sulfur of its dying breath. For the thousandth time, Mazareem wondered if Abimelech knew it could never have been Rowen the Dragonslayer who had killed his last true child. The title and the throne should have been Mazareem's. Not once had Rowen's blade pierce dragonflesh.

Blood boiling, Mazareem grasped the hilt of the sword and tensed to wrench it from the ancient skull. The weathered grip still felt familiar beneath his cold fingers.

"Don't be a fool," Mazareem muttered to himself as the vision released him. He let go of the weapon and with it the memory. That life was forever lost to him. Nothing could be gained by clinging to artifacts of the past.

Behind the skull, spirits danced above the haunted bones, their hazy forms little more than flickering shapes of light. In all of Haverfell, this might be the one place where the barriers between the physical and the spiritual were the weakest. As he moved beyond the head of the fallen tyrant, the power of the place surged through Mazareem's senses and threatened to overwhelm him. Squatting inside the towering ribs of the beast, he closed his eyes and breathed deep, basking in the maelstrom of energy that swirled around the dead dragon.

When he had mastered himself, Mazareem removed a stick from beneath his cloak and started scratching a symbol in the dirt. The magi were beyond his ability to influence by magic—a guardian watched over them in the spirit plane. However, their traveling companion had no such protection, and he had been touched by shadow once before. Such a man was marked for life.

"You've answered my call before, Azmon," Mazareem said into the night. "And you will do so again."

Crouched beneath the dancing spirits, kneeling in the ribcage of a long-dead foe, Mazareem grinned to himself. Before his quarry left the Wraith Wood, at least one more of his enemies would die.

Chapter 20

MARIEL TRIED NOT TO scream. She stood in the open air of the training ground in the center of her fortified home. Garius stood at her left, five guards at his back. Tarathine and Saredon stood on her right. They stared across the courtyard in tight-lipped silence.

Opposite their small group, a squad of the regent's personal soldiers accompanied three priestesses of Abimelech. A reaver watched from the sidelines, silent and sinister. The senior priestess stood in the center of the courtyard, a golden chalice in her hands.

"You misunderstood, I'm afraid," the priestess said, raising the chalice toward Mariel. "All must partake. Even you."

"My lord husband will deal with you when he returns," Mariel said in barely controlled fury. "Until then, I demand that you leave this place. This is the private estate of the High Reaver, and you're trespassing."

The priestess glanced at the sullen reaver. The man stepped forward. He wore dark plate similar to Kaiser's, his helmet adorned with a profusion of short spikes instead of horns. Their needle sharp points glistened in the sunlight. A black cloak hung from his shoulders, its edges dragging on the sandy ground. A giant, white 'V' emblazoned on the cloak signified his position as the Fifth Reaver. He carried a massive, two-handed battle axe that he planted before himself. When he spoke, his words rang out deep and hollow from within his armor.

"The High Reaver is not ignorant of what we do here," the reaver said. "Before his departure, the lord regent informed him of the necessity of this ritual. Your lack of discipline reflects poorly on your husband. No doubt were he with us, he'd take you in hand. You and your household will comply with the requirements of the priesthood, or you'll suffer the consequences."

Mariel swallowed hard. "At least send the children away."

The priestess shook her head sharply. "They stay. There's no shame in partaking of Abimelech's blood. The sooner they learn that, the better."

With swift strides, the priestess covered the distance between them and held the chalice out toward Mariel. Hands trembling, Mariel accepted the cold metal cup and held it as if it were a serpent. Garius was tense at her side. Mariel had no doubt that if she cast the cup into the dirt, Garius and his men would fight and die at her side. And then her children would die. They would kill her last of all.

"You can force me to drink, but you cannot make me believe," Mariel said.

"One precedes the other," the priestess said with a cruel smile. "You will learn."

Mariel raised the chalice to her lips. She took the smallest of sips, and yet the liquid seemed to force itself upon her. As if it had a will of its own, the vile concoction thrust itself into her mouth and clawed down her throat.

Mariel gagged and took a step back. She almost dropped the chalice, but the priestess darted forward to snatch it from Mariel's hand. Mariel felt like she had swallowed corruption itself. It settled into her stomach like rot, then crept through the rest of her body. She trembled, unable to stop the spastic twitch of her muscles.

While Mariel struggled against the effects of the liquid, the priestess moved to Garius, and then to the guards behind him, ensuring that all took their fill from the chalice. Only the children were spared.

Once the ritual was complete, the priestess returned to the center of the courtyard. "Abimelech is pleased with your choice," she said. "Soon, I think, you will come to understand the benefits of faith in our god. After all, the only other option, is…"

Rather than finish her statement, the priestess looked meaningfully at the reaver who still stood with his axe grounded in the sand. "Come," she said, turning to leave with a swish of her robes. "We have done you the courtesy of calling at your door first of all, my lady. We have many lesser houses to visit before this day is done."

The dark procession filed out of the courtyard. No one spoke until they heard the front gate shut with a thud. When at last they were sure the priestess and the reaver were gone, Garius dropped to the ground retching. Tarathine and Saredon looked up at Mariel with huge, terrified eyes.

Mariel knew she should comfort them, say something to assuage their fears, but a black pride gripped her soul, and the only words she could find to speak were angry and hurtful. "Run along," Mariel snapped at the children. "I'll tend to you later."

Tarathine looked shocked, and Saredon's face crumpled. With Saredon's hand firmly in her grip, Tarathine fled the courtyard with her little brother in tow. Mariel scowled at their backs, angry at them and herself, and struggling to understand why. Had she not raised her children to be stronger than this? They would never survive what was to come if this trifling display had upset them so.

Behind Mariel, two of the guards exploded into heated argument. In the time it took her to turn around, they were at each other's throats. Only Garius seemed unaffected by the rage that had consumed the rest of them.

"Be silent!" Mariel screamed at the quarrelling guards. They whirled on her, ready retorts on their lips, but one look at her face was enough to silence them. "I don't know what the ritual has done to us, but I'm not myself, and neither are the rest of you. Until this foulness passes, you will sequester yourselves away somewhere private. Don't you dare argue with me, or I'll have you in stocks for a week. Now go!"

Mariel punctuated her last words by raising a rigid arm and pointing at the nearest arched doorway that led out of the training yard. One by one, the guards glared at her and then moved to obey her order. When she and Garius were alone, he tried to speak.

"M'lady," Garius said, "I—"

"I meant you too, Garius. Get out of my sight."

The captain of the guard looked hurt, but he nodded and left her alone.

Trying to get herself under control, Mariel expelled a great breath through her nostrils and focused on slowing her breathing. When her vision no longer throbbed red, and she trusted herself to take a step without screaming at the sky, Mariel left the courtyard and moved through the house to her private study. There she could wait out the influence of the dark ritual.

After a few hours of solitude, Mariel felt herself reasserting control of her soul. The anger and pride lingered, but it sat in the back of her mouth with an aftertaste like iron instead of an all-consuming force that dominated her will. The rot in her stomach had turned sour, and she suspected she would be sick. She thought of Tarathine and Saredon, regretting her harsh words to them. Before she could work up the courage to go find the children and apologize, the door to her study slowly opened.

To Mariel's surprise, the old, wizened head of Ursais peeked around the door at her.

"Can I come in?" he asked.

Unable to compose a response in her state of surprise, Mariel nodded and beckoned the old man forward. He stepped into the room and shut the door quietly behind him.

"Garius let me in," Ursais said. "I saw the priestess and her pet reaver come and go and bided my time until I thought the effects of the ritual would have worn off. Are you okay?"

Tears filled Mariel's eyes. She shook her head and wiped at her cheeks with the back of a hand. "Oh, Ursais, it was horrible. I've never tasted anything so vile. It wanted control—it wanted to use me."

Ursais gave her a sorrowful look. "If you wish to fight it, you must understand that the ritual doesn't add anything that's not already there. It merely unlocks what's already inside you. Abimelech preys on the darkest parts of our nature, coaxing it to the surface, and then exploiting it for his own purposes."

"You speak as if Abimelech is real. Don't tell me you believe he exists."

"He exists whether I believe in him or not," Ursais said. "Abimelech is very real, and very dangerous."

"Then what's the point of defiance? The kingdom is his, and soon all the people will bend the knee in his name. You told me of the Shrouded King, and I believed you. But what good is faith if there's no hope?"

"Don't give in to despair," Ursais said. "Even now, the Shrouded King is moving against Abimelech. This was his kingdom once, and it will be so again. The magus that your husband hunts is the key. Through the magus, the power of the Shrouded King is made manifest. If they can survive to strike back against Abimelech, we have a fighting chance."

"Then we are lost," Mariel said, her voice empty of emotion. "My husband has killed magi before. He'll succeed in this task as he does all others."

"Perhaps, but perhaps not." Ursais took her hand in his, kindly eyes crinkled with a smile. "Your husband has spared heretics as well, has he not? Let us hope a while longer, Mariel."

— —

Parenthia's exhausted horse clattered to a stop before the gates of Castle Vaulkern. She slid down to the cobblestones. The animal's chest heaved, its dying breaths whistling in its nostrils. Parenthia had not eaten in almost a week. It took every bit of willpower she possessed not to slaughter the animal in the street and gorge herself on horseflesh. She abandoned the doomed creature. The filthy beggars of her congregation would see to its remains soon enough.

Parenthia rehearsed what she would say as she entered the castle. Somehow, she had to make the regent see that the events in Oakroot had not been her fault. She had gone hunting one magus and had been ambushed by two—had been betrayed most foully by her strongest servant. Surely Regent Trangeth would understand that she had done all she could.

The halls of Castle Vaulkern were empty and silent. Humans were no longer allowed here, and Abimelech's children preferred the cathedral. Regent Trangeth ruled from the castle because it was the seat of the kingdom's power. He haunted these abandoned corridors with only his guards for company.

In the hallway outside the throne room, two of the regent's guards stood, sentinels in black armor. They did not move or speak as Parenthia approached, but the doors were open, indicating that the regent was within. Parenthia forced herself to walk between the guards without hesitation.

Inside the grand room, Regent Trangeth sat at the base of the High King's dais at a large wooden desk of stained oak. His chair was a throne of sorts, but nothing like the resplendent seat at the top of the platform behind him. The former seat of High King Rowen himself, the castle's true throne looked out over the court as if from a mountaintop. None of Abimelech's children could come near to that throne without being struck down, and now it sat in shadow and dust, unused for millennia.

Regent Trangeth did not look up from his desk at Parenthia's entrance. Even in silence, the regent's presence filled the grand room. She moved to stand before him and waited as he finished reading a scroll on the desk in front of him. Finally he removed the weights holding the scroll open, rolled it back up, and returned it to its case. That done, he sat back in his chair and looked at Parenthia for the first time.

He frowned. "Why do you insist on wearing such a vulgar appearance? You can conjure any manifestation of beauty you desire, and you choose... *this.*"

"Are we to find the humans beautiful now?" Parenthia asked. "Are we to pattern our lives after theirs, such that we become indistinguishable from the enemy?"

"They're no more our enemy than are the cattle that graze in the fields outside this city."

"If only Abimelech could hear your—," Parenthia started to snarl. Trangeth overrode her.

"Don't threaten me with the name of our lord and father," Trangeth snapped. "As High Priestess, you pretend to know his will. Tell me, have you ever spoken with him?"

Parenthia did not answer. Trangeth knew she had never gone before Abimelech.

"You were raised to the position of High Priestess because you showed promise," Trangeth said. "Never forget that what has been given can also be taken away. Now, I cannot help but notice that you've returned to Northmark months ahead of schedule, and you appear to be alone. I assume an explanation is forthcoming."

Parenthia took a deep breath and plunged ahead. "I alone survived the inquisition to Oakroot."

Regent Trangeth said nothing, but his gaze sharpened as his eyes focused on Parenthia.

"We went seeking one magus, but we found two," Parenthia said. "The Tenth Reaver, Kaiser Pellathor, manifested the prophesied powers. When we tried to subdue him, we were ambushed by a second magus who was lying in wait. We could not withstand their combined might. To my knowledge, I'm the only one who escaped."

The regent remained silent for a long time. He leaned back in his chair and stared at Parenthia, chin resting in his hand. Parenthia tried not to fidget. Her fear grew with the silence. She imagined Trangeth ordering his guards to run her through on the spot.

"And the First Reaver?" Trangeth finally said.

Parenthia lowered her head. "I saw him fall. He did not rise."

Trangeth sat up straight and started to sort the stacks of parchment on his desk. He spoke as he worked. "I trust I don't have to remind you that Abimelech's children are not created equal. The First Reaver was important to me, and you've ruined my plans for him with your incompetence. Not only that, but you allowed two magi to slip through your fingers. Tell me why I shouldn't strip you of your position and cast you into darkness."

"I don't know who the other magus is, but I know Kaiser," Parenthia said, desperate to convince the regent of her worth. "I can capture and subdue him. His family is the key. Give me two weeks. Within that time, he'll come to Northmark to save them. He'll not leave here alive, I swear it."

"Mazareem warned me of sending you to deal with the magus," Trangeth said. "I gave you a chance because I despise him and his disgusting hound, but even the most unsightly of tools have their uses. I should have trusted him to deal with this threat and kept you in Northmark, playing at being high madam for the cattle wearing that soft flesh of yours."

Parenthia kept her head down and bit her tongue. Giving voice to her rage would only make things worse. Mazareem would soon return to Northmark, and she needed to be prepared.

"Very well," Trangeth said. "You have until Mazareem makes his way back here. If you've not dealt with Kaiser before then, I'm turning over the task to him. Should that happen, your time as High Priestess will be at an end. I'll decide what to do with you when the time comes. If you wish to avoid a great deal of suffering, don't disappoint me again."

Parenthia bowed low and turned to exit the throne room.

"One more thing," Trangeth said, as if he had remembered a minor matter that needed her attention. "With two magi running free, we cannot pin all our hopes on a pair of overactive corpses. You know what must be done."

"You mean—"

"Yes," Trangeth interrupted, "release the wights."

Parenthia glanced over her shoulder at Trangeth, wanting to make absolutely sure she had understood his command.

Trangeth gave her a cruel smile. "Consider your debts paid if they elect not to spare you."

With a shudder, Parenthia turned away and left the throne room on swift feet. Rather than retrace her steps back to the front of the castle, she turned aside at the entrance to the throne room. When she found the stairs down into the bowels of the fortress, she started the long descent to the lowest levels.

The door that led to Mazareem's prison chambers came and went, yet Parenthia did not slow. She had only been this deep once before, many years ago. The stone walls became damp, weeping moisture from the cold earth they held at bay. Beneath her feet, the slick steps were invisible in the darkness between torches. Fetid air rose from the yawning abyss in the center of the circular staircase. Parenthia imagined that if she slipped and fell into that empty blackness, she would plummet to the center of the earth.

Finally, Parenthia reached an ancient wooden door covered in creeping fungus. Set in an iron hook, a single, weak torch flickered next to the door. The steps continued down into the darkness, but Parenthia could not see any more torches below her. She had no desire to know what horrors lay beneath this level.

Parenthia pushed the rotting door inward, and the hinges squealed with the effort of opening. She found absolute blackness inside, so she plucked the torch from its place and held it in front of her as she stepped into the hallway beyond. Rusted iron doors lined the long hall. Each door had a small window about the size of her hand. Some of these openings were filled with bars, and others were sealed with metal plates. Parenthia stopped in front of a door with its window covered in metal mesh. It reminded her of mail.

From within the cell, Parenthia heard a sigh of pleasure.

"It bringsss ussss light," a voice said, the words slithering on the edge of hearing.

"Abimelech calls, and you must obey," Parenthia said. She fought to keep her voice level, to show no evidence of the fear in her heart.

"Yesss, yesss, we obey," the voice whispered.

"I place a task before you and release you to see it done," Parenthia said. "Two magi roam free in the Kingdom of Haverfell. You will find them, and you will kill them."

"Magusss will die," the voice said. *"Releasssse ussss."*

Parenthia could not stop her hand from trembling as she raised the bar from the door. She released the latch and stepped back. The door banged open and a flurry of dark shapes filled the corridor. Parenthia screwed her eyes shut, waiting for the cold touch of a wight that would snatch the life from her. The touch never came.

When Parenthia opened her eyes, the hallway was empty. She allowed herself a small smile—she had survived. Her ordeal was over. Parenthia's next service to Abimelech would be a pleasure.

Chapter 21

MARIEL TALKED WITH URSAIS long into the evening. Outside the windows of her study, dusk crept over the walls of the fortified palace. The sickness in her stomach and the turmoil in her heart passed, replaced by sympathy for the children. She needed to go to them and try her best to apologize, explain that she… had not been herself, earlier. But before she could bid Ursais goodnight, Garius burst into the room, wild-eyed.

"What is the meaning of this, captain?"

"Apologies, my lady," Garius said, ducking his head. "I've come from the front gate. One of my agents from the city came with a report…"

"Well, what is it?" Mariel asked.

The guard captain's eyes flicked between Mariel and Ursais. He swallowed hard and said, "This man watches the royal district. He monitors the comings and goings from Castle Vaulkern." Here, Garius paused, as if he dreaded what he had to say next. "Parenthia has returned to Northmark, alone, and riding a horse nearly dead from exhaustion. She went straight to the castle, no doubt to speak with the regent."

Mariel fell back in her seat, the strength suddenly gone from her limbs. Ursais leapt to his feet and started pacing.

"This isn't good," Ursais said.

"The inquisition must have failed," Garius said. "Why else would Parenthia abandon it?"

Ursais and Garius grew more animated and agitated as they talked, but Mariel said nothing. The news settled in her being with a numbing chill. In her heart, she knew what must have happened. For Parenthia to return alone, either Kaiser had finally defied her will, or he was dead. In either case, her husband was Tenth Reaver no longer. The father of her children, their only sure protector, was either a corpse or an outlaw.

"We have to escape Northmark," Mariel said, cutting through the heated conversation between the two men.

Both Ursais and Garius stopped and looked at her. Garius was incredulous, but Ursais's face bore a look of grim determination, and he nodded at Mariel's words.

"You can't be serious," Garius said, shaking his head. "There's no way out, and besides, where would you go?"

"What did you expect me to do with this information?" Mariel asked. "Sit here and wait for Parenthia to come for my head?"

"There's a formal process to follow," Garius said. "You can appeal to the regent for protection until Kaiser's fate is known. None of the other reavers can touch us without an investigation. Parenthia's word alone is not enough."

"What if it is? What's to stop her, or the reavers?" Mariel shook her head. "Before today, I trusted the laws of this kingdom. But when they invaded my home and forced their profane ritual on me those laws became tyranny. I'll not sit here like a caged rat while I wait for them to decide what to do with me and my children."

"She's right, Garius, and you know it," Ursais said. "We have to act now, tonight, before it's too late."

"If your suspicions are correct, Parenthia might be on her way here this very moment," Garius said. "How do you propose we escape?"

"There's a system of secret tunnels beneath this district," Mariel said. "Only a few of the reavers know about them. Kaiser showed me the hidden door in our cellar in case we ever needed to flee."

Garius's eyes widened in surprise. "And here I thought I knew everything about this palace."

"I'm sorry, Garius," Mariel said gently. "It's not that Kaiser doesn't trust you. He just thought that the fewer people who knew of the tunnels, the better."

"So be it," Garius said with a nod. "I swore to Kaiser that I'd protect you to his absence, and my only loyalty is to his family. I'll do as you command."

"Thank you," Mariel said, rewarding Garius's steadfastness with a smile. "Collect the children and meet me in the cellar. If we can get out of the city tonight, we'll make for my family in Arwic. We can figure out what to do next when the immediate danger has passed."

With a smart salute, Garius turned on his heel and left the room. Mariel rose from her seat and moved to follow. She stopped at the desk to pluck a small pouch of coins from a drawer.

"Come with me," Mariel said to Ursais. "If Parenthia's on her way, it won't be safe to leave the through the front gate. You can escape the palace with us."

Ursais fell into step with her as they walked quickly through the hallways of the estate.

"Kaiser is alive, I know it," Ursais said. "Don't give up hope."

Mariel faltered, almost tripping when Ursais spoke. "There's one thing I know beyond a doubt," she said when she recovered her balance. "It would take all the powers of heaven and hell to kill my husband. If Kaiser's fallen, he took an army with him."

They reached the cellar stairs. Mariel stopped in her tracks, surprised to find a guard at the top of the steps that led down into the underworks of the palace.

"Is everything alright, m'lady?" the soldier asked as he inspected Mariel and Ursais.

"Yes, everything's fine," Mariel answered. The man was new — she did not know his name.

"Are you sure?" the soldier asked, making no move to step aside. "Shouldn't you be in bed this time of night?"

Mariel's anger flared. "Who do you think you are, to question me in my own home? If you wish to stay a member of the Tenth Reaver's guard, step aside."

The soldier looked like he wanted to refuse, but after a heartbeat of hesitation, he gave her a smile and moved out of the way.

Before Mariel and Ursais could start down the steps, Garius rounded the corner with a sleepy Tarathine and Saredon in tow. He had given them enough time to get dressed.

At the guard captain's appearance, the soldier perked up again.

"What's going on, captain?" the soldier asked. "Where are you taking the children?"

"It's none of your concern," Garius snapped. "Who ordered you to patrol in here? Get back to the wall."

"Forgive me, sir. I thought protecting the High Reaver's family was my concern. I would hate for something to happen to them while he's away."

Something in the soldier's voice plucked a chord of fear in Mariel's heart.

Garius froze mid-step. He slowly turned to face the man. "Do you have a problem, soldier?"

"No problem, captain," the soldier said, still smiling. "We're all loyal subjects of the kingdom here, right?"

"Indeed," Garius said, his voice strained. "Now get out of here before I put you in stocks for disobeying orders."

The soldier lingered a moment too long, scanning each of their faces in turn. When Mariel was sure that Garius would lose his patience, the soldier nodded and made his way down the hallway. They watched his retreating back, waiting until the soldier disappeared around the corner before starting down the cellar steps.

"Every year it gets harder to find men you can trust," Garius muttered as they descended the stone stair.

At the bottom of the steps, Mariel opened the heavy wooden door just a crack, giving them enough space to squeeze through one at a time. Once inside the cellar, she pushed the door closed. Garius took a stout wooden chair and propped it underneath the door handle.

"You think that's necessary?" Mariel asked.

"Best to not take chances," Garius said.

"What's going on, mother?" Tarathine asked, her voice quavering.

"It's an adventure, like in one of your stories," Mariel said, taking the girl's hand and giving it a comforting squeeze. "Just follow me and Garius, and watch out for your little brother."

A solitary torch burned on one of the stone columns that supported the house above. Mariel took this torch from its hook and moved deeper into the cellar. At the far northern corner of the palace's foundations sat stacks of crates filled with old armor and weapons. Anything Kaiser did not have an immediate use for in the training area above got stored down here. Behind these crates, a grid of iron bars had been pounded into the stone wall from which weapons, armor, and shields could be hung and displayed.

Mariel approached this metal grid. She held the torch above her head so that she could inspect the items hanging on the wall. When she found the one she was looking for, an ornate buckler with a gilded "M" emblazoned on its surface, she hooked her fingers over it and pulled downward.

Instead of coming free of the grid, the shield clicked downward, triggering a hidden lever. With nothing more than a whisper of passing air, an entire section of stone next to the metal grid fell away, leaving a rectangular hole the size of a doorway.

The children gasped, and Garius swore underneath his breath.

"You're sure these tunnels are safe?" Ursais asked as they stared into the pitch-black darkness.

"No, I'm not," Mariel said. "I've no idea what's waiting for us in there, but we don't have any other choice."

Kaiser had instructed her to only use the tunnels in the most extreme circumstances. The palaces of the other reavers connected to the same network of underground passages, and there was no way of knowing who frequented the tunnels.

Garius took the torch from Mariel and stepped into the dark doorway with his sword drawn. When the rest of them had moved inside the cramped corridor, he put his shoulder to the stone slab of a door and heaved it shut.

With the torch held out in front of him, Garius led them into the darkness. The short tunnel in front of them soon intersected with a larger passage that ran under all of the palaces on this side of the street. They turned right, hoping that it would carry them under the wall of the royal district and up to the city above.

Garius moved slowly, intent in pausing at every intersection to listen. Ursais urged caution, and as they crept along, the old man scanned the floor, walls, and ceiling for traps.

After several hundred painfully slow paces, Mariel stumbled on an incline in the floor beneath her feet. Soon, they had to crouch to avoid bumping their heads into the ceiling of the tunnel. After a few minutes of crawling, they reached the end of the passage. An ancient piece of rotted rope dangled from the ceiling, and they looked up to see the underside of a rusted metal trapdoor.

Garius tugged on the rope. It disintegrated in his hand. He extinguished the torch and reached up to put his back against the door. With a push, it gave way, squealing horribly. Mariel winced at the noise.

Garius went first, and Mariel urged the children forward. Ursais insisted on being last, so Mariel went next. When she climbed out of the hole, she found herself standing in a small storehouse. Crates were stacked to the ceiling, and she could see a tiny avenue of open space that would allow them to reach the door.

Hope surged in Mariel's chest. This just might work. She turned to help the frail Ursais climb out of the tunnel. When they were all free of the hole, she lowered the trapdoor back to the floor. As it closed, she heard an audible click. Surprised, Mariel tried to open the door again, but it would not budge. She told herself not to panic; they wanted to escape, not hide in the tunnels.

Garius started toward the door with the children close on his heels. Mariel and Ursais followed, squeezing through the stacks of boxes. She could discern the outlines of the crates in the darkness, but little else. Insects scattered beneath her feet, and Mariel clamped her mouth shut to prevent from crying out. Finally, they reached the outline of the door. Garius made eye contact with her in the faint light. With a deep breath, Mariel gave him a nod, and he pushed the door open.

The secret tunnel had deposited them hundreds of paces from the royal district. Mariel could not even see the reavers' palaces over the tops of the surrounding buildings. They moved toward the head of the alley. Garius paused before stepping into the street, and Mariel moved to stand by his side. Street lamps lined the road, pools of orange light in a world of shadows.

"I can't see a damned thing," Garius said. "There could be an entire army hidden out there. Let me scout the street. I'll be back in the blink of an eye."

Garius made to step forward, but Mariel put a restraining hand on his arm. "No," she said. "Let me go first. If anyone's waiting for us, they'll not reveal themselves for you. Keep the children safe."

"My lady, don't ask me to abandon you."

"I'm not asking, I'm commanding," Mariel said, putting as much steel in her voice as she could muster.

Garius lowered his head. "As you wish."

Mariel gave both Tarathine and Saredon a quick hug and then stepped out into the street. She composed herself and walked with purpose. When she paused under the streetlight, Mariel scanned the area for signs of movement. Had they made it this far undetected?

Nothing moved in the darkened streets for a moment. Then, a hundred paces to the north, a dark figure stepped from the shadows and into the light.

Mariel's heart sank. She knew that silhouette from earlier in the day. The spiked helm of the Fifth Reaver cast a sinister shadow on the cobblestone street. A second figure stepped to the reaver's side, and Mariel recognized the guard that had questioned them at the top of the cellar stair.

Anger surged in Mariel's heart. She forced herself not to look back at the alleyway where Garius, Ursais, and the children hid. She bolted into the darkness, racing in the opposite direction. The guard and the Fifth Reaver took off after her, flickering from lamplight to lamplight, hellish apparitions hard at her heels.

Mariel was rounding a corner blindly when the blow felled her. All her world was black pain for a moment. Then she was on her hands and knees, gasping for breath, motes and tears swimming before her eyes. A soft, clammy hand grabbed her beneath the chin and jerked her face up. Ill-fitting folds of black robes and pale flesh blotted out the street lamp above.

Mariel tried to jerk her face away but the grip was iron. "What brings you out at this hour, my lady?" Parenthia asked, caressing Mariel's cheek and grinning widely. "Haven't you heard the saying? Only the guilty run."

Chapter 22

MAZAREEM LOOKED AT THE world through another man's eyes. In his mind, he knew that his physical form still crouched beneath the dragon bones at the heart of the Wraith Wood, but his consciousness inhabited the body of another. He had invaded the being of the man called Brant.

Had the magic Mazareem used on Brant in Oakroot not still clung to the man, he would never have been able to find his prey on the spiritual plane. But here in the Wraith Wood, the whispers of shadow that still lurked in Brant's soul called to Mazareem like a fire in the darkness.

Brant lay on his back in the road. Together, they stared up at the dark trees out of the same set of eyes. Mazareem sensed Brant's panic, but he held the man's will in a merciless grip. The faint sounds of Brant's sleeping companions could be heard nearby, and through Brant's thoughts, Mazareem learned their names. Lacrael breathed long and slow, the rhythmic cadence of exhausted slumber. Kaiser snored. Mazareem hoped their dreams were sweet, for they would never wake. Azmon was coming.

A strange apparition floated down from the trees and hung in front of Brant's face. Adrenaline and fear surged through Brant, but Mazareem kept him pinned to the earth with the power of his possession, helpless and immobile. The spectre looked like a hazy cloud of faint light, hovering above Brant for a moment before coming closer. Mazareem's spell prevented Brant from crying out, even though the man thrashed against the mental barriers.

Lines appeared within the apparition as it started to take on shape and definition. Mazareem watched with Brant, entranced, as an image of horror took form in front of their eyes. The head of a grinning demon materialized out of the light, its huge, ragged tongue lolling out of a mouth full of wicked teeth. It grinned down at Brant. Mazareem could *feel* the thing's hunger and desire. Brant tried again to struggle, to scream, but Mazareem held him fast.

The demon wraith opened its mouth wide and rushed at Brant's face. Flesh burned and then went cold as the thing sank into his being. A third presence joined Mazareem and Brant in the single body. Individual muscles contracted and released, commanded by an exquisite, inhuman level of control. Maniacal laughter echoed as the demon explored Brant's physical form.

"I summoned you, and you will obey," Mazareem said to the demon, his words echoing within the confines of Brant's mind.

"Azmon knows you, man of shadow," Azmon said, turning his attention to Mazareem. "Who gave you the power to bind Azmon to your will? He tires of your games."

Unable to speak or break free of Mazareem's hold on him, Brant cowered before Azmon's voice. Even Mazareem shuddered as the demon's words slid into his mind like poisoned thorns.

"The source of my powers are none of your concern," Mazareem said. "Do as I command, or I'll banish you back from whence you came."

"Speak your desire," Azmon said. "If it amuses Azmon, he will act."

"Take control of this man," Mazareem said. "Rise up and kill his companions. Do this, and I'll turn his body over to you for a time."

After a moment of silence, Azmon said, "This pleases Azmon. So be it."

Against his will, Brant sat up. Azmon noticed the sleeping Lacrael for the first time. His overpowering surge of lust caused Brant to scream out in his own mind, throwing himself against Mazareem's spectral bonds. The demon ignored him.

The fingers on Brant's hand twitched as Azmon experimented with his newfound body. Mazareem sensed its satisfaction. The demon crawled Brant's body to where Lacrael slept, and fingers quested toward the dagger at Lacrael's waist. With the hilt between thumb and forefinger, Azmon pulled the weapon from its sheath.

Brant went berserk. He called upon every power known to god and man to set him free. He challenged Mazareem and Azmon, demanding that they face him. Mazareem almost lost control of him as he tore at the foundations of his own soul, seeking a way to free himself.

"Kill her!" Mazareem commanded Azmon. "I cannot hold him back much longer."

Azmon drew back Brant's hand, the point of the dagger aimed at Lacrael's heart. At the last instant before the demon struck, a brilliant gold light flared from under Lacrael's shirt. Mazareem and Azmon reeled, and Brant seized the opportunity. For a heartbeat,

Mazareem's power over Brant's will weakened. Brant surged forward, smashing through Mazareem's prison of shadow and taking back control of his body.

Brant screamed a challenge at Azmon, and in the battlefield of his mind, Azmon took on its true form. A body appeared to support the floating head, and the fiend grew to tower over Brant. It had the shape and tail of a salamander, but walked upright like a man. Its head was huge, with a massive, grotesque mouth that could swallow a Brant whole. Putrid, open sores covered its wrinkled, hairless body.

Mazareem appeared next to Brant, taking the form of a man wrapped in shadow. He raised a hand to renew the bonds that held Brant in check, but Azmon's power stopped him.

"No," Azmon said. "You had your chance. Now Azmon takes control."

"You cannot defy me," Mazareem said, struggling against Azmon's growing influence. "I called you to his place. I hold your true name in the palm of my hand."

Despite his words, Mazareem felt the summoning ritual slipping away from him. Brant's sudden defiance had given Azmon the chance he needed to break free of Mazreem's spell. Now they were locked in a battle for full possession of Brant's body.

Azmon sneered at Mazareem, the expression stretching across his huge, toothy maw. Rather than attack, the fiend locked Mazareem in his fell gaze. Red eyes flashed like blazing rubies, and an onslaught of horror crashed into Mazareem's soul.

Barely able to withstand the assault, Mazareem lowered his head and screwed his eyes shut. Corruption and hate flowed into his being with tangible force. He saw himself in the demon's eyes: a morsel, a trifle of flesh to be consumed and discarded. Azmon was as old as the world itself. Visions of ages long past filled Mazareem's thoughts. He watched empires rise and fall. He saw the armies of dragons and men shine in glory for a brief moment before crumbling to dust where the worm ate their flesh and the hounds of the pit lapped up their blood.

Only Azmon endured. Mazareem sensed the demon's amusement at his feeble defiance, and he knew that he was doomed. Azmon toyed with him. When Azmon tired of this game, he would devour Mazareem's soul and murder Lacrael and Kaiser in their sleep. The demon would walk the world for a time, using Brant's body to spread chaos and pain.

Azmon took a step forward, and in Brant's mind, writhing worms and black vines tore at the ground beneath the demon's feet. Mazareem cast about for a way to fight back, for a chance at salvation. A sliver of golden light passed through his eye and penetrated the fog of his thoughts. It shone like a single ray of sunlight breaking through a blackened sky. Mazareem focused on this beacon of hope, and the image of an amulet around Lacrael's neck surged to the forefront of his thoughts. The image had come from Brant. Azmon had reacted to the pendant, and it was the only chance they had.

Mazareem understood that he had no choice but to release Brant. Without giving Azmon any hint of what had passed between the two of them, Mazareem gave Brant control of his body and turned his powers to resisting the demon. Azmon surged forward in a rage at this betrayal.

With a heroic effort, Brant cut the amulet loose from Lacrael's neck with the dagger in his hand. He pulled it out of her shirt and placed it in his open palm. The metal burned white hot against his flesh—all three of them felt the pain. Azmon jerked in agony, the demon's body contorting in a grotesque seizure.

While Azmon suffered, Brant faced down Mazareem's shadowy presence. "I know you," Brant said.

"Yes, yes, we've met before," Mazareem said in impatience. "I scoured your soul on the floor of your quaint little store. It was nothing personal, I assure you. Now, cast aside that amulet so that I can deal with Azmon. He's a danger to the both of us until I can banish him back to his plane."

"You must think I'm crazy," Brant said. "I... I can sense you. You're in the forest somewhere nearby."

Brant left the road behind and plunged into the trees.

"What are you doing?" Mazareem shouted.

Brant did not answer. The thick mass of thorns flinched away from his feet, and he ran on open ground. Azmon howled and tried to overpower both Mazareem and Brant, but the amulet restrained the demon.

Mazareem tried to confuse Brant as he crashed through the dark forest. He conjured an army of shadows to confound Brant's path. Brant was almost blind in the darkness, and he tripped and fell often, cutting his face and arms, but he never slowed. He dodged the trunks of gnarled trees as his feet pounded the earth, and he covered mile after mile, always running toward the source of the power touching his mind. Nothing Mazareem did deterred Brant from his unerring course.

When at last Brant stumbled into a clearing, Azmon had gone quiet. Mazareem had given up trying to stop Brant and was now only concerned with surviving the next few minutes.

Brant stepped forward. A menacing growl sounded from the shadows on his right, and a massive form shot out of the darkness. Still locked in Brant's mind, Mazareem gave a cheer for Worm. He really was a good dog.

The hound slammed into Brant's side, sending him sprawling. Brant lost his dagger as he fell. The beast jumped on him in an instant, pinning Brant on his back with giant paws. Brant got his hands around the animal's thick neck just in time to prevent his head from being bitten off. Jaws snapped in front of Brant's head — hot saliva splattered his face.

Worm's flesh sizzled under the dragon amulet in Brant's palm. Brant pulled his hand into his chest and thrust it straight up into the hound's jaw. The golden pendant struck bone and a flash of blinding light exploded in front of Brant's face. Worm yelped in pain and leapt away.

Mazareem roared in anger.

Brant pulled himself to his feet and stumbled toward the bones in the center of the clearing. The ethereal lights floating in the sky plunged to the earth and swirled around him. Faces appeared when they flashed in front of his face—spirits and demons screamed in silence, pushed into a frenzy by Brant's intrusion into their sacred place.

Crouched in the center of the skeleton's ribcage, Brant spotted a robed figure kneeling over a series of symbols drawn in the dirt. Powerless now to stop Brant or escape his mind, Mazareem stared at himself through the shopkeeper's eyes. The jagged circles and shapes in front of Mazareem glowed with blue fire.

"I know what you're thinking," Mazareem said in Brant's mind, struggling to maintain a reasonable tone, "and I wouldn't, if I were you."

"I know damned well what you'd do if you were me," Brant rasped out loud as he stumbled to a stop behind the kneeling form of Mazareem. After sucking in a great, shuddering breath, he drew back his palm and slammed the amulet into the back of Mazareem's hooded head.

At the same instant, Brant and Mazareem's worlds disappeared in a cataclysm of white light.

— —

Mazareem groaned.

When Brant had touched the amulet to the back of Mazareem's head, pain like Mazareem had never known exploded in his body. It had felt like every drop of blood in every vein started to boil. He had tried to cry out, but no sound came. Blood had poured from his nose and ears. Mazareem had thought that the time had come at last—that he would finally die.

His killer would not be the magnificent prince of dragons whose corpse he had fallen under, mind you. No, Mazareem's killer was to be a tubby backwoods merchant. The indignity would be a fittingly cruel coda to a long and cruel existence. Had a similar thought crossed the dragon's mind in his final moments? Mazareem wondered.

When the pain eased, Mazareem opened his eyes and found himself staring up at the sky between the white pillars of the dragon's ribs. The brute was still dead, and Mazareem still survived. On the eastern horizon, a faint light waged war against the night, the encroaching gray a herald of the new day. The coming dawn had chased away the spirits that haunted the darkness.

Mazareem sat up. When he moved, Worm jumped on him, the hound's huge tongue slurping at his master's face and neck. Mazareem gently pushed the dog away. His hand came back bloody. Worm whined as Mazareem inspected the animal's wound. The flesh of the dog's neck and jaw had melted away, revealing the raw white of bone beneath. Had Worm been a mortal beast, the injury would probably have been fatal. The workings of tendon and muscle were visible, and Mazareem peered through the ragged hole into the animal's torso.

"We'll patch you up when we get home," Mazareem said. The effort of speaking made his head spin. He looked around—his oafish nemesis was nowhere to be seen.

Something had gone terribly wrong. Not only had Brant resisted the possession of the strongest demon Mazareem could summon, he had found his way to this glade. Mazareem knew about the golden amulets of the Dragonslayers, but he had never seen them imbued with such power. This was an omen that warranted further study. Ideally somewhere handsomely appointed and dry, with refreshments on hand.

With another groan, Mazareem pulled himself to his feet with the aid of a nearby rib. He touched the back of his head with the tips of his fingers. He did not find blood, and he suspected the ritual had protected him from an injury as gruesome as Worm's.

Whatever that lunk had done, he had interrupted the spell. Azmon's summoning was incomplete. A small part of Mazareem worried that he may have just loosed an evil on the world worse than Abimelech. He had no idea what the consequences of this might be, but he fervently hoped that they would fall squarely on Azmon and Brant. They deserved each other.

Mazareem had done what he could to slow the progress of the magi. Now he had no choice but to return to Northmark. Worm needed tending, and he needed to rest and recover. A man of his age only had so much energy for dabbling in the dark arts and accosting magi in haunted forests.

With Worm at his side, Mazareem limped from the forest clearing. As he slipped through the trees, he put Brant and the magi out of his mind. Instead, he started to mentally catalog the books in his library that might shed light on the magic of the dragon amulet. He could not risk tasting its power a second time.

— —

Lacrael woke before Kaiser. She reached a sleepy hand to her chest, feeling for her amulet out of habit, then sat up in alarm. Brant was nowhere to be seen. She scrambled to her feet, calling Kaiser's name.

Kaiser snapped awake in an instant. He was up and ready to fight before Lacrael could fill her lungs to say that Brant was missing. When he saw no immediate threat, he relaxed. "So the merchant ran home. Can't say that I blame him."

"I can't believe this," Lacrael said. "He took my dagger and amulet."

"There you have it," Kaiser said. "He took the one thing that might be valuable and snuck away in the night. He's probably miles down the road back to Oakroot by now."

"That doesn't make any sense. He must have had a reason."

"He had two of the best: fear and greed."

"What if something happened? What if he's in trouble?"

"Then at least his troubles aren't ours any longer. We'll move faster without him."

Lacrael turned in place while she peered into the surrounding trees.

"I'm serious," Kaiser said, "there's no way we're going to look for him. I promise you, he's running back home with his tail between his legs."

Lacrael could not deny Kaiser's logic, but in her heart she did not believe that Brant had stolen from her and then run away like a coward.

"I'm going," Kaiser said, taking a step down the road. "If you want to search for him, you should at least come with me to Thornhold first. We'll reach the city by nightfall. You won't survive chasing after him if you don't resupply."

Kaiser left Lacrael standing in the path. She looked for some sign of Brant one last time, but found nothing. Thorns choked the forest on every side. If he had ventured into the trees, his trail would have been obvious. Fighting back frustration and confusion, Lacrael followed after Kaiser.

They walked in silence for an hour. Lacrael made no attempt to catch up, content to walk twenty paces behind Kaiser. The sun rose above the Wraith Wood, but precious little light penetrated the tangled canopy above their heads.

Sometime near mid-morning, Kaiser stopped in the road ahead of her. When Lacrael had almost drawn even with him, he said, "It appears I was wrong."

Lacrael stopped next to Kaiser and followed his gaze. Thirty paces in front of them, a man lay sprawled on the side of the road. He was filthy and covered in blood, but Lacrael recognized Brant in an instant. She rushed forward with a cry.

Brant moaned when Lacrael knelt next to him and placed a hand on his forehead. His eyes fluttered open, and he looked up at her with haunted eyes.

"What happened to you?" Lacrael asked. Brant looked terrible. He was covered in dirt. His arms, face, and chest all bore hundreds of cuts and scrapes.

"I don't know," Brant said weakly. "I fell asleep on the road, and I woke up here. I remember bits and pieces of a crazy dream, but I don't know how much of it was real. I saw the man from Oakroot. Mazareem. I think he followed us, hoping to finish what he started with me."

"Can you move?"

Brant sat up. Lacrael's amulet was cradled in his open palm. "I must have taken it in the night," he said, as shy as he had been a short month ago. "I think it offered some protection against Mazareem's curses."

Lacrael plucked the pendant out of his palm and tied the broken thong around her neck. She was pleased to find Brant, but she was overjoyed to have her grandfather's amulet back. When she glanced back up at Brant's face, she went still. A sudden change had come over him. His handsome face was marred by a harshness Lacrael had never seen in the gentle man. Something sinister looked out of his eyes.

"Are you okay?" Lacrael asked, her voice almost stolen by the surprising change in Brant.

In answer, Brant snarled and lunged at Lacrael. His hands found her throat before she could react. Fingers like iron dug into her neck, and Lacrael crashed to the road under Brant's bulk.

Stars exploded in Lacrael's vision. Brant's lips were pulled back from his teeth in a terrible grin. She could not cry out, could not even draw a breath. Before she lost consciousness, an armored thigh slammed into the side of Brant's head. His weight fell away from her body as he rolled away from the attack.

Brant surged to his feet, hurling himself at Kaiser. Kaiser tried to dodge Brant's attack, but the enraged merchant moved too fast. Brant hoisted Kaiser over his head as if he weighed nothing and hurled him into the thorns along the side of the road. The black bushes convulsed as they swallowed Kaiser's armored form.

Faster than Lacrael could believe possible, Brant whirled to face her. He stalked forward, hands extended toward her like claws.

"Brant, what are you doing?" Lacrael choked out through her burning throat. "Please stop!"

Brant's grin only widened. Beneath Lacrael's shirt, her amulet felt hot against her skin. Desperate now, Lacrael yanked the pendant out into the light of day. The instant his eyes fell on the golden dragon, Brant stopped in his tracks. He looked confused, his gaze flicking between the amulet and Lacrael's face.

Lacrael climbed to her feet. "Do you know who I am?" she asked.

"Y-yes," Brant said, nodding his head. "You're Lacrael."

"Why did you try to kill me?" Lacrael pressed, fingers massaging her sore throat as she talked.

Brant's face crumpled as tears welled up in his eyes. "I don't know. I was only watching. I couldn't control it. There's—there's something terrible in here with me."

Behind Brant, Kaiser's spectral swords flared into life within the thicket of thorns. With shouts and curses, he hacked his way out of the carnivorous undergrowth. When he regained the road, Kaiser's armor bore a hundred scratches. Black thorns were embedded in his exposed skin, trickles of blood oozing from the tiny wounds.

Kaiser advanced on Brant, murder in his gaze.

Lacrael jumped between Brant and Kaiser. She still held the amulet high where Brant could see it.

"Get out of my way," Kaiser growled.

"No," Lacrael said, shaking her head. "Brant isn't himself. Something strange happened to him in the night."

"All the more reason to feed him to the thorns."

"I won't let you kill him," Lacrael said. "He's in this mess because of me. I'll watch over him."

Kaiser stared at her, and for a heartbeat, Lacrael feared he would defy her. Finally, the ethereal blades vanished from Kaiser's hands.

"His life is in your hands," Kaiser said. "If you lose control of him even once, he dies."

Lacrael nodded. Without another word, Kaiser turned on his heel and marched away down the road. Hands shaking, Lacrael turned back to Brant.

"Thank you," Brant whispered.

"Don't thank me," Lacrael said bitterly. "If not for me, you'd still be in your shop in Oakroot."

Brant did not reply.

Lacrael offered the amulet to him. "If wearing this keeps you sane, then you'd better keep it on you. Can you walk?"

"I can run if you need me to," Brant said with a nod, taking the amulet and securing the leather thong around his neck.

Together, they set out after Kaiser. Lacrael struggled to control her racing thoughts as they hurried to catch up. Thornhold waited, and something in her heart told Lacrael that the Wraith Wood was not yet finished with them.

Chapter 23

KAISER HIKED WELL AHEAD of Lacrael and Brant as they covered the last few miles to Thornhold. Every so often, he glanced back to check their progress. Brant stumbled along in a daze. Whatever had happened to the timid merchant had turned the man into a monster. Kaiser replayed over and over again in his mind how easily Brant had bested him. Without his newfound powers, Kaiser would have been helpless in Brant's hands.

Lacrael had gone silent as she walked alongside Brant. Doubtless she wondered at the change in Brant too. Kaiser imagined she was taking it rather hard. The sooner they reached Thornhold and went their separate ways, the better. Traveling with Lacrael and Brant was becoming complicated, and complications were not something Kaiser could afford.

With every step that Kaiser took, he felt himself pulled toward Northmark with all haste. Visions of his family in chains haunted his dreams. The fear for their safety never left him while he was awake. Parenthia would have arrived at the capital by now. Kaiser believed she would keep his wife and children alive to bargain with, but that did nothing to assuage his growing dread.

"Won't it be dangerous if someone in Thornhold recognizes you as a reaver?" Lacrael said from behind him, speaking up for the first time in hours.

"No one knows my face," Kaiser said over his shoulder. "I'm as safe as you in a crowd."

"It's not your face I'm worried about. It's that ridiculous armor."

Kaiser almost tripped as he looked down. With a silent curse, he realized she was right. Even though he wore less than half of his full harness, the make and quality were still unmistakable. No one would know he was the Tenth Reaver, but his armor, adorned with spikes and skulls, marked him as a reaver without a doubt.

"You're right," Kaiser said. "I don't know what I was thinking."

He hated to do it, but he saw no other choice. With Lacrael's help, Kaiser stripped the rest of his armor off and did his best to hide it underneath a thicket on the edge of the road. The padded undergarments seemed odd on their own, so he removed those too.

"Thornhold is a proper city as far as the kingdom is concerned," Kaiser said as he disarmed, "but everyone knows that it's a haven for outlaws. Reavers don't come here unless chasing an extremely dangerous fugitive. Don't let your guard down and assume that everyone is your enemy."

When they were finished, Kaiser looked like a simple laborer, dressed in nothing but a drab cloth shirt and pants. He hung his coin purse around his neck where it would be hidden beneath his shirt. Kaiser paused. He looked Brant up and down.

"What is it?" Lacrael asked.

"I'm not walking in there with him unsecured," Kaiser said. "We need a reason for being out here, and he gives us one. We're bounty hunters, and he's our bounty." He knelt over his discarded armor and used one of his spectral blades to cut away lengths of leather straps and buckles. When he finished, he had enough tied together to wrap around Brant's hands and wrists several times.

Lacrael looked on as Kaiser tied Brant's arms behind him. Kaiser tested the bonds, satisfied that even with his impossible strength, the merchant would have difficulty breaking free. Brant accepted the restraints without a word of protest.

"Alright, let's go," Kaiser said.

They reached the outskirts of Thornhold several miles later. High walls had been erected between the trees to hold the thorns out. The creeping briars piled up against this barrier, but could not climb over to claim the city beyond.

Protected by the walls, Thornhold sprawled beneath the dark trees of the Wraith Wood. The buildings were set close together, leaving room for only narrow paths and alleyways on the forest floor. Walkways and platforms hung suspended from the trees above, used by the denizens of Thornhold to move quickly through the city.

Kaiser led the three of them through the eastern gate. Guards watched from above as they passed under a walkway suspended ten feet above the road. They entered the narrow corridors between the buildings, forced to walk single file in some places. When they reached an intersection big enough for the three of them to huddle together, Kaiser turned to speak with Lacrael and Brant.

"I said I'd travel with you to Thornhold, and so I have," Kaiser said. "Now it's time for us to part ways. I've no time to search for these mysterious allies of yours. You're on your own from here."

"Wait," Lacrael said as Kaiser turned away. The fear and desperation in her voice caused Kaiser to pause. "I can't stop you from leaving. But please, don't abandon us like this. We don't know anything about this place. At least help us find somewhere to start looking."

"I'm bound for Northmark," Kaiser said. "What you do now means nothing to me."

Kaiser left Lacrael and Brant staring after him. He pushed the look of sorrow on Lacrael's face from his mind, instead focusing on the need to reach his family as quickly as possible. Kaiser walked hard, making for the far side of Thornhold. He needed supplies, but he wanted to be free of the Wraith Wood. On the other side of the forest, he could find a horse and cover the remaining distance to Northmark in a matter of days.

It took Kaiser the better part of an hour to navigate the confined warren of a city. More than once he had to backtrack to find his way after wandering down a dead end. He ignored the watchers that stared down at him from the rooftops. Few people traveled the city on the ground, and he knew he was conspicuous in his clumsy efforts to find his way. One hooded figure in particular seemed to take a special interest in him, shadowing Kaiser's movements no matter where he went.

Kaiser was about to confront this stalker when he turned a corner and found himself in the midst of a group of men. They were dressed like mercenaries and stood with their shoulders resting on the walls of the nearby buildings. Arms crossed, the burliest of the bunch looked Kaiser up and down.

"Welcome to the finest street in all of Thornhold," the man said with a smile that did not reach his eyes. "Those who pass betwixt these hallowed walls come away blessed. Many a painful ailment has been cured on this stretch of road. You'll understand if we request a toll of you to continue on. Let's call it a token of good faith, a reward for those who keep this sacred place safe."

"I don't want any trouble," Kaiser said. Above his head, a crowd started to gather on the rooftops to witness the confrontation.

"No trouble here, friend," the burly man said. "Simply grace my palm with some coin and you can go on your merry way."

Kaiser did not have time for this. He took a step back. "I'll find another way."

"Now you'll have to pay me for wasting my time," the man said, hoisting himself up from where he leaned on the wall. At his back, the rest of his men followed his lead. Hands went to weapons.

"You don't want to do this."

The bandit laughed. "You should have paid when you had the chance. Now we're going to take everything you've got. I'm feeling generous today, so I'll spare most of your fingers."

Drawing his sword, the man stepped forward. The air sizzled as Kaiser's ethereal weapons burst into existence. He lunged forward, slicing at the bandit leader's armored forearm. The ghastly blade passed through metal and flesh without resistance, crimson blood splashing on the walls of the alleyway. Kaiser swept by the man, leaving him staring at his stump of an arm in stupefaction.

In the close confines of the narrow alley, the remaining three bandits could not avoid Kaiser's deadly swords. He ducked a clumsy swing and counterattacked, shearing through sword and buckler to tear into the flesh beneath. The bandits screamed and fell over themselves as they struggled to retreat.

One man, braver than the others, tried to get inside Kaiser's guard. He slipped beneath Kaiser's glowing blades and aimed a vicious stab at Kaiser's guts. Kaiser sucked in his stomach and twisted away—the enemy's sword pierced his shirt, and he felt the cold steel slide across his skin.

Kaiser struck at the man's exposed head. The bandit's skull sliced open as easily as a rotten melon, and he collapsed into the dirt. Terrified now, the other two bandits threw down their weapons and fled. Kaiser turned back to the leader. The man stared at him with a mixture of horror and awe, clutching his stump and stumbling backward.

"What are you?" the man asked.

For an answer, Kaiser snarled and slammed both of his swords into the man's chest. The bandit gasped, shuddered, and slumped back against the wall. He slid down into the dirt street, leaving a bloody streak on the wooden building.

Footsteps thudded on the rooftops overhead as the crowd scattered. Kaiser headed down the alley at a jog, but before he reached the next intersection, horns of alarm were bellowing out across the city.

Kaiser turned the corner and found the hooded stalker from the rooftops standing in the middle of the street, blocking his path. The phantom swords still glowed in his hands. "You'll join your friends if you don't get out of my way," Kaiser said as he advanced.

The cloaked stranger pulled back her hood, revealing dark skin and a head of blazing red hair.

"They're not my friends," the woman said. "I'm here to help you. Those horns mean the gates are sealed. Unless you want to fight off the entire city, you must come with me. Right now."

Kaiser swore under his breath. Thornhold might be a den of thieves, but they looked out for each other. Public murder would be met with swift and terrible retribution.

"Lead on," Kaiser said, dismissing the swords from his hands. "But I warn you, if you lead me into an ambush, I'll slaughter you and everyone else that stands in my way."

The woman inclined her head as if acknowledging that Kaiser's threat was perfectly understandable. Without another word, she turned and moved to a ladder hidden in the wall of a nearby building. She scampered up to the rooftops without looking back. Kaiser reluctantly followed her up.

Once they were on the rooftops, the woman dashed across the elevated pathways with sure feet of an acrobat. Kaiser managed not to make a fool of himself, but he struggled to keep his balance. If she wanted to, the woman could have lost him easily.

Finally, the woman hopped down onto the roof of a nearby building. Without a word, she opened a wooden hatch and disappeared down a ladder. Wary now, Kaiser followed at a much slower pace.

When Kaiser reached the bottom of the ladder, he looked around. The space was small and crowded with wooden crates and iron-banded chests stacked floor to ceiling. Kaiser stood in the center of the room, which held a few chairs, a table, and a stack of folded sleeping cots. Candles on the table provided the only light.

Lacrael and Brant sat at the table, along with one of the biggest men Kaiser had ever seen. Lacrael's eyes widened when she saw Kaiser.

"Allow me to make the formal introductions," the red-haired woman said at Kaiser's side. "My name is Niad, and I'm the first mate of the *Golden Dawn*. Seated at the table with your companions is Captain Gustavus. We've been waiting for you."

Kaiser still had not taken his eyes off of Gustavus. Gustavus's mane of brilliant blonde hair was tied back behind his head. His bare forearms, as thick around as one of Kaiser's thighs, rested on the table before him. Kaiser saw curly yellow hair poking out of Gustavus's low cut shirt. The man had more hair on his chest than most men had on their entire body. Gustavus was beyond handsome—he was statuesque.

A much smaller man stepped out of the shadows behind Gustavus. He observed Kaiser with piercing eyes, and Kaiser knew the man's gaze missed nothing.

"That's Parnick," Niad said, nodding to the small man. "He's our master at arms."

Gustavus leaned forward. The table creaked under his bulk. "I expected one of you, not three. I don't like being surprised. If you're who I'm supposed to find, you'll have a sign or a token. Now's the time to show it."

Kaiser glanced at his former companions. Brant sat as still and expressionless as a rock. Lacrael had removed the restraints from his arms. Her brow knit in concentration at Gustavus's words. When understanding dawned on her, she leaned over and lifted the amulet out from beneath Brant's shirt. It rested against his chest, gleaming and golden in the candlelight.

"What's the matter with him?" Gustavus asked. "Can't he tend to himself?"

"He's not accustomed to rough travel," Lacrael said, her eyes darting to Kaiser before she responded. "He's had a hard time of it."

Gustavus stared at Brant for a long moment before grunting and turning away. "So you've got the token. That means we can get down to business."

"Our ship is a trading vessel," Niad said when she noticed Kaiser inspecting the crates that filled the room. "These are some of the captain's personal stores, buried away until the tides turn."

Kaiser nodded, but said nothing. His eyes found the food laid out on the big table. It looked like the remains of a meal, but to Kaiser it seemed that the table still held a feast. His stomach rumbled. "I've not eaten in days. Break my fast and I'll listen to what you have to say."

Niad glanced at the table in surprise. "There's no need for you to eat our scraps. I can do better than that."

"Go ahead, use our limited stores to make our guests at home," Gustavus said when Niad started rummaging around in a nearby crate.

"There's nothing wrong with showing a little hospitality," Niad said.

Gustavus crossed his arms and muttered something under his breath but did not press the issue.

Kaiser sat next to Lacrael and waited. Niad brought a loaf of bread and a fresh wheel of cheese. While Kaiser, Lacrael, and Brant tore into this, Niad found some salted meat and sat that before them as well. Between the three of them, they ate every crumb.

Lacrael finished first, and absentmindedly played with a nearby candle while she waited for Kaiser and Brant to eat their fill. Her fingertips brushed the flame, and in response to her caress, the fire wrapped itself around Lacrael's hand and danced across the skin of her forearm. Gustavus watched with furrowed brows.

"It's not just the fire I summon," Lacrael said when she noticed Gustavus's gaze. "I can control any flame. I can't feel the heat."

When at last the three of them had finished eating, Gustavus rested his big hands on the table and gave Kaiser, Lacrael, and Brant an appraising stare. After a moment of silence, he leaned forward and said, "Had your fill? Good, because it's coming out of Niad's pay. I've told you my name and trade. Now it's your turn."

"My companions are Lacrael and Brant," Kaiser said, speaking before Lacrael could open her mouth. "Lacrael is a hermit from the deep woods of Nogard Forest, and Brant is a merchant from Oakroot."

"Did he run into a tree?" Gustavus asked, taking in the scratches and cuts on Brant's face and shoulders.

"He had a run in with the thorns," Kaiser said. "I did too, if I'm honest."

Gustavus's eyes lingered on Brant before turning back to Kaiser. "You've neglected to tell me your name."

Kaiser took a deep breath. A man like Gustavus might be able to help save his family. But for Gustavus to be of any use, he had to know the truth. "I am Kaiser, Tenth Reaver of Northmark."

Gustavus did not flinch, but Niad and Parnick both gasped. Daggers flashed in Parnick's hands faster than Kaiser could blink. Niad reached for the scimitar on her hip.

"Starting to regret that hospitality?" Gustavus asked his first mate with a smirk.

"I'm sorry cap'n," Niad said. "I had no idea."

"Calm yourselves, both of you," Gustavus said, motioning for Parnick to stow his blades. "I'd wager all the wealth in this room that he's not here to arrest us." Gustavus grinned at Kaiser, revealing his perfect teeth. "Isn't that right?"

Kaiser forced himself to relax. Rather than answer Gustavus's question, he held up a hand and summoned one of his spectral swords. The weapon blinked into existence, its transparent blue blade shimmering in the weak torchlight.

Gustavus's eyes widened, and he shook his head in wonder. "Fate has a cruel sense of humor. You've become what you've spent your entire life trying to destroy."

"It wasn't my choice."

"Two magi," Gustavus said, incredulous. He stared at the ceiling for a long time. When he looked down, a change had come over him. "This changes everything."

Gustavus reached into an inner pocket of his greatcoat and withdrew a golden amulet that matched Lacrael's. He placed it on the table between them.

"You bear one of these, so I trust you know what it means," Gustavus said. "I'm one of the last Dragonslayers. To my knowledge, there's only ten of us left across the four realms. We swore an oath to watch for the return of the High King, and should the opportunity present itself, to commit all of our ability and resources to hasten his coming.

"The legends of our sacred order say that the High King cannot die. His throne sits empty, but the grave cannot claim him. The enemy hides his majesty behind a shroud of darkness and corruption. They can't sever his spirit from the mortal world, so they try to erase his memory from history.

"But the High King still lives, and he fights back from the spirit plane. With the power he still possesses, he raises up champions to fight against the enemy. The legends passed down through the generations of our order are clear: a champion will be chosen from each realm, and when all four stand together, they'll have the combined might to defy Abimelech and deliver the High King."

Gustavus paused to allow the weight of his words to sink in. The skeptic in Kaiser still fought against the idea that a shrouded savior would break free of his prison and deliver Haverfell from Abimelech's oppression, but he could not deny that Gustavus's words affected him.

"We've been preparing for your coming," Gustavus said. "I expected to find one champion. Two have never survived long enough to stand together in the same realm. For both of you to be sitting here means that the High King's power is waxing. His return is imminent, and if I can get the lot of you out of here alive, maybe we'll see it done."

"There's only one problem," Kaiser said. "I'm not leaving."

Chapter 24

KAISER WATCHED THE EFFECT his words had on Gustavus. Up to this point, Gustavus had been calm and collected—in control. Now he exploded.

"What the hell do you mean, 'you're not leaving'?" Gustavus thundered. "Why the blazes are you here then?"

"I'm on my way to Northmark," Kaiser said, remaining calm in the face of Gustavus's anger. "Word of my… conversion will have already reached the capital, and my family is in grave danger. I'm going to rescue them or die trying. If you want my help, you'll aid me."

Gustavus fell silent. He snatched up his dragon amulet with an angry swipe and returned to the inside pocket of his coat. His gaze shifted to Lacrael. "You're with him on this?"

"You've been watching for us in Thornhold," Lacrael said. "But I waited for Kaiser to appear for four years. My grandfather, a Dragonslayer like you, sent me to this realm to find the next champion. And now that I've found him, he wants to charge headlong into the heart of the enemy and risk everything."

Lacrael glanced at Kaiser before continuing. "I don't want the last four years of my life to have been a waste, but I can't ask Kaiser to abandon his family to join us. My grandfather taught me to oppose tyranny, not force it on others."

After Gustavus had considered Lacrael's words for a time, he said, "Suppose I agree to help you. What's your plan?"

"You have a ship," Kaiser said. "Infiltrating Northmark and finding my family won't be hard. It's getting out alive that I need help with. If you dock in the harbor and wait for me, I'll sneak into the city, free my family, and bring them to your ship. Help us escape into the sea and I'll sail with you to the ends of creation if you wish."

"The *Golden Dawn* makes her home far beyond the edges of any map," Gustavus said with a cryptic smile. His grin faded with his next words. "Your plan would put my ship and her entire crew at risk."

"You're a smuggler," Kaiser said. "I'm confident you could sail into Northmark, tweak the High Priestess's nose, and be away before anyone was the wiser."

"There's no doubt about that," Gustavus said with a snort. "The question is: is it worth the risk?"

"That depends," Kaiser said. "Were you serious with all that fancy talk of a sacred order and Shrouded King, or was it just a mummer's farce to lend a sense of grandeur to the miserable life of a pirate?"

"Pirates pillage and rape other ships on the open sea," Gustavus growled. "I do neither. It's bad for trade."

"My apologies," Kaiser said. "Does 'miserable life of an outlaw' suit you better?"

"I should just throw you in irons and take you with us."

"You're welcome to try," Kaiser said. A spectral scimitar flashed into being in one of his hands.

"You're about as agreeable as a mule with hemorrhoids," Gustavus said.

Kaiser fixed an impassive stare on Gustavus and did not respond.

After a tense moment of silence, Gustavus threw up his hands and said, "Fine, we'll help you. But mark my words: we'll sit in the harbor and wait for you and nothing else. Don't expect any heroics. My crew is *my* family, and I'll not trade them for yours."

"Fair enough," Kaiser said with a nod. "I can infiltrate Northmark far easier alone, so you'll take these two with you to the coast. If I leave now, I should be able to reach the city within the week. Does that give you enough time to reach your ship and sail north?"

"You're giving the orders now, is that it?"

"Do you take issue with anything I've said?" Kaiser asked, his voice hard.

After a heartbeat, Gustavus grated out, "No. We'll make for King's Port in the morning. We should arrive in Northmark harbor at the same time you reach the city."

"How will I know your ship?"

"You won't," Gustavus said. "We'll be watching for you. If you make it to the docks, we'll reveal ourselves."

Kaiser pushed himself away from the table and got to his feet. "I've a long road ahead of me still. Before I leave, you don't happen to have any equipment hidden in these crates of yours, do you?"

Gustavus crossed his arms and stared Kaiser down. Kaiser's gaze never flinched. He let his question hang in the air as he waited

Gustavus out. Finally, Gustavus sighed and dropped his arms. He waved Niad toward a nearby crate, and Kaiser moved to follow the woman.

Niad cracked the crate open, revealing an assortment of simple leather armor and crude blades. Her eyes flicked to Gustavus and then back to Kaiser. She leaned close and whispered, "Last year we were hired to supply a revolt in the tropics with weapons and armor. The deal fell through, and he's been trying to offload this stuff ever since."

Kaiser searched through the crate until he had found enough mismatched pieces to cobble together a suit of armor. It did not fit well, but it was better than nothing. He took the least rusted and pitted sword he could find, tying it at his waist to complete the outfit.

"You look like a down-on-his-luck mercenary," Niad said. "That's no way to sneak into a busy city. Wait here."

Niad disappeared into the piles of crates, leaving Kaiser to stand alone in the shadows. Back at the table, Gustavus and Lacrael were deep in a quiet conversation. Brant sat in his chair with his head lowered. Kaiser had almost been rid of his dead weight and mysterious affliction, but Lacrael insisted that he remain with the party. Managing him would be her problem.

"Here," Niad said, thrusting a dark piece of clothing into Kaiser's hands. It was a long, hooded travel cloak.

Kaiser shrugged into the cloak. The supple leather coat hid his armor and weapon, and if he pulled the hood down low, it would obscure his face.

"My thanks," Kaiser said.

"Don't mention it," Niad said with a smile. "It's not every day that I see someone face down the cap'n."

They returned to the table, interrupting Gustavus and Lacrael's conversation. Gustavus looked Kaiser up and down.

"Must you dote on him like a love-struck maiden?" Gustavus grumbled. "That's one of the good coats. It would fetch a hefty price in the north."

"Stow that talk," Niad snapped. "You've always known there were other men in the world just as stubborn as you are. Now you've met one. Don't whine about it."

Gustavus glowered, but did not respond.

"If there's nothing else, then I'll see you in Northmark," Kaiser said.

Niad smiled and wished him all haste, Lacrael looked concerned, and Gustavus only glared. Without another word, Kaiser hoisted himself up the ladder to the roof. He closed the hatch behind him and set out across the rooftops of the city. He estimated he had a few hours before nightfall, and he intended to put as many miles between him and Thornhold as possible before he was forced to stop.

— —

Lacrael watched Kaiser go with a sinking feeling in her gut. In the short time they had spent together, she had come to rely on his indomitable presence. Was she doing the right thing, sending him on his way after waiting four years to find him?

As Lacrael watched Kaiser disappear up the ladder and out of sight, she felt alone again. She had no reason to distrust Gustavus and his companions, but they were strangers to her. At Lacrael's side, Brant sat still and mute, staring at her with sorrow-filled eyes.

"By the hungry abyss, that's the hardest man I've ever met," Gustavus said when they heard the hatch on the roof close. "He's one of the reasons I've avoided Haverfell the last few years. As Tenth Reaver, he's made life miserable for us smugglers."

"Well, he's on our side now," Niad said.

"Sure, if he survives."

Niad smiled at Lacrael. "We'll be heading out before the dawn. You and your friend should get some rest. I'll show you where you can set up some cots and have a little privacy."

At Niad's prompting, Lacrael rose from the table and moved to grab one of the cots stacked nearby. Brant remained seated. Lacrael paused and looked at him.

"Brant... ?" Lacrael said, her voice trailing off as he turned his head to look at her, his face contorted into a horrible grimace of a smile which passed in an instant. The chair under Brant scraped the floor as he pushed it back and stood up. He followed Lacrael to the cots without a word.

Niad led them to the back of the warehouse. Behind a wall of crates, they had just enough room to unfold their cots out of sight of the table in the center of the crowded room.

After making sure they were situated, Niad returned to the table. Lacrael lay on the uncomfortable cot and listened to Brant's heavy breathing. She wondered if she should tell Gustavus and Niad about what had happened to Brant. Maybe she was foolish for removing his restraints. After a few long minutes of agonizing about what she should do, Lacrael heard a strange sound coming from the other side of the warehouse wall. It sounded like a hundred tiny legs were scratching at the outside of the wood.

Eager for an excuse to get up from the cot, Lacrael got to her feet and went to ask Niad and Gustavus about the noise. She found them sitting at the table, nursing drinks poured from a dark bottle.

"Can't sleep?" Niad asked when she looked up at the sound of Lacrael's footsteps.

"There's a strange noise on the other side of the wall," Lacrael said.

"You don't know about the bugs?" Niad said in surprise. She sat her cup down on the table. "Come, I'll show you. It's an interesting, if disgusting, sight."

Niad stood from her seat and moved to the ladder that led to the roof. She scampered up the rungs with the dexterity of someone used to scaling the rigging of a ship. Lacrael followed after, wishing she had half of Niad's grace.

Once on the roof, Niad moved to an edge and peered down toward the forest floor. Curious, Lacrael did the same. At first, she could not figure out what she was looking at. The ground below appeared to be moving.

"Here, this will help," Niad said. She picked up a rag lying at their feet and lit it on a nearby torch. When it was burning brightly, she tossed it over the edge of the roof. It fluttered to the narrow gap of forest floor between the buildings, and the black carpet covering the earth recoiled from the fire with a screech.

Lacrael gasped. Before it died, the flame revealed gigantic insects the size of cats. Their armored shells glinted in the firelight, and huge pincers snapped in anger at the heat. As they scrabbled against the buildings, Lacrael noticed that the three feet of wood nearest the ground were covered with metal.

"Thornhold has to contend with more than just thorns," Niad said with a laugh. She had enjoyed Lacrael's reaction. "Those nasty little bastards are why there are no doors or windows on the ground level. The people that live here call them scabbers. They only come out at night, and they'll eat anything, living or dead. Trust me, you don't want to fall down there."

Both horrified and fascinated at the same time, Lacrael stared down at the insects in awe. She was about to say something when Gustavus's voice floated up out of the hatch to them.

"Damnation, woman, get back down here and finish this bottle with me!"

"He's still upset about Kaiser," Niad said. "I'd best go keep him company. Stay up here as long as you like, just make sure you close and secure the hatch behind you. As far as we know, scabbers can't fly or jump, but we all sleep better knowing they can't get in."

Lacrael nodded, and Niad vanished back down the ladder. The minutes stretched, and when Lacrael was certain she had been standing there longer than an hour, she finally decided to face the anxiety in her heart: she had to confront Brant. She needed to know if she could trust him.

The sound of someone climbing out of the hatch interrupted Lacrael's thoughts.

"I didn't mean to stay up here so long, Niad," Lacrael said. "I'll come down now."

No one answered. Lacrael turned to look toward the hatch and saw Brant standing on the roof at the top of the ladder. He held her amulet in the palm of his hand.

"Brant, we need to—," Lacrael started to say. Her words caught in her throat when Brant stepped forward into the torchlight. His face bore a look of pure torment. His cheeks were wet with tears.

"I'm rotten on the inside," Brant said. "There's a monster wrapped around my soul. I can't control it; I can't even fight it."

Lacrael took a step back. The open air beyond the edge of the rooftop loomed behind her. "You didn't do this to yourself," she said. "It's not your fault."

Brant laughed, the sound filled with pain instead of humor. "That doesn't change what I've become. There's a voice in my head screaming for me to kill you. The only thing that holds it back is this amulet."

"We can fight this," Lacrael said, trying not to let her voice quaver. "If the amulet is able to restrain whatever's inside you, then there's hope. We're not completely helpless."

"I'm dangerous. You should lock me up and leave me here."

"No," Lacrael said vehemently as she shook her head. "I won't leave you behind. If not for me, you'd still be working your shop in Oakroot. Keep the amulet on you, and if the struggle becomes too much for you to bear, come to me. I'll do what I can to help."

Brant stared at the rooftop beneath his feet for a time as he considered Lacrael's words. Finally, he looked up and whispered, "Thank you."

"Don't thank me until we find a way to free you from this curse," Lacrael said. "How much control does the amulet give you? Are you still yourself if I'm holding it?"

"I don't know," Brant said. "But I think we should find out."

Brant stepped forward and offered the dragon pendant to Lacrael. She took from it his hand, letting the amulet dangle from her fingers by its leather thong. Lacrael watched Brant's face. Muscles in Brant's neck twitched. His hands open and closed, but he did not lunge for her.

"I'm still in control," Brant rasped. "But I can feel rage building inside me."

Lacrael decided to take a risk. She needed to know how far she could push Brant. Without warning, she wrapped a fist around the pendant, hiding it from Brant's view.

Brant blinked once and then snarled. His face twisted with inhuman fury, and his hands leapt toward Lacrael's throat.

Lacrael removed her hand from the amulet. Brant froze, his arms still raised to strangle her. As awareness came back to him, so did the shame. His face crumpled as he understood what he had almost done.

"It's better that we know what your limits are," Lacrael said.

Brant only nodded his head in agreement.

"We should get some sleep," Lacrael said, handing the amulet back. "The next few days are going to be rough."

Brant took the pendant from her hand without looking at her. He moved to descend the ladder into the room below. Lacrael followed, and soon they were lying on their cots in the darkness.

Within minutes, Brant's snores echoed off of the crates stacked around them. Lacrael stared into the shadows for a long time. She felt responsible for the horrors Brant had endured. His life as he knew it was over and Lacrael was to blame. She had said the words that she thought Brant needed to hear, but did she believe them? How could she trust him? What if she had to face the evil that lurked inside him?

Lacrael shuddered and tried to push the thought of using her powers against Brant out of her mind. To distract herself, she thought of Kaiser, and she wondered if he was happy to finally be traveling alone.

Chapter 25

KAISER PUSHED HIMSELF HARD and cleared the Wraith Wood in two days. Without Lacrael and Brant slowing him down, he set a brutal pace that even he could not maintain for long. Unlike the eastern road out of Thornhold, the western path bore travelers. Dressed as he was, Kaiser drew looks of open suspicion, and he went out of his way to avoid interacting with anyone.

When he finally reached the edge of the forest, Kaiser breathed easier. The blue sky overhead felt like a long-lost friend. He glanced over his shoulder at the twisted trees of the Wraith Wood, amazed at how oppressive the simple lack of light could be. By now Lacrael, Brant, and Gustavus and his crew should be well on the way to King's Port. Kaiser put his head down and spurred himself to greater speed.

The heavens rotated above Kaiser, night and day unerring in their cycles, oblivious to Kaiser's need for haste. For two days he never stopped except to buy, trade, or steal horses as he was able. On the eve of the second day, the highlands of the central kingdom rose out of the northern horizon. At Kaiser's pace they would take a day to cross, and then he would descend into the great coastal plains. Into Northmark.

Kaiser decided to rest for a few hours on the third night to replenish his strength and give his horse some relief. The altitude of the highlands would sap the beast's stamina if he was not careful. As a full moon rose overhead, he lay beside a fast-running stream and stared up at the starry sky. He tried formulate a plan in his mind for getting into Northmark, but his thoughts kept turning to his family.

In the company of Lacrael and Brant, Kaiser had shown no fear. To show emotion in his world was a sign of weakness that others would exploit in an instant. Now alone, horror threatened to overwhelm Kaiser. In the dark places of his mind, he imagined that his family already suffered, that they looked for his coming to deliver them and he did not appear. Kaiser could see little Saredon's face twisted in pain and confusion as he cried for a father who did not come.

The thought almost made Kaiser leap up and press on through the night, but he steeled himself. He would need his strength if he was to save his family. If he arrived too weak to fight, he would die alongside them. With great effort, Kaiser closed his eyes, emptied his mind, and let sleep take him.

The next thing Kaiser knew, he was sitting at the campfire across from the mysterious stranger. He now wore leather armor, and the scenery had changed to match the sprawling fields of the open kingdom, but the rest of the dream was the same as before.

"Lacrael says she knows who you are," Kaiser said.

"Don't say it," the stranger said, raising a hand to forestall Kaiser. "Speak that name here and all my work is undone."

"You act as if that should concern me."

"What of your wife, or your young son?" the stranger asked. Kaiser could not see his beneath face his hood, but he thought he heard a smile. "Perhaps their hopes aren't so small? Perhaps I chose the wrong champion from the right family."

"The only words I'll have from you on my family is how I can save them," Kaiser growled.

"I'm trying to save *you*, Kaiser," the stranger said, showing anger for the first time. "Even if you deliver your family from the lair of Abimelech, they're still doomed if you don't scrape away the scales covering your eyes. You're the most powerful man amongst powerful men, and this has fostered within you a delusion that you can withstand the whole world! I believed the same once, and all who I loved suffered for it."

"You did this to me!" Kaiser cried. "You brought the enemy down on my head and put my family in danger. Any harm that comes to them will be at your hands—not mine."

"You lack perspective. What you cannot see is that your path always ended in destruction. I've given you a chance."

"Now you want me to believe that you can see the future?"

"I catch only glimpses of what might be, but it doesn't take a prophet to predict that the sheep dwelling amongst wolves will be devoured."

"I'm no sheep," Kaiser said, his voice hard.

Now the stranger smiled broad enough to see. "You only say that because you've never suffered under the fangs of the predator. They've seduced you, tried to make you like them, but at every turn you resisted. Now their patience has worn thin, and you'll see them for what they truly are."

Kaiser did not respond. All he could think about was Parenthia's dragon face and reptilian eyes.

"I've come to warn you," the stranger said. "Slaves of darkness have been loosed from the dungeons beneath Northmark. The cries of suffering that follow in their wake echo across the spirit plane. They're waiting for you in the pass that splits the highlands. If you don't defeat them here, they'll hound your steps all the way to the city.

"Beware the physical forms these golems of shadow and bone wear. The power you wield alone will not destroy them. You must strike at their spirit—you must sunder their souls from the mortal plane. Remember my words. You'll understand when you face them."

Before Kaiser could respond, the stranger rose from where he sat on the other side of the fire.

"I've lingered too long," the stranger said. "Sleep now, and dream no more."

The dream vision faded before Kaiser's eyes, and he slipped into a deep, peaceful slumber. He did not wake until the warmth of the sun touched his face. When Kaiser's eyes opened, he sat bolt upright. He had not intended to sleep through the morning. With a curse, he jumped to his feet and tacked his horse as quickly as he could. Soon they were trotting north once again, as fast as Kaiser dared.

The miles passed beneath the horse's hooves, and Kaiser climbed into the highlands without noticing. Only after midday did the conspicuous lack of travelers on the road penetrate his thoughts. Kaiser slowed the horse's pace, recalling the stranger's warning.

Within the next several miles, the mountains hemmed the road in and the highway split the highland range through a narrow gap carved out of solid rock. A small trading post had been built at the mouth of this passage. If an enemy waited in ambush, Kaiser expected to fight them there.

When the few buildings of the trading post came into sight, Kaiser knew something was wrong. There should have been people moving between the few wooden shacks and two-story inn. He approached to a distance of about a quarter mile, then stopped to consider the scene in front of him.

From his vantage point atop the horse, Kaiser could see corpses scattered on the cold ground between the buildings. Dead bodies did not bother him, but the way these clung to the ground set him on edge.

Kaiser slipped down from the horse's back and crept forward to investigate. With a thought, he summoned the spectral scimitars into his hands. Kaiser stopped by the first corpse he came to—he had never seen so much blood pooled under a single dead body. The way the slain man lay in the grass seemed strange.

Kaiser was a battle-hardened warrior and thought he had seen every horror of war that man could imagine, yet when he flipped the corpse over, he gagged and almost retched. The carcass flopped on the ground like an empty sack of skin.

In fact, as Kaiser looked closer, he concluded that it *was* an empty sack of skin. The dead man's bones had been removed. When Kaiser's eyes fell on the slack, empty face, he yanked his gaze away. He had no desire to discover how an entire skeleton had been separated from the flesh it supported.

THE TENTH REAVER

Disgusted and unnerved, Kaiser moved on. The trading outpost was small. He only counted twenty bodies, but they had all been given the same treatment as the first. A trail of blood led from each corpse to the steps of the inn in the center of the huddled buildings. Kaiser stared at the wooden structure and contemplated his options.

He could make for the pass and try to outrun whatever horror waited inside, but the stranger from his dreams had warned him that this enemy would pursue him all the way to Northmark. Despite his need for haste, something inside Kaiser snarled at the idea of walking away from this travesty. This wholesale slaughter and mutilation of innocent people could not stand. Whoever or whatever had done this needed to die.

With a silent curse to the fate that had led him here, Kaiser stepped toward the inn. He climbed the stairs and pushed the double doors open. In the great room beyond, he found a vision out of hell itself.

The bloody bones of the fallen people outside were stacked in the center of the room. Flies and insects covered the floor of the inn, feasting on the remains. In front of the bone pile, four monsters faced Kaiser. They were human in form only. Instead of skin, their bodies appeared to be made out of black tar. As Kaiser watched, that tar shifted and flowed like mud, revealing gnarled bones beneath.

A gash opened in one of the monster's faces, and words slithered like oil into Kaiser's ears. *"Magussss. We've been waiting for you."*

"You did this?" Kaiser asked in growing horror.

"Yessss. Come, let usss show you."

At this, the four creatures turned and dove into the skeleton pile. The tar of their bodies splashed and dissipated when it struck bone as they sank out of sight, disappearing like water down a drain. For a long moment, nothing happened. Then the heap of discarded skeletons twitched.

Kaiser watched in disbelief as the entire pile rose from the floor. Threads of black tar knit the shifting mass together as it rose to tower over Kaiser's head. The remains of twenty people were reborn as a golem of bone and shadow.

The thing roared and charged at Kaiser. He slashed at the monster with his swords, ethereal blades biting deep, but the golem's bulk smashed into him and sent him flying. He crashed through the doors behind him and rolled to a stop in the yard in front of the inn.

As Kaiser scrambled to his feet, the golem tore into the wall standing between them. He watched in awe as the monster tore oak apart like it was kindling. Bits and pieces of wood stuck to the reanimated bone and were incorporated into the golem.

The golem stepped out of the inn, the roof sagging and collapsing behind it. With another roar, it leapt through the air, bearing down on Kaiser with remarkable speed. He dove out of the way just in time—the two-handed slam that would have flattened him landed harmlessly in the dirt. The ground trembled with the force of the blow.

Kaiser spun on his heels and went on the offensive. He dashed inside the golem's reach, slashing at legs, chest, and arms. He had no idea if the monster had a weak spot. Kaiser's blades severed the black threads holding the thing together, and bones fell away from the unholy construct.

As Kaiser's swords carved it up, the golem roared in frustration. Kaiser jumped back to avoid a flailing arm and then paused as the monster changed its shape. The thing split down the center, and the two pieces sloughed off to form smaller golems. The monsters picked up all the pieces Kaiser had hacked away and absorbed them back into their bodies.

For the first time in his life, Kaiser was at a loss. How the hell was he supposed to beat this thing? The stranger's warning came back to him, but he had no idea how to strike at the monster's soul.

Kaiser backpedaled as the two golems moved to flank him. As he had done in Oakroot, he reached down inside himself and touched the power burning in the core of his being. Raw energy coruscated through his veins. The sky darkened overhead—lightning flashed in the clouds. The golems paused only long enough to glance upward before advancing toward him again.

With a shout, Kaiser unleashed the power overflowing inside him. Jagged bolts of lightning flashed down, impaling the golems and incinerating the very air around them. They collapsed into piles of smoking bone.

As the echo of the lightning strike faded from Kaiser's ears, a garbled laugh rose from the ground. One after the other, the four tar-like monsters sprouted from the fallen bones. They flowed across the earth toward Kaiser, surrounding him before he could react.

Desperate now, Kaiser lashed out with his power a second time. The creatures exploded when lightning touched them, disintegrating into puddles of goop and bone, but when the sky cleared overhead, they rose to fight again.

Kaiser let go of the storm and raised his swords. The next time the monsters attacked, he met them head-on with the ethereal blades. Fighting for his life, Kaiser whirled and danced between his four inhuman opponents. The burning scimitars carved great gashes in the bodies of the creatures, but every grievous wound that Kaiser inflicted repaired itself in a heartbeat.

The golems pressed Kaiser with relentless efficiency. They never stopped moving as they circled and probed his guard, denying Kaiser even a moment's rest. Soon, Kaiser's assault had turned into haggard defense, and it took every bit of focus and ability he possessed to ward off the blows of the enemy.

High overhead, the sun started to sink into the western horizon. Minutes stretched into hours and Kaiser's arms began to burn. For every blow he parried, the next one came perceptibly closer to landing. His breathing became ragged in his chest. One of the creatures lashed out at his head—Kaiser stumbled as he dodged the attack. A gash appeared on the monster's face, and its sinister laugh invaded Kaiser's thoughts. They sensed his weakness. With renewed frenzy, the golems rushed at Kaiser.

Kaiser was at the end of his strength. He tried to spin on his toes, striking out in all directions at once, but the monsters were too fast. One of them hit Kaiser in the legs, another in the shoulder, and he toppled to the ground. Kaiser tried to roll when he hit—the golems held him fast with their sticky tar. Three of the enemy pinned his arms and legs while the fourth stood over him.

"Take hisss bonessss," the creatures said in unison.

As the golem contorted above him, twisting itself into some horrible implement of torture, Kaiser closed his eyes and tried to summon the power inside him. Exhaustion threatened to overwhelm him. He could sense the power within, but he could not grasp it—it slipped through his weary fingers every time he tried to take hold of it.

Kaiser flinched when a sticky substance touched his chest. He did not open his eyes, but he felt the golem flowing over him, molding its body against his. Despair welled up inside Kaiser, and his doomed family filled his vision. Words of apology and love spilled from his lips.

The golems laughed.

With his eyes closed and his gaze turned inward, Kaiser sensed something strange about the laughter. It reverberated in his ears, but it also assaulted his soul. Kaiser latched onto this spiritual assault, following it back to the source. As the golem's viscous flesh crept up Kaiser's neck toward his mouth, he fought for understanding with every bit of strength he had left. Kaiser screamed as something deep inside him woke—he gasped as the spirit plane washed over him. At the same instant, the golem plunged itself into his open mouth.

Kaiser gagged and opened his eyes. He no longer looked on the physical world. The creatures standing over him were no longer monsters of black tar—they were the spirits of men. They stared down at Kaiser with gaunt faces, wisps of blue smoke rising from their transparent bodies. Their faces were contorted in a rictus of hungry anticipation.

Rage filled Kaiser. These were not demons—they were men. With a thought, Kaiser banished the foul spirit consuming his body. The spirit lurched backward, looking down at Kaiser in surprise. Kaiser sucked a deep breath into his chest and roared his fury at the sky. The sound hit the spirits like a tangible force, and they fell away from Kaiser.

Kaiser climbed to his feet. He looked down at his incorporeal body and found the twin scimitars hanging at his waist. With a snarl, he drew the blades and advanced toward the enemy that now cowered before him.

The spirits feared him, but they stood their ground. When Kaiser plunged a sword through the nearest spirit's chest, their attitude changed. The ghost of a man writhed on Kaiser's blade, screaming and flailing before winking out of existence in front of Kaiser's eyes. Kaiser turned to face the remaining three spirits. They looked at him with horror, and as one they turned and fled.

Kaiser stepped after them to give chase, but a flicker of movement from the steps of the inn caused him to stop. Swords up, Kaiser oriented himself toward this new threat. He found the hooded stranger from his dreams walking toward him.

"That was well done," the stranger said, "but you cannot stay here. It's too dangerous. Those things were a nuisance compared to what hunts on this plane."

Before Kaiser could respond, the stranger raised a hand to Kaiser's forehead and the spirit plane receded. Kaiser closed his eyes and shook his head. When he opened them, he looked out on the ruined trading post. He could feel the warmth of the sun on his skin again.

Kaiser trembled. He had never encountered evil like this. What could turn the echo of a man into such a monster? What would possess a spirit to collect the bones of the living? If this was the power of Abimelech, then Lacrael was right: he must be defeated.

The horse was nowhere to be found. Kaiser did not blame the animal for fleeing. With weary steps, Kaiser left the trading post behind. He pulled the hood of his cloak tight and entered the pass. As far as he knew, Kaiser was the last living person in the highlands.

He pressed on toward Northmark, a solitary figure on an empty road, leaving the dead where they lay behind him.

Chapter 26

MARIEL STARED OUT THE window at the rooftops of Northmark spread out beneath her. The suite behind her was fit for a king, but it was still a prison. Parenthia had locked her in one of the highest towers of Castle Vaulkern.

Footsteps echoed in the hallway outside. Parenthia had placed Mariel in an ancient wing of the castle, far from any other occupied room. She alone visited Mariel, personally delivering her food along with hollow gestures of sympathy and reason. It was almost enough to spoil her appetite, but Mariel endured their visits with as much civility as she could manage. She did not doubt that her captivity could be made less pleasant at the foul woman's whim.

The door to Mariel's suite creaked open, the hinges loud from disuse. She sat on the bed with her hands folded in her lap. With one hand, Parenthia pushed the door open and backed inside. She did not bother closing it behind her—there was nowhere for Mariel to run.

"A special treat today," Parenthia said in her best sing-song voice as she sat the platter she carried on the table in the center of the suite. "This is straight from the regent's table."

Without a word, Mariel moved to the table and began to eat. Her movements were mechanical, and she chewed in silence without looking up. Parenthia sat opposite with a dramatic sigh.

"If you talk to me, things will go easier for you."

Mariel gave no indication that she heard.

"We found your children," Parenthia said. Mariel's head snapped up and the repulsive priestess smiled, her veneer of concern unable to conceal her delight. "Did you truly think they would get away? If you help me, I can let you see them."

"You lie."

"I've no reason to lie to you," Parenthia said with a sad shake of her head. "The cooperation I desire from you is for your own sake, not mine. You and I both know that Kaiser will return to Northmark. When he arrives, what happens to your family is up to you."

"You intend to kill him," Mariel said between mouthfuls of food. "You'll get nothing from me."

"Your husband is a magus. Do you understand what that means? I saw him single-handedly cut down two hundred of the kingdom's finest soldiers. You know the man hasn't got a merciful bone in his body—or have you forgotten what he did to your own family? Kaiser is a danger to himself and everyone around him, including you. And there's something I've not told you: he's not alone."

Mariel returned her attention to the food, determined not to give ear to Parenthia's lies.

"There's a second magus, a woman," Parenthia said. "She travels with Kaiser. I saw her with my own eyes. She's young, beautiful, and wields power over fire like you wouldn't believe."

Mariel stopped chewing as Parenthia's words sank in. Then she swallowed her food and said, "Good. Maybe she can burn your horrid cathedral to the ground."

"Damn your foolishness," Parenthia shouted, "I'm trying to help you!"

"You've a funny way of showing it," Mariel said, glancing at the open door behind Parenthia.

Parenthia visibly worked to calm herself. "I'm the only chance you have of survival. Neither of us can change what your husband has become, but I might be able to convince the regent to pardon you and your children."

"Let me see them first."

"You must provide me a gesture of goodwill before the regent will allow that."

"You've taken everything from me and locked me away from the world. What can I possibly give you?"

"Sign a written confession that you do not, and never have, believed in the return of the High King, denounce your husband as a heretic, and partake in the ritual of Abimelech's blood in the public square of the cathedral."

Mariel stared at Parenthia for a long time. The silence stretched, and Parenthia's demands hung in the air between them.

Finally, Mariel said, "I'll never do it."

"I can't guarantee your children won't suffer if you refuse," Parenthia said.

"You don't have them."

Parenthia surged to her feet, her face twisted in fury. She hooked a hand over the back of the wooden chair and hurled at the wall behind her. The chair shattered into splinters against the hard stone.

"I'll burn you on a pyre in the public square!" Parenthia shouted.

"If you hurt me or the children, Kaiser will kill you," Mariel said quietly. "You said yourself that he is without mercy."

Parenthia froze mid-tirade. Mariel's words had been spoken in a meek voice, but they stripped Parenthia of her anger and confidence in an instant. "Your confidence in your husband is misplaced," the priestess snarled. "Abimelech will crush him into dust and sprinkle the ashes of his bones on your grave."

Parenthia turned away before Mariel could respond and stormed from the room. She slammed the door behind her, and Mariel heard the lock click into place with a turn of the key.

Mariel sagged in her chair. She raised trembling hands to her face as tears began to spill down her cheeks. There was not a waking moment that Mariel did not worry about her children.

"Please, Kaiser," Mariel whispered. "We need you."

— —

Mazareem approached Northmark from the east. With Worm at his side, he walked down the middle of the king's highway. Worm suffered, his ragged breathing and exposed wounds enough to stop men staring in their tracks. In his haste, Mazareem had cast aside any attempt at subtlety. Their fellow travelers gave them a wide berth, some going so far as to abandon the road altogether when they came near.

SANDELL WALL

Terror suited Mazareem just fine. He was in a foul mood and inclined to snatch the life out of the next idiot that spoke to him. His head still ached from the failed summoning of Azmon. The trip to Oakroot should have been a simple venture. Left alone, Mazareem could have identified and neutralized the magi without throwing the kingdom into chaos. Now, thanks to Parenthia's incompetence, Mazareem returned to Northmark empty-handed, and the magi were on the run. Apart from dear, sweet Parenthia's death, the whole misadventure had been a waste.

The sinister spires of the Tarragon Cathedral rose into view first, stabbing up from the city like needles arranged on a torturer's table. He could not see Castle Vaulkern from this angle, but the peak of the mountain to the north marked the direction in which the fortress lay.

Mazareem smiled to himself. Of all living souls, he alone could remember a time when the mountain had not looked down on the city. Modern maps had only begun to display it within the last hundred years. If the people who lived within its shadow knew its truth, they would flee Northmark in droves.

When the entrance to the city came into view, Mazareem frowned. A cordon of guards blocked the road, and a queue of travelers waited to be inspected before being allowed into Northmark. No doubt word of the disaster in Oakroot had preceded him.

The last of the long line of travelers looked over their shoulders as Mazareem approached. Glances of curious indifference turned to fear as they scrambled to get out of his way. Soon, Mazareem and Worm stood in front of the squad of soldiers obstructing the road. Their black plate marked them as the regent's personal guard.

"You've got to get to the back of the line," a swarthy sergeant said after giving Mazareem and Worm a once-over. The man's gaze lingered on the wounded hound, but he remained suspiciously and discourteously unimpressed. Three more soldiers moved to stand behind the sergeant.

"Step aside," Mazareem rasped.

The sergeant chuckled. "You might scare the peasants with your act, but you're in Northmark now. You'll follow the regent's law, or you can turn around and slink back to whatever cave you crawled from."

Mazareem lost with little patience he still had. With a snarl, he stepped forward and grabbed the sergeant's helmeted face. His long fingers wrapped around the sides of the man's head. The other three soldiers reached for their weapons.

"Don't move," Mazareem said, the power of the command causing them to freeze.

Lines of frost appeared beneath Mazareem's hand, spreading like frozen spider webs across the sergeant's helmet. Mazareem tightened his grip on the man's head as the power flowed out of him. The sergeant moaned, his armor rattling as his limbs trembled.

"I can drag your lifeless husks to the regent and explain to him how you accosted me on the road, or you can let me pass and save yourselves a great deal of pain," Mazareem said.

"Our apologies," one of the soldiers stammered. "We didn't know you were one of the regent's men. You can pass."

Mazareem released the sergeant. The man fell back, his mouth open in a silent scream. The flesh of his face had turned blue. His companions caught him before he collapsed to the ground.

"Will he survive?" one of the soldiers asked in a panicked voice.

"Men never do," Mazareem said as he stalked into the city.

The cries of confusion and despair faded behind Mazareem when he turned the nearest corner. Regent Trangeth would not be amused, but he should have trained his soldiers to have better manners with weary travelers. Certain weary travelers in particular.

Mazareem made straight for the throne room when he finally reached Castle Vaulkern. As he and Worm passed by the stair that led down into the dungeons, he clicked his tongue and pointed down the dark steps. Worm obeyed without hesitation. The hound knew the way to Mazareem's lair.

The guards outside the throne room made no move to stop Mazareem as he stalked through the open doors. He pulled the hood back from his smooth scalp and strode into the grand room. The empty high throne drew his eye, and Mazareem imagined Rowen's ghost staring down at him.

A soldier stood in front of Regent Trangeth's desk, giving a hurried report. Mazareem crept up to loom behind the man. Regent Trangeth's eyes flicked up to Mazareem's face and then back down to the soldier giving the report. The soldier's voice faded and broke off, then he stepped out of the way.

"I've just been told that a dark stranger killed one of my sergeants and infiltrated the city," Regent Trangeth said.

"Come now, I'm no stranger," Mazareem said with a smile that showed his teeth.

Regent Trangeth dismissed the soldier with a flick of his fingers. With one last terrified glance at Mazareem, the man beat a hasty retreat from the room.

"Do whatever you like to the humans, but the children of Abimelech are *forbidden,*" Regent Trangeth said, his voice shaking with fury.

"I beg a thousand pardons," Mazareem said. "I've such a hard time telling the two apart."

"There will come a time when you no longer hold Abimelech's favor. Pray I'm not alive when it happens, because it's a short fall from your prison to the wights cells."

"Every regent before you has said the same... yet I remain."

"Enough. You're still compelled to serve me, so do your duty. What happened in Oakroot?"

"Parenthia, in her hubris, led the inquisition into an ambush. She fled while a pair of magi slaughtered what remained of her forces and burned Oakroot to the ground. Not only that, but she interrupted my investigation before it could bear fruit. In another day or two, I would have been able to warn her of the danger."

Regent Trangeth waved a hand in annoyance. "I know all of this from Parenthia herself. What have you done in the wake of her failure, or are you as useless as she is?"

Mazareem blinked. "You know this... from Parenthia."

"Yes."

"Because she is already here, working to bungle things even further."

"I'll soon lose my patience if you do not begin telling me things I don't already know," Regent Trangeth said.

The regent's frustration paled in comparison to Mazareem's anger and disappointment. If Trangeth was ready to pardon her failures, Mazareem would have to deal with Parenthia himself. Twelve more years waiting to be summoned to another of her debacles would be an unbearable torment. Trangeth would thank him once she was gone, however much he prized the lives of Abimelech's brood.

"I tracked them as far as the Wraith Wood," Mazareem said, regaining his composure. "I almost took possession of a human that travels with them, but there were... complications. When I left their trail to return here, they were fast approaching Thornhold."

Regent Trangeth absorbed this information in silence. He leaned forward to consult a map unrolled on the desk before him. After a few minutes he said, "Parenthia believes Kaiser will come here. I suspect she's right."

"You speak of her as if her words carry weight," Mazareem said. "Need I remind you that Abimelech doesn't suffer failure?"

"Don't you *dare* presume to speak to me of Abimelech," Regent Trangeth said, his voice deadly quiet. "You're a man's corpse, nothing but dead flesh held together by power you cannot understand. I was born with Abimelech's blood in my veins. You lap up what precious scraps you're given, just like your hound."

"And yet you hesitate to do Abimelech's will," Mazareem said, not flinching from the regent's murderous gaze. He wondered if he would have to kill him as well. Trangeth would not be the first regent to fall by Mazareem's hand.

To his credit, Regent Trangeth realized the danger before it was too late and backed away from the confrontation. "I've little love for her, but Parenthia has grown powerful, and it's not as simple as ordering her execution. That damned priesthood of hers would incite the city to riot and storm the castle. Northmark already teeters on the precipice of chaos. They're calling Pellathor's wife a martyr in the streets."

"Give me military command of Northmark and I'll subdue the city, take care of Parenthia, and solve your magus problem in one stroke," Mazareem said. "That's why you keep me locked up below this castle after all: to solve your problems."

Regent Trangeth's eyes widened at the suggestion, and Mazareem waited for him to work out the implications and consequences of such a drastic move. "You're a bound servant of Abimelech," the regent said, thinking out loud. "If he permits you to chastise his child for her mistakes, it is not for us to question his will."

"His wisdom is unfailing," Mazareem said, bowing his head piously.

"So be it," Regent Trangeth said with a nod. He removed the golden signet from his finger and held it out across the desk. "Take this ring. With it, you will command Northmark's forces in my name. When you've taken care of Parenthia and the magus threat, you'll return it to me at once."

"As you wish," Mazareem said, smiling as he slipped the heavy golden ring onto one of his long fingers.

Mazareem turned and left the throne room without another word. The wheels of his mind were already turning. He would set his plans in motion as soon as possible, but first he needed to visit his hidden sanctuary. Mazareem followed after Worm as he descended the dark stairs into the bowels of Castle Vaulkern.

Worm was lying in the first room, his huge head resting on his front paws. The hound was so tired that he did not even raise his head when Mazareem entered.

"I'll tend to you in a moment, boy," Mazareem murmured to the animal as he moved through the first room and into the second.

After an excursion to the outside world, Mazareem always returned in a weakened state.

The smaller room of the prison suite contained hundreds of books and the peculiar oddities Mazareem had collected over a thousand years of occasional exploration. In the corner of the room, a stone font had been carved out of the wall. Black liquid dripped from a small hole in the rock to collect in the font's basin. The deep bowl was almost filled to overflowing.

With shaking hands, Mazareem dipped a cup into the dark liquid and then drew it to his lips. The vile concoction slid down his throat and into his belly. He gasped and placed a hand on the wall to steady himself as the familiar fire burned through his veins. When his trembling stopped, Mazareem refilled the cup and retraced his steps to the main room.

Mazareem knelt at Worm's side and placed the cup beneath the hound's nose. The exhausted dog lapped up the concoction, and Mazareem stroked the his head while he waited.

"It seems we've the luxury of a reasonable overseer," Mazareem said. "But for the first time in a millennium, the fates are moving. I've lived long enough to learn that change brings opportunity, and nothing is permanent. I'll not be the slave of god or king."

Worm leaned into Mazareem's hand in appreciation of the affection.

"You and I were meant for greater things than this, boy. When the time is right, we'll reclaim our freedom."

Taken by sudden inspiration, Mazareem got to his feet and moved into his studio. He stared at the canvas for a long time, contemplating the lines of her face and the color of her hair. With a smile, Mazareem reached for the brush resting on the easel.

Chapter 27

LACRAEL SLUMPED IN THE saddle as her horse clopped down the road to King's Port. Brant rode alongside her, looking as awkward in the saddle as she felt. Gustavus, Niad, and Parnick trotted ahead of them. They had been traveling hard for two days, but it seemed like a casual stroll after the brutal pace Kaiser had imposed. Gustavus had picked up horses at the first stable they encountered outside the Wraith Wood.

Despite Lacrael's persistent attempts to reach Brant, he refused to talk. He had withdrawn into himself after Thornhold. He rose with the dawn and rode at her side without saying a word. When he collapsed to the earth at night, he rolled over with his back to her. Lacrael knew he suffered, but she could think of no way to help him. She missed the clumsy, awkward merchant from Oakroot. In her heart, Lacrael feared that the old Brant might be gone forever.

They left the Wraith Wood behind, and Lacrael wondered at the open plains stretching out before them. She knew only the harsh desert wasteland of her homeland and the shadowy confines of the Nogard Forest. As the kingdom finally cast off the last vestiges of winter, the rolling hills exploded in a vibrant sea of colors. Her mind struggled to accept that so many flowers could exist in one place.

"If I never see a forest again, it'll be too soon," Lacrael said as they made their way through the plains.

Niad glanced over her shoulder. "It's a marvel, isn't it? You've got to see it to believe it."

"What would these people think if they could see Vaul?" Lacrael asked. Niad was the first person she'd met from her realm since her grandfather had sent her through the portal four years ago. Lacrael hoped that finding her was an omen that they still held true to Garlang's quest.

"Bah," said Niad, "they'd never believe it. They're spoiled. They don't appreciate how easy their lives are here, or how much they have to lose."

"On the contrary," said Gustavus. "If I wasn't afraid that this world would sink so low as to spawn more like Niad, I'd sell the lot of you for a clipped silver and enjoy what peace and quiet I could."

Niad took her cue and began to sing a bawdy sea shanty. Parnick joined in, somewhat to Lacrael's surprise, and then Gustavus in spite of himself. Lacrael had to admit that they made for cheerier company than Kaiser. Or Brant, of late.

King's Port appeared on the horizon at noon. The sun hung directly overhead, its rays beating down on the distant rooftops. Beyond the port town, Lacrael got her first glimpse of the sea. She stared in wonder at the immensity of the endless blue expanse. They were going to sail across that?

"The ocean's as big as a desert!" Lacrael blurted.

Gustavus laughed. "It's just as deadly, too. That water might look refreshing, but you can't drink it. The sun will bake you on those rolling waves just as easily as if they were dunes."

As they neared the city, a change came over Gustavus, Niad, and Parnick. Their casual banter and singing stopped. The three sailors checked their weapons, made sure packs were secure, and conferred quietly amongst themselves. Once they had reached a decision, Gustavus turned to Lacrael and Brant.

"We've little reason to expect trouble in the city, but it's best to be prepared," Gustavus said. "There are several miles of streets between us and the docks. The *Golden Dawn* should be waiting for us, but we've got to reach her without attracting attention to ourselves. If we're questioned, here's the story: we ventured inland to find new crew. We're returning to our ship with the two of you."

Lacrael nodded, but Brant did not respond.

"Is he going to be more trouble than he's worth?" Gustavus asked, glaring at Brant.

"I'll make sure he cooperates," Lacrael said.

Gustavus held Brant's gaze for a long minute before turning away. "See that you do," he said over his shoulder.

The highway into King's Port was a gruesome spectacle. Gibbets and suspended cages lined the road into the outskirts of the city. Lacrael peered into each cage they passed, horrified fascination riveting her. Most held rotting skeletons, but a few of the pitiful prisoners still lived.

Lacrael's heart hurt for them. These people had been strung up and left to die. Too weak to beg for mercy, their eyes pleaded for salvation instead. Lacrael finally looked away when her gaze fell on an emaciated woman that looked to be her own age.

"There are so many," Lacrael said, keeping her voice low as they passed between the rows of cages on each side of the road. "Are they all criminals?"

"They've not broken a single damned law," Gustavus said, his voice savage. "The priesthood strings them up on the slightest suspicion of heresy."

Gustavus flicked his reins and trotted into the city without a glance at the cages. Disturbed and unable to look away, Lacrael followed at a slower pace. Before they disappeared into the maze of streets, she glanced back. Every prisoner with the strength to raise their head was watching Lacrael. She shuddered and turned away.

Even to Lacrael's inexperienced eye, King's Port seemed like it should have been a bustling, cheerful city. Constructed from white stone, and topped with patterned roofs of wood from the nearby forest, the buildings looked like something out of a fairy tale. Cobblestones paved the streets, and wrought iron lampposts decorated every corner. And yet a pall hung over the city.

Gustavus ordered them to dismount at a stable by the road. They turned over their horses and proceeded into the city on foot. The few citizens that Lacrael spotted going about their business were furtive and wary. Instead of the sounds of children playing or the noises of industry and commerce, they were met with silence as they passed between the quiet buildings. Every door was shut and every window barred. Lacrael felt conspicuous—there was no way their passing went unnoticed.

As if sharing Lacrael's assessment, Gustavus picked up his pace. His long coat slapped against the backs of his boots as he lengthened his stride. No one spoke, but Larcrael guessed that Gustavus intentionally avoided the busiest streets. More than once, he ducked into a narrow alleyway and they had to walk single-file to follow him.

Finally, they stepped out from between two towering warehouses and onto the wharf that led to the docks. Lacrael stumbled when the harbor full of ships came into view. Their masts rose into the sky like a forest stripped bare by the winter. The rest of the city might be as silent as a graveyard, but here people were hard at work. Great storehouses lined the docks, and a steady stream of cargo moved between their dark warrens and the holds of the ships that bobbed in the water.

"Blast it all," Gustavus said, adding a few more colorful curses under his breath.

Lacrael tore her gaze from the activity on the docks to find out what had upset Gustavus. She followed his gaze and found a squad of soldiers patrolling along the wharf. A man dressed in rich clothes strolled lazily in front of them. Spotting Gustavus, he changed course and headed in their direction.

"Can you melt them with your fire?" Gustavus asked Lacrael.

Lacrael blanched, unable to tell if Gustavus was serious. "Since Oakroot, I can't really control more than a small flame. I might destroy the entire harbor if I tried."

"I'd pay to see that," Gustavus muttered. "Forget I said anything. Let me do the talking."

Lacrael stood silent and patient as the soldiers approached. When they stopped in front of Gustavus, the man at their head inspected each member of their party in turn. His eyes lingered on Lacrael. She fidgeted under his gaze. Finally, he returned his attention to Gustavus.

"Fine afternoon for a stroll, Captain Gustavus," the man said.

"What do you want, Chasius?" Gustavus asked. "You've been paid three times over. Get out of my way."

"I'm afraid it's not that simple anymore," Chasius said. "Times are changing. The regent is tightening his grip on King's Port. I cannot allow one of the kingdom's greatest criminals to come and go from my harbor!"

"I'll double your normal rate," Gustavus said.

Chasius blinked.

"Triple," Gustavus said.

Chasius smiled and held up four fingers.

"I'll sail away with an empty hold if I pay you that much," Gustavus said.

Chasius shrugged and held out his upturned hands. "That's not my problem."

"After this, our arrangement is over," Gustavus said. "Send someone to the ship to collect within the hour. I sail with the tide."

Gustavus moved to walk past Chasius and the soldiers, but the man stopped him with a raised hand.

"Our… relationship has been profitable for me, so I'll do you one last favor," Chasius said. "I have one of your crew in lockup. He drank more than he could handle and roughed up a local wench. Come with me and I'll turn him over to you."

"How charitable of you," Gustavus growled. He waved for the rest of them to follow after Chasius.

Lacrael walked along the wharf, awestruck by the towering ships and the bustle of activity. Chasius led them to an official building on the side of the docks. At a command from Chasius, the squad of soldiers waited outside.

Inside the building, Lacrael found a stout counter facing the door. Behind this counter, a wall covered with shelves and slots was filled with parchment and books.

"Just this way," Chasius said, indicating a long hallway.

Chasius stepped through an open door at the end of the hall. Lacrael followed close behind Gustavus, and she almost ran into his back when he stopped short.

"You traitorous bastard," Gustavus said.

Chasius stood in the center of the room next to a man in dark armor. The man wore a black cloak and his helm grinned at them, the face of a demon wrought in silver metal. His hands rested on the hilt of a greatsword, its point digging into the floorboards beneath his feet.

Around the perimeter of the room, a squad of soldiers waited with weapons drawn. Brant, Niad, and Parnick stumbling to a halt behind Lacrael when they saw.

"Reaver!" Niad cried, her hand reaching for her sword.

"No!" Gustavus rumbled, his hand raised to stop Niad from drawing her weapon.

Niad froze. No one else moved. They were outnumbered four to one.

"I'm not accustomed to being called 'traitor' by outlaws and smugglers," Chasius said into the silence. "Let alone murderers."

"I've made you a rich man, and this is how you repay me?" Gustavus said.

"They came seeking the... man you killed," Chasius said. "What did you expect me to do? There's not enough wealth in the world to convince me to lie to a reaver. They've given me a full pardon for luring you here. I do apologize. I'm afraid things are about to become very unpleasant for you."

Chasius turned and strolled away, making to exit the room by a different door. He paused on the threshold and said, "Don't worry about the *Golden Dawn*. I'll handpick her next captain myself. She'll be in good hands."

When Chasius had gone, the reaver's deep voice thundered from behind his helmet. "Gustavus, you are under arrest for the murder of an agent of the regent, for treason, and for heresy. You will throw down your weapons and come with me. The only other option is suffering."

Instinctively, Lacrael touched the fire that burned at the core of her being. She could incinerate the reaver and his soldiers with a wave of her hand. Yet since Oakroot, Lacrael could not bring herself to trust in her power. Even in full control, once she began, she might have burned the entire building down and her friends with it.

There was only one way out. Lacrael turned to bury her face in Brant's chest. He stiffened beneath her touch. She raised her face to look into his eyes.

"I need you, Brant," Lacrael murmured. She pressed her mouth to his, at the same time wrapping her arms around his neck. While Brant recovered from the shock of being kissed, Lacrael untied the knot in the thong on the back of his neck. When she had worked it loose, Lacrael pulled back and held her face close to his.

"I need you to kill them all," Lacrael said. In one swift motion, she yanked the dragon amulet from beneath Brant's shirt, spun behind him, and shoved him toward the reaver.

In the space of three steps, Brant transformed into a juggernaut. He roared as he charged. Gustavus, Niad, and Parnick were caught flat-footed. They drew their weapons and backpedaled as Brant bore down on the reaver.

The reaver never hesitated. He hefted his greatsword, bringing it to bear in a devastating two-handed swing that should have cut Brant in half. Brant swatted the blade aside as if it were a toy. He slammed a fist into the reaver's helmet—metal crunched and the reaver went flying backward.

Along the sides of the room, the soldiers recovered from their surprise and rushed at Brant. He met their charge head-on. Brant danced through their midst, moving so fast that Lacrael had trouble tracking him. He never picked up a weapon, instead snapping necks and tearing arms out of their sockets.

One soldier leapt onto Brant's back. Brant reached over his head, wrapped his fingers around the soldier's neck, and with a mighty heave, flung him across the room to smash into the far wall.

Twenty soldiers quickly became ten, and soon only two remained standing before Brant. He reached out, grasping a head in each hand, and slammed the helmets of the last two soldiers together. Armor crumpled, and they dropped to the floor like stones. Blood covered the floor and splattered the walls. The dead and dying lay at Brant's feet.

"By the black depths, what is he?" Gustavus asked in a quiet voice.

Lacrael stepped forward, the dragon amulet dangling from her hand.

"Brant, come to me," Lacrael commanded.

Brant looked at her. He grinned through the blood that covered his face. That grin sent a spike of fear through her heart. Lacrael forced herself to take another step toward him.

"That's a pretty trinket," Brant said in a voice that was not his own.

Lacrael started to worry that he would not come back to himself, but when she took the last step to stand before him, his shoulders slumped. Brant looked at her in horror.

"What did you make me do?" he whispered.

"You saved our lives," Lacrael said. She handed the amulet back to Brant.

Brant looked at the dead and broken men scattered around the room. He raised his hands in front of his face—they were crimson. Without warning, he bent over at the waist and puked on the floor. While Brant retched, hands on his knees, Gustavus moved to Lacrael's side.

"You're going to explain what the hell just happened, but right now we have to get to the ship," Gustavus said.

Lacrael nodded. "What about your imprisoned crewman?" she asked.

"That was a lie that I should've seen through," Gustavus said. "None of my crew would do something so stupid."

Before leaving the room, Gustavus went to inspect the fallen reaver.

"You don't attack a reaver and leave him behind without making sure he's dead," Gustavus said. He felt for a pulse, and finding none, pulled his hand back with a low whistle. "Knocked dead with one punch. Never thought I'd see a thing like that."

Lacrael placed a hand on Brant's back. "Can you walk?" she asked.

Brant straightened and wiped his mouth with the back of his hand. "I can manage," he said.

Once they were outside, Gustavus stomped down the dock, and Lacrael and Brant had to jog to keep up. Niad and Parnick seemed to anticipate Gustavus's movements—they never had any trouble staying at his side.

They circled the harbor, staying clear of the frenzy of activity at the center of the docks. On the far northern side of the quay, a ship floated at the end of a single long jetty. Lacrael had not seen a ship before today, but after one glance, she knew that Gustavus's vessel was a craft of incomparable beauty.

Compared to the crude, clumsy ships that floated in the center of the harbor, Gustavus's vessel kissed the sea like an arrow waiting to be shot from a bow. Its aggressive lines were nothing like the boxy tubs from which mountains of cargo were being removed. Lacrael felt an instant kinship with the ship, and she wanted to learn everything about it. For now, she contented herself with gazing at the ship in admiration.

Gustavus, Niad, and Parnick all hiked up the gangway without hesitation. Lacrael paused at the edge of the dock. She looked down into the dark water lapping against the pylons of the pier. There had never been any reason for her to learn to swim and being unable to see the bottom of the harbor gave her a sinking feeling in the pit of her stomach.

On the far side of the harbor, a cry went up, and people started running toward the harbormaster's office.

Niad's head appeared over the rail of the ship above them. "It appears your friend's handiwork has been discovered," she said. "Do you need help getting aboard?"

Lacrael's face turned red at the thought. After prodding Brant to go ahead of her, she stepped onto the gangplank and climbed aboard the *Golden Dawn*. Niad led them across the deck to the door of the captain's cabin. She stepped aside to let them enter and then followed them into the room.

Gustavus waited for them in front of a great wooden desk. Without his greatcoat on, his loose, flowing shirt did little to hide his impressive physique.

"I'd hoped to find Chasius on board," Gustavus said. "That's a score I'll have to settle another day. The two of you will stay in this cabin until we sail from the Haverfell coast. I trust every member of my crew with my life, but only Niad and Parnick the truth of what we're about. It's better for everyone involved if it stays that way until this insanity is over."

Lacrael and Brant nodded.

Gustavus raised an eyebrow at Brant's response. "So he's not gone out of his mind after all. Where did you learn to fight like that? I've never seen anything like it."

"I'm sorry," Brant said, stumbling over his words. "I don't mean to be any trouble."

"You slaughtered a reaver and twenty men *barehanded*, and you want to apologize?" Gustavus asked, shaking his head. "As long as you're aboard my ship, you'll wear irons. Do you have a problem with that?"

Brant hung his head. "No."

Niad stepped up behind Brant and clapped his wrists in iron chains.

"What is he?" Gustavus asked Lacrael. "You had best give me a damned good reason to not fill his pants with cannon shot and toss him into the sea."

"He's cursed, somehow," Lacrael said, struggling to explain. "We lost track of him for a night in the Wraith Wood. When we found him the following morning, he was like this. A man named Mazareem did this to him. Only the dragon amulet keeps him sane."

"Mazareem...," Gustavus said, a faraway look in his eye. "I know that name. He'd best get comfortable in those manacles. We need to cast off. I'll return to the cabin once we're underway. Until then, stay quiet and stay out of sight."

What that, Gustavus and Niad left them alone in the captain's cabin. Brant slumped to the floor, and Lacrael knew she should go to him, but she could not resist watching the crew make the *Golden Dawn* ready to sail. She peered through the small window that looked out on the deck. Men and women scrambled up the rigging to unfurl sails. Lacrael gasped when the sunlight struck the sails — they were *gold!* They reflected the light with a brilliant yellow sheen.

From somewhere over Lacrael's head, Gustavus's voice roared out a command, and the ship began to drift out to sea. The sails snapped against their restraints, filling with wind and propelling the vessel forward. Her view was limited through the little window, but Lacrael saw the edges of the harbor come and go as they made for the open sea.

Lacrael was so entranced by the sight of the ocean that she leapt back in surprise when the door to the cabin swung open. Sunlight silhouetted Gustavus's huge form for an instant before he closed the door behind him.

"We got out just in time," Gustavus said. "The harbor is swarming behind us. No doubt Chasius will pin the slaughter on us the first chance he gets. He may live to regret his choices before this is done. The regent will be far less forgiving after the murder of a reaver."

Gustavus slapped the inner hull that formed one of the walls of the cabin. "This is a Praxian ship. There's nothing else like her in these seas. Everyone who lays eyes on the *Golden Dawn* knows her. We'll have to disguise her to sail into Northmark."

Before Lacrael could ask how to disguise a ship, the door swung open again and Niad and Parnick entered the room. Lacrael and Brant were forgotten as the captain and his lieutenants planned out their route to Northmark. Lacrael listened and tried to make sense of it, but she struggled to understand the unfamiliar nautical terms they used. After a time, Gustavus, Niad, and Parnick exited the cabin to set their plans into motion.

Lacrael and Brant ate when food was brought, and slept when they got tired, but for the most part they sat and waited. Gustavus did not spend much time in the cabin, and when he did, he did not want to be bothered. Lacrael watched him consult charts and maps, and she longed to ask him what they meant, but she dared not ask.

On the second day at sea, the *Golden Dawn* dropped her anchor in a hidden cove on a stretch of uninhabited coast. Lacrael overheard Gustavus and Niad arguing about whether the location was safe. Outside the little window, Lacrael watched as the crew climbed all over the ship in a flurry of activity. When they were finished several hours later, the ship had been transformed.

The golden sails had been replaced with standard white canvas. The crew removed the smallest mast and laid it lengthwise on the deck, covering it with stacks of crates and half-filled sacks. Lacrael had seen great planks of wood come out of the hold go over the side of the ship, and the pounding of hammers had reverberated through the hull for a solid hour. From her vantage point within the cabin, the ship no longer looked like the *Golden Dawn*. Lacrael could only imagine what it looked like from a distance.

When the disguise was complete, Gustavus entered the cabin. Without a word, he moved to his giant desk, put his shoulder against it, and pushed it across the floor. He grunted with the effort, but the massive piece of furniture slid aside to reveal a hatch beneath.

Gustavus lifted the hatch and stood to look at Lacrael and Brant. "We'll reach Northmark by sunset," he said. "The ship should avoid suspicion, but I'm worried they'll want to inspect us. You'll be safe in here. I'll join you when we're near the port. I can't risk being recognized up on deck."

"Who will captain the ship?" Lacrael asked.

Gustavus scowled. "Niad. Best not to dwell on that part."

Lacrael and Brant got to their feet and went to stand by the hatch. A ladder descended into the belly of the ship.

"There's a fully furnished room down there, with beds and a head," Gustavus said. "It's no prison. We use it to smuggle people out of danger. They pay better than you."

Brant went first. The chains of his manacles clattered against the wooden rungs of the ladder. Lacrael followed after. At the bottom of the ladder, she found a cramped room just big enough for her and Brant to move about. The only light came from the open hatch overhead. Six cots were bolted to the inner hull of the ship, one on top of the other. She could hear the gurgle of water through a hole in the floor at the back of the tiny room. If that was the toilet, Lacrael decided that she would not pee for a day or two.

"It's kind of cozy," Brant said. He sat on one of the lowest cots, and his weight caused it to creak.

"Yeah, cozy like a coffin," Lacrael muttered. "I'll be glad when this is over. I'm tired of hiding."

Lacrael sat opposite Brant and looked across the cramped space at him. He would not meet her gaze. Lacrael knew they needed to talk, but she did not know where to start. For now, it was easier to just say nothing.

Gustavus joined them several hours later. He brought a sack of food and a lantern with him. When he reached the bottom of the ladder, the hatch overhead was sealed. Gustavus dropped the sack on the floor and hung the lantern from a hook on the wall.

"It's in Niad's hands now, gods be good," Gustavus said. "Let's hope Kaiser appears on time, or this is all for nothing."

Chapter 28

KAISER GAZED UPON NORTHMARK with disgust. The city boiled out of the landscape like a putrid scab on diseased flesh. The horrors of the last few days had confirmed the suspicions that had been growing in Kaiser's heart for years: Haverfell was rotting from within. Northmark was the source of the corruption. From here, the infection spread throughout the kingdom like a plague. And Kaiser's family was in the thick of it.

He rehearsed the plan in his mind as he covered the last few miles to the capital. The most Kaiser could hope for was that Parenthia had slaughtered his personal guard but kept his family hostage. His first task was finding out what had happened in his absence and where his wife and children were being held. The only person he could safely ask was Ursais. Kaiser had no idea how to find the old man, but he had to try.

On the outskirts of the city, Kaiser encountered a long queue of travelers waiting to be admitted. A squad of bored soldiers blocked the road. Kaiser sucked in his breath. The soldiers wore the black plate of the regent's personal guard and inhuman faces. They were dragon spawn, like Parenthia.

Panic surged in Kaiser's chest. Could they detect that he was a magus? He scanned the surrounding buildings, but did not see any signs of an ambush. The soldiers seemed oblivious to Kaiser's presence, so he decided to wait patiently in line. When a soldier finally waved him forward, Kaiser did his best not to flinch away from the creature's scaly face.

The soldier looked Kaiser up and down. "That's a fancy getup. What's your purpose in Northmark?"

"I'm here looking for work," Kaiser said, using the first excuse that popped into his head.

"You picked an odd time to come looking for a job. I'll need your weapons before you can enter. We're confiscating all blades on the regent's orders."

Kaiser loosened the scabbard on his waist and handed it to the soldier. Despite himself, his gaze lingered on the dragon spawn's face. From this close, the creature truly was monstrous. Yellow eyes with dark slits for pupils looked out of a face covered in black scales. Wicked teeth lined a wide, red mouth.

The creature narrowed its serpentine eyes. "Is there a problem?"

"No, of course not," Kaiser said, shaking himself.

"Move along then," the soldier said. "Hail Abimelech, and don't forget the festivities at the cathedral later today."

Kaiser entered Northmark, leaving the soldier behind. If Parenthia was holding an event at the cathedral later, she would be distracted. Perhaps he could use that to his advantage. First he had to find Ursais. The beggar had always accosted Kaiser near the castle, so he made for Castle Vaulkern.

As he strode through the streets of the city, Kaiser sensed that something was wrong. He had lived in Northmark for most of his life, and he had survived by keeping his finger on the pulse of the city and its people. Before he left with the inquisition, the citizens had been downtrodden but stolid. Now there seemed to be an undercurrent of imminent violence everywhere Kaiser looked.

The streets were no less crowded than he remembered, but the people huddled together in small groups. When Kaiser neared, they faced him with open hostility, not turning to speak to each other again until he was well beyond earshot. Even the beggars and gutter rats watched him with contempt.

Now that he was paying attention to the signs, Kaiser started to notice smashed windows and gutted buildings. It seemed to be completely random. One house in a row of ten would be destroyed, and on the next street, every house had been broken open and looted. Where were the families that had lived in these homes? What had incited the people to violence?

A small voice in his mind whispered Mariel's fear: that this was the effect of the mass consumption of Abimelech's blood. Kaiser shook his head to dispel the thought. Whatever the cause, Kaiser did not care. All that mattered was getting his family out alive. Once they were safe, Northmark could tear itself apart.

Kaiser reached the castle district and executed a thorough search of Ursais's usual haunts. The avenues between the stone houses of Northmark's wealthy were deserted. He covered every street twice, but saw no hint of the old man. Frustrated, Kaiser paused on the corner of an intersection. If he lingered in the district any longer, he was going to draw attention to himself. Better to enter a local tavern and ask if anyone had seen the old beggar.

Unaccustomed to frequenting such places, Kaiser chose a tavern at random. The moment he stepped into the dark room, he knew he had made a mistake. At this time of day the place was empty, save for a barkeeper covered in greasy black hair. He looked up from the back as Kaiser turned on his heel to leave.

"Don't be shy! Come in, be welcome. We're open, and I've got plenty of ale."

Annoyed with himself, but having no better options, Kaiser turned back to the owner of the tavern.

"Come, have a seat," the man said, pulling a chair out from a table. Kaiser sat as the man moved to the back of the room to draw two tankards from a keg of ale. When he returned to the table, he plunked one down in front of Kaiser and sat down at the same table.

"First one's on the house," the owner said. "My name's Pilk, proud owner and operator of the Pig Tickler."

Kaiser eyed the dirty tankard and the smelly tavern owner with distaste.

"Tis a bleedin' shame what's happening out there," Pilk said, oblivious to Kaiser's reservations. "I've not had more than two customers in here at once since the riots started."

"They've been bad?" Kaiser asked.

"Oh, aye. Ever since the priesthood declared a culling on all heresy, the city's been on the verge of war. I'm sure you've heard. Anyone who refuses to drink the blood of Abimelech is open game. Their possessions, their homes, even their women are free for the taking if you can rouse a big enough mob."

Pilk's words hit Kaiser like a punch in the gut. Without thinking about it, he lifted the tankard and took a long drink of the sour ale. He was hardly bothered by the foul taste.

"Can't say that I've not been tempted to join in," Pilk said. "Why shouldn't I profit some when everyone else is divvying up the loot? But then I see the face of my blessed mother. She would never have taken the cup."

With a grunt, Pilk tilted back his flagon and drained the last of his ale, then slammed the empty stein on the table with a loud thud. He followed this performance with a tremendous belch.

"I'm surprised to find anyone in my tavern on this afternoon," Pilk said when the echo of his burp had faded. "Everyone I know has gone to the execution. I've never had the stomach for a public bloodletting."

"Who's being executed?" Kaiser asked, raising the tankard to his lips for another drink and trying to decide when to ask about Ursais.

"The wife of the Tenth Reaver," Pilk said. "They've had her strung up in the cathedral courtyard for—"

Kaiser's tankard slipped through numb fingers, smashing to the floor and interrupting the man.

Pilk jerked back in his chair. "By the teats of a dragon, you scared the hair off my toes!" he said when he recovered. He squinted at Kaiser through the gloom. "Are you unwell?"

"You said the execution is happening at the cathedral?" Kaiser asked, his voice rasping in his throat.

"Well, yes, but it's probably over by now," Pilk said. He opened his mouth to say something else, but Kaiser was already halfway to the door.

Kaiser almost crashed into the door jamb as he raced from the tavern. Pilk's surprised voice rang out behind him. Kaiser's feet hit the cobblestone street outside, and he turned himself toward the distant cathedral. The spires of the Tarragon Cathedral were visible over the tops of the city buildings, but it was still several miles away.

Kaiser lowered his head and charged through the streets of Northmark. He pushed his body to the edge of physical ability, throwing himself into every stride, every footfall. After half a mile, his calves burned. He called on a lifetime of training and exercise, demanding that his legs go faster with every heartbeat. The roads were almost empty, but the few people who witnessed his mad dash stopped and stared.

With the image of Mariel tied to a stake spurring him on, Kaiser covered the few miles to the cathedral in mere minutes. If Parenthia had Mariel that meant she must have the children too. Kaiser was out of options. He would storm the cathedral and rescue his family, fight his way through Northmark to the docks, and hope that they found the *Golden Dawn* waiting.

When Kaiser neared the cathedral, he barreled around a street corner and came to an abrupt stop. A squad of five soldiers blocked the road. He recognized the spiked helm of the Fifth Reaver. Kaiser swore under his breath—the reaver had seen him running and was moving to intercept him. He prepared his mind for killing and stepped toward the soldiers.

"Where are you headed in such a hurry?" a soldier asked.

"I'm just going to join the crowd," Kaiser said without slowing. He nodded at the large mob he could see at the far end of the street. A wall of people blocked the road. Their backs were turned to the empty street, every neck straining to look into the open square in front of the cathedral.

"Not without answering my questions, you're not," the soldier said, raising an armored hand to stop Kaiser in his tracks. The Fifth Reaver watched the confrontation in silence.

Kaiser spun around the soldier's arm and summoned his spectral weapons at the same time. He twirled the swords in his hands, lashing out to the left and right. The transparent blades sliced through armor, flesh, and bone. One soldier died in an instant, Kaiser's strike separating head from neck—the second fell away with a garbled cry, blood seeping through a gash in his breastplate.

The remaining soldiers drew their weapons and faced Kaiser in the street. Their eyes flicked down to his burning blades and back up to his face. The Fifth Reaver stepped forward, hefting shield and battleaxe.

"Get out of my way," Kaiser snarled.

Two of the soldiers faltered, lowering their weapons, but the Fifth Reaver lunged forward with a cry, committing them to the fight. Despite the fear on their faces, the soldiers raised their blades and fanned out to surround Kaiser.

The reaver advanced on Kaiser with his shield raised. With a few quick slashes, Kaiser carved the sides of the shield away with the smoking edges of his swords. Nothing remained but the metal boss. The reaver tossed the ruined shield aside, but he did not waver. Under different circumstances, Kaiser would have applauded the man's courage—now he only wanted the reaver to die.

With a shout, the reaver aimed a chop at Kaiser's chest, the attack intended to drive him back into the blades of his comrades. Kaiser stepped into the blow, allowing the tempered steel axehead to whisper past his body. Kaiser looked into the reaver's eyes as he plunged one of the ethereal swords into his chest. The breath went out of the reaver with a pitiful gasp, and he dropped to the street in a clatter.

As the reaver fell, Kaiser ducked low and spun backward, anticipating a strike from behind. He lashed out to his left, using his momentum to carry him out of harm's way. Blades seeking his flesh stabbed at the air. Kaiser's blind strike caught one of the soldiers above the knee, severing the leg clean off.

Kaiser rose from his crouch, twin swords at the ready. He faced the final soldier. At his feet, the wounded man's cries echoed off the surrounding buildings. One of Kaiser's weapons flashed down, silencing him forever. The surviving soldier flinched and took a step back.

"Run or die," Kaiser said, "I don't care which."

The soldier dropped his sword and shield and sprinted away down the street. Kaiser let his glowing scimitars vanish into thin air. No one seemed to have noticed the skirmish yet. Every eye was turned toward the events unfolding in the square before the cathedral.

Kaiser stepped over the dead men in the street without a second glance. Dread gripped his heart as he moved toward the back of the crowd. He briefly contemplated tearing into the mob with his spectral blades, but discarded the idea immediately. He would never get his family to safety if he had to fight off the entire city.

From his vantage point at the end of the street, Kaiser could not see a thing over the heads of the crowd. He slipped into the throng, pushing aside anyone who would not give way. A few angry faces turned toward him, but their curses died on their lips when they looked into Kaiser's eyes. After one glance at his face, they moved meekly out of his path.

On the rooftops surrounding the square, Kaiser spotted dragon spawn soldiers in the black armor of the regent's personal guard. They watched the crowd with vigilant eyes, most holding a bow with an arrow nocked on the string. He caught glimpses of alleyways full of the regent's soldiers. Kaiser could feel the jaws of a trap closing around him, but he was committed now.

Finally, the focus of the mob's attention came into view. A wooden scaffold had been constructed in the public square in front of the cathedral. A single massive log rose from the center of the stage. The entire thing was a giant pyre, and Mariel stood with her hands tied behind the center stake. Her feet were hidden in a pile of kindling. Parenthia stood on the platform in front of Mariel, a sword in one hand and a torch in the other. As Kaiser moved deeper into the mob, the sound of the orator's voice rang out over the crowd.

"Citizens of Northmark, there is a disease in your midst!" Parenthia shouted. "This plague is silent, invisible, and deadly. If left unchecked, it will bring doom down on your heads! Do you know of what I speak?" Here Parenthia paused for effect. She thrust her blade into the sky and screeched, "It is the disease of heresy!"

Parenthia flourished her sword and turned to face Mariel. "Even the most powerful among us can fall prey to the lies of the unbeliever."

Mariel did not flinch as Parenthia leveled the sword at her chest.

"This woman's husband has corrupted himself with the powers of a magus," Parenthia said. "I watched with my own eyes as he slaughtered hundreds of loyal Northmark soldiers. I watched as he butchered innocent acolytes, as the demonic fire of the magi laid waste to a humble town! Only by Abimelech's grace was I spared."

Parenthia turned toward the crowd and lowered her voice in a conspiratorial manner. "I dare not speak to you of their perversions, for they are far too horrible to recount."

"Tell us!" a voice near the front of the crowd shouted.

Parenthia smiled, her voice rising back to a shout. "He satisfied himself with their bodies and then consumed the flesh of the dead! He and the second magus, that burning she-devil, consummated their unholy lust in the very streets and bathed in the blood of their victims!"

Mariel shook her head violently, her composure cracking. "She lies!" Mariel cried out. "The High Reaver would never do such a thing!"

"Silence!" Parenthia roared, spinning back toward Mariel. "I give you one last chance at salvation. Bear witness, citizens of Northmark! She can deliver herself from the fire if she but denounces the wickedness of her husband."

Around Kaiser, the crowd responded to Parenthia's display with the appropriate gasps and shouts, but they seemed subdued. He noticed that pockets of men did not respond at all, instead muttering amongst themselves and huddling closer together. The crowd was divided and on edge. Not everyone here wanted to see Mariel burn.

Kaiser placed a hand on the side of a large, bearded man blocking his way. Underneath the man's cloak, he felt the unmistakable hardness of a blade. The man whirled toward Kaiser in alarm. Kaiser shook his head and raised a finger to his lips. The man looked uncertain, but he nodded and stepped aside to let Kaiser pass.

With only several hundred paces between Kaiser and the platform, Parenthia's voice changed, and he knew he was running out of time.

"Will you condemn the heresy of your husband and submit yourself to the will of Abimelech?" Parenthia said, her voice thundering across the square.

The crowd went silent. Mariel hung her head. "Never."

Tears sprang to Kaiser's eyes. His heart ached at the suffering of his wife, but he wanted to shout for joy at the strength of her spirit.

Parenthia turned back to the throng with her arms spread wide. "Let no one call Abimelech unmerciful. Thrice have I given her the opportunity to save herself, and thrice has she refused. All that's left now is for her to burn."

Mariel raised her head. She did not raise her voice, but her words still carried out across the crowd. "Killing me won't stop him. He'll come for you."

Parenthia laughed, pandering to the crowd. "She clings to the belief that her demon-possessed husband will save her. Pity her, Northmark, and see that you never suffer her fate." She turned toward Mariel, holding the torch in her hand high. "Kaiser has abandoned you along with your false king. May you find deliverance in the fire, for there's none to be found here."

Now only fifty paces from the pyre, Kaiser stopped and closed his eyes. He dove deep into the growing well of power that suffused his soul, chasing currents of lighting down into the core of his being. The sky darkened over the square. Kaiser opened his eyes—twin blue swords flashed in his hands. Lightning slashed down, striking his body and filling him with terrible energy. Sparks danced behind his eyes.

All around Kaiser, the crowd scattered in terror. Parenthia turned toward the disturbance.

"I've come for you, Parenthia," Kaiser said, his voice booming like thunder. "Untie my wife and I'll make your death swift. Harm her, and I'll tear the cathedral apart brick by brick and bury you in the rubble."

Parenthia only smiled.

Chapter 29

KAISER SHOUTED AT THE stragglers to get out of his way. He did not want to kill innocent people, but if they did not move, he would cut them down. He strode forward, the power of a storm roaring inside him and demanding to be unleashed.

Atop the platform, Parenthia dropped to her knees and worked at something out of Kaiser's sight. Tears streamed down Mariel's face, and she struggled at the bonds that held her to the stake. Before Kaiser reached the platform, Parenthia surged to her feet in triumph. Kaiser watched in confusion as the High Priestess cut open her palm and sprinkled blood on the wooden platform.

"She's casting a spell!" Mariel screamed, the warning far too late.

Kaiser snarled and tried to charge the scaffold. Instead, he staggered, the strength suddenly gone from his limbs. The spectral swords in his hands disappeared, and he fell to his knees. Kaiser's vision flickered wildly, one instant seeing the platform and his wife, the next peering into the spirit plane. Somehow trapped between the planes of the living and the dead, Kaiser could not move.

Parenthia moved to the edge of the platform and pointed down at Kaiser. "Behold, the demon himself! Now watch, as the strong arm of Abimelech defends his people from the perversions of the wicked."

The words seemed to be some sort of signal, and Parenthia looked toward the regent's soldiers on the rooftops in anticipation. Nothing happened. From where he struggled on his knees, Kaiser saw the black-clad soldiers draw back, leaving Parenthia on her own.

A riot of expressions flashed across Parenthia's face. "You would betray me?" she screamed. "I am Abimelech's High Priestess!"

Parenthia took up sword and torch and whirled toward Mariel. "I'll kill the both of you and demand the regent's head as my reward," she snarled.

Kaiser watched, helpless, as Parenthia plunged her blade through Mariel's stomach. Mariel's body spasmed as the blade passed through her abdomen and out her back. Parenthia dropped the torch on the kindling before turning away. The dry wood caught fast, and the flames licked at the bottom of Mariel's bloody dress.

When Parenthia attacked Mariel, the crowd went berserk. Men and women threw off cloaks, drawing old swords, axes, and even gardening shovels and hoes. They brandished anything that could be made into a weapon. Some seemed intent on defending Mariel, pushing their way to the front of the square, but they were soon attacked by their neighbors. Faces contorted with aimless, animalistic rage, they tore into each other. The square turned into a bloodbath.

Parenthia hopped down from the scaffolding and stalked toward Kaiser. She drew a long, wicked dagger from beneath her robe as she came. Kaiser was mesmerized by the silvery embroidery on her robe, glinting in the sunlight as she walked. How had he never noticed before? It was not a seven-limbed tree bearing strange fruit—the symbol of Abimelech's priesthood was a great, roaring dragon with seven heads.

"You've grown stronger," Parenthia said when she stood over Kaiser. "In another day or two, that spell might not have held you." She smiled down at him, the expression grotesque on her reptilian face. "I could have made you great. I could have shown you pleasure like you cannot imagine. Now you'll die, another tragic footnote in the history of this pathetic kingdom."

Behind Parenthia, Mariel still lived. She was using the sword protruding from her back to saw at the ropes that tied her wrists. She gasped and shuddered at the pain wracking her body with every movement, but she did not stop.

Parenthia lowered the blade of the dagger to Kaiser's throat and took a fistful of his hair in her hand. She yanked his head back, exposing his jugular. The melee swirled around them as the blood-drunk citizens of Northmark waged war on one another.

"Wait," Kaiser managed to growl between teeth that would not open.

"For what?" With a savage jerk, Parenthia drew the blade across his throat. At the same instant, Mariel sawed through the last of the ropes that bound her to the stake. With a cry, she fell forward. When she hit the wooden platform, she slapped a bloody hand out at the sigil holding Kaiser prisoner.

Kaiser felt Parenthia's dagger bite into the soft skin of his throat, and then he could move again. He twisted his head in the direction of the cut, letting the dagger score his flesh. It sliced deep, but did no lasting harm. Kaiser rolled once and leapt to his feet. His swords returned to his hands with a thought.

"No!" Parenthia screamed. "This is not the will of Abimelech! How can he let this happen to me?"

Parenthia died with her question on her lips. Kaiser cut her down with his glowing scimitars, her sundered body falling to the earth in three pieces. Black, foul smelling blood stained the dirt beneath her corpse.

Kaiser lurched toward the pyre. The flames were spreading down the scaffolding. Soon the entire thing would collapse in a pile of ash and cinders. Kaiser tripped up the steps and found his wife lying on her back staring at the sky. One bloody hand lay in the center of a ruined heptagram. She had smothered the flames on her dress, but her feet were black and charred to the bone.

Mariel's head turned toward Kaiser. He started to weep. She smiled at him. "I'm beyond the pain, my love."

With tender hands, Kaiser lifted the body of his wife and carried her from the burning platform. She tried to wrap her arms around his neck, but could not summon the strength. Kaiser knelt in the dirt of the courtyard with her in his lap. He tried to pull the sword from her stomach, but even the smallest of tugs on the hilt made her shudder.

"I don't think I can remove it and keep you alive," Kaiser said through his tears.

"It's okay," Mariel said. "It's enough that I got to see you again."

Kaiser trembled and lowered his head to press his face into Mariel's hair. "Damn the Shrouded King to the pit of the foulest hell. He set me on this path that led us here. I never wanted this power."

"Shhhh," Mariel said, somehow finding the strength to raise a hand to Kaiser's face. He leaned his cheek into her caress. "Don't say such things. My eyes have seen the glory of his coming in you. You are blessed, my love. I consider my life a small price to pay to see the wickedness of Abimelech defeated."

Mariel sank back into Kaiser's arms, exhausted with the effort of speaking. "Promise me...," she said, losing her breath before she got the words out. "Promise me you'll use your power to serve the High King. You don't have to believe, but you must fight."

Kaiser closed his eyes and bowed his head. He wanted to give her an answer, yet the words would not come.

"The children still live," Mariel said, the strength in her voice fading fast. "Find Ursais and Garius. They're hiding in the city. They need you, Kaiser. Live for them when I'm gone. Fight for them."

There were a hundred things Kaiser wanted to say. He wanted to apologize for not being strong enough to save her. He wanted to tell Mariel how proud he was of her strength. He wanted to tell her how thankful he was to have been her husband, but all he could do was nod as great, heart-rending sobs wracked his body.

Mariel gasped, and her eyes found Kaiser's with a sudden urgency. "Tell me you love me," she said.

"I love you," Kaiser said. "With all my heart, I've loved you every day since I first met you, and will keep loving you until the day I die."

Mariel smiled. The strength left her body, and she slumped back as her eyes closed for the last time. Kaiser crumpled, pressing Mariel's body against his chest and rocking back and forth. His cries of grief turned into a moan that started as a pitiful whimper and grew into a roar of all-consuming rage. He tilted his head back and shouted his fury and pain at the sky.

"The High Priestess is dead!" a voice shouted over the sounds of battle. "Kill the magus!"

The regent's troops rushed into the square. Kaiser lowered his gaze from the clouds and saw the dark forms of the regent's personal guard pushing their way through the rioting mob. Their swords lashed out, felling citizens in indiscriminate slaughter. On the rooftops surrounding the square, archers tried to find a clear shot on Kaiser where he knelt, but their aim was thwarted by the press of bodies.

Kaiser remained on his knees with Mariel's limp body in his arms. He watched the enemy come, watched their hideous reptilian mouths open as they shouted at each other. The crowd surged away from the soldiers' killing blades, and the dragon spawn soon faced Kaiser over open ground. When he made no move to rise and fight, they slowed their advance and approached with caution. At least forty of the regent's own guard fanned out to face Kaiser.

"By the order of the Regent of Northmark, you've been condemned to death," a captain of the regent's guard shouted. "Give yourself up and plead for his mercy, or die here and now."

Kaiser did not answer. Instead, he leaned down to kiss Mariel's forehead. Grief and rage warred in his heart until they became one, and when the tears dried on his cheeks, all that remained in his soul was emptiness, an infinite void that demanded bloody vengeance.

The sky over the square turned black, the clouds turning in a maelstrom that centered on Kaiser. The first rank of the regent's guard inched forward. Shields up, swords held low and ready, ten heavily armored soldiers moved to within fifteen paces of Kaiser.

When Kaiser did not react, they came closer, and he could hear their nervous breathing.

"The fight's gone out of him," one of the soldiers said.

"Careful," the captain said. "A beaten dog is still dangerous."

Kaiser closed his eyes. As if in response to the murderous need in his heart, the power inside him surged. He felt anchored to earth and sky, a conduit for energy that could not be harnessed, only unleashed.

"My wife believed in you," Kaiser said, conjuring an image of the mysterious stranger from his dreams in his mind. "She gave her life for that belief. If her sacrifice meant anything, if faith in your return is worth a damn, give me the power to destroy those who put her to death."

The instant the words left Kaiser's lips, thunder spoke from the dark sky. A presence filled him, and he knew he was not alone. Kaiser's head jerked up—his eyes snapped open as the fury of a storm poured forth from his soul. He roared with the thunder. Now only five paces from him, the regent's guard stopped in their tracks, their reptilian eyes going wide with terror.

Lightning stabbed down, ten brilliant spears of energy. White-hot power slammed into the regent's guards. The ten soldiers nearest Kaiser died instantly. They collapsed in a clatter, smoke rising from armor that had been fused together by the wrath of the heavens. The last remnants of the mob fled in terror, running or limping or crawling as their injuries allowed.

Kaiser's hair stood on end as the air around him crackled with electricity. He gently lowered Mariel to the earth, his gaze lingering on her beautiful face before he stood to face the remaining soldiers.

At least thirty of the enemy remained. They glanced at each other, trying to determine who had the courage to lead the next charge.

Arrows flickered through the sky from the nearby rooftops. Kaiser watched the missiles speed toward him with curious detachment. He felt no fear or concern. When the first dark arrow flashed down toward his chest, a tendril of lightning shot out, reducing the wooden shaft to smoking ruin. The metal arrowhead dropped into the dirt at Kaiser's feet.

Kaiser summoned the twin spectral blades into his hands as the hail of arrows was disintegrated. He stepped over the still form of his wife, saying a final goodbye to her in his heart. The regent's soldiers locked their shields together as Kaiser approached. He strode toward them without urgency, lightning flickering into each arrow as it came.

Ten paces from the shield wall, Kaiser blasted its center with a bolt of energy from the black clouds swirling above his head. The earth shook with the force of the explosion—soldiers went flying. With their line broken, the regent's guards charged Kaiser in a desperate bid to avoid the lightning.

Kaiser strolled through their midst, a reaper wielding blades that shimmered like the blue summer sky. The enemy moved as if they fought underwater, their faces twisted in killing rage, but their swords moving so slowly that Kaiser simply stepped around the clumsy swings. His ethereal blades danced, carving bloody carnage in the ranks of the enemy.

When Kaiser stabbed a glowing sword through an armored chest, his victim dropped like a puppet whose strings had been cut. He spun around a pitiful thrust and lashed out at the attacker's neck. Kaiser's burning scimitar sliced through armor, muscle, and bone without any resistance. The helmeted head fell one way, the body another.

The numbers of the regent's guard dwindled quickly. Soon only three remained, and they backed away from Kaiser toward the alleyway from which they had come. From the nearby rooftops, the archers renewed their futile attack. Annoyed, Kaiser raised a hand and swept his arm in the direction of the rooftops. Lightning smashed into the buildings, gouging flaming holes in metal and stone. The archers scattered. The remaining three soldiers turned and ran.

Kaiser stood alone. The cathedral courtyard was scattered with hundreds of the dead and dying, the only fruit of Abimelech's unholy tree. The moans of the wounded and suffering citizens echoed off the surrounding buildings. As his murderous rage receded, Kaiser's thoughts turned toward his children. He could not fight all of Northmark and save them too. He had no idea where to find Ursais, but he knew where Garius would hide.

Before Kaiser could take a step to leave the courtyard, a great rumble shook the city from the north. He turned his gaze to the mountain peak that rose over the northern rooftops. A thunderstorm circled its summit, and as Kaiser watched, it spread quickly over the sky. Darkness clawed through the clouds, leaping across the horizon and blotting out the sun. When this storm reached the maelstrom of clouds over Kaiser's head, it swallowed them up.

The presence that had filled Kaiser since he knelt over Mariel abandoned him, and Kaiser gasped at the sudden absence. His twin scimitars still glowed in his hands, but he no longer felt the immense power of heaven and earth flowing through him. As the sun disappeared behind roiling black clouds, Kaiser spurred himself into motion. He jogged out of the courtyard, certain that the crash of thunder in the north meant that he needed to escape the city as fast as possible.

Outside the cathedral square, Northmark had turned into a war zone. Blood ran in the gutters. Even the fortified houses had been torn open and ransacked. As Kaiser ran through the city, he caught glimpses of great mobs of people spreading through the streets like a single organism of destruction.

Intent on avoiding unnecessary confrontation, Kaiser kept to the back alleyways. He dismissed his spectral swords, not wanting to draw attention to himself. Women and children cowered in the shadows of the narrow lanes between buildings. Men wounded in the streets dragged themselves to relative safety in the dark passages.

Kaiser pushed through them all, ignoring their cries for help. Northmark had brought this devastation on itself. Once, as Tenth Reaver, it had been his concern. No longer. Now all that mattered was finding his children and getting them to the harbor.

In the years that Kaiser had served as Tenth Reaver, assassination and assault on his family had been a constant threat. Taking great care to keep his actions from the knowledge of the priesthood and the other reavers, Kaiser had constructed safe houses throughout Northmark. These secret hideaways had enough food and supplies to keep his family fed for months. Garius knew of one of these safe houses, and Kaiser had no doubt that the captain of his guard would take children there to keep them safe.

The slums of Northmark seemed untouched by the rioting. With a sigh of relief, Kaiser stepped out of an alley into a quiet street. A strange scream rang out from the dark passage behind him. Kaiser whirled, ethereal blades flashing into existence in his hands. The biggest hound Kaiser had ever seen stared at him from the shadows. Its blunt, scarred snout stood level with Kaiser's face, dripping blood.

Kaiser took a menacing step toward the animal. It did not flinch. Instead, it turned around and disappeared back into the alley. The hairs on the back of Kaiser's neck stood on end. He was being tracked. With a silent curse, Kaiser turned and sprinted toward the safe house.

Chapter 30

KAISER KICKED OPEN THE door to the decrepit house. The rickety door slammed against the wall and almost fell off its rusted hinges. Trash covered the floor inside. A rotting, tattered rug in the center of the main room was the only sign that the place had once been inhabited.

With quick steps, Kaiser moved through the tiny, three-room house to the smallest chamber at the back. Stains covered the ancient wooden walls. He knelt before one dark splotch in particular and pressed his hand against the wall. A section of the wood panels swung inward without a noise. Kaiser's heart sank when he saw only darkness inside, but he ducked his head and crawled inside anyway.

"Garius, Tarathine, Saredon—are you in here?" Kaiser whispered as he raised himself to a crouch in the pitch black of the hidden room. He could see little of the tiny space with his body blocking the light from the hatch behind him.

"F-father?" a tiny voice said.

Kaiser's heart jumped in his chest. "Tarathine!" he said, the words coming out in a ragged gasp.

Something clattered to the floor, and a small form hurtled out of the darkness and slammed into Kaiser's chest. Tarathine pressed her face into Kaiser's neck and sobbed. Kaiser gripped his daughter in a fierce embrace, his face pressed into hair that smelled like her mother.

They clung to each other for a long moment until Kaiser pulled gently away. "We have to get out of here," he said. "Where's Saredon?"

"I don't know! He went with Ursais. Garius went to try and save mother," Tarathine said, swiping a hand at her tears. She darted away into the darkness and came back with a loaded crossbow. "He left me with this."

"Damn them for splitting the two of you up, and damn that man's bravery," Kaiser said, shaking his head. "I can't fault him for the attempt, but he's probably dead."

Tarathine gasped.

"I'm sorry," Kaiser said. "You should know the truth. Your... your mother's dead. I was with her when she died. Northmark has gone insane. I've got to get you and Saredon out of the city. I don't know where Ursais has him, but I can get you to safety first. There's a ship waiting at the docks that will get us out of here."

Tarathine wilted as Kaiser spoke. He pulled her into his arms as she wept even harder than before.

"I know girl, I know," Kaiser said, stroking Tarathine's hair. "I killed the men who did it. Now you've got to be strong. It's what your mother would want."

Tarathine pulled back and looked him in the eye. She looked so much like her mother that Kaiser almost started weeping again. "Did you kill all of them?" she asked.

"I did," Kaiser said, his voice trembling.

With a sharp nod, Tarathine stopped crying.

"Good girl," Kaiser said. "Now follow me."

Kaiser turned and crawled back into the light. Tarathine followed close on his heels, crossbow still in her hands. Together, they crept back to the main room of the abandoned house. Now that he had Tarathine at his side, Kaiser felt vulnerable. As they made for the street, he mapped out the quickest and safest route to the docks in his head.

With Tarathine one step behind, Kaiser stepped into the empty road. He scanned their surroundings and froze. "Get behind me," he hissed to Tarathine.

The hound from the alley had returned with its master. A tall, hooded figure stood in the middle of the street with the dog at his side. He grasped a long, black walking stick in his right hand, and his left rested on the animal's back. Kaiser had seen the man once before, outside the general store in Oakroot.

Kaiser kept himself between Tarathine and the dark stranger as they crossed the street. He would find another route to the docks. As Kaiser made to guide Tarathine into a side street, the stranger's voice boomed out.

"I'd rethink that course of action," the stranger said. "Worm has been tracking you, but he can kill just as easily. He'll tear the girl's throat out before you can stop him, I promise you."

"Who are you, and what do you want?" Kaiser asked.

"My name is Mazareem. I must thank you for dealing with Parenthia, though I'm sure you'll agree things would have been easier for us if you hadn't botched the job in Oakroot." The stranger began scratching a symbol in the dirt of the street as he talked. Kaiser gritted his teeth and held his ground, fearing for Tarathine. "I'm afraid I cannot let you leave Northmark. It's nothing personal, but if you surrender, I can guarantee the girl will be spared."

With a thought, Kaiser summoned his spectral blades into his hands. Behind him, Tarathine gasped in surprise. "I'm taking my daughter and we're leaving this city," Kaiser said. "You can let me pass, or I can bury you next to your hound."

Mazareem laughed. "That's an interesting trick. Let me show you mine."

There was no choice. Kaiser sprang forward as Mazareem removed a vial from beneath his cloak, pulled the stopper, and poured it out on the image he had scratched in the dirt. Lines of green fire ignited when the liquid splashed to the furrowed earth.

Kaiser staggered halfway to Mazareem—his burning scimitars vanished. Darkness smothered his soul. He closed his eyes and saw the spiritual plane. A hundred ravenous shadows swarmed him, dragging him down with their cold talons. Kaiser tried to fight them off, but there were too many. Tarathine screamed as Kaiser flailed his arms against the phantom assault.

Every time one of the wraiths touched him, Kaiser felt the empty coldness of death seep into his body. He tried to take a step toward Mazareem, but his legs nearly buckled as the strength was leeched from his being.

"Speak to him, child," Mazareem said. "Tell your father that the harder he resists, the more he'll suffer. You wouldn't want me to have to hurt him, would you?"

Tarathine raised her crossbow and aimed it at Mazareem's chest. "You leave my father alone!" she shouted.

"Go on then, loose your bolt," Mazareem said with a grim chuckle. "Who will you shoot, me, or the dog?"

The tip of Tarathine's crossbow wavered as she moved it back and forth between Mazareem and his hound.

With a flourish of his cloak, Mazareem spread his arms wide. "Make your choice!"

Tarathine chose. The crossbow fired with a meaty *ka-chunk,* the shock of the release nearly jerking the weapon from her hands. Kaiser watched the bolt flash across his vision straight at Mazareem's breast.

Puncturing flesh with a gruesome *thunk,* the bolt struck Mazareem a little left of the heart. He never tried to avoid the attack, arms spread as Tarathine took aim and fired. His body absorbed the impact of the bolt slamming home with the smallest of shudders.

Mazareem grinned at Tarathine, reached down, and plucked the bolt from his chest. He inspected the bloody head before dropping it on the ground. Dark liquid oozed from the wound, but Mazareem showed no indication of pain.

"Wrong choice," Mazareem said. He raised an arm and pointed at Tarathine. "Worm, kill."

Worm sprang forward. At that same instant, a cry rang out, and a soldier charged into the street between Tarathine and the animal. "You'll not have her, you foul bastard!" Battered, bloody, but still standing, Garius raised his shield to meet Worm's charge head on, the boss of his shield cracking the hound in the nose. His sword stabbed up and under the shield, biting deep into the flesh of the dog's throat.

Canine yelps of pain filled the street as Worm crashed to the ground. The hound thrashed as Garius flailed at it with his blade. In the frantic struggle, Garius danced around the writhing dog and kicked at the green fire that burned in the dirt. Mazareem's spell fell away, and the shadows swarming Kaiser vanished.

Garius glanced over his shoulder as Kaiser recovered from the assault.

"Get her out of here!" Garius shouted. "I'll take care of this."

Mazareem blindsided Garius, flinging something at the man's face. Kaiser opened his mouth to shout a warning, but he was far too slow. Garius was struck in the cheek, and the captain of Kaiser's guard screamed. Kaiser caught a glimpse of flesh sloughing off bone and white skull beneath. He did not wait to see what happened next. Shoving Tarathine on ahead of him, Kaiser ran into the side street.

Kaiser took his daughter's hand in his as they raced through the slums of Northmark. Mazareem would not know their destination, and Kaiser hoped to throw him off the trail by taking an indirect route to the docks. His only hope was that Garius had injured that damned hound badly enough that it could not follow their scent.

After half a mile, Kaiser risked a look back. The streets behind them were empty. Tarathine struggled at his side, and Kaiser slowed his pace.

"I want you to run as hard as you can, and when you can't go any farther, I'll carry you," Kaiser said. "Do you think you can keep going?"

Between deep breaths for air, Tarathine nodded.

"Good girl," Kaiser said, squeezing her shoulder. "Now let's go."

Tarathine ran hard, but she only managed another few hundred paces at Kaiser's pace. When she faltered, Kaiser knelt so that she could climb onto his back. After she was secure with her arms locked around his neck, Kaiser set out again.

They left the slums behind and entered the war-torn harbor district. The damage here looked recent. Fires still burned in the looted buildings, and dazed survivors picked through the ruins. One man looked up as Kaiser trotted past. He saw Tarathine on Kaiser's back and raised his hands to his mouth to shout a warning.

"There's a war being fought on the docks," the man said. "You'll find no safety there!"

Kaiser nodded his thanks, but did not alter his course. If the docks were under siege by the mob, all might be lost. Either they would find the *Golden Dawn* waiting for them, or they would die.

The sky overhead was the color of dirty steel. Clouds swirled, and thunder rolled across Northmark like the harbinger of destruction. Lightning clashed far up in the heavens, angry gods dueling over the city's fate. Tarathine pressed herself against Kaiser's back, clutching him tighter at every peal of thunder.

When they neared the docks, Kaiser slowed his pace. In the brief moments of peace between thunderclaps, he heard the shouts and sounds of a pitched battle ahead of them. Kaiser sat Tarathine on her feet near the end of a road that led into the harbor.

"Wait here," Kaiser said. "I'm going to see what's happening."

Tarathine did not like to be left behind, but she nodded that she would obey. Kaiser crept forward, making sure to stay behind a stack of crates that hid him from the harbor's view. He found chaos when he peered over the top of the wooden crates.

The mobs ransacking the city had converged on the harbor. Two battle lines faced off against each other, thousands of furious citizens screaming obscenities at each other. Caught in the middle, guardsmen and sailors fought tooth and nail to drive the more courageous looters back. Kaiser spotted burning ships on the northern side of the harbor. Their crews had been slaughtered and their cargo spread on the wharf like the guts of a dead animal.

Kaiser scanned the ships floating on the water, fighting the rising desperation in his heart. How was he supposed to find the *Golden Dawn* in this mess? He caught a flash of orange in the corner of his eye. He held his breath, waiting for the stab of light to appear again. When it did, he knew he had found his target. He knew that spark of fire. Lacrael was using her power to defend the ship.

The *Golden Dawn* floated in the center of the harbor in the midst of the thickest fighting. Her crew manned the decks, standing next to Lacrael as she flung fire at any looter who ventured too close. Even to Kaiser's untrained eye, they appeared to be making ready to cast off. The only thing preventing them from escaping the harbor was the press of panicked ships between them and the open ocean. Kaiser swore. He had to get Tarathine to that ship before they pulled away from the dock.

"Are we going into that, father?" Tarathine said from his side.

Kaiser almost jumped out of his skin. "Shades of heaven, girl. I told you to wait back there!" He slowed his breath and willed his heart to stop racing. "Yes, we've no choice but to risk it. There's nowhere else to go. I want you to get on my back again."

Tarathine wrapped her arms around Kaiser's neck, and he stood behind the stack of crates.

"Whatever happens, don't open your eyes, and don't let go."

Kaiser sucked down two deep breaths, stepped out from behind the crates, and ran into the chaos. He summoned his swords into his hands as he ran. With Tarathine on his back, Kaiser hurdled corpses and dodged puddles of blood. On his right, the back of the nearest mob pressed forward and surged back as the tides of battle changed. He made it halfway to the *Golden Dawn's* jetty before anyone noted his presence.

A cry went up on the nearest ship, and as the warning spread, arrows started to thud into the dock around Kaiser. Whatever power had protected Kaiser from the arrows of the enemy in the cathedral courtyard had abandoned him. "Keep your head down!" he shouted to Tarathine over the sounds of battle. She burrowed her head into the back of his neck. The sailors' missiles whizzed past his head and skipped under his feet.

Kaiser skirted the warring mobs to his right and dodged the arrows of the ships on his left. As he neared the *Golden Dawn's* dock, his heart sank. A guard shack sat on the wharf, and the harbor guards blocked the pier with a line of shields and pikes.

"Make way for the Tenth Reaver!" Kaiser shouted as his feet pounded the wooden planks.

The cry earned him a few seconds of confusion. Terrified men peered at him over the tops of their shields. The points of pikes wavered, the men that wielded them unsure if they should stab Kaiser or let him pass.

"Weapons up!" a voice bellowed, but the warning came too late. Kaiser ducked under the steel point of a pike and tore into the makeshift shield wall. His blue scimitars hacked bloody chunks out of the harbor guards. Kaiser spun as he dashed through their line, trying to protect Tarathine from their blades.

The dock behind the guards was wide open. Any looters that had penetrated this far had been slain—many by the archers still in port. Arrows rained down from the ships on both sides. Kaiser grunted as a broadhead slammed into his left bicep. The metal point bit deep, but he did not slow.

Moored at the very end of the pier, the *Golden Dawn* floated alone. The onslaught of arrows died away as Kaiser passed the other ships. Ahead of him, a spark of fire flashed on the deck of the *Golden Dawn*, followed by a loud report and a puff of smoke. The bullet bit into the dock in front of Kaiser, throwing up a cloud of splinters. Kaiser clenched his eyes shut against the stinging bits of wood.

Another gun fired, and Kaiser thrust one of his glowing swords up over his head. On the deck of the ship, a voice rang out, and the guns fell silent. Kaiser slid to a stop at the end of the dock. The *Golden Dawn* floated about twenty paces from the end of the pier. Lacrael appeared at the rail.

"You've made it just in time!" Lacrael called out to Kaiser. "We can't stay here any longer, else we'll never leave."

"I've got my daughter," Kaiser shouted back. "How do we get her aboard?"

Lacrael ducked out of sight, returning a moment later with Gustavus at her side. The massive captain began stripping down to his breeches. "Toss her into the water," Lacrael called. "Gustavus will fish her out."

Kaiser set Tarathine on her feet and looked her in the eye. "I know you can't swim, but you've got to trust me. This is the only way out of the city. Do you understand?"

Tarathine's eyes were huge, but she nodded at Kaiser's question. Kaiser pulled her to his chest, and she hugged him so hard he thought his ribs might crack.

"I love you, Tarathine," Kaiser said. "I have to go and find your brother. I'll be back."

"I know you will, father," Tarathine said. "I love you too."

"It's now or never!" Gustavus roared. The *Golden Dawn* had drifted to forty paces from the dock.

Kaiser lifted Tarathine's slight form in his arms. His left arm gave out, and he almost dropped her. Biting his tongue against the agony of the arrow digging into his muscle, Kaiser spun once, and hurled Tarathine out over the open water. She did not make a sound as she fell, disappearing below the dark waves with a tiny splash.

Gustavus dove into the sea at the same time, and he swam hard toward where Tarathine had vanished. When he reached the spot, he kicked his feet over his head and swam straight down. Kaiser held his breath as he watched the water. After what seemed like an eternity, Gustavus resurfaced with Tarathine in his arms.

"Now you!" Lacrael called from the deck of the quickly receding ship. Parnick and a second burly sailor stood ready to dive in and retrieve Kaiser.

"I'm not done here," Kaiser shouted. "I have to find my son."

"The gods damn your worthless hide," Gustavus roared as he was hoisted out of the ocean by a rope. A soaked Tarathine clung to him. "You agreed to this if we helped you!"

"The deal was that we would save my family! My wife is already dead for your damned High King—I'm not leaving my son!"

"Kaiser, look out!" Lacrael cried.

Kaiser whirled. Claws digging deep into wooden planks, oozing black blood, heedless of the arrows peppering his hide, Worm barrelled toward him down the long pier. The hound had tracked him all the way here.

"Come on, then!" Kaiser yelled at the beast. He braced himself for impact, twin swords up and ready.

Worm slavered at the mouth, white foam spraying from his terrible jaws. The dog never slowed. Kaiser tried to dodge out of the way, but Worm was not fooled. The hound struck him with the force of a charging horse. Kaiser's swords plunged deep into the beast's chest—he screamed as Worm's teeth tore into his wounded shoulder. They both went over the edge of the dock. Dark water rushed up to meet Kaiser, and his mind went blank as the cold ocean swallowed him.

Kaiser flailed against the sea. His injured arm refused to work, and instead of rising to the surface, he sank. Below him, Worm dropped like an anchor. The animal did not even try to swim. Kaiser stared down into the depths of the harbor, lungs burning, as the hound sank into shadow, jaws stretched wide in what Kaiser swore was a sinister grin.

Chapter 31

LACRAEL CRIED OUT IN horror as Kaiser sank beneath the waves. Tarathine rushed to the railing of the ship and Lacrael wrapped her arms around the girl, afraid she might try to jump in. Brant stood with them, helpless and sullen in his iron manacles. Footsteps pounded on the deck, and Gustavus's huge form shot past. He dove into the harbor, outstretched arms knifing into the water.

Lacrael held her breath when Gustavus left the surface and followed Kaiser down. After a few agonizing heartbeats, Gustavus exploded back into the air, Kaiser's body supported by one huge arm.

Niad shouted orders, turning the loading crane out over the harbor. Gustavus wrapped the dangling rope around his forearm and allowed himself to be yanked up and out of the water. The small crane lifted him through the air as if he weighed nothing. Kaiser hung limp from the captain's arm.

When Gustavus hit the deck, he turned Kaiser over his knee and started to pound on his back. The force of the blows caused Kaiser to jerk, and he gagged as buckets of water poured out of his mouth and onto the deck of the ship.

Kaiser waved his good arm in a plea for mercy, and Gustavus relented. He let Kaiser roll off his knee and flop onto his back. Lacrael released Tarathine, and the girl rushed to her father.

"I have to get back," Kaiser said as he tried to sit up.

"The only way off this ship is straight to the bottom of the harbor," Gustavus said. "I just pulled your arse out, but I can toss you back in with half the trouble."

Kaiser shook his head. "My son—," he coughed, "I have to save him."

"The docks are lost," Gustavus said. "We're sailing out of here right now, or we'll never leave."

"No, damn you!" Kaiser tried to shout, but the words came out as a croak. "I can't leave him."

"I don't want to leave a child behind, but there's not a blasted thing I can do for your boy," Gustavus said. "I risked everything on this gambit, and now it's going to hell. If your son's still safe in that mess, pray he'll stay that way. Like as not you'd get him killed, dragging a boy through this, and we'd all be dead by the time you do."

Gustavus strode away toward the helm without another word. Kaiser tried to stand, but his legs would not cooperate. Lacrael stepped forward to offer her shoulder.

With help from Lacrael and Brant, Kaiser struggled to his feet. "My son's still in the city," he said, choking on the words.

Lacrael grimaced. "We have to get out of here. Gustavus is right: you've done everything you could."

Kaiser looked away from Lacrael, unwilling or unable to look her in the eye. Even Brant looked anguished at the man's plight. He knew as well as anybody what it felt like to abandon his family and his home, Lacrael thought. It was an experience they had all shared.

"None of us want to leave your family behind," Lacrael said. "But we must live to fight another day. If we survive, there's a chance we can come back and save him."

Lacrael helped Kaiser limp to the side of the ship that faced the city. When they looked out on the destruction raging through the harbor, Lacrael shared his despair. The mobs were swarming over the ships too slow to cast off. Had they not sailed the moment they did, the *Golden Dawn* would have been lost, and any chance at escape lost with her.

On the end of the dock, Lacrael spotted a tall, dark figure standing alone. Brant stiffened at her side.

"That's him," Brant said, "that's Mazareem."

Lacrael placed a hand on Brant's arm. "As long as you wear the amulet, he has no power over you," she said.

"The harm's already done," Brant said in anguish. "He turned me into a monster. Both of you did." He left the deck for Gustavus's cabin.

Lacrael watched him go, weary at heart and seemingly unable to comfort anyone. One day Mazareem would answer for his crimes. Maybe if she could see that done and see Brant home again, he would be able to heal.

"Lacrael!" Gustavus roared from the command deck. "Get your miserable sack of guts up here!"

Lacrael checked that Kaiser and Tarathine were okay, then dashed away to answer Gustavus's order. She found him at the ship's wheel, gripping it fiercely.

"The harbor's more clogged than my bowels after a feast of Coriddian cheese," Gustavus said. "I need you to clear us a path."

Gustavus pointed toward the open sea, and Lacrael followed his gaze. Between the *Golden Dawn* and freedom, eight other ships blocked the narrow passage between the stone walls that blunted the force of the ocean's waves. In their panic, the ships had fouled themselves so badly that several of them had crashed into each other. As more ships won free of their besieged moorings, the harbor would soon be so crowded that escape would be impossible.

"I don't know if I can," Lacrael said, shaking her head. "The last time I unleashed the full fury of my power, I destroyed an entire town."

"That's what I like to hear!" Gustavus shouted over the rising noise. "Incinerate everything but us, and we'll sail out of here on the burning tide."

Lacrael glanced over her shoulder at Kaiser and Tarathine. She considered all that they had suffered to get this far, all that Brant had suffered, and she knew that she could not let their sacrifices be in vain. Her grandfather had died for this chance—she had to try.

With a sharp nod to Gustavus, Lacrael turned and sprinted toward the bow of the ship. When she looked out over the roiling waves, Lacrael took a deep breath and closed her eyes. She counted to ten, opened her eyes, and began to weave threads of fire out of thin air. The crew of the *Golden Dawn* shouted and swore in surprise at the sight of burning flames on the deck of the ship, but Gustavus bellowed them into silence.

The fireball between Lacrael's hands grew until it hung in the air like a burning sun. Gustavus pointed the *Golden Dawn* straight into the snarl of ships and ordered the sails opened. As the crew scampered along the high rigging, loosing sails and securing lines, Lacrael released the flaming orb, and it shot across the water toward the massed ships.

Lacrael's magus fire struck the ocean mere paces from the hull of the nearest ship. The fireball detonated with tremendous force, sending a surge of waves outward from the point of impact. The clump of ships bobbed like corks.

"Again!" Gustavus roared from the helm. "Try to push them to the left!"

Lacrael's hands were a blur of motion as she summoned another burning missile. She launched this one in haste—her aim was off. The fireball slammed into the side of one of the ships, consuming its hull in an instant. Lacrael tried to shut out the screams of sailors as the sea rushed into the gaping cavity in the side of the vessel. Fire leapt across the deck of the ship, climbing to eat the sails faster than she would have believed possible.

"A wayward shot," Gustavus called. "Keep pouring it on them!"

Trembling now, Lacrael started to craft another fireball. The *Golden Dawn* struggled to make headway against the waves tossed up by Lacrael's constant barrage. She launched four more fiery spheres of magus fire, and a clear path opened up to the mouth of the harbor, but their ship made no progress.

"To the stern, now!" Gustavus shouted as he wrestled with the wheel. "If you blasted them out of the way, you can propel us forward."

Lacrael ran toward the aft of the ship. She stumbled as she moved, nearly overwhelmed by the immense strain of drawing on so much of her power. Hanging over the rail at the rear of the ship, Lacrael summoned the biggest fireball she could conjure and sent it hurtling into the ocean below. She almost tumbled into the sea as the *Golden Dawn* launched forward, propelled by the explosion.

— —

Kaiser barely kept his feet when the ship shot forward. Tarathine sagged against him, using his weight as an anchor. The *Golden Dawn* leapt across the waves as if she hungered for freedom as much as her captain and crew.

The sky overhead had darkened to almost the absolute black of a starless night. A roar echoed out across the roiling clouds like no thunder Kaiser had ever heard. It was the roar of a god walking the face of the earth, a god whose anger would shake the very foundations of the world. The sound obliterated thought. Tarathine screamed, and Kaiser's soul quaked with dread.

Every eye turned toward the north. They could no longer see the mountain in the darkness, but flashes of lighting revealed seven massive necks in the clouds over Northmark. Kaiser's mouth sagged open. The mountain had become a monster.

"Look alive, you bastards!" Gustavus bellowed over the chaos. "You've woken the Lord of Dragons himself!"

The *Golden Dawn* picked up speed. Kaiser hung on for dear life as the ship crashed through the turbulent harbor. They swept by the sinking ship. Magus fire still burned, floating in deadly pockets on the surface of the water. A cry for aid from the surviving sailors went up as the *Golden Dawn* sailed past, but Gustavus ignored their pleas for mercy.

Kaiser held his breath as the mouth of the harbor came into view in front of them. The gap between the walls was about three times the width of their ship.

"Hold fast!" Gustavus yelled.

With one final explosion, Lacrael propelled the *Golden Dawn* toward the open sea at fantastic speed. The ship rode the crest of a wave that crashed against the walls of the harbor, but it carried them through the narrow gap and into the ocean beyond. A cheer went up from the crew, and Kaiser sagged against the rigging in relief.

"Shut your holes!" Gustavus shouted. "We're not out of this yet."

Rain finally started to pour from the black sky. A storm came on them out of nowhere as the dragon over Northmark roared again. As the waves rose higher and higher, lightning flashed down, each strike moving closer to the ship. This was no natural squall. When the lightning found them, it would pound them into dust.

An image of Lacrael sitting in the warehouse in Thornhold thrust itself to the forefront of Kaiser's mind. He remembered the flame of a candle dancing along her dark skin. If she controlled fire, maybe he could command lightning.

"Get me to the top of the ship!" Kaiser screamed into the storm. The wind tore the words from his mouth and cast them out over the roiling waves.

Kaiser knelt his mouth down next to Tarathine's ear. "Go to Gustavus. Tell him I can save the ship."

Tarathine nodded and launched herself toward the helm. Kaiser watched with his heart in his throat as she battled against the rolling deck of the ship. She was so slight that the wind might pluck her up and carry her away. Tarathine climbed the stairs to the command deck and disappeared from sight. A heartbeat later, Gustavus landed on the deck in front of Kaiser with a solid thud.

"Take me to the top!" Kaiser shouted, pointing at the sails overhead. "I can stop the lightning!"

With one huge arm, Gustavus scooped Kaiser up. Draped over the man's broad back, Kaiser clung to Gustavus's neck with his good arm and hung on for dear life as the captain hurled himself up the *Golden Dawn's* rigging.

At the top of the highest mast, Gustavus placed Kaiser on a small circle of wood just big enough to sit on. With deft hands, Gustavus secured Kaiser's legs to the ship with rope, slapped him on the back, and then plummeted down toward the deck far below.

When Kaiser raised his head to look out over the churning sea, he almost fainted. Northmark had disappeared in the storm behind them. All that existed was the *Golden Dawn*, the furious ocean, and the hurricane. Rain pelted his face, and the wind tore at his body. Tied down to the top of the mast, Kaiser felt like an infant strapped to a raging bull.

A bolt of lightning flashed down only twenty paces away, and Kaiser prepared himself for the next attack. He reached down inside of himself, drawing up any scraps of his power that still remained. Kaiser was so weary that his soul ached, but the power responded to his call.

The clouds flashed and another lightning strike stabbed down toward the *Golden Dawn*. Kaiser raised his hands and *compelled* the energy to hit him instead of the ship. The jagged bolt of light twisted and changed direction mid-air, slamming straight into Kaiser's chest.

Kaiser screamed. His teeth rattled in his head. Every muscle in his body went rigid. The lightning receded as quickly as it had come, leaving Kaiser reeling from the impact. When he could think again, he looked down.

His clothes were on fire. Kaiser swatted at his chest and legs, smothering the flames. Smoke rose from a hole blasted through the armor on his chest. Unblemished flesh lay beneath the charred leather. He tore off his ruined breastplate and cast it into the storm. Pain like he had never imagined radiated throughout his body, but he still lived. He could deal with pain.

The assault from the heavens rained down again and again, and every time, Kaiser called the lightning to his breast. He started weeping after the third strike. His tears mingled with the rain, and he felt like his pain connected him to the storm. The fury of the sky matched the turmoil in his soul. Thunder boomed so close over Kaiser's head that he thought it might pluck him from the top of the mast and tear him limb from limb.

With Kaiser shielding the ship, the *Golden Dawn* battled the ocean to distance itself from the coast. Lacrael no longer launched fireballs into the sea, so the ship resorted to traveling under the power of its own sails. Between lightning strikes, Kaiser glanced down to see the frenzied crew doing everything in their power to keep the ship afloat.

As they moved away from Northmark, the strength of the storm waned, and the time between strikes lengthened. Kaiser began to catch his breath, then alarm surged through him when he spotted a rocky outcropping jutting up through the waves. If Gustavus did not change his course, the ship would slam into the ring of rocks within minutes.

Kaiser tried to shout a warning down to the captain—he could barely hear his own voice over the swirling wind. With hands numb from cold, Kaiser struggled with the knots that secured his legs to the mast, but he was no sailor. The knots held fast.

Helpless, Kaiser watched the ship rush toward the rocks in agony. They had fought so hard to escape, and now they were going to be undone by a circle of stones.

Unimpeded by the storm now, the *Golden Dawn* leapt across the waves. Kaiser grimaced and braced himself for impact. When the rocks were fifty paces away, a strange green light ignited in their center. The light spread to form a swirling, jade maelstrom suspended above the surface of the sea. Dumbfounded, Kaiser forgot to be concerned.

The prow of the *Golden Dawn* aimed at the heart of the green portal. A cheer went up from the deck below Kaiser when the ship touched the otherworldly green light. Kaiser blinked, and reality shifted.

When Kaiser opened his eyes, he found himself on a tranquil sea. The sun rose high overhead in a clear sky, its heat a blessed warmth. Kaiser turned, scanning the horizon in every direction. Behind them, Northmark was gone. The entire coast of Haverfell had disappeared. They were in the middle of nowhere.

As Kaiser tried to understand what had happened, Gustavus's head popped up.

"Hey, you survived," Gustavus said, grinning. "I had a wager going that you'd been fried to a crisp."

"What happened?" Kaiser asked, his voice cracking as he forced the words through a raw throat. "Where are we?"

Gustavus smiled. "Welcome to the realm of Praxis, my homeland. Here, let me get you down."

Kaiser watched Gustavus make short work of the knots that had defied him. When he was free, Kaiser slid down onto Gustavus's back and allowed the captain to carry him down to the deck.

"I don't understand," Kaiser said as Gustavus sat him on his feet. Kaiser almost collapsed, and Lacrael jumped forward to catch him. "Where did Haverfell go?"

"There're more worlds than the one you know," Gustavus said. "This one is called Praxis, and it's my home. I had no intention of returning anytime soon, but with Abimelech dropping the sky on us, I didn't think we had any other options."

Gustavus reached into the open collar of his shirt and withdrew the gold chain he wore around his neck. The golden dragon amulet winked in the sunlight. "These are the keys to the portals. One final gift from High King Rowen. Abimelech might be able to follow us, but not through the same portal."

Now Kaiser did collapse. Tarathine dropped to the deck next to him, and Kaiser wrapped his arms around her. For the first time in his life, Kaiser felt very small. Everything he had known, everything he had lived for, had just disappeared in a swirling cloud of green light. Mariel was dead. Saredon was lost. Kaiser hugged Tarathine to his chest and closed his eyes. Curled up on the wet deck of the *Golden Dawn*, Kaiser let exhaustion take him.

Chapter 32

KAISER FLOATED IN NOTHINGNESS. Warm currents buffeted his body, and he let them carry him to and fro. He knew that he was unconscious. He needed to wake and face whatever came next, but he could not force his eyes to open. Some force outside of himself compelled him to rest.

After a time, colors and lights began to form in the void that surrounded him. Soon, Kaiser found himself sitting in a little rowboat bobbing on a vast, empty sea. The mysterious stranger sat across from him. Neither spoke, and Kaiser struggled with the riot of emotions boiling up in his heart.

"I grieve for your wife," the stranger finally said.

Kaiser closed his eyes and bowed his head. "I should hate you, but I can't find any more anger to spare within myself."

"I didn't set you on this path," the stranger said. "You were already walking it; I only opened your eyes."

"She died believing in you," Kaiser said. "Her last wish was for me to see this through."

"Will you?"

"Do I have a choice?"

"Of course. If you wish to turn your back on those who risked everything to save you, I cannot stop you. However, the problem with choice is that you think you control the outcome. A rat in a maze can choose to turn left or right, yet in the end it's still just a rodent in a trap."

"Is that supposed to help?"

The stranger smiled. "Do you know why I talk to you and not Lacrael? I talk to you instead of her because you challenge everything I tell you. She would charge into the pit of hell without question if I asked her too. Her loyalty is commendable, yet it worries me. I'm no god, Kaiser. My word isn't infallible. I fight for a vision of the future where the enemy is defeated, but there's no guarantee that we'll win. I need your skepticism. Without it, I'm loosing arrows in the dark."

"I'd feel better if you *were* a god."

"So would I," the stranger said with a chuckle.

"I left my son in Northmark," Kaiser said, his voice hollow.

"Saredon is in good hands," the stranger said. "I'll do my best to watch over him. It took every bit of power I possess to restrain Abimelech while you escaped through the portal, but I think I can shield Saredon's presence from him."

Kaiser stared at the watery horizon and thought of Saredon alone in the corrupt city at the heart of the enemy's power. All Kaiser could see was Saredon's terrified face. He stared up at his father, wondering why he had been abandoned. Kaiser pushed the thought aside before his heart broke in two.

"What would you have me do now?" Kaiser asked, his voice raw.

"Just as Lacrael waited for you in Haverfell, you must find the champion of this realm," the stranger said. "I can't reveal to you who it is, else you would tip my hand before I'm ready. They have to arrive at the both correct time and location, and even then there's a chance I fail. All I can tell you is that you're in the right place, and now you have to watch and wait."

"Damn your cryptic nonsense."

"There's another reason I chose to speak to you," the stranger said, the corners of his mouth upturned in a small smile. "You remind me of myself. Now go, the others are waiting for you."

The vision of the stranger, boat, and sea faded before Kaiser's eyes. As the dream vanished, sounds penetrated his slumber, and he felt the gentle rocking of the ship underneath him. Kaiser opened his eyes and found himself lying in a gently swaying hammock. He turned his head to take in his surroundings.

Kaiser guessed he was somewhere in the bowels of the *Golden Dawn*. The hammock hung from the walls of a tiny room. Tarathine sat next to him on a stool. She was reading a book and had not noticed him wake. Kaiser watched her for a few long minutes before disturbing her. Every time he looked at her, his heart ached for Mariel.

"Is that a good book?" Kaiser asked, his voice weak.

Tarathine's head jerked up. "Father!"

The book dropped to the floor as Tarathine smothered Kaiser in a hug. He raised his arms to return her embrace and discovered that his left arm and shoulder had been cleaned and bandaged.

"How long have I been out?" Kaiser asked, the words muffled with his face pressed into the top of Tarathine's head.

Tarathine pulled back. "You've been asleep for two days. I need to go tell them you're awake!"

"Can you bring me some food first?" Kaiser asked, his stomach suddenly protesting his involuntary fast.

With a nod, Tarathine dashed from the cabin. Kaiser laid back in the hammock and listened to the creaking of the ship. After only a few minutes, Tarathine returned bearing a tray of cheese, bread, and cold meats.

"The cook said this is from the captain's personal stores," Tarathine said, placing the tray on the stool next to Kaiser. "He said you deserved it, after saving the ship like you did."

Kaiser grunted his thanks as he stuffed his mouth. Tarathine watched him eat. He devoured everything on the tray. Kaiser's stomach still growled, but at least he felt like he would survive now.

"I'll go get them," Tarathine said, turning to dash from the room again.

"Wait," Kaiser said, raising a hand to stop her. "I think I can walk. I'll go with you."

Legs trembling, Kaiser slipped out of the hammock and stood on the floor. The subtle rocking of the ship almost tripped him up on his first step, but Tarathine darted forward to offer her support. With her help, Kaiser staggered through the door and into the hold of the *Golden Dawn* beyond.

They walked through a long hallway full of closed doors. At the end of the hall, hammocks filled a large open space, suspended from the ceiling in sets of three. Tarathine led Kaiser up a set of stairs to the next deck.

On this level, Kaiser could see the entire length of the ship. Massive tubes of iron lined the deck, pulled back from square hatches in the side of the hull. A few sailors loitered around, casting curious glances at Kaiser as he limped by.

"Gustavus says these are guns, father," Tarathine said as they walked past the metal cylinders. "Can you imagine what they must sound like?"

Kaiser struggled to comprehend this idea. The exotic firearms Gustavus and his crew carried were fantastic enough. Kaiser had never imagined there might be guns big enough to blast a hole in a castle.

Tarathine helped him up one last set of stairs and they stepped out on the top deck of the ship. The brilliant sunlight almost blinded Kaiser, and he raised a hand to shield his eyes. All around them, the sailors of the *Golden Dawn* were busy laboring under the watchful eye of Niad.

At Kaiser's appearance on the top deck, a voice rang out.

"You're awake!" Lacrael called, striding toward them with ease over the rolling wooden planks beneath her feet. Brant followed behind her, stumbling along and looking sick. The merchant from Oakroot had lost weight. Kaiser noted his manacles with approval.

Lacrael stopped short of Kaiser. He saw in her eyes that she wanted to hug him, but he did not encourage her. "I'm sorry about your wife," she said.

"You look like a natural born sailor," Kaiser said, deflecting her sympathy. The grief in his heart was too powerful, too recent, to be shared with anyone.

"I've decided that I love the sea," Lacrael said, her face lighting up with a huge smile. "Not in my wildest dreams did I ever see anything so wonderful."

"What about you?" Kaiser asked Brant. "Did you ever imagine you'd be sailing across an unknown world?"

Brant grimaced. "As far as I'm concerned, everything since Oakroot has been a waking nightmare."

Lacrael sobered quickly. "Speaking of dreams, did *he* speak to you?"

A thud on the deck caused Kaiser to glance over his shoulder. Gustavus had appeared as if from thin air. The big captain grinned at Kaiser's surprise.

Kaiser turned back to Lacrael. "Your so-called High King did visit me. He says we're to watch and wait for the coming of the next champion."

"After all that's happened, you still doubt who he is?" Lacrael said with a frown.

"Until I've good reason to no longer doubt, I'll continue to do so," Kaiser said. "He's not named himself to me. Believe what you wish. I want truth, not faith in a legend."

Gustavus slapped Kaiser on the back. "Spoken like a true reaver. Don't worry, a few weeks under the Praxian sun will set you straight. It'll boil the sense right out of a man."

Kaiser winced at the blow. Together, the five of them stared out at the flat expanse of endless ocean. In every direction, Kaiser saw nothing but blue. With his good hand, he squeezed Tarathine's shoulder.

"That life is over," Kaiser said into the warm breeze. "I'm a reaver no longer. I don't know what we'll find on that far horizon, but with her dying breath, Mariel told me to fight, and so I will."

Epilogue

URSAIS LIMPED THROUGH THE slums of Northmark. The city bled like an open wound. A week had passed since Mariel's execution sparked the riots. Entire districts still resisted the regent's troops, but everyone knew the inevitable outcome. The regent and the priesthood of Abimelech had seized complete control of the city, and they were using the chaos as a pretext to purge those who refused to submit to their rule.

When Kaiser escaped, the regent had gone mad. Anyone who had ever whispered High King Rowen's name was being dragged into the street and slaughtered. Ursais was only safe because all of his friends were already dead, murdered by the regent's personal soldiers.

To the north, the mountain peak had been stripped bare, a winter's worth of snow gone in a day. He shuddered. Northmark was full of the foolish and the willingly blind; they saw only what they wanted to see. To them, it was obvious that the vicious winds of the sudden squall had swept the snow away. But Ursais remembered the terrible dragon in the sky. If only for a short time, Abimelech had woken.

After looping back over his path several times, taking great pains to ensure he was not followed, Ursais darted into a dark, narrow alley. At the end of the stinking corridor, Ursais ducked into a hole in the wall. Crouched as low as his old back would allow, he waddled several paces through darkness until he felt a flap of fabric hanging in front of him. He pushed it out of the way and crawled into a tiny, but well-lit room. The hidden space was as clean and furnished as he could make it.

Saredon raised his head from a cot at the back of the room. The boy's eyes were red from crying again. Ursais wanted to comfort the child, but there was nothing he could do to ease the boy's sorrow.

"I've learned some good news, my boy," Ursais said, shuffling over to sit on the cot at Saredon's feet. "Someone saw your father carrying Tarathine onto the ship he escaped on."

Saredon sniffled. "Why didn't he come get me too?"

"Your father was attacked," Ursais said. "He was tossed into the sea before he could make his way back into the city. Don't worry now, he escaped with your sister. He would have come for you if he could—there's no doubt in my mind of that."

Saredon lowered his head and started to sob quietly into the cot. Ursais placed a hand on the boy's back. He wanted to weep with the child, but forced himself to be strong.

"We've got to be strong, child," Ursais said. "Kaiser will come for us when he can. Until then, we have to survive. Here, there's something I want you to have."

Ursais got up from the cot and shuffled over to the one brick wall of the room. He worried a loose brick free near the floor and reached his hand into the hole. Saredon had stopped his crying and sat up to watch.

"Aha, there it is," Ursais said, pulling out cloth-wrapped bundle. He moved back over to where Saredon sat on the cot.

Slowly, hoping to communicate his reverence to the boy, Ursais unwrapped the object in his hand. When the ragged fabric fell away, a golden amulet in the shape of a roaring dragon rested in the palm of his hand. Saredon stared at it in wonder.

"I want you to wear this," Ursais said. "It will keep you safe in ways that I cannot. You must keep it secret: no one else can know you have it. Can you do that?"

Eyes wide, Saredon nodded his head.

"Good lad," Ursais said. He picked up the amulet by its leather thong and slipped the cord over Saredon's head.

Saredon looked down at the amulet, holding it out from his body with his hand.

"This will keep you safe until your father comes," Ursais said. "I know he wants you to be strong. Can you do that, my boy?"

Saredon looked up at Ursais. For the first time since hearing of his mother's death, he smiled through his tears.

— —

Mazareem knelt over Worm with needle and thread in his hands. The hound had not stopped trembling since crawling out of the bottom of the harbor. Mazareem had feared him lost, but when he heard news of a dead monster on the beach, he had found Worm hanging onto life. With the help of a few soldiers, Mazareem had returned the injured dog to his private sanctuary beneath Castle Vaulkern.

Two jagged holes gaped in the animal's chest where Kaiser's swords had pierced flesh and bone. Mazareem sewed them shut and treated them with a stinking salve. He placed a bowl of black liquid beneath Worm's snout. He would heal, in time. As long as Mazareem found him and stitched him back together, Worm could survive anything, even decapitation.

"You're my greatest success," Mazareem sighed, patting the hound on the head. Men, women, dragon spawn, demons, horses— Mazareem had been betrayed by every kind of creature he had ever met, save Worm. Worm was one of a kind.

Worm let out a low whine as he lifted his muzzle just high enough to lap out of the bowl. Behind Mazareem, footsteps echoed in the hall. The door to his cell was still open, but with the magi fled, he suspected that the regent would soon try to seal him in again. Mazareem twisted the regent's golden signet on his finger, mulling his options. He was loathe to overplay his hand. Perhaps twelve years of restoring Worm and celebrating Parenthia's downfall would not be so bad.

Mazareem got to his feet and waited for his visitor to appear. He masked his surprise when a young woman wearing the robes of the High Priestess appeared.

"They've chosen another so soon?" Mazareem asked.

The woman inclined her head. "The priesthood requires leadership. I'm honored to have been chosen."

"You're quite welcome, my dear. Have you come to lock me away?"

"Nothing of the sort," the woman said. "I've come to summon you to speak with the regent."

"Ah, just the man to make one eager for a decade of solitude. Very well, tell him I'll be along shortly."

The woman frowned, but nodded and turned to disappear down the hall.

"I'll be back soon, boy," Mazareem said, looking down at the now-sleeping Worm. "Don't strain yourself while I'm away."

Worm's ears twitched at Mazareem's voice, but the hound showed no other reaction. With a sigh, Mazareem left the cell and climbed the stairs up to the castle proper. From the other room, the finished painting of the woman saw him leave.

Mazareem found the regent in the throne room, seated in his usual place behind his massive desk. Regent Trangeth was bent over a piece of paper, scratching away with a quill.

"If you're looking for this, take it and lock me away again," Mazareem said, sliding the regent's signet from his finger. "I'm tired. You've matters well in hand."

Regent Trangeth glanced up from his writing. He looked as if he had swallowed something foul, but he did not speak. Instead, he reached down and opened a drawer in his desk. He pulled something from within and tossed it onto the desk between them.

Mazareem's heart quickened as the object thunked against the wood. It was a single red scale, about as big as Mazareem's hand with his fingers outstretched. Etched into one side of the scale, a strange symbol glowed like fire. Mazareem knew that symbol. It was a draconic summons.

"You know where to go," Regent Trangeth said.

"Oh I suppose it will do," Mazareem said, swapping the golden ring for the burning scale, "but you drive a hard bargain."

"Get out," Regent Trangeth snarled.

Mazareem grinned at the regent before making his exit. Such a summons was the ultimate honor amongst Abimelech's children, and Trangeth had never received one. Mazareem tucked the scale into his cloak and strode from the castle. Rest could wait. Antagonizing Trangeth alone would make the trip to Abimelech's lair worthwhile.

The mountain to the north of the city stood several miles from the outskirts. It took Mazareem the better part of an hour to leave Northmark and reach its lowest slopes. The main highway wound around the mountain, giving it a wide berth. Mazareem stepped off the road and onto a narrow track that ascended steeply upward.

Instead of climbing toward the peak, the path circled the base of the mountain until it ended at the mouth of a cave. Outside this cave, two guardians in black plate stood watch. Their hands rested on the hilts of greatswords, points grounded in the dirt between their feet. They did not move or speak as Mazareem approached, but he knew better than to try and enter the cave without their permission.

Mazareem removed the scale from beneath his robe and held it out for the guardians to see. After several long minutes, a voice sounded behind one of the dark helmets.

"You may pass."

"You're so kind," Mazareem said. He pocketed the scale and entered the cave.

Inside, the mountain was hollow. Darkness hid most of the interior, but Mazareem's imagination completed the picture. Where

Abimelech's children used illusion magic to appear human, Abimelech himself slumbered outside Northmark disguised as a mountain.

Mazareem stopped thirty paces from the mouth of the cave. Inky blackness surrounded him on all sides. The daylight streaming through the portal behind him seemed miles away. He trembled with excitement and anticipation.

Far overhead, a red glow blossomed in the darkness. Mazareem peered upward in fascination as two ruby eyes swung down from on high to pierce him with their gaze. One of Abimelech's many heads hung in front of Mazareem, disembodied in the black void.

Red scales gleamed beneath the fire of Abimelech's eyes. Teeth as long as a man lined a mouth that could gulp Mazareem down like a mere morsel. This close, Mazareem could feel the dragon's breath. He fought the urge to step back in the face of the withering heat. He almost felt young again.

"My children know to kneel in my presence," Abimelech said, his voice grinding like the shifting of the earth. Mazareem felt the words reverberate in the core of his bones.

"If you wanted groveling, you should have summoned the regent."

The ground shook beneath Mazareem's feet as what passed for a dragon's chuckle rumbled in Abimelech's throats.

"Your bravado is foolish, but amusing," Abimelech said. "My children carry out my will, bringing my vengeance to fruition, but you have proven yourself to be a valuable tool over the past millennia. I know the lust for immortality that burns in your heart. Bring me the heads of the two magi that escaped from my clutches, and I will give you what you seek. That scale you carry will unlock the portals to the other realms. Although his body is my prisoner, Rowen still lives, and as long as his accursed magic guards the pathways between the realms, you can go where my children cannot."

"I'll not survive long away from my cell beneath the castle," Mazareem said.

"Grind a fragment of the scale to dust, mix it with the blood of any living creature, and it will sustain you," Abimelech rumbled. "You may range far with this new freedom, but never forget that your soul belongs to me."

Mazareem smiled, a million thoughts racing through his head at the possibilities now open to him. "The magi are as good as dead."

"See to it that you do not fail," Abimelech said. "Do not return to me empty-handed."

Without another word, Mazareem turned from the dragon and strode out of the cave.

About the Author

Sandell Wall is a computer programmer/business analyst by trade. He lives in Michigan with his wonderful wife and growing baby boy. He has embarked on a personal quest to write a million words. This book represents the fulfillment of one tenth of that quest. *The Tenth Reaver* is his fourth book and the first entry in a new series. He hopes his readers enjoyed the book. He is excited to keep writing and to create new worlds for his readers to explore!

You can visit his website at http://www.sandellwall.com. He would love it if you stopped by and joined his mailing list.

Made in the USA
Middletown, DE
04 October 2023

40159961R00209